Judy Nunn's career has been long  faceted. After combining her interna career with scriptwriting for tele decided in the '90s to turn her hand to prose.

Her first three novels, *The Glitter Game*, *Centre Stage* and *Araluen*, set respectively in the worlds of television, theatre and film, became instant bestsellers, and the rest is history, quite literally in fact. She has since developed a love of writing Australian historically based fiction and her fame as a novelist has spread rapidly throughout Europe, where she has been published in English, German, French, Dutch, Czech and Spanish.

Her subsequent bestsellers, *Kal*, *Beneath the Southern Cross*, *Territory*, *Pacific*, *Heritage*, *Floodtide*, *Maralinga*, *Tiger Men*, *Elianne*, *Spirits of the Ghan*, *Sanctuary*, *Khaki Town* and *Showtime!* have confirmed Judy's position as one of Australia's leading fiction writers. She has now sold over one million books in Australia alone.

In 2015 Judy was made a Member of the Order of Australia for her 'significant service to the performing arts as a scriptwriter and actor of stage and screen, and to literature as an author'.

Visit Judy at judynunn.com.au or on
: facebook.com/JudyNunnAuthor

JUDY NUNN

Black Sheep

WILLIAM HEINEMANN: AUSTRALIA

WILLIAM HEINEMANN

UK | USA | Canada | Ireland | Australia
India | New Zealand | South Africa | China

William Heinemann is part of the Penguin Random House group of companies
whose addresses can be found at global.penguinrandomhouse.com.

Penguin
Random House
Australia

First published by William Heinemann in 2023

Cover photography courtesy Stocksy and Alamy
Cover design by Adam Laszczuk © Penguin Random House Australia Pty Ltd
Artwork on p. iii, head of a sheep, vector sketch by La puma, courtesy of
Shutterstock; on p. 265, pocket watch, ink sketch, hand drawn vector illustration
by Nata_Alhontess, courtesy of Shutterstock; artwork on pp. 5, 133, 383 drawn
by James Mills-Hicks, Ice Cold Publishing
Internal design by Midland Typesetters, Australia
Typeset in 12pt Sabon by Midland Typesetters

Printed and bound in Australia by Griffin Press, an accredited
ISO AS/NZS 14001 Environmental Management Systems printer

A catalogue record for this
book is available from the
National Library of Australia

NATIONAL
LIBRARY
OF AUSTRALIA

ISBN 978 1 76134 012 3

penguin.com.au

MIX
Paper | Supporting
responsible forestry
FSC® C018684

We at Penguin Random House Australia acknowledge that Aboriginal and Torres
Strait Islander peoples are the Traditional Custodians and the first storytellers
of the lands on which we live and work. We honour Aboriginal and Torres
Strait Islander peoples' continuous connection to Country, waters, skies and
communities. We celebrate Aboriginal and Torres Strait Islander stories, traditions
and living cultures; and we pay our respects to Elders past and present.

With love and thanks to my dear friend and agent,
James Laurie

PROLOGUE

QUEENSLAND, 1881

Seated on his customary log by the camp fire, George Wakefield recited the old nursery rhyme slowly, the methodical cadence of his Midlands accent lending added force to the words.

'Baa baa Black Sheep,
Have you any wool?
Yes, sir, yes, sir,
Three bags full;
One for the master,
One for the dame,
And one for the little boy
Who lives down the lane.'

Having completed his recitation, he leaned forward – elbows on knees – and gazed down at his six-year-old son, cross-legged on the ground beside him. The look in the boy's eyes was one of expectancy, but also mystification. Young James had heard the nursery rhyme often – he'd heard many a nursery rhyme from his father in the past – but this time when he'd joined in, knowing it off by heart as he did, he'd been silenced.

'No, no, Jimmy,' his father had said. 'Listen very carefully to the words, each and every one of them, for I'm about to explain to you their meaning. You're of an age to learn now.' And then he'd started his recitation all over again with even greater deliberation.

Now the wide-eyed boy stared up at his father in wordless anticipation. He was about to learn something. James liked to learn things.

'Who do the three bags go to, Jimmy?' George asked.

Oh that part was easy. 'The master and the dame and the little boy,' he answered.

'And who do you think they are?'

Not so easy. Not so easy at all. What did his father mean? James was confused. He shook his head.

'I'll tell you a story,' George said in answer to his son's understandable bewilderment. 'Hundreds of years ago, way back in the Middle Ages, England's King Edward needed to finance his wars. So he raised the tax on wool something terrible. Sheep and wool were of great value in those days, you see, very important to the country's economy.'

George grinned knowingly, he was a shearer after all. 'I suppose that proves some things never change, eh? Wool's as valuable as ever it was, and probably always will be.' He gazed about at the typical outback bushland. 'Don't know what this country would be without it.'

'Anyway,' he went on, getting back to his story, 'these hefty taxes were most unfair to those on the land. For every bale of wool sold, a third of the money went to the King, a third went to the Church – of course you've always got to keep the Church happy,' he added with a touch of cynicism, 'and a third went to the poor shepherd who'd done all the hard work.'

He gave his knee a self-congratulatory slap as he summed up. 'So there you have it, Jimmy lad, the master and the dame and the little boy are the King and the Church and the shepherd, that's who. "Baa Baa Black Sheep" is a very, very old nursery rhyme, son, and like many a nursery rhyme it has a hidden meaning.'

James, fascinated, was about to speak. But there was more to come.

'And do you want to know why the sheep is *black*?' his father asked meaningfully.

The boy nodded. Yes, he certainly did.

'Back then black cloth was popular . . .' George paused, giving the matter a moment's thought, he wanted to get things right. '. . . probably for funerals, there was a lot of death around in those days. But black dye was hard to come by, which made black cloth very expensive. And what do you think that meant?'

A telling pause as father and son's eyes remained locked.

'It meant black wool could be taxed more heavily,' George said, 'that's what it meant. No need for black wool to be dyed, see?'

James finally gave voice. He had the answer. 'So the black sheep were the most valuable ones,' he announced triumphantly, delighted that he now understood the nursery rhyme with such clarity. He'd never seen a black sheep himself. He only wished he could. Perhaps they didn't have black sheep in Australia.

'Aha! That's what they *say* . . .' George held up a staying hand in order to halt the boy's assumption. 'But there's another point of view altogether.'

Once again James fell silent.

'Black cloth may have been popular,' George said, 'but there were other colours that also found favour, particularly with the ladies . . .' He wasn't actually sure about this detail and wished to be fair. 'Or so I would reckon upon, knowing ladies as I do.' It was true, he had known quite a few ladies in his time, and he doubted feminine tastes had changed even over several hundreds of years. Ladies liked a spot of colour.

'But black wool *cannot* be dyed,' he declared, this time with absolute certainty. 'Black wool can produce only black cloth. In which case the black sheep might well be the *least* valuable.'

In the gathering dusk, George's eyes searched those of his son, seeking the intelligence he knew lay within. James was a bright boy.

'So which is it do you think, Jimmy?' he asked. 'Is the black sheep the most valuable in the flock, or is he the least valuable of them all when his wool goes to market?'

James knew he was being put to the test, and having no wish to be found wanting gave the matter serious consideration.

'I suppose it depends upon the demand of the day, Pa,' he said after a pause. 'Whether people want black or whether they want colour.' An intelligent answer, but James had more to say. 'Although if the person who *owns* the sheep is really smart, he might *control* the market. He might *tell* the people what they want. You've always said people like to have a leader.'

George gave a loud, proud guffaw. He had indeed said just that. *People are like sheep, son,* he'd said, *they need a leader.*

'Good boy,' he applauded, 'good answer.' *My son will go far,* George thought.

PART ONE

CHAPTER ONE

George Wakefield was an enigmatic figure to most, even something of a mystery. An Englishman from Cheshire, where he'd been a shearer, he'd arrived in Australia in 1878 with a three-year-old boy. No wife. Just the boy. Which was highly unusual. He was appealing company; handsome, bearded, with a lean, fit body, ice-blue eyes that beguiled and an easy smile; a man's man respected by his peers, and to women highly attractive. But despite his pleasant personality, he remained a mystery. What were the details of his background, his family, his wife? No one knew. And if anyone asked, they received a politely delivered answer brief enough to invite no further query. His wife had died in childbirth, so he'd brought his son to Australia. He'd heard shearers had a good life down here. A winning smile, and that was that.

His son had received little more information, apart from the fact that his mother had been Irish and her name had been Molly.

'And if she hadn't died giving birth she would have loved you very much, Jimmy,' his father had fondly assured him. And again, that was that.

Young James didn't even know where he'd been born, but as the years passed this didn't appear to bother him. If ever he was asked where he came from he'd say, 'Right here. Right here in Longreach.'

The region of Longreach in Central Western Queensland was the only home James had ever known, so it seemed rightful he should claim it as his. Yet 'home' in the literal sense didn't really apply. Most of the boy's life was spent camping out under the stars with his father who worked as an itinerant shearer during the season, a farmhand during the layoff and occasionally as a labourer in one of the small local towns that appeared to be springing up throughout the area.

It was during one of these layoff periods when George was working in the township of Aramac that James' life underwent a radical change. The year was 1882, he was seven years old, and the change arrived in the form of widowed schoolteacher Harriet Brereton.

Harriet had fallen under the spell of George Wakefield upon their very first meeting, just as George had planned she should. Upon his employment as a builder's labourer in the rapidly expanding town, he'd been delighted to discover it boasted a school, which had opened only four years previously. *How wonderful,* he'd thought; he hadn't known there was a school anywhere in the region. Upon further discovering the school was run by a forty-year-old widow, he'd thought *how even more wonderful,* and he'd set out, sight unseen, to woo her. Harriet Brereton would fit his plans perfectly, or rather she would fit the plans he had for his son.

'James is a very bright boy,' he said as the three of them sat in her poky office at the rear of the neat, weatherboard structure that constituted the school. He'd made sure they'd arrived shortly after school hours so that the pupils, admittedly not many in number, had left for the day.

The discovery that Harriet Brereton was a rather plain little woman did not in the least deter George who now channelled upon her the full force of his charm.

'He's had no formal education, but he can read quite well nonetheless, can't you, Jimmy lad?'

He cast an affectionate smile at his son, who grinned back and nodded eagerly.

'Taught him myself I did,' George went on in the humblest of fashion, although with the knowledge she'd be impressed, 'to the best of my ability anyway.'

'Very admirable, Mr Wakefield.' Harriet was indeed impressed, particularly as many itinerant workers were illiterate, but what impressed her most was the relationship between father and son, which she found touching, and also more than a little puzzling. *How remarkable that a shearer should travel the countryside with such a very young child,* she thought. She wondered what had happened to the mother, or to the mother's family, or to the man's *own* family for that matter. Surely the child could have been left in the care of others. From her personal experience, having worked on a sheep station in the past, she knew this to be the case under normal circumstances.

'I must admit, however, I did have some help in my tutorship . . .' Aware of the favourable impression he was making, George continued to play 'humble' and, picking up his kitbag, which sat on the floor beside him, he produced the book.

'*Popular Nursery Tales and Rhymes*', he said, opening the cover to display the beautiful frontispiece of a mother gathering her children around her. '*With One Hundred and Seventy Illustrations*', he quoted, smiling winningly at the schoolteacher. 'It was the illustrations that interested James most in the early days,' he admitted, 'but over the past year or so he's taken to reading the words for himself, haven't you, Jimmy?'

Another vigorous nod from James. 'Yes, I like reading the words,' he said. He'd been told how to perform, that he must put on a show, and he wasn't about to let down his pa.

'And these days his favourite part is learning some of the stories *behind* the nursery rhymes, isn't it, son?'

'Yep.' James' eyes lit up. He wasn't putting on a show now. 'I like the gruesome ones best. My favourite's "Mary, Mary, Quite Contrary" because of all the torture and the executions.'

'I see.' Harriet wasn't prepared to admit that she didn't know the story behind 'Mary, Mary, Quite Contrary', although she determined to look up the nursery rhyme's background in her encyclopaedia, which might hopefully provide the answer. 'And where did you get the book, may I ask, Mr Wakefield?'

'It belonged to my wife.'

'Ah.' This was a matter of far greater interest to Harriet, and she was wondering how to pursue the subject. But there proved no need.

'She died in childbirth.' George halted any further enquiry with his customary blunt rejoinder.

'Oh I am so sorry to hear that.'

'Thank you, ma'am.' Another smile, warm and respectful this time, and they got down to the business at hand.

James was enrolled in Aramac State School that very day and within just two weeks George and Harriet had become lovers.

Their affair was conducted most discreetly. If seen together during daylight hours, they were perceived as a caring father communicating with the woman responsible for his son's education. Given the ten-year age difference, who would ever have thought the mousey little schoolteacher with her bony body and her wire-rimmed spectacles would have been of any interest to the handsome young shearer anyway? During the darkest hours of the night, however, when George surreptitiously visited Harriet's cottage, a different scenario altogether played itself out.

Harriet's sexuality being finally unleashed after four years of widowhood, she gave herself to her lover with complete abandon. Despite her prim appearance and her adherence to the image she chose to present given her position in the town, Harriet Brereton was an extremely sensual woman.

'Well, well,' George remarked delightedly the first time they made love, 'still waters run deep, eh?'

She hadn't been insulted. Not in the least. She'd laughed instead. The sexual relationship she'd shared with her husband had always been robust, and four years was a very long time.

Harriet's husband, Albert, had been a foreman at Aramac Station. They'd been employed as a couple in 1870, Harriet serving as governess to the boss's two children. Over the years they had not been blessed with children themselves, which had been a profound disappointment to Harriet, and also a great source of guilt for she held herself solely responsible. But she and Albert had been happy at Aramac Station nonetheless. Aramac was a fine home to many.

During the 1860s in this western central region of Queensland, the traditional tribal land of the Iningai, pastoral occupation had taken hold of great swathes of territory. Before long, sheep stations had sprung into being, some large with their own facilities, including stores, workers' accommodation, smithies and the like. Aramac was one of the earliest of such stations, and when the region's first township was established in 1875 it was deemed only right it be named after the thriving sheep station that had pioneered the colonisation of these bountiful pasture lands to the west.

By the late 1870s the township of Aramac, with its neat weatherboard houses, boasted four stores, three hotels, three butcher shops, a post office, a bank, a courthouse and a surgery. And in early 1878, a school!

The school had proved most fortuitous for Harriet Brereton, whose husband had died just three months prior to its opening. Poor Albert. An accident. A mundane, meaningless, commonplace accident with the direst result.

The whole episode had been foolish. Farcical even. A fall from his horse! How had that happened? Albert was a marvellous rider, as skilled as the Aboriginal stockmen the station employed, which was true testament to his horsemanship, for as Albert himself had professed on many an occasion *'those boys can really ride!'*. And if by some odd chance he *were* to take a fall he'd pick himself up and get back on the animal as all riders did.

But not this time. This time, when he'd left the boys penning the sheep and whirled off to bring in a couple of breakaways, his horse had stumbled. And that too was a farce. Betty was Albert's favourite stockhorse, as sure-footed as any on the property. Betty never stumbled. But she did that day. Heavily, too, and on stony ground. Betty broke her knees and had to be shot where she lay. Albert broke his neck and was dead before the boys could get to him.

Harriet was deeply distressed by her husband's death, but despite an appearance some perceived as 'mousey', she was tough and resilient, like most women accustomed to life in the outback.

When a replacement foreman and his wife were employed, as was standard procedure – the station preferring to hire couples for positions of importance – Harriet applied for the post of teacher at the new school and moved into town.

Now, four years later, she was a highly respected member of the community, considered indeed to be one of the most important citizens in the small township, responsible as she was for the education of its children.

Harriet and George's clandestine affair continued, their nightly trysts conducted twice a week arousing not a shred of suspicion. The back door of Harriet's cottage was shrouded by bushes and George's comings and goings were seen by none. He would arrive and leave under the cover of darkness, sneaking back to his lodgings and the room he shared with young James, who regularly slept through his father's nocturnal wanderings. And even were the boy to awaken, there would be no cause for alarm.

'I like to take a bit of a walk now and then in the dark,' his father had told him. Just in case.

George very much enjoyed his affair with Harriet. He'd been most gratified to discover her lack of inhibition, which was an added bonus to his plan. And as the weeks passed he found also that he rather enjoyed Harriet's company. That too was a bonus. They would talk in the dead of the night, about all sorts of things; she was a woman who held strong views, particularly on politics. George realised he could learn much from Harriet Brereton. Which was no surprise, she was a schoolteacher after all. She was teaching his son, and she was teaching him too.

Theirs was an amicable relationship. And one could not deny that he paid in kind. George took pride in the knowledge that he satisfied Harriet's sexual appetite, taking care always to make sure that he did.

There was one step in their lovemaking, however, that he would *not* take.

'Stay,' she whispered time and again. 'Stay inside me. Please, George. Stay inside me.'

But he never did. She had told him she was infertile, that there was no need for preventative action, and he had no doubt she was right, besides which she was surely already past child-bearing age. But George was reluctant to take the risk and always withdrew before ejaculation. He had no wish to be saddled with another child.

The weeks became months and then, winter over, spring beckoned. Shearing season. George needed to be on his way. He must now carry out the plan he had set in motion from the very start of their relationship.

'What say if James were to stay here with you,' he whispered in the dark, as if the idea had just occurred to him while they lay together sated, the sweat of their bodies mingling despite the cool of the night. 'I have no wish to interfere with his learning, Harriet. Education is of the greatest importance, as you of all people know only too well.'

She didn't reply instantly, unsure of her own reaction, which was complex. She loved George, she knew that much, although she'd never told him so, and she never intended to. She'd been dreading the onset of the shearing season and the knowledge that he would leave. This would certainly be a way of assuring his return to her. But did she dare? There was her reputation to consider. Did she dare risk compromising her position in the town?

George knew exactly what she was thinking, but he'd planned well in advance how to combat the problem.

'We'll keep everything above board, there'll be no cause for suspicion,' he coolly assured her. 'I'll pay for the boy's lodgings. You have a spare room. James will be a tenant, a pupil of yours who needs a roof over his head, as simple as that.' He drew her to him and kissed her gently. 'I'll call on you when school's out tomorrow, shall I? When some of the mothers will be collecting their children?'

She could hear the smile in his voice.

'We'll discuss the proposition right out in the open for all to see. The whole town knows of your devotion to your pupils. Taking in the young son of a widowed shearer with no family would be seen as an act of kindness.'

George had already made sure that it would. Over the past two months he'd ingratiated himself most successfully with the townspeople. Everyone liked George Wakefield, particularly the women, all of whom considered him a wonderful father. They talked about the fact what's more.

'So devoted to his son, isn't he?'

'And to his son's schooling. Why he said to me only the other day, "My boy's education is the top priority in my life." Not many fathers like that around here.'

'*There certainly aren't,*' some protective mothers would say. '*Most want their sons working by their side from the age of eight. Boys are to be men by the time they're ten.*'

Other mothers, particularly the wives of farmers, might disagree. '*And that's just as things should be. We need all the workers we can get.*'

But the women were of one accord when it came to George Wakefield. He was without doubt a fine father.

'*He'll miss the boy when he's out on the road, but he's determined to do the right thing. The right thing the way he sees it, anyway. And that's the true measure of a father's love, that is.*'

George was genuine in his desire for the boy to have a decent education, and he would indeed miss his son when he was out on the road. But he knew also that life during the shearing season would be easier without James, for he'd be able to stay in the shearers' quarters with the other men instead of having to set up camp at night. Previously the boy had been left during the day in the care of the sheep station's housekeeper, or cook, sometimes even the station owner's wife, but during the nights the two had always camped out together. A child of that age could not be housed in the shearers' quarters.

The stage successfully set, all went according to plan. No one suspected for one minute there was any personal relationship between the young, widowed shearer and the middle-aged schoolteacher. When the shearing season was over and George returned, he reclaimed his son and the two stayed together in lodgings, the boy attending school, the father seeking work around the town or at nearby farms. George Wakefield continued to be viewed by the townspeople as the finest of fathers and Harriet Brereton as the most devoted of teachers, while their twice-weekly trysts told an altogether different tale.

During the several years that followed, the status quo was maintained, but there was one upon whom the subterfuge took its toll.

Young James Wakefield's existence had undergone such a radical change that he was left confused. Throughout the whole of his short life there had been no one but his father; now it seemed he led two different lives. And this second life involved a woman, the only female influence he had ever known. Like everyone else, he was unaware of the relationship between his father and his schoolteacher, but when he sat down at the little dining table with Harriet Brereton, he felt an intimate connection. He pictured her as his mother. He even fantasised about it. What would it be like, he wondered, to be gathered in her arms and cuddled the way he'd seen other mothers gather their children to them? The way the mother in the beautiful frontispiece of *Popular Nursery Tales and Rhymes* gathered her children to her.

The fantasy grew and grew, until on one occasion he was bold enough to put it to the test.

'Goodbye, son.'

It was shearing season and once again his father had delivered him, together with his kitbag and small travelling case, to the schoolteacher's house where they now stood on the verandah, Mrs Brereton having gone inside.

'I shall leave you to make your farewells, Mr Wakefield,' she'd said and closed the door behind her.

'Goodbye, Pa.'

James accepted the hearty pat on the shoulder and watched as his father strode down the front steps and mounted the eight-year-old mare that was waiting patiently, untethered and loaded with gear. Red Nell was a fine animal. 'The best horse I've ever had,' George maintained.

'You behave yourself now,' his father instructed.

'Yes, Pa.'

A touch of heels and Red Nell set off at a trot down the dusty street.

The boy waved to his father, who didn't look back, but raised an arm high in salute to the son he knew would be waving.

James waited until Red Nell was out of sight, then picked up his travelling case, opened the door and went inside.

She was setting out a pot of tea and cups and saucers, together with a plate of biscuits on the small central dining table.

'You may put your things in your room, James,' she said without glancing up, 'and then you may have some tea.'

He slipped his kitbag from his shoulder, set down his case and crossed to stand beside her.

She was a small woman, and being tall for his age, James was only an inch or so shorter. She stopped setting the table and stood erect, rigid-backed, a query in her eyes. Was there something he wanted?

There was.

James wrapped his arms around her and rested his head in the crook of her bony shoulder, hoping to feel her arms encircle him. But they didn't. Instead, he felt her whole body tense.

'We'll have none of that, boy,' she said, her voice as hard and bony as her shoulder.

But James, urged on by his long-held imaginings, nuzzled his head closer. A longing. An ache.

Still, Harriet would have none of it. She made no move, her voice, as always, proving her weapon of control. 'Stand up straight, boy. This instant, do you hear me? Do as you're told.'

He did. And they stood facing each other. Eye to eye.

Her voice didn't altogether soften, but it did lose a little of its harshness. She was instructing him now, rather than issuing orders. 'You're nearly ten, James, far too old for mollycoddling. And you must remember always that I am your schoolteacher, not your mother. Is that understood?'

'Yes, Mrs Brereton.'

'Now take your things to your room. Wash your hands in the water basin and we'll have some tea. Would you like that?'

'Yes, thank you, ma'am.' His father always called her 'ma'am' and James knew the term to be respectful. Furthermore, it made him sound 'grown up', the way she obviously wanted him to be.

'Good boy.'

He picked up his kitbag and travelling case and went through the kitchen to his little room out the back. He had learned his lesson. He would never again seek a cuddle. Besides, he decided, she was right. He was too old to be mollycoddled. But oh how he did so admire Mrs Brereton.

Harriet felt saddened as she watched him go, aware that he longed for the mother figure he'd never known. She'd always taken care to avoid any show of maternal affection, but it was difficult at times for she felt a great fondness for the boy. She'd even occasionally thought with regret that he might have been the son she and Albert had so desperately wanted all those years ago. But this boy was not her son, and he never would be. This was the son of a man with whom she was having an affair so furtive most would consider it sordid. A man who would no doubt disappear as soon as she no longer served a purpose in his life.

Although still in love with George Wakefield, Harriet did not delude herself, as she once had, that her love might one day be reciprocated. At first she had wondered, and possibly even with some hope, whether he might come to see her as a mother for his son. But she'd soon realised she was no more than a convenient combination of teacher and landlady, so she'd played the role accordingly.

George, for all his warmth and his charm, and – yes –
even his affection, which appeared genuine, remained a
mystery. And the more Harriet tried to solve the mystery,
the more confused she became. What of his background?
What of his family? He said nothing of his wife, the mother
of his child. Had she really died giving birth? Was she dead
at all? Perhaps not. Perhaps he'd deserted the poor woman
and run away with the boy. The more evasive George was
about his past, the more Harriet tortured herself with
possibilities.

'Tell me about your life, George,' she would beg. 'Please.
Please tell me about yourself. I long to know you.'

But the answer that came back in the darkness remained
the same.

'What's to tell, my love?' he'd say. He always called her
'my love', a term of affection, which she adored while also
recognising the irony. 'The past is the past, nothing worth
the telling.' Then that smile in his voice and the touch of his
fingers in her most intimate place. 'As for me? Well now,
I think you know me only too well, wouldn't you say?' And
within barely a minute they'd be making love again.

Harriet could do nothing but wait for the affair to end;
for the time when he would tire of her or no longer have
need of her. But in the meantime, she couldn't help herself.
She loved him. Or rather she loved the reawakening of a
passion she had long thought dead. That was a love of
sorts, wasn't it? That was surely enough. But she knew
deep down she wanted more, much more. She wanted all
of him.

'Stay inside me, George, please stay inside me,' she continued to beg on occasions.

But still he withdrew before his final moment, as if by
habit, as if he hadn't even heard her pleas.

Then came the night in midsummer when he surprised
her. It was the fifth year of their affair and this was the

first visit he'd paid to the cottage following his return from shearing. His first visit to the cottage under the veil of darkness, that is. He had of course collected James that very same day, a Sunday as usual, at around noon. The boy had been waiting with his kitbag and travelling case, and the customary procedure had been played out on the front verandah for the benefit of passers-by.

'Much obliged, Mrs Brereton.' The tip of his battered bush hat, the money pouch, detached from his belt, changing hands. 'I hope he's been a good lad.'

'He has indeed, Mr Wakefield.' The discreet depositing of the money pouch into the pocket of her apron. 'You have a fine boy there. No trouble at all.'

'Thank you, ma'am.'

George picked up his son's travelling case, and Harriet didn't even watch as they set off down the street, the father leading the chestnut mare, the boy beside him chatting away nineteen to the dozen. Their boarding house was only five minutes away. She stepped inside the cottage, closing the front door behind her, knowing she would be counting the hours, hungering for his return in the dead of the night.

Their lovemaking was torrid. He had satisfied her completely, as he always did, and was nearing his own climax. She remained clinging to him, expecting any minute he would break away from her and withdraw. But he didn't. Instead, he stayed buried deep inside her, and as Harriet felt the shudder of his release, she found herself quivering with far more than the aftermath of her orgasm. Their trembling bodies now fused, she was engulfed by a euphoric sensation that could only be love. She heard herself saying the words she had never intended, but which now simply had to be said.

'I love you, George.'

He stayed right where he was, he too still quivering, still breathing a little heavily, and she heard his smile as he smoothed the hair back from her face and kissed her with all the tenderness of a true lover.

'Course you do, my love. Just as I love you.'

George had decided it was time to humour Harriet. She was so valuable to him, he'd be lost without her. Besides, any danger was past. She'd have to be in her mid-forties by now, far too old to conceive. And where was the harm in telling her he loved her?

Over the months that followed, he maintained the practice and also the endearments, knowing how much it pleased her, and Harriet remained in a state of euphoria. This was surely a love beyond even that she'd shared with Albert. How she longed to legitimise her relationship with George, to live openly with the man she loved. But she knew this would be impossible.

'You'd lose the respect of the whole township, my love,' George had said, 'they'd never accept you as their teacher.'

And George, of course, was quite right. So their clandestine affair continued as always, twice-weekly trysts and no more.

Summer gave way to autumn and then winter was upon them – mildly pleasant, although the nights were chill. The weeks passed and with the approach of spring Harriet wondered how she should break the news, or more importantly how it would be received. She was sure by now. Sure of the unbelievable fact that she was pregnant. At forty-five! Approaching forty-six even! A miracle! During all those years she'd been barren she'd presumed the fault lay with her, but the problem must have been Albert's.

'You told me you weren't able to have children,' he said as they sat hunched over the little table, the kerosene lamp between them, the cottage's curtains drawn. She had wanted to see his face when she told him. 'You said you were infertile.'

'I thought I was,' she replied in all honesty. 'My husband and I tried for years to have a child.'

'Are you sure?' He seemed more in a state of disbelief than anger. 'You're too old to conceive, surely,' he said, peering at her in the dim light. *Good God,* he thought, *she looks all of fifty.*

'I thought that too,' she admitted, 'but it's happened. I really am sure, George.'

'Ah. Well now . . .'

She tried to read his reaction, but it was impossible; true to form he was giving away nothing.

'What should we do?' she asked, hardly daring hope, but longing to hear him say, '*Why we'll get married, my love, and James shall have a little brother or sister.*'

'We must think upon that, my love,' he said, allaying her fears with a comforting smile. 'It's certainly a matter deserving of thought. Now shall we turn off the lamp and adjourn to the bedroom?' A look of concern. 'Or would we be putting the little one at risk?'

'No, no, we wouldn't be putting the little one at risk,' she said hastily, thrilling to the care she saw in his eyes and the caress she heard in his voice. 'I can assure you, no risk at all.'

There was nothing to think upon. As they made love, George knew exactly the path he would follow. He would leave early for the shearing season this year and he would take James with him. It was a pity Harriet had spoilt their perfect arrangement. A greater pity, too, that the boy's education was to be halted earlier than intended, but the lad was soon to turn thirteen, which was schooling enough. He was an early developer what's more, tall for his age and even beginning to show facial hair. He could well pass for fifteen. They'd be able to bunk in together with the other shearers and James could work as a rouseabout.

Beneath him, Harriet began to softly moan her pleasure, but as he drew her ever nearer to ecstasy George's mind was elsewhere. He'd buy the boy a horse tomorrow. *Yes,* he thought, *no more riding double-backed on Red Nell. James is becoming a man. He'll need a horse of his own.*

Harriet didn't discover he'd gone until two days later. On the Tuesday when young James Wakefield didn't turn up for school.

'Where's James?' she asked, her eyes scanning the classroom casually while she felt her pulse quicken with a sense of foreboding.

'He's gone,' Davey Bridges piped up. Davey's father, a smithy by trade and a highly successful businessman, owned the stables and blacksmith shop on the outskirts of town. 'His dad bought a horse from my old man yesterday. They took off early this morning.'

'I see.'

Harriet barely remembered getting through the rest of that day. But she must have, somehow, because late afternoon saw her back in her little cottage, her mind made up and her future firmly mapped out.

She would not let George Wakefield destroy her. She would tender her notice to the school and leave town before her condition was beginning to show. She had funds enough put by. She would give birth in secret, after which she would apply for a teaching position in another school far from Aramac where she would be a widowed woman with a child.

Harriet had always been strong. Now possibly stronger than ever because she had a purpose. The child she had longed for. She was even grateful to George Wakefield. He'd given her the greatest gift imaginable.

George felt not a shred of remorse in deserting Harriet Brereton. She had meant nothing to him. But then no one did. No one except James. There had been one other; just one other person for whom he had cared. Molly. They hadn't been married, but he'd loved her, in a way and with a force he'd never before known. Molly had awakened in him an emotion stronger than he'd ever imagined possible. But Molly had died in childbirth.

George Wakefield was not only a mystery to others, he was a mystery to himself. He had no idea why he was devoid of the normal feelings visited upon most human beings. He'd felt nothing for his parents, nothing for his siblings and nothing for his peers. Compassion, empathy, sympathy, affection, even friendship, all were foreign to him. He'd learned to feign the signs: the caring smile, the soothing voice, the gestures of camaraderie, and always the charm; charm was his specialty. But throughout the whole of his life people had meant nothing. Until Molly. Molly had been just like him. They'd recognised themselves in each other instantly. She too had cared for no one. Until she'd met him. Suffering the same affliction, they'd belonged to one another in a world to which they were alien. And then she'd died, and he'd been once again set adrift.

Far from hating the child whose arrival had killed the only person he'd ever cared for, George had treasured the boy. James was all he had left of Molly.

George Wakefield knew himself to be a strange man, but of one thing he was certain. He loved his son.

CHAPTER TWO

George had painstakingly taught his son all he knew, and the boy was a quick learner. Now just turned sixteen, James had graduated from the shed duties of a rouseabout and could handle blade shears as well as the next man. Admittedly, it would be some years before he would qualify as the gun shearer he was intent upon becoming, but even at this tender age the lad's focus and commitment was a matter of considerable pride to George.

'I'm going to be as famous as Jack Howe,' James declared to his father in all seriousness; Jack Howe was his hero.

'You'll have to muscle up a bit, boy,' his father replied with a laugh. The gun shearer Jack Howe, whose feats were legend throughout Central Queensland, was a giant of a man with massive hands and wrists like steel. No one could match him, although many tried. Shearing shed tallies soared high above normal as men hopelessly attempted to compete with Jack.

'I *will* muscle up,' James said, still in deadly earnest. 'By the time I'm twenty I'll be muscled up good and proper, Pa. You just wait and see.'

'I'm sure you're right, Jimmy.' George's smile was indulgent. He didn't think it likely himself; the boy didn't have the potential build of a Jack Howe. In truth it was a constant source of wonder to George that others accepted his son as older than his years, for James, although now as tall as the average man, still openly bore the bloom of youth, fresh-faced, fair-haired, blue-eyed and boyish.

George took great pains to disguise this fact, encouraging the growth of a sparse beard to which he'd add some grime from the cooking fire. At first he'd tried tousling James' hair, but it had only added an attractively adolescent rakishness, so he'd opted for a dirt-stained bush hat instead.

Regardless of his efforts James remained, in his father's eyes anyway, no more than a youth. Others, however, accepted the lie the two had constructed between them. Others saw James Wakefield as an impressive young man.

George had come to the conclusion that it was his son's manner rather than appearance that gave the impression of maturity. James' intelligence, and his intensity, was far beyond his years. When he trained his full focus on a person, as he very often did, he made a startling impact. It was clear the boy genuinely found others a source of great interest; the antithesis of his father, whose show of interest in those about him had always been feigned.

I suppose it's a good thing he has the capacity to care, George thought, vaguely gratified that his son hadn't inherited the curse of apathy with which both his parents had been afflicted, *so long as it doesn't land him in trouble.*

Father and son were currently lodged in Barcaldine where they had more or less based themselves these days, the township being central to the industrial union action with which George had become involved.

Barcaldine was only forty-two miles south of Aramac, but George never feared Harriet Brereton may come looking for him with a claim he had fathered her child. If she were to do so he would deny it anyway. He never gave Harriet a thought. At least not on a personal level, although from time to time he would recall their conversations about unionism. Harriet had had firm political opinions, principally from the farmers' perspective, which George had found most interesting. *Handy,* he now thought, *having views from both sides. Very handy knowing exactly how your enemy thinks.* Yes, he'd learned quite a bit from Harriet.

The once sleepy township of Barcaldine had sprung into prominence as the terminus of the Central Western railway in 1886, and in doing so had replaced Aramac as the region's major outback town. The busy railhead had also become a natural focus for the development of unionism, drawing together as it did seasonal and casual workers. Shearers, shed hands, navvies and carriers all gathered at the Barcaldine railway station where a sense of mateship and mutual support was born of financial hardship and the need to bring about change.

In 1887, discussions leading to the Central Queensland Carriers' Union were held under the shade of the giant ghost gum that towered in the broad, dusty street right outside the railway station. That same year the Queensland Shearers' Union was formed at the nearby township of Blackall, and the following year the Central Queensland Labourers' Union was established in Barcaldine. It was the combined power of these three unions that became the driving force behind the Australian shearers' strike of 1891.

The giant ghost gum, hailed the 'Tree of Knowledge', had by now become a symbol of unionism for it was under this very tree that the strikers held their meetings. A year later this same tree would be the chosen site for the reading of the manifesto that would lead to the formation of the Australian Labor Party.

A series of events paved the way to the inevitable strike of 1891. The founding of the Pastoral Employers' Association at Barcaldine in 1889 was a direct response by farmers to union activism, and a retaliatory move was made to reduce shearers' pay rates. As a result, many workers were quick to join the unions, swelling their ranks and pushing membership numbers to a premium. Barcaldine, now the central meeting place of union representatives and pastoralists alike, quickly became a cauldron of unrest. Anything and everything was brewing. By 1890 only severe wet weather prevented direct confrontation, but in January the following year, with pastoralists ignoring union demands and pressing shearers to sign freedom of contract forms, union representatives finally called a strike. Employers refused to negotiate and immediately set about employing non-union labour from the south. The fight was on.

The shearers were angry. And none more so than George Wakefield.

'We're joining the men at Lagoon Creek, Jimmy,' George told his son as they hastily gathered their belongings at the lodging house. 'Strikers are pouring into town and setting up camps and we need to be with them. Strength in numbers, boy. We must stick together.'

James wasn't in the least surprised. He'd been to the volatile union meetings with his father; he'd known it was only a matter of time before things would come to a head.

They packed their gear, saddled their horses – Red Nell and James' young gelding, an amiable four-year-old called Barnaby – and headed for Lagoon Creek on the outskirts of town where large numbers of strikers, many armed, were setting up a camp site and digging in for the long haul.

An anxious Queensland government dispatched police and soldiers to the area, none of which deterred the strikers, who responded by staging processions through the town, carrying burning torches and chanting union slogans. Daily, they rallied outside the railway station protesting not only the arrival of police and soldiers, but above all the rapidly burgeoning number of non-union labourers. Fists raised in anger, cries of 'scabs!', 'traitors!' and 'turncoats!' were hurled at the newcomers with alarming ferocity.

By March, the carriers and railway workers had come out in sympathy and the hordes of men gathered beneath the Tree of Knowledge had swelled exponentially, the giant gum having become the landmark location of protest meetings. Barcaldine was by now the focus of the whole country's interest. Further military reinforcements arrived. Arrests were made and leaders incarcerated. Armed conflict was expected any day.

On the 1st of May the strike reached its zenith, with one of the world's first May Day marches taking place in Barcaldine. The *Sydney Morning Herald* reported that of the 1340 men taking part, 618 were mounted on horseback; that the leaders wore blue sashes and the Eureka Flag was carried; that the banners included those of the Australian Labor Federation, the Shearers' and Carriers' Unions, and another simply inscribed 'Young Australia'. The *Labor Bulletin* reported that chants and cheers were given for 'the Union', 'the Eight-hour Day', 'the Strike Committee' and 'the Boys in Gaol' . . .

The reports carried by the newspapers made impressive reading. Clearly word was out; the general populace was being informed; people were taking notice. Yet to what purpose? Nothing was being achieved, no new ground was being broken. As time progressed it seemed a stalemate had been reached. No, not a stalemate, something far worse, or so it appeared to the most diehard of strikers. Apathy. Submission. The arrest of their leaders had slowed the momentum . . . heavy rain had set in, limiting movement, as had occurred the previous year . . . many of their compatriots were starting to disperse . . . Was it to end like this? Their noble cause surrendered without a whimper?

The mere thought aroused fresh anger, and fuelled by a sense of helplessness and frustration, fights broke out. Lawlessness replaced the legal right to protest, and violence became the order of the day.

The wide boulevard of Oak Street, the main artery of Barcaldine, was flanked by the railway station on one side, and pubs and stores along the other. It was normally an expanse of dry dirt, and always a busy, but peaceable, site. Yet the wet weather had reduced it to a broad soggy mess, and rage had turned it into an ugly place.

'Deserters! You're cowardly bastards, the whole damn lot of you.'

There were fierce altercations in every bar in Oak Street, but the Royal Hotel was the favoured pub of many of those from the Lagoon Creek camp and it was here a particularly aggressive fight broke out one Saturday night in late May.

'Oh leave it be, Douglas,' one of the accused responded wearily, 'the strike's over. I've got a family in Longreach, it's time to go home.'

There were cries of 'hear, hear' from other strikers who'd announced they were leaving. 'Yeah, time to call it a day . . .' they yelled. 'We've done enough . . .' 'We've families to feed . . .'

But Douglas Fenshaw wasn't having a bar of their excuses. 'Go home then,' he roared, 'go home, you bloody traitors!'

'Who're you calling a traitor?' One of the men took exception to the term in no uncertain manner. A big, burly Irishman called Tom Hennessy, known by all and feared by any who'd been foolhardy enough to cross him. 'You want to take care bandying around a statement like that, my friend.' He picked up his rifle, which was propped against the bar beside him, and raised it threateningly. 'You want to be very, very careful. I suggest you take that back right now, Douglas. And I suggest you apologise.'

Douglas said nothing, but glared at Tom unafraid, aware the rifle was just for show. With the police and military still patrolling the streets he wouldn't dare discharge a firearm.

The bar had quietened, men waiting expectantly.

Tom returned the rifle to its place against the bar. Douglas had been right, it was just for show; he used it to frighten the scabs as they stepped off the train. Besides, Tom Hennessy needed no rifle to arouse fear in another.

'You'll live to regret those words, I can promise you, if you don't tell me right now that you're sorry,' he said and with eyes still menacingly trained on Douglas, he addressed the man who stood next to him at the bar. The man he knew as his friend, one who was bound to side with him.

'What do you say, George? I deserve an apology, do I not?'

George Wakefield replied without hesitation, although he didn't know why he answered as he did, for as a rule he avoided confrontation. He'd taken care to cultivate a friendship with Tom Hennessy simply because it was to his advantage to do so. Hennessy was strong, a gun shearer who was looked up to by most. But George was as devoted a union man as Douglas, and Hennessy was proving a disappointment.

'No, you deserve no apology,' he announced loud and clear. 'You're a spineless traitor, Tom, and you should run off with your tail between your legs like the rest of your lily-livered friends.'

An uproar ensued. Douglas gave a loud hurrah and was quickly joined by his mates. Those who'd decided to leave town took umbrage at the depth of the insult and a scuffle broke out. Blows were exchanged.

All of which went unnoticed by Tom Hennessy, who'd turned to the man he'd presumed was his friend.

'You bastard,' he said incredulously, as if he couldn't quite grasp what he'd just heard. Had his mate really ratted on him in such a way? Was it possible?

But the eyes that met his said yes, it was.

'You fucking disloyal little bastard.' Grabbing George by the collar with his left hand Tom pushed the man's back hard up against the bar. 'You'll pay for that,' he growled, raising his right hand high, fingers balled into a giant fist.

'Leave my pa alone.' Young James, standing nearby, leapt to his father's defence. 'Leave him alone, Tom! Leave my pa alone.'

James tried to drag Hennessy off his father, but the big Irishman, still with a hold on George's collar, swatted him away effortlessly and he fell to the floor. Then Tom once again balled his fist. He'd teach this puny Englishman a lesson all right.

George in the meantime had made no attempt to defend himself. He knew he was no match for Tom Hennessy and was prepared to take a beating. Arms outspread he gripped the bar behind him and braced himself. He'd no doubt cop one king hit and be out to it; he'd seen Hennessy in action, the man never needed more than one blow. *Come on, Tom, give it your best shot,* he thought. *Let's get it over and done with.*

Having swatted away the nuisance son, Tom's right hand was now lowered, and the blow came from a different angle than originally intended. His intent had been to break the Englishman's nose, indeed to smash it into his face and leave him a bloodied pulp. The blow's trajectory now coming from beneath, however, speared the nose upwards, the cartilage within piercing the brain. A killer blow. Death was instantaneous.

Even in the relatively dim glow cast by the pub's gaslight it was clear George Wakefield was dead. Sprawled back upon the bar, his eyes stared blankly at the ceiling, unmistakably the eyes of a dead man.

Having scrambled to his feet, James gazed in horror at his father. 'You've killed him,' he said in a disbelieving whisper as around them the scuffle was rapidly turning into an all-out brawl. Nobody else seemed to have noticed the dead man among them. 'You've killed my pa.' James' voice was louder now, louder and accusatory, but still no one noticed.

Tom Hennessy too was staring at the body that lay before him. He too was surprised. He hadn't intended to kill George. 'An accident,' he said. And it was. An accident, simple as that. One punch and the man was dead. How had that happened? A freak accident that's how. Nobody could accuse him of murder.

But the boy could. And the boy did.

Tom Hennessy felt the barrel of a rifle pressed to his temple, and he turned to face his own firearm aimed unwaveringly at his forehead.

'You murdered my father,' James said. His voice was icy, emotionless, and the hands that held the rifle were rock-hard steady. 'You'll pay for that.'

They'd been Tom's own words, and Tom knew in that instant he was a dead man. A wave of fear overtook him as he looked into the young man's eyes and saw the cold, hard purpose there.

Then the crack of a rifle shot, and the back of Tom Hennessy's head blew away, his brains splattering the bottles that sat on the shelves of the bar.

Sudden silence.

Men remained frozen, some poised about to take a punch, others about to receive one, but no one moved. What was going on?

In the brief hiatus, James dropped the rifle and dived for the pub's front doors. Within only seconds he was out in Oak Street, hearing behind him the consternation as men discovered the dead bodies and the mayhem that surrounded them.

He raced to where he and his father had left their horses, slipped the reins from the tethering post and mounted

Barnaby. Then, leading Red Nell, he took off through the wet, gloomy night for the camp at Lagoon Creek, already aware that people were gathering about the Royal Hotel. Possibly authorities too, police, military . . . He didn't turn back to look.

It was drizzling when he arrived at the camp. In the light cast by various kerosene lamps that burned here and there from other men's tents, he could see the glint of raindrops dimpling the lagoon's black surface. He didn't light his lamp, the one his father had rigged that hung from their tent's central pole. That would be to invite comment. He knew his neighbours well. 'Where's your pa, Jimmy?' they'd be bound to enquire for the two were inseparable. He lit a candle instead, placed it in a candle-holder and shielding the splay of its light hastily set about packing. He sifted through his father's kitbag, taking only the barest of necessities and transferring them to his; best he travel light. Items of value were of the greatest importance for he would need money. His father's highly valued blade shears were instantly included, a good work knife and several tools that would come in handy. He avoided weighty objects where he could, but when he discovered the book, he couldn't resist including it. *Popular Nursery Tales and Rhymes.* Yes, he decided, the book had to come with him, and he shoved it into his kitbag.

He rolled up his swag, gathered the billy can and the several other cooking utensils they travelled with, the kerosene lamp and the items of food that remained, and within only minutes he was ready to go.

He gazed about the tent, checking for any item of importance he may have overlooked. The swag where his father had slept just the previous night remained rolled out on its weatherproof groundsheet. The imprint of its owner might possibly be discernible if he stared closely enough and if he had the wish to see it. But he did not stare closely, and he had no such wish. In his determination not to panic, James had put all thought of his father aside. George Wakefield's dead eyes would return soon enough. He snuffed out the candle and left.

He rode all that night, keeping Barnaby at a modest pace, leading Red Nell, still saddled although he'd loosened the girth, and noon the following day saw him arrive at Blackall situated on the Barcoo River to the south.

James knew Blackall. Like all shearers, he and his father were well acquainted with the major townships that had grown as service centres for the pastoralists who'd set up their stations in these rich grazing areas of Central Western Queensland. Why his personal hero, Jack Howe, was a Blackall man. In fact, Jack Howe was well on his way to becoming one of Blackall's most famous citizens.

As James wended his weary way to the stables and smithy shop that he knew to be in Thistle Road, he thought of Jack Howe, and he wondered if his plan to emulate the famous gun shearer would ever come to fruition. Surely not. Not now he was destined to be labelled a murderer. He must leave this area, he must quit the sheep industry; he must disappear altogether. The thought saddened him; he'd had such plans, such dreams and all had involved being the best man with a set of shears. Just like Jack.

For the first time, he thought of the man he'd killed. Tom Hennessy. Tom had been a gun shearer. How could such a thing have occurred? Tom had been one of them. *I killed one of our own*, he thought, *the man wasn't scab labour, he wasn't a traitor. He was one of us. A shearer on strike. How could I have done that?*

It was then George Wakefield's dead eyes returned. James saw his father staring glassily at the ceiling and he knew exactly how he had done what he did. *Tom Hennessy murdered Pa*, he thought. *Of course I had to kill him.*

James remembered the man's look of sheer terror when he'd realised he was about to die, and thinking upon it he found himself savouring the moment. *'You'll pay for that,'* he recalled saying, just as Tom himself had said, and he relished the memory. He knew he always would. The truth of the matter was, James had enjoyed killing Tom Hennessy.

'This horse isn't nine years old, you lying young bastard,' the stables owner said accusingly as he inspected Red Nell's teeth, 'she's twelve if she's a day, possibly even thirteen.'

'Oh really? Is she?' James played the innocent. No longer with the need to appear older than his years he used his boyish looks to his advantage. 'I'm sorry, sir, I didn't mean to lie, truly I didn't,' he said, with the winningly wide-eyed gaze of youth. 'The bloke I bought her from a year or so back told me she was eight and I took him at his word.'

Bob Mainsbridge saw no reason to disbelieve the boy; naiveté wasn't a crime. He gave a good-humoured wink. 'A word of advice, sonny,' he said, 'you want to become a better judge of horse-flesh or you'll end up being well and truly taken for a ride.' He chortled as he made the customary joke, a regular part of his banter when dealing with the uninitiated. 'But I admit she's a fine animal with a number of years in her yet. I'll take her on.'

They agreed upon a price for the horse and the saddle and bridle that went with her and parted ways. James was more than happy with the transaction. Red Nell, after all, was fourteen years old, going on fifteen. He'd been sorry to say goodbye to her, but reminded himself she was only a horse.

He visited the second-hand goods shop in Shamrock Street. Here he sold his father's top-quality knife in its embossed leather sheath, regretfully as it was a fine knife and he would have liked to have kept it. However, he would need whatever money he could lay his hands on if he was to successfully evade the law, for he had no cash of his own. His father, who'd looked after their joint earnings, would have died with his money purse on him. George Wakefield would never leave cash back at camp. No man would.

James sold other possessions of his father's too. The felt bush hat, kept for best and in excellent condition; the shaving kit wrapped in kidskin, complete with small enamel bowl, camel-hair brush, nail scissors and strong, leather sharpening strap: George had always taken pride in his appearance, keeping his cheeks smooth and his beard well trimmed. James, who had his own razor and modest shaving kit, intended to remain clean-shaven from now on, not only in order to disguise his appearance, but by way of personal preference. He'd not enjoyed the dishevelled look he'd been forced to adopt; he liked a clean-shaven face.

Having sold what he could, with the one exception of his father's beautifully maintained blade shears – which having been of such importance to George he simply could not bring himself to sell – he headed south-east and after travelling several miles pulled off the main road to set up camp in a secluded spot beside the river. It was getting dark and he was thoroughly exhausted. As was Barnaby. James unsaddled, watered and brushed down the horse, leaving the animal tethered and grazing while he collapsed onto his swag without even taking off his boots. He expected to fall asleep within minutes given his state of fatigue, but he didn't. Sleep evaded him as, for the first time since the killings, images of his father flooded his mind.

James had blanketed all thoughts of George Wakefield. He had known from the start that in his fight for self-preservation he must continue to do so, but right now there was no escaping the man. James could see and hear him, the father whom he'd adored for the whole of his life, his hero.

George: seated by the campfire reciting 'Baa Baa Black Sheep'. 'Is the black sheep the most valuable in the flock, or is he the least valuable of them all when his wool goes to market?' Then the proud guffaw of approval at his young son's answer . . .

George: telling the stories behind the nursery rhymes they'd both so loved. 'Mary, Mary, Quite Contrary'. 'Oh there's a good one for you, Jimmy. The silver bells and cockle shells, why they're instruments of torture. And those pretty maids all in a row, why they're just *some* of the Protestant women our good Queen Mary executed; there were plenty more, I can tell you. Oh dear me yes, a charming poem.' And another guffaw . . .

George teaching him to ride on Red Nell: 'Don't haul on the reins, son, she has a delicate mouth. Speak to her with your thighs and your knees – and your heels when neces-sary, just a light tap – they're communication enough with a horse like Nell. And above all, talk to her Jimmy. A loyal horse loves the sound of your voice . . .'

George teaching him how to shear a sheep: 'You hold 'em this way, Jimmy, the grip on the animal is the all-important part. Now watch me closely, boy . . .'

On and on it went. As James fell into a fitful sleep, the sight and the sound of the father whose loss he mourned was everywhere.

It was still dark when he awoke. And cold. Colder than he'd expected, but it was the end of May, he reminded himself. At least the wet weather had held off. He longed to light a fire and boil the billy, but didn't dare. He needed to put more distance between him and Barcaldine and Tom Hennessy's splattered brains. He wolfed down some salted pork, stale bread and cheese, filled the water bag, saddled Barnaby up and once again took to the main road.

James had a plan firmly in place. His destination was Brisbane, around 600 miles south-east. Vast though the state of Queensland was, these towns to the north, particu-larly those of the central pastoral area, were linked by a grapevine of itinerant workers. Word spread far and fast in such places. He needed to lose himself in the seething mass of a city where people cared nothing for the stories of others.

It would be a long trek on horseback. Barnaby was strong, but James was aware he must not panic and attempt to drive the animal too fast. Roughly thirty-five miles a day at a walking pace should suffice. That would see him reach Brisbane in a fortnight or so, around mid-June. In the meantime, he would camp well away from the main road, and visit towns only when he needed to purchase fresh supplies. The authorities were no doubt already on the hunt for him. He could well be a wanted man by now.

He maintained his plan religiously for close on a week until he was struck by an unseasonal bout of wet weather. After suffering a wretched night camped out in the open it was obvious he would need to seek shelter.

The next township was Roma in the Maranoa region, and he boldly fronted up to one of the several pubs that lined the main street.

'I'd like to book a room if I may,' he announced to the woman behind the reception desk, displaying a bravura he didn't feel. Had word reached this far south? Would the police be called? Was he about to be arrested? 'And I wish to stable my horse for the night,' he added with a further air of authority.

'Yes of course, sir.' The publican's wife, a beefy English-woman called Mabel, smiled, thinking what a very good-looking young chappie he was. 'Would you mind signing in?' she asked, dipping the nib of her pen into the inkwell and opening the ledger that sat on the counter.

'Pardon?' James was caught out, he hadn't expected this.

'Your name, sir. For the book.' She smiled again, swivelling the ledger about to face him.

'Yes of course,' he replied smoothly and took the pen from her.

Without a moment's hesitation, he wrote 'Brereton', then returned her smile and passed back the pen.

'James Brereton, ma'am,' he said, 'how do you do.'

Mabel was impressed. *Not only good-looking,* she thought, *but a gentleman to boot. Refreshing in one so young.*

'Most obliged, Mr Brereton. Mabel Dainty at your service. Nice to meet you, I'm sure. Welcome to the Roma Hotel.'

An hour later, with Barnaby safely housed in the stables, James treated himself to a decent hot meal and a comfortable bed for the night.

Well, well, how has this come to pass? he wondered as he switched off the gas lamp and settled himself between the crisp cotton sheets. *You signed the name and you said it out loud. Does this mean it is now who you are?*

James had no idea why he'd given the name 'Brereton'. In the need to avoid 'Wakefield' it had just popped out somehow. His mind had been blank, no other name had presented itself. The choice had been purely instinctive. Did he still harbour deep-seated feelings for Harriet Brereton, was that it? Despite her insistence upon being no more than a schoolteacher, she remained the closest thing to a mother he'd ever known. Was that why he'd taken her name?

No matter, he decided, *it's just a name, no more, but a name other than Wakefield and that is important.*

He drifted into a sleep more blissful than he'd known for some time and awoke with fresh resolve, with the feeling even of being reborn. And in a way he was, wasn't he? James Wakefield had ceased to exist. He was now James Brereton, another man altogether.

Throughout the remainder of his journey, when weather conditions dictated he should, James had no qualms staying overnight in a hotel. His new identity lent him a sense of impunity. He was bolder now. With his clean-shaven face he knew he appeared younger, quite different from the image he'd presented in Barcaldine. And no one was looking for James Brereton, were they?

He arrived in Brisbane on the 12th of June, or rather he arrived on its outskirts. Even here he found the busyness daunting. The bustle of industry, the people, the horse-drawn traffic; he'd never seen anything like it. But this was what he wanted. Here lay the anonymity he sought.

His accumulated funds now sadly diminished, he sold Barnaby, together with his tackle, to one of the many stables and saddleries that abounded along the main road into town. He was sorry to say goodbye to Barnaby, they'd been through so much together, but he reminded himself once again that, like Red Nell, Barnaby was only a horse.

Then, shouldering his kitbag and swag, he walked the last mile or so into the city centre where here, more than daunted, he was rendered agog with amazement.

On either side of the broad streets were buildings taller than he'd ever seen. Grander too. Some were solid edifices with shapes and patterns sculpted into their stonework, others ornate with wide balconies and moulded lace-iron railings, here and there yet others boasted towers. And again the traffic ... There were open buggies, fancy carriages, wagons and drays, and even a horse-drawn bus, which had to be carrying at least ten people. He'd never seen a bus before, he hadn't even known buses existed.

Deciding that the inner-city hotels, which to him appeared most opulent, were probably out of his price range, James made enquiries of passers-by that led him to a modest lodging house near the main railway station. Here he booked himself in for a full week, during which time he intended to line up some paying work, most likely

as a labourer; he'd noted a number of building sites about
the city.

At the lodging house he was once again expected to
sign in.

'A request of management, sir,' the efficient young clerk
at the front desk explained, 'all new residents are required
to sign in.'

James did so with alacrity. He was accustomed to the
procedure by now and had developed an impressive sig-
nature. 'James Brereton', he wrote, adding a flourish to
the 'n' and a bold stroke beneath, signifying the powerful
character of one who would sign himself thus.

He found a job the very next day, upon enquiry at a
site in Queen Street, barely a five-minute walk from the
lodging house, where an extension was being made to one
of the city's fine hotels. He'd been right, constant building
was taking place around the ever-burgeoning state capital
of Brisbane. There was plenty of work to be found for a
strong, fit young man like James Brereton.

But his sense of complacency was about to be shattered.
On the 15th of June, newspapers screamed the latest bulletin. He didn't even need to buy a paper, assaulted as
he was by the newsboys in the streets and the headlines
emblazoned on the posters surrounding the newsstands.

'Shearers' strike over! Read all about it!' the newsboys
hollered.

'FAILED STRIKE OFFICIALLY CALLED OFF,' the
posters announced.

He quickly purchased a copy of *The Brisbane Courier*
from a boy who was doling them out left, right and centre
from a pile tucked under one arm. Leaning against a lamp
post, he read the lead article.

Shearers were apparently outraged, not only that their
demands had been denied, but that the strike had been
officially declared over. *'There will be repercussions,'*

union leaders announced. '*The strike is destined to have far-reaching effects upon the Queensland government,*' the shearers and their fellow unionists proclaimed.

So it's over, James thought, *at last it's over.*

The strike itself may have been over, but as subject matter for discussion the ramifications of its aftermath was more popular than ever. Particularly at the modest lodging house near the railway station, which James now realised had been a poor choice on his part as it was an intermittent home to many itinerant workers, particularly railwaymen and carriers, all of whom had been heavily committed to the strike.

'How dare they call it off just like that!' Syd raved.

The very day the news was published, James stood alongside other residents in the lodging house's common room where men gathered about the urn with their tin mugs to serve themselves the tea that was laid on in the late afternoon.

'Who the hell do they think they are!' Syd was a carrier and a rampant unionist. 'Men died fighting for their rights and these bastards think we'll *forget* that? They think we'll just walk away and *forget* that some of our mates *died* for the cause? Well bugger them, I say!'

Syd was quickly joined by several fellow protesters and very soon names were being mentioned. Names of places and names of men. Blackall and the leader of the Queensland Shearers' Union, Barcaldine and the organisers of the Central Queensland Labourers' Union.

Upon hearing the reference to Barcaldine, James shrank back against the wall, willing himself into the shadows. Of course Barcaldine would come up for discussion, he told himself. Barcaldine was the site of the strike for God's sake.

Then he heard mention of Lagoon Creek, and he froze. He glanced surreptitiously about at the faces in the room.

Do I know any of these men? he wondered. *More importantly, do any of these men know me?* One or two were starting to look alarmingly familiar. But were they? Or was it just his mind playing tricks?

He began to edge his way along the wall towards the open door. The lodging house had been more than a poor choice, he told himself – it had been a downright mistake.

Among the cacophony of men's voices now raised in competition it was difficult to follow the actual conversation, which seemed mostly about the protests, the processions, the military and the police. Then, jarringly, a man's name was thrown in, calling a brief halt to the discussion.

'Tom Hennessy.' The voice was Syd's. 'Wasn't there myself, but did you hear about him?'

A short pause followed before . . .

'Yep,' a man said, 'had his head blown away in the bar at the Royal.'

James was by the open doorway now. He slipped out quietly, not closing it behind him for fear of drawing attention to his departure, and as he crept away to the side door that led to the street he heard the conversation continue.

'Another bloke died that night at the Royal,' the man went on. 'I was there. I knew him. A bloke called George Wakefield.'

His father's name was the last thing James heard as he stepped into the street, closing the door behind him. If he'd stayed a moment longer he would have heard the man say . . .

'They reckon it was George's son murdered Tom Hennessy. Leastways he disappeared and they haven't been able to find him.'

But James didn't need to hear those words. He knew already that he must leave this city. His recently developed sense of security had deserted him in an instant; no longer could he afford to be complacent.

He walked the streets deep in thought, and as he walked, the streets seemed somehow smaller. Brisbane was not the vast city he'd presumed it to be, the place where a man could disappear. Brisbane was full of Queenslanders. It was no more than a big country town, really. Here the shearers' strike was on everyone's lips, and it would be for some time.

They won't leave it alone, James thought, *Queenslanders will keep gnawing at the strike like dogs at a bone.*

He needed a bigger city, he told himself, a more cosmopolitan city. And from all he'd read and heard, what could be bigger and more cosmopolitan than Sydney?

Two days later James caught a train south.

CHAPTER THREE

1892 ushered in a depression unlike any Australia had ever known. People were suffering, and it was common knowledge things were only going to get worse. A sense of desperation was pervading the country.

Young James Brereton, who had been in Sydney for well over six months, was doing better than many for he had a steady job and a roof over his head.

'You're a bit on the young side, aren't you, laddie?' the publican at the Great Western Hotel, a bullish Scot by the name of Clyde McTavish had sneered. And Clyde felt he had every right to sneer – what was a pretty boy like this doing fronting up for a job that demanded a man? The Great Western was a Surry Hills pub after all, not a bloody teashop in some genteel part of town.

'I'm nearly twenty,' sixteen-year-old James had boldly replied, 'and I'll take any work you have. You just try me out, sir. You'll not find me wanting.'

Clyde hadn't believed for a minute the lad was nearing twenty – seventeen, eighteen perhaps, no more – yet there was something about him that impressed the Scotsman. What was it? Something in his manner, in his bearing, in the intensity of his gaze. *This is no soft boy,* he thought, *this boy has grit.*

'It'd be menial work,' he warned, 'and by that I mean

hard labour, loading and unloading beer barrels for the main part.'

'I'm strong, sir,' James assured him. 'Much stronger than I look.'

Yes, I believe you are, Clyde thought. 'The wages wouldn't be anything to write home about either. There's a depression on, as you're no doubt aware,' he added drily. 'But you'd work an hourly rate and if you prove yourself up to it, you'd make enough to get by.' *Another thing in my favour,* Clyde thought, *I could no doubt pay you less than I would a man.*

'That's fine by me, sir.' James nodded briskly, trying to disguise his elation.

'All right laddie, I'll give you a go.' The Scotsman offered his hand. 'Clyde McTavish,' he said.

'James Brereton, sir, how do you do.' James returned the handshake with an iron-like grip in order to impress.

'Report here tomorrow at noon, James, and we'll take things from there.'

'I shall. Thank you, sir.'

James hadn't been able to believe his luck. This was the first pub he'd visited in search of work, simply because it was the nearest pub to the boarding house he'd moved into several days previously. The one that the railwayman had directed him to.

'Take that road over there and up the hill,' he'd been told when, upon arrival at the Sydney Railway Terminal, he'd made enquiries about modest accommodation. He'd found, as a rule, railway workers were well acquainted with cheap lodging houses, and Sydney had proved no exception.

'When you get to the top, cross over Bourke Street,' the obliging railwayman, a Londoner by the sound of him, had explained. 'Big main road, you can't miss it. Then a block down Fitzroy take a little road to the right, Marshall Street. A row of boarding houses there, cheap as dirt they are. Mind you,' he'd warned, 'the landlord's a right bastard. If you don't have your money in hand when he collects the weekly rent, you're out on your arse before you can say Jack Robinson.'

'Many thanks, my friend, I'm most obliged.'

'Good luck to you, son.' The Londoner had watched as the young man set off up the hill, donning his battered felt hat and hoisting his kitbag over one shoulder. *You can't half tell he's from the bush,* he'd thought.

James had noted the Great Western Hotel as he'd passed where it sat on the corner of Bourke and Fitzroy streets. An impressive two-storey brick building with a fine corner façade of decorative design. If he settled in this area he might apply for a job there, he'd told himself.

The Cockney railwayman's advice had proved most helpful and that very day James moved into one of the boarding houses at the top of Marshall Street. From the outside these were colourful little workers' cottages, built of stone and pleasing to the eye, but inside the rooms were tiny, deprived of sunlight, dank and gloomy. Not that James cared. Beggars can't be choosers, he'd told himself, and he'd quickly discovered the area very much to his liking. Surry Hills was within easy walking distance of the city, the harbour, the docklands and the parks, everywhere he wished to explore. And explore, he did.

James had found Sydney overwhelming from the outset. The sheer size of the place: the beauty of its deep-water harbour, dotted with tantalisingly pretty little bays; the tangle of streets that weaved their way up from the docks, criss-crossing each other like a giant maze; the endless laneways designed for night-soil collection that burrowed like rabbit warrens behind the rows and rows of suburban dwellings; and the houses themselves; above all, it was the houses that had intrigued him. Some were imposing, standing several storeys high, others squat, little taller than a man, and yet all were conjoined, huddled side by side as if for comfort.

To James, who had spent his life surrounded by vast open spaces and bushland, the huddled houses seemed somehow absurd. Had the first English settlers found this immense land so fearsome they'd felt the need to cluster themselves together like bees in a hive?

But it was the very cluster of Sydney that was exciting. The tangle and the jangle of the city, the hurly-burly, and the hustle and the bustle of thousands going about their business heedless of those about them. *Where people exist in such numbers, individuals are not noticed,* James thought, which suited him perfectly. Sydney was a jungle, and in the fight for survival no one cared about others. Here indeed was a place where he could successfully disappear.

After four days of exploration, with funds running low, he'd discovered a further aspect of Surry Hills that appealed. The suburb abounded with pubs. It seemed there was one on every major corner. And the very first pub he'd approached, just a half a block from his boarding house, had a job for him. Sydney was definitely destined to become home.

Now, over six months later, James had settled comfortably enough into his new life. He'd even embarked upon an affair with a girl called Betsy who worked at the bakery down the street. It wasn't really an 'affair' as such, but they copulated regularly in his dingy little room at the boarding house. Betsy was in her early twenties and no virgin, but then James hadn't been a virgin either, his father having taken him to a brothel in Barcaldine when he was barely fifteen. George Wakefield had considered if his young son was to play the role of a man then he should become one. And James had heartily embraced the experience. There had been quite a number of prostitutes since then.

Although not 'in love' with Betsy, he enjoyed her company and would rather have liked their relationship to be a bona-fide affair. He'd never had an affair. Money, however, was the problem. He couldn't afford to woo her in any way, a dinner out, even a bunch of flowers being beyond his rigorously observed budget.

James was thankful for his job at the Great Western Hotel, particularly given the ever-worsening depression and the fact that so many were unemployed, but the pittance Clyde McTavish paid barely covered his rent and living expenses, let alone a treat for Betsy. He'd decided to seek extra part-time work, perhaps even another job altogether. Where though? Should he join the hordes that queued up early each day at the docksides of Sydney? It was said dock labour paid well. But upon enquiry of several regular drinkers he'd befriended in the Great Western's bar he discovered the dockside queues had increased tenfold of late, not only due to the depression, but to the recent drought that had hit New South Wales and showed no sign of abating. Already men of the land were coming into the city in search of work, he was told, and many more were destined to follow.

'This drought's here to stay, I can promise you,' one man said dourly. 'I got mates on the land, a brother too. Des and me was brought up near Wagga. Farmin' folk are either goin' broke or they're goin' mad, and Des reckons if they're not one or the other yet, they soon will be.'

'And I'll tell you something else besides,' another informant added in a bid for one-upmanship, 'you'll never get a job on the docks unless you've got the right contacts. It's who you know at the wharfs, and that's a fact.'

James wisely decided against seeking dockside employment, aware that even if he *were* to land a day's work now and then, he'd have to take time off from the pub in order to do so and would risk losing his current job. Clyde would certainly view his actions as a sign of disloyalty. He was in a quandary. Until the subject of Sunday closing came up, and the person who unwittingly fed him the ideal solution was none other than Clyde himself.

'I don't know how they get away with it,' Clyde grumbled one Monday morning as they sat in the near-empty bar downing a beer. Unlike some pubs that opened at six in the morning to cater for night-shift workers, Clyde didn't open his doors until ten, and when business was slow he often invited James to share a beer with him. Clyde liked James. Besides which, the boy was proving not only a hard worker but versatile; he regularly served behind the bar these days and the customers found him most personable. Clyde saw no point in paying him above their agreed regular hourly rate of one shilling, however. Times were tough.

'But they do,' he went on belligerently, the subject obviously a source of great irritation, 'and they make good money what's more.'

'I thought pubs weren't allowed to open on Sundays,' James said in all innocence.

'They're not,' Clyde barked. 'The *Licensing Act of 1882*, laddie. It's bloody well illegal to trade on a Sunday! But there are some who do, and they bloody well get away with it.' He gave a snort of derision. 'Particularly those bastards in Woolloomooloo. Shit, Monty bloody Farrell operates late every Sunday night catering to God only knows what sort of clientele and the coppers never touch him.' Clyde downed the last of his beer and slammed the empty glass on the counter in a gesture of disgust. 'I tell you, the policing in this city's a downright disgrace. It's not fair for honest publicans like me who follow the law to the very letter.'

Clyde McTavish had not the least desire to trade on a Sunday. Six days a week suited him perfectly and the Great Western was a popular pub offering decent upstairs

accommodation and doing excellent bar business downstairs, particularly on Fridays and Saturdays. But the
thought that other publicans were raking in huge profits by
operating illegally rankled to the extreme. Not that Clyde
would ever report the likes of Monty Farrell and others of
his ilk. There was honour among publicans. They would
never rat on one another.

'It's a crime, that's what it is,' he continued to growl,
unaware that he had just fed the perfect idea for extra
work to his young employee.

Woolloomooloo, James was thinking, *late nights
Sundays.* He wondered whether it was worth it. If by any
chance he managed to land a job, would Clyde find out?
Sydney publicans shared a strong network and Clyde obviously knew this Monty Farrell bloke, or at least knew *of*
him. Was it worth the risk?

Then James heard his father's voice. *'Nothing ventured,
nothing gained, son'* – one of George Wakefield's favourite
sayings – and the decision was made. Late afternoon the
following Sunday saw him walking down Bourke Street to
the docks.

Woolloomooloo, fondly referred to as 'the Loo' by its
residents and those acquainted with the area, was a once-
picturesque, harbourside suburb with a very chequered
history. Nestled less than a mile east of Sydney Town in a
horseshoe-shaped valley overlooking a particularly pretty
bay, it had been considered in the early days of settlement
an ideal location for those who could afford to build grand
homes. The upper echelons of colonial society had reacted
accordingly and the gentrified houses of the wealthy had
soon graced the slopes of Woolloomooloo, making it possibly the city's most elite suburb.

Those days were long gone. The decline of the Loo
had begun with the draining of the mangrove swamps
in the 1850s and the construction of a new semi-circular

wharf in 1866. The new Cowper Wharf had expanded the suburb, leaving space for further development, and over the next two decades small workers' houses, and pubs, brothels, gambling dens and other venues catering to all forms of debauchery had sprung into being in order to accommodate a now maritime-focused population. The imposing homes of the gentry, who had long since vacated the area, had either crumbled away through neglect or been converted to cheap, overcrowded boarding houses.

Now, towards the end of the century, the Loo was a tough place, considered by most to be highly unsavoury. Fights regularly broke out in the pubs around the wharf, and also at the fish markets that stood on the corner of Plunkett Street and Bourke. The larrikins of the Plunkett Street Push were furthermore infamous for terrorising innocent passers-by 'just for the fun of it'. And for the most part they could get away with 'just having fun' because the police had given up keeping a close eye on the area. The constabulary possibly saw little point in doing so, considering the Loo a world of its own that could look after itself. And this may have been true. No one cared much about the Loo anymore. Here people could do pretty much what they wanted. There was a certain 'freedom' to be found in Woolloomooloo for those who sought it. Which is probably why Monty Farrell's illegal Sunday trading did so well. Secrecy was a commodity very much embraced by some.

From halfway down the hill of Bourke Street, James' eyes scoured the valley of Woolloomooloo and the bay below; the fish markets on the corner of Plunkett Street; the glut of tiny houses untidily piled together; and most particularly the pubs dotted here and there around the wharf. *Which one would be Monty Farrell's?* he wondered. He'd walked to Woolloomooloo any number of times – over the past six months he'd walked everywhere within at least a two-mile radius of Surry Hills – but he'd not examined the Loo's pubs. He hoped Monty Farrell's would prove easy to find.

It did. At the bottom of the hill, turning right into Cowper Wharf Road and following the curve of the bay, there it was. The Crown and Anchor. A modest hotel, attractive enough although not as impressive as the Great Western, it bore a sign out the front that read 'Monty's Bar', and in smaller letters, 'Late Night Hours: Finest Ales and Liquors'. This had to be it.

James tried the main front door that led directly to the bar. It was locked. There was no lamplight inside and the pub appeared closed. Cupping his hands, he peered through the bay windows that looked out over the street. The glass of the windows was frosted, prettily displaying a crown and an anchor looped together with the name of the pub ornately lettered beneath. Like most hotels the frosted windows were designed not only for decorative purposes, but to create privacy for those who frequented the premises. Nevertheless he could detect movement inside. Someone was there, he was sure of it.

He knocked. No answer. He knocked again, louder this time. There was a sound from within and the door opened.

The man who stood there was of average height, average build, bearded as most men were, particularly those of middle-age as he was; there appeared nothing at all remarkable about him.

'We're closed,' he said, no belligerence in his tone, a simple statement of fact. 'We're always closed on a Sunday.'

'Oh.' James decided to call his bluff. 'I was told you operated late nights on Sundays and I was wondering if you might have a job.'

The man looked him up and down silently, taking in every detail, in a way James found just a little peculiar.

'Is there any chance I might have a word with Monty Farrell?' he asked boldly. 'I believe he's the publican here.'

'Down the side street,' the man said, and James detected the slightest hint of an Irish accent. 'Down the side street and round the lane to the back.' He gave a jerk of his head to the right. 'I'll let you in there.'

The door closed.

James did as instructed, taking the street to the right and circling around via the lane to the rear of the pub. As he arrived, the back door opened. He stepped inside.

'Come on through,' the man said, turning abruptly to lead the way down the passage.

James obediently followed. They walked past a narrow staircase, which presumably led to the upstairs accommodation, and then into a small side office. The man closed the door behind them, then turned to once again examine James in the light that spilled from the gas lamp in a wall bracket. Although barely five in the afternoon, the office was gloomy.

'Where did you hear that we operated on Sundays?' he asked.

James sensed he was being put to the test. 'In a pub,' he replied airily. 'Some bar or other.' He gave a careless shrug. 'Can't remember where.'

The man nodded, his eyes still shrewdly assessing the newcomer. The answer satisfied. 'And you're after some work?'

'Yep.' James tried not to sound too eager. 'Only on Sundays though, I've got a regular weekly job.'

'Well now, we might just be able to find a spot for you,' the Irishman said, relaxing, his brogue a little stronger now. 'Fact is, your type might prove quite popular with our Sunday regulars.'

James wondered what exactly his 'type' was.

'Monty Farrell,' the man said, thrusting out his hand. 'What's your name, boy?'

So this was the infamous Monty Farrell, James thought.

He felt a little disappointed as they shook. He'd expected
Monty Farrell to be something colourful, something larger
than life, but the man was so very ordinary.

'David, sir,' he replied, 'David Howe.' He'd come
prepared with an alias, and what better surname than
Howe? He could be Jack Howe's little brother.

'Any experience with bar work, Dave?'

'Yes sir, a little.' James hoped he wouldn't be asked
for specifics. He certainly wasn't about to say the Great
Western.

But Monty wasn't remotely interested in specifics. He'd
been surprised the boy had given a surname. The turnover
of Sunday workers was considerable, they came and went
on a regular basis, and no one ever had a surname.

'Bar work's a bonus, but no matter, you can work the
floor if need be. Right then.' Monty clapped his hands
together, startling James somewhat. 'Can you do tonight?'

'I certainly can, sir.'

'Enough of the sir, boy,' Monty said, opening the office
door and once again leading the way along the passage.
'I'm Monty to one and all.'

'Right.' James didn't much like the way Monty called
him 'boy'. It sounded somehow demeaning.

'Seven-hour shift, two shillings an hour,' Monty said
over his shoulder as they went, 'eight till three in the
morning. You all right with that?'

He opened the door and James stepped outside.

'Yes that's fine.' *A whole fourteen bob for one day's
work,* James thought. Twice as much as Clyde paid him.
'Thanks, Monty,' he said, 'thanks very—'

'See you at eight. Come round the front.'

The door closed.

James walked up the hill of Bourke Street and in his
dingy boarding-house room made himself a cheese sandwich with bread that was more than a little stale. Then two

and a half hours later he spruced himself up and walked down the hill again.

The month was April, the night was fine with just the slightest nip of autumn, and the gas lamps of Bourke Street cast a pretty light. At the bottom of the hill there were fewer gas lamps. Woolloomooloo was always a little gloomier than the suburbs that towered above it, particularly on a Sunday. The raucousness of Fridays and Saturdays lit up the Loo, but Sundays were quiet, sleepy even.

Not at the Crown and Anchor. Monty's Bar was far from sleepy.

James was let in at the door to the main bar and lounge by a man standing watch outside, vetting all those who entered. Should anyone make an enquiry that appeared suspicious they would be told the bar was closed and that a private party was being held, invitation only. No such enquiry was ever made. Monty had a financial arrangement with the police, who were happy to leave him alone so long as there was no trouble. They mostly steered clear of the Loo in any event.

Inside the bar, the lamps in the wall brackets were turned down lower than those of most pubs. James rightly assumed this was in order not to attract undue attention, but there was something else about the place that differed from most pubs. Certainly from the Great Western anyway. It was the clientele, or rather their manner. They were quieter, less rowdy. This too he presumed was in order not to attract attention, they were, after all, drinking illegally. But as the evening wore on, he was surprised that voices weren't raised a little louder; as a rule the more men drank the noisier they became. Not here. There was a secretiveness about this place, something furtive. Men came and went. New arrivals circled the bar and the lounge as if searching for something. Some sat sharing drinks and conversing quietly, others left together, and

some continued to prowl, chatting here and there, making
contact before moving on.

James surveyed the scene from behind the counter while
busily serving alongside the other barman on duty, a young
man in his early twenties called Pete. He was mystified, but
also intrigued. What was it about this place?

'Hey there, Dave,' Monty called from a table where
he was seated with a well-dressed man in his forties, the
two apparently doing business. 'See to the floor, will you.
Maxie and Rupe are having trouble keeping up.'

Maxie and Rupe were two general hands, also in their
early twenties, who were clearing away glasses and washing
them up for re-use. James dived out from behind the bar in
order to collect glasses, and a minute or so later the realisation hit him. As he went from table to table, he noticed
the pair tucked in a corner among the shadows. They were
standing close together and at first he thought they were in
intimate conversation. But no. They were kissing. The way
a man and a woman would. Sensually, sexually.

The sight shocked him to the core, he'd never seen anything like it, and he instantly averted his gaze. But as he
continued on his rounds, eyes flickering about the room,
he realised this explained the very 'difference' that pre-
vailed in Monty's Bar. These were not normal men. These
were men seeking other men for sexual purposes. Yet they
all *looked* normal. How could that be? At a glance one
would never have picked them as deviants.

James was more than shocked, he was horrified. He
had heard of the existence of such men. He recalled the
time when a rouseabout had been beaten up. The shearers
and the shed hands had taken quite brutally to the young
man, who was a stranger newly arrived from the city, and
he'd asked his father why. He'd been around fourteen at
the time.

'What did he do, Pa? Why are they bashing him?'

'He's a deviant, son,' George had replied, 'a sexual pervert.' In response to his son's obvious bewilderment, George had spelled things out in no uncertain terms. 'Men like him are not normal, Jimmy,' he'd said, 'they're degenerates. Men who mess around sexually with other men. Pay them no heed, son, they're nothing to do with us.'

George had played no part in the violence himself, but nor had he come to the man's assistance. He'd just stood by watching disinterestedly. He hadn't cared either way. George Wakefield never did.

James vividly remembered that day. *So these are degenerates*, he thought, gazing around, taking in the scene while trying not to stare. Degenerates, deviants, sexual perverts, yet they looked so very normal. More than normal. For the most part they looked rather stylish, upper class even, not like the rough and rowdy mob of regulars that drank at the Great Western. And in ordering their drinks they'd been most polite. James was confused.

He carried the pyramid of glasses he'd collected to the basins that sat behind the bar and as he washed them he pondered the situation. The shock had worn off and he could think a little more clearly. What was he to do? Should he leave the place? Walk out in high dudgeon? But why? These men had done nothing to personally threaten him. If they wanted to kiss one another, he could look away, and whatever they got up to behind closed doors was surely their own business. Who was he to pass judgement?

He looked at Maxie and Rupe, who'd washed and dried their own collections of glasses and returned to the lounge. With less work to do they were now chatting amiably, socialising with the customers as if there was nothing amiss. And he looked at Pete happily serving behind the bar. None of them appeared in the least disturbed by the behaviour or the nature of the pub's clientele.

James came to the conclusion that he'd over-reacted, that it had been the shock, nothing more. *Takes all sorts,* he told himself. Besides, it was barely eleven o'clock, four hours to go and he needed the money. He dried the glasses and returned to his work behind the counter.

Twenty minutes later Monty and the well-dressed man he'd been chatting to sauntered up to the bar.

'Oi, Dave,' Monty said, 'this is Charles, a friend of mine. He has a request to make of you.'

'Hello, Dave.' The man offered his hand.

James shook obligingly, but he was taken aback. By all appearances the man was wealthy; the cloth-covered buttons of his grey coat and matching waistcoat – James had never even seen cloth-covered buttons before, they must be handmade – the heavy gold chain of his pocket watch, the man himself, mid-forties and fleshy, oozing the confidence of the rich. Surely it was unusual for a publican to introduce his well-to-do friends to his barmen, and particularly on a first-name basis.

'Hello,' he said, wondering what the request could be.

Charles smiled affably. 'I'm after a bartender and waiter for a private party I'm throwing, and I just remarked to Monty, "what about your boy there, he looks frightfully efficient".' A further affable smile to Monty who grinned by way of reply, then back to James. 'What do you say, Dave?'

The man's voice was plummy, typical of the privileged English upper classes, and James felt a mixture of discomfort and dislike, aware he was being patronised.

'When would the party be, sir?' he asked.

'Why now of course, boy, this very evening.'

'But it's nearly half past eleven.' James stared in disbelief. Was the man making some sort of joke?

'So? What of it?'

'Well, it's a bit late for a party, isn't it?'

Charles laughed indulgently. 'My parties always start late,' he said. 'But they're very exclusive and they pay very well, I can assure you. A guinea for your *bartending* services.' There was mockery in both his smile and his tone. 'You won't find that rate of pay at your average hotel now, will you?'

A pause followed, James darting a look to Monty expecting him to make some comment, but Monty said nothing.

'So what do you say, Dave?' Charles gave the counter a confident slap with the flat of his hand. 'Have I found myself a barman?'

'I'm afraid not, sir. Not tonight anyway. I'm booked to work here until three in the morning. Perhaps another evening—'

'Oh go along, son,' Monty said, his tone suddenly and surprisingly avuncular, 'it's fine by me, we can manage without you.' He reached a hand into his coat pocket, drew out a fistful of coins, and meticulously counted some onto the bar. 'There you are, seven shillings for tonight's work, a half a shift, right?' His smile, too, was avuncular. 'Run along with you now, Dave,' he said. 'A guinea, my goodness, you can't knock back that sort of money.'

James pocketed the coins, but remained hesitant, looking from one man to the other, bewildered. The night was becoming progressively stranger.

'Follow me,' Charles said, 'the party's right nearby, just a short walk.'

And collecting his jacket, James followed the man out the main doors and into the street.

Monty watched them go, thinking what an excellent performance the boy had given. But then he'd been impressed by Dave – if indeed that was the boy's name, which he very much doubted – from the moment he'd met him. Such a good-looking lad. So young and yet at the same time so self-assured. And the way he played the innocent was most effective. Everyone knew those of homosexual persuasion found innocence arousing. Dave was good all right, Monty thought, far better than the other three boys he had on tonight.

Monty's Bar was not a brothel. Rather it was a well-known venue where, on Sunday nights (and Sunday nights only) men could safely mingle with those of their own kind. It was also known among Sydney's homosexual society that the young male staff Monty employed were available for hire, so long as Monty himself was suitably remunerated.

Outside, James kept pace with Charles, who walked briskly along the waterfront before turning into the backstreets. He remained suspicious, but not frightened. More than anything he was puzzled. *What's going on?* he wondered.

'Only a block or so now,' Charles assured him as they turned yet another corner. Then barely a minute later, 'Here we are.'

They'd arrived in front of one of the many narrow two-storey terraces that abounded in the Loo. It could have been an attractive house, but due to neglect by an uncaring landlord was squalid and ill-kempt.

Charles opened the front door, which he'd left unlocked, having visited the premises an hour or so earlier to ensure the setting was as he wished. He'd rented the house a number of times in the past, although only ever on a Sunday. The place served as a brothel throughout the week, the lease being held by a pimp who farmed the services of three whores. The women refused to work Sundays and the pimp was always happy to sub-let.

James eyed the house warily. Behind the curtained front windows a gas lamp burned. *Hardly the place for a rich man's party,* he thought. Nevertheless he followed Charles inside. His suspicions were by now well and truly raised, but he remained unafraid, confident he could look after himself should there be any trouble.

As Charles closed the door behind them, James looked about the room, which was clearly the main living area of the house, a narrow set of stairs to the side no doubt leading up to the bedrooms. It was sparsely furnished; two Carver chairs and a table upon which sat a whisky decanter and glasses, a mantel over the small grated fireplace and, most incongruously, a washstand with basin and water jug in one corner, and a bed beside it. *Strange*, he thought.

Charles strode to the table where he took off his coat, threw it over one of the chairs and poured two glasses of whisky.

'Where's the party?' James asked.

'It's here.'

Charles thrust the glass at him, but James didn't take it, shaking his head instead – he didn't enjoy hard liquor.

'Where are the guests?'

'They're here too.' Charles returned James' glass to the table and downed half the measure he'd poured for himself. 'You and me, Dave, we're the party.' He dipped his fingers into the breast pocket of his vest and produced a coin, which he placed on the table. 'There, as agreed, one guinea. Now let's get started.' He swigged the rest of his whisky, dumped the glass on the table and seating himself in one of the Carvers, lounged back, legs splayed out before him.

'Get started on what?' James registered something unsavoury was called for, but he had no idea what it might be.

Charles laughed delightedly, the boy was proving rather fun. 'Well let's begin with a strip, shall we?'

'A what?'

'Take your clothes off, boy, show me the goods. Nice and slow now, I like a bit of a tease.'

James stared at the man, aghast. Charles was stroking himself, the bulge in the crotch of his tailored trousers appallingly evident.

'I think there has been some misunderstanding, sir,' he said, aware of the slight tremor in his voice.

'Oh dear me, we have been mistook, have we?' The man's laugh was lascivious, as he started undoing his trousers. 'Poor innocent boy, eh? Very good, very good.' Now he was attending to the buttons of his fly. 'Oh dear me, dear me, yes.' Now he'd wriggled himself free and his engorged penis was revealed. He clasped its base, waving it like a baton. 'Come on, boy,' he growled in deadly earnest, 'get down here and give me your mouth.'

James stood dumbfounded. 'I don't . . . I don't . . .' He meant to say 'I don't understand', but the words wouldn't come out.

Charles was suddenly annoyed. The boy's pretence of innocence was no longer appealing. The game had been fun, but it was time to call a halt. Leaning forward, he hauled off his boots then stood and divested himself of his trousers. But for his stockinged feet he was naked from the waist down and might have presented a ludicrous figure in his shirtsleeves and vest, a healthy erection poking through the crisp white cotton of his shirtfront, were it not for the threatening glint in his eyes.

'You don't what?' he scorned. 'You don't wander Hyde Park and the Domain at night selling your wares? Course you do, boy, I've seen you there.' He hadn't, but he'd occasionally seen pretty boys like this around the well-known haunts, and he'd had them what's more. Ripe young meat. 'Now stop playing games and get on with the job.'

But the boy was backing away, repulsed by the sight of him, which only served to anger Charles all the more.

'Do what I'm paying you to do,' he hissed, and grabbing the boy he tried to force him to his knees.

But the boy resisted, standing firm. He was obviously stronger than he appeared.

'What are you playing at, boy?' Charles demanded. 'Is it more money you're after, is that it?' He didn't wait for an answer. 'If so then get to and earn it,' he snarled and he hurled the boy onto the bed.

Caught off balance, James landed heavily on his back and was jolted out of his numb-like state. This was now a physical attack, and as Charles straddled his chest, thrusting a revoltingly rock-hard erection into his face, James' anger surged to the surface. How dare this pervert attempt to practise his vile ways upon him.

Beyond the swollen penis was the man's face looking down at him, equally ugly, equally disgusting, and reaching up James grasped Charles' throat in his hands. Rage lent him strength. More than rage. Outrage. He squeezed harder and harder. Then harder still, a vice-like grip.

Charles fought to free himself. Terrified eyes bulging in their sockets, he clawed desperately at the hands but to no avail. The hands were like steel, the hands of a shearer.

James felt his thumbs dig deep into the man's flesh, he heard the guttural animal sounds from within the man's throat, and maintaining his hold he rolled off the side of the bed to land on the floor, the man now beneath him, kicking and struggling. Frantic fingers raked his face, nails drew blood, but James was unaware as he dug deeper still, using the weight of his body to bear down, the man's eyes bulging wider and wider as if they might pop from their sockets.

On and on it went, the futile thrashing, until gradually the sounds grew fainter and the struggle weaker. Still James refused to relinquish his grip. Then finally there were no more sounds and the body beneath him was limp. All was silent. Silent and still. Charles was dead.

It was only then James released his hold. He rose to his feet and looked down at the dead man. He felt not the slightest shred of emotion. No anger, no guilt, no fear of recrimination. Why should he? Instead, he passed judgement. The man deserved to die.

Cold, hard practicality took over and crossing to the chair he rifled the pockets of Charles' jacket and trousers. A number of gold sovereigns and three treasury notes for twenty pounds each. *A whole sixty pounds,* he thought, *a couple of years' salary. I can live like a king on this.* How did the man happen to have such a healthy amount of cash on him in the midst of a depression when people were starving? James judged him for that too.

He pocketed the money, together with the guinea that still sat on the table and was about to leave, but one more glance at the body made him aware he'd overlooked something. The fob watch. That would fetch a very good price.

Kneeling beside the dead man, he detached the watch and chain from the pockets of the vest and, opening it, checked there were no identifying initials or inscriptions. There were none. *Good,* he thought.

Then he turned off the gas lamp, plunging the room into darkness, and stole out into the streets of Woolloomooloo.

CHAPTER FOUR

That night changed James forever, or so he firmly believed, for that was the night he lost his innocence. *How naive I was,* he thought, *how they must have been laughing at me.* But any humiliation he might have suffered at the memory was quickly salved. *They won't be laughing at me now though, will they? Charles certainly isn't.*

James didn't regret having killed Charles and he felt no guilt for having done so. Just as he'd felt neither regret nor guilt the previous year when he'd killed Tom Hennessy. Both killings had been justifiable. He'd been avenging the death of his father and he'd been defending himself from an attack by a deranged pervert. Where was the wrong in either? The fact did remain, however, that now at the relatively tender age of seventeen he had killed two men. People would judge him for that. *And people would be wrong,* he thought, *both men deserved to die.*

But there was one element James could not justify. One indisputable element he could not even *explain.* He had *enjoyed* killing these men. He clearly recalled the moment of their deaths. The abject fear in Tom Hennessy's eyes upon realising he was about to die . . . The bulging terrified eyes of Charles upon recognising his fight for life was in vain . . . On both occasions James had relished the power he'd wielded. This was surely cause for worry. Where had it come from, this detachment? This ability to kill with such apparent ease? He'd not been prone to violence as a child, his father had been known by all as a peaceable man, a good man who cared for others. Was there something inherently wrong with him? James wondered.

Whatever the case, he knew from that night on he would never be the same again.

At first he was a little concerned about what might happen when the body was discovered. The murder of a wealthy man like Charles would not go unreported; there were bound to be repercussions. He had no fear of Monty assisting in whatever form of investigation might take place, for Monty Farrell would keep well clear of any involvement with the police. But there would surely be enquiries.

There were not, however. James scoured the newspapers daily, and there was no mention of a rich man found strangled to death in Woolloomooloo.

Unbeknownst to him, the answer was simple. The murdered man had been Charles Grenfell, and Grenfell's Imported Furniture, Fittings, Fashion and Drapery Emporium was renowned for the superior quality of its products and therefore, by association, its family. The remaining brothers who ran the business were not about to let it be known that one of their own had been murdered in a Woolloomooloo brothel. And Charles' wife, who was aware of her husband's predilection for young men, was not prepared for this sordid detail to become known to the family, particularly her two daughters. Better for all concerned if Charles Grenfell had simply died of a heart attack.

As the days passed and fear of investigation appeared needless, James relaxed. He'd been forced to field some comments about the scratches on his face, however.

'Looks like fingernails to me,' Clyde had jovially remarked when he'd reported for work on Monday. 'You been fighting a girl, laddie?'

To which he'd laughed in a man-to-man way. 'Just a bit
of a scuffle with a bloke who couldn't fight,' he'd said.

'What happened to your face?' Betsy had asked on the
Wednesday when he'd snuck her into the boarding house
late at night for their mid-week assignation.

Same reply. 'Just a bit of a scuffle.'

She'd peered at him closely in the light of the kerosene
lamp that sat on the bedside table. 'They look like fingernails to me,' she'd said suspiciously, but as he'd already
removed her blouse and was caressing the fullness of her
breasts through the thin cotton of her chemise, she'd become
distracted and hadn't bothered enquiring any further.

After they'd sated their lust and lay comfortably
entwined, Betsy had intended to ask again – not that she
had any ownership rights on him, she was aware of that,
but she did give him her body on a regular basis, which
surely accounted for something – but his next comment
had taken her so completely by surprise she'd forgotten all
about the scratches.

'Do you want to do something special on Sunday?'

'Like what?' She looked at him blankly. A walk in the
park was the most they ever got up to. *Apart from fucking*,
she thought.

'Oh I dunno.' He gave a careless shrug. 'I could take you
out to lunch, a trip on the harbour, the races, whatever
you like.'

'Where'd you get the money for that?'

'A poker game.'

His boyish grin was enough to set her heart aflutter. She
knew he was too young for her – *nineteen my arse,* she'd
thought when she'd asked him how old he was – but God he
was handsome and, as it had turned out, bloody good in bed.

'All right then. You can take me to lunch.' A saucy smile
lit up her plump and prettily dimpled face. 'And then a
ferry ride on the harbour.'

So James embarked upon his first bona-fide affair. Betsy Brown from the bakery became 'his girl'.

He moved into grander lodgings, a large three-storey terrace boarding house in Bourke Street, not far from the Great Western Hotel, where he had the whole of the basement to himself. The house had been advertised as 'prestigious accommodation' and every morning the land-lady served a hearty breakfast on the ground floor. Luxury!

Steps led directly down from the main street to the front door of the basement, where inside was gloomy, as base-ments tended to be, but compared to his poky little room in the Marshall Street cottage there was more than ample space and, above all, there was privacy. His regular trysts with Betsy (usually mid-week, a Wednesday or Thursday and always Sunday) no longer required skulking about in order to avoid others.

James quickly adapted to his new home. He enjoyed the company of his fellow tenants over the breakfasts that the landlady, an English woman called Edna Pusey, cooked each morning. The other tenants numbered seven men in all, one elderly gent in a room on the ground floor, which also housed the landlady's quarters, and another three on each of the first and second floors. They were office workers for the main part, or travelling salesmen who came and went, but the rooms were fully occupied as a rule, the house well known for providing 'superior lodgings'.

'We're a home away from home here, I can assure you,' Edna would warmly say, welcoming each guest into the house with such a proprietorial air that everyone assumed it was hers.

It wasn't. Edna Pusey was not a landlady at all, but a live-in housekeeper hired by one Broderick Ratcliffe to ensure both his property and its impeccable reputation were maintained. Broderick had a number of properties

billed as 'prestigious accommodation' and therefore a
reputation to maintain. He didn't care in the least if Edna
wished others to perceive her as a woman of some means,
a widow who had converted her home to a lodging house.
It was to his advantage that she should, so long as she
carefully vetted the tenants, kept the place spotless and the
books meticulous, incoming rentals and outgoing expenses
to be painstakingly noted to the very last penny.

All of which Edna did while relishing the role she had
created for herself as the genteel, middle-class woman
she wished to be. Those with an acute ear for accents,
however, might have picked up the slightest hint of a twang
normally associated with the streets of London.

'I shan't be able to offer any lower a rental rate, despite
the fact you're booking in on a long-term basis, Mr Brereton,' she'd warned him during their initial interview.
'I would dearly love to of course,' she'd added with feeling,
'given this terrible depression we're suffering, but sadly the
hardship affects us all, so . . .' A hopeless shrug had said
the rest.

Upon her employer's instruction, Edna *had* recently
lowered the rental rates.

'We don't want rooms sitting vacant, Mrs Pusey,'
Broderick Ratcliffe had told her. 'People are unable to pay
top prices during these trying times and it's best we maintain full occupancy.'

Edna had considered herself more in a position than
Mr Ratcliffe to judge the rental rates apposite to the
current circumstances. Mr Ratcliffe was clearly unaware
that it was easy to maintain full occupancy with so many
men arriving from the country in desperate search of work.
It was easy to sift out those who could and those who
could not afford the higher rate. Young James Brereton,
Edna had decided, was one who could, judging by the fine
cut of his jacket. She'd been right.

'Whatever the rental, I'm willing to pay,' James had said before she'd even quoted the terms.

Edna was pleased. This would mean another several extra shillings a week that she would not have to declare to Mr Ratcliffe, but which she could put towards the running of the household. In no way did she consider she was robbing her employer, rather she was improving the quality of his lodgings. She hired a girl who arrived each morning shortly after breakfast in order to do the washing up before setting about the many tasks demanded in the upkeep of a large house. Edna found household chores irksome herself. The general cleaning, the changing of the bedlinen, the delivery and collection of laundry to and from the local washerwoman were all the duties of the hired help. This allowed Edna ample time to address the true responsibilities of a landlady. There was the shopping to be done, and most importantly the preparation of breakfast for her guests, which she very much enjoyed. Guests became family to a widowed landlady who might otherwise have been lonely rattling around the large house she'd once shared with her husband.

Edna Pusey was not widowed. Edna Pusey had never married. A tall, angular woman, oddly fleshless, all bones and now in her mid-forties, Edna was destined to remain a spinster for the rest of her life. But she accepted her lot, enjoying a status she might never have known had it not been for Mr Ratcliffe and the position he'd granted her. And there was now further pleasure to be found in the person of her brand-new tenant. Edna very quickly took to young James Brereton. Such a fine boy! So handsome, so charming and, above all, so respectful. Why, he might have been the son she'd never had.

From their very first meeting, James had determined to make an impression upon his landlady who, although one of the plainest women he'd ever met, was obviously well bred. He considered her instant acceptance of him a sure indication that he'd moved a rung or two up the social ladder. The thought pleased him greatly. He intended to acquire style.

James had embraced the new life his freshly procured wealth afforded, while also taking care not to flaunt himself too ostentatiously for fear of arousing suspicion. He even continued to work for his pittance at the Great Western Hotel. Not because he needed to, but because he liked the companionship on offer, particularly as Clyde now employed him full-time behind the bar. He did, however, invest in a set of new clothes and a fine pair of boots, discovering the pleasure to be found in smart apparel.

'My, my, very fancy,' Clyde had remarked, looking him up and down with a querying eyebrow that plainly said *'how come?'*

'A poker game,' James had replied, the glib response having rapidly become his catch phrase.

'You're quite the card sharp, aren't you laddie,' Clyde had commented, with a wry mix of admiration and disbelief.

'Yes,' James agreed, 'I am adept, this is true. But a fair bit of luck comes into play as well,' he added modestly, 'the way the cards fall, you know.'

'Oh aye.' A grave nod from Clyde, but a cheekily disbelieving gleam in his eyes. 'I know that for sure. Oh aye'—another grave nod—'always the fall of the cards.'

James decided it best not to be too flashy around Clyde.

Betsy, however, was another matter altogether. He could spend whatever money he wished and whenever he wished in Betsy's company. She showed no particular interest in how he'd come by it. 'You're very good at cards, aren't you?' she'd remarked on one occasion, after which she'd made no further comment. To Betsy, where the money came from was inconsequential.

He'd converted the three twenty-pound treasury notes to manageable cash, which he kept under lock and key in the small wooden deposit box he'd purchased for the purpose. The box lived on the floor of his wardrobe beneath his old kitbag, and along with the stash of coins inside was the gold fob watch and chain. He hadn't yet sold that. He hadn't had the need.

James had not only embraced his new lifestyle, but also his new union with Betsy. As indeed had Betsy. Now that she was 'his girl', the two shared an altogether different relationship, and Betsy thrived on the role she played in his life.

'No, no, that's all wrong, James. It must go over here against this wall so that the gas lamp is just above it.'

James obliged, dragging the chaise longue to the other side of the basement.

'There, you see?' Betsy clapped her hands together delightedly. 'The lighting is perfect.'

Lighting was very important to Betsy, who considered it mandatory to the creation of a romantic atmosphere, which James found just a little confusing. He didn't recall lighting being of any particular importance during their frenzied couplings in the poky room at Marshall Street. But he presumed, and rightly so, this was all part and parcel of a relationship that was now a bona-fide affair.

'It's an odd-looking sofa,' he said, eying the piece critically. 'Why does it only have a backrest at one end?'

'Because it's not a sofa, silly,' Betsy said with a superior air. 'It's a chaise longue.' She rolled the term around on her tongue as if pleasuring in the taste as well as the sound. 'Like the classy people have.'

'Oh.'

Betsy was making a lot of changes to the basement. She was furnishing it to her taste, or rather to the taste she wished to acquire, for the items she insisted he purchase were not inexpensive. James supposed he didn't mind, although he'd been quite content with the bare basics included in the rental; a bed, a wardrobe, a chest of drawers that served also as a washstand with basin and jug, and a diminutive corner desk and chair. Betsy had insisted, however, that they needed another chair and a small dining table for two.

'That way we can have candle-lit suppers on a Sunday night,' she'd said, her face rapturous at the mere thought.

And so they had. On Sundays she would bring special delicacies from the bakery; puffy pastries and jam tarts and sweet macaroons. They'd eat them that night in the flickering candlelight that issued from the three-stemmed candelabra, and they'd sit at the little table sipping the port wine she'd demanded he buy, out of the cut-crystal glasses she'd claimed were essential.

'All the best people drink port wine,' she'd declared.

James didn't have the heart to tell her how very much he disliked the taste of port wine.

Edna Pusey did not at all approve of Betsy, whom she mentally referred to as *Mr Brereton's bit of fluff*. She had of course never met Betsy, but she'd seen the girl serving behind the counter of the bakery up the street, and she'd certainly spied her through the ground floor's front sitting-room window.

Edna always knew when Mr Brereton had his *bit of fluff* stay over, because he didn't come up for breakfast the following morning, which he otherwise would have between half seven and eight. That was when she'd go to the front window that looked out over the street and, sure enough, on the dot of half past eight, there would be the girl skipping up from the basement, bold as brass, not a care in the world. *Brazen hussy*, Edna would think. Furthermore, on a Sunday the girl would arrive in broad daylight with a brown-paper parcel from the bakery, and more often than not a bunch of flowers or a fancy little knick-knack of some sort with which to decorate the basement. *As if she owns the place,* Edna would think, outraged, *as if it's her bleeding home!* Edna didn't like Betsy one bit. That girl was far too common for Mr Brereton.

Betsy *was* coming to think of the basement as home. Why should she not? she asked herself. She had a regular fella now and this was his home, which surely meant it was her home too. She even suggested as much to James.

'I should move in here with you,' she said one day, gazing around admiringly at the cosiness of the basement, at the pretty, feminine touches she'd added; the vase of flowers on the table, the cushions on the chaise longue, the china ornaments on the chest of drawers.

James was startled. 'Why?' he asked. 'Why would you want to do that?'

'Oh for goodness sake, James'—she gave her dimpled smile—'just look around and you'll see why. I've made this place real nice, haven't I?'

'Yes,' he agreed, nonplussed nonetheless. He'd indulged her every whim, enjoying spending his money on her, enjoying her delight in every new purchase, but he hadn't considered for one minute she might be making a home for herself. He was aghast at the mere thought of their living together. 'I don't think that would be wise,' he said awkwardly, feeling caught out.

'Oh? And pray tell why not?' Her response was arch.

He decided to give her as honest an answer as possible, but in doing so he found himself fumbling. 'Because this is *my* world, Betsy, this is my personal world where I can be on my own,' he said. 'I need my privacy. I need a place that's mine, and mine alone . . .' He tailed off.

'I see.' Her tone was icy now, Betsy was furious. *I see all right,* she thought. *It's your world, is it? What about* mine? *I go to all the trouble to make your 'world' pretty, but*

I'm only allowed in it when you're after a fuck. She wasn't about to make a scene though. She liked the way James bought her things that took her fancy; no one had ever done that before. 'Very well,' she said, playing the scene with wounded dignity. 'We'll say no more on the matter.'

'You do understand, don't you, Betsy?'

'Yes, of course I do.' She understood perfectly and she'd made an instant decision what's more. She would stop insisting he buy beautiful things for his bloody basement, she would insist he buy beautiful things for *her* instead.

Over the ensuing weeks, to make up for any hurt he may have caused, James continued to indulge Betsy's whims, but he suspected the end may be in sight. After only three months 'his girl' was becoming intrusive. And she was, furthermore, an expensive commodity. He was made particularly aware of this one Sunday when she paraded her latest acquisition from Grenfell's fashion department. She'd seen the bonnet in a Bloomingdale's catalogue at the Grenfell Emporium some time back and he'd agreed to buy it for her, but he hadn't known it would be so expensive.

'Yes, it's very pretty,' he agreed as she twirled about the basement, although he wasn't really paying much attention, his mind somewhere else altogether. Given the rate at which he'd been going through his funds recently he'd soon need to sell the fob watch and chain. The realisation came as a shock. Betsy was starting to wear thin.

Sensing her lover's interest might possibly be waning, Betsy decided there was only one course of action to be taken. She must get pregnant. James was young and naive, he wouldn't recognise the trap she was laying. And although being from the bush he was a little rough around the edges, he was at heart a gentleman. He would never desert her in her hour of need. *He's a soft one all right,* she told herself. *He'd marry me, I know he would.* The more she thought about it the more the idea appealed.

She'd like to be married. Besides, she was twenty-three years old; high time she found herself a husband.

She embarked upon her course of action the following Sunday after they'd spent a pleasant day together out on the harbour. Their favourite Sunday outings always involved lunch in a tea house at Circular Quay followed by a ferry trip, after which they would walk back up to Surry Hills, cutting through Hyde Park, clutching their coats and scarves about them to ward off the winter chill. Not this Sunday though. This Sunday there was the smell of spring in the air, a fine late September day so unseasonably warm that, even on the ferry, they hadn't needed the coats they'd taken with them.

She'd brought the delicacies from the bakery to the basement that same morning, and she'd checked that he'd purchased a fresh bottle of port wine. She'd even set the candles into the candelabra, thus ensuring everything would be perfect.

It was not yet dark when they returned, but the basement being a gloomy place even in the middle of the day, he was about to turn on the gas lamp.

'No, don't,' she said, tossing her coat onto the chaise longue and taking the hatpin from her straw boater. Her hair, simultaneously released, bounced down around her shoulders most attractively as she intended it should.

The boater joined the coat on the chaise longue and he watched as she fetched the candelabra from the corner desk, placed it on the small central table and proceeded to light the candles.

'Let's keep everything romantic, shall we?'

'If you wish.' James didn't mind in the least. He'd wanted to make love before they'd left that morning; it was their usual practice. But she'd kept him at arm's length.

'Later, James,' she'd whispered, even as she'd kissed him tantalisingly. 'It's such a beautiful day outside, let's make the most of this glorious weather. *Please,*' she'd whispered again with greater insistence, easing away from him as he'd grasped her breast and thrust himself at her. *'Please, James, please!'*

He'd been forced to give in, albeit reluctantly.

Now there was no stopping him.

She laughed as he kissed her, groping for her breast with one hand while clumsily attacking the buttons of his trousers with the other.

'Careful,' she said, 'you'll set the place on fire,' and she pulled away to extinguish the still lighted match in her fingers.

He quickly divested himself of his trousers to stand there half naked, his erection boldly evident.

In blouse and skirt, she'd discarded her belt and now raised her arms, her eyes focused upon him, smiling as she reached behind her head to undo the fastening of her modest, high-necked, long-sleeved blouse.

He wasn't sure why, but he found both the action and her expression extraordinarily erotic.

'Will you undo the rest for me, please?' she said, turning her back to him.

He fumbled with the blouse, wanting to rip it from her, but the very sound of her voice stayed his feverish fingers.

'Do take care, James,' she said playfully, 'this is such a pretty blouse, a favourite of mine, I wouldn't want to spoil it.'

Her voice was teasing him, eking out the pleasure, and he was aware of her hands, now waist height, reaching behind her back, undoing the fastening of her skirt, which was nipped in at the waist to flow free to the ground, the design accentuating the generous hour-glass proportions of her body. The fact that she was helping him undress her added immeasurably to his excitement.

The skirt dropped to the floor just as he finished undoing the blouse and, turning to face him, she wriggled her arms free, the blouse also dropping away. She stood before him in her tantalisingly flimsy mid-calf-length undergarment of light cotton and lace – Betsy never wore a corset – and stepping over the clothes that lay on the floor, she reached out her hands to his collar.

'Your turn,' she said, honey-toned, seductive, and she slowly started undoing his shirt buttons.

James was riveted to the spot. This was far more erotic than usual. Normally they undressed themselves, more often than not in haste, and sometimes barely at all, he dropping his trousers, she pulling off her drawers and lifting her skirts. For all Betsy's insistence upon a romantic setting, their couplings were invariably driven by a sense of urgency.

His shirt dropped away to join the other clothes on the floor and he stood naked, aware of her eyes roaming his body approvingly. He reached forward to undress her further, but her smile and the slightest shake of her head halted him.

Betsy was not yet done. This was why she'd worn her combination undergarment, in circumstances like this so much more effective than separate chemise and drawers.

Her eyes locked with his, and very gently she slid one lacy strap over a shoulder, then the other lacy strap over the other shoulder.

James watched, mesmerised, as the flimsy garment hung there, the swell of her breasts all that kept it in place.

Then arms hanging loosely by her sides, just the briefest tug of her fingers and the undergarment slithered daintily to the floor.

James had lost count of how many times they'd been naked together in bed, grunting and heaving and satis-fying a lust that was mutual. But this was the first time she had presented herself to him in such a way. A way in which to be studied. More than studied. Admired. He was awe-struck.

'You're beautiful,' he said.

'So are you.' She held out her arms. This was exactly how she wanted him. In awe of her, overwhelmed by who she was and all she had to offer.

Then they were making love. He was imbedded in her, plunging deep within her body. She was engulfing him, dragging him in ever deeper. Familiar territory for both, their passion mounting equally. He was lost in her and she was meeting his every thrust. But at the very peak, at the point of no return, something changed.

Betsy had always been in charge at this moment. Just as he was about to ejaculate she had always twisted her body free. Every single time. But not this time. This time she clung on, clenching herself around him with a muscular strength that was nothing short of astounding.

It was the very strength of her that shocked James from his complete distraction, and in that instant he pulled free to spill himself on the rumpled bed linen.

They collapsed gasping for breath to lie side by side, gazing up at the ceiling, at the flickering shadows cast there by the candles. Then finally . . .

'Why did you do that?' he asked.

'Do what?' she replied in all apparent innocence.

'Keep me inside you,' he said, rolling to face her, studying her expression in the dim candlelight.

She rolled on her side to gaze back at him. 'I couldn't help myself,' she said tenderly, 'I was overcome. I didn't want to leave you.' She raised a hand, fingers softly stroking his cheek. 'Oh my darling James, I do love you so.'

'No you don't.' His voice was brusque and he sat up, breaking the moment, not even looking at her as he made his accusation. 'You did that deliberately, didn't you?'

She sat up also, deeply offended. 'How could you suggest such a thing,' she said, appalled. 'I was carried away by my love for you . . .'

'You're trying to trap me, aren't you, Betsy?'

He turned to her, the intensity in his eyes more than a little unnerving, but Betsy's performance did not falter.

'Trap you into what, my love?' She remained the picture of hurt bewilderment.

'Into getting you pregnant of course,' he snapped. 'That's what you were trying to do just then.'

Betsy sensed she was fighting a losing battle, but she was certainly not prepared to admit defeat. She gave a worldly laugh instead. 'Oh James,' she said with a warmth of affection that managed to sound patronising, 'you're very young. Babies don't happen that easily. One careless moment doesn't result in a pregnancy.' She'd been hoping it would herself, but even if it hadn't she'd been presuming he would enjoy their new carefree form of lovemaking to the point where the inevitable would occur. 'To think so is naive, my dear.' Her expression changed to the penitent. 'But I shall take care never to lose control again as I did, I promise you.' A girlish moue. 'Do you forgive me?' A winsome pout of the lower lip. 'Please say you do.'

James was vaguely amused by her change of tack. *Young. Naive.* That's what she'd called him. And yet after treating him like an ignorant schoolboy she was now all of a sudden playing the coquette. Did she really consider him so incredibly gullible? *Would she feel differently,* he wondered, *if she knew I'd killed two men?*

He stood, picking up his trousers and hauling them on.

'Time to go, Betsy,' he said.

'Oh.' She was taken aback and made no move. 'Where?'

'Come on now, get up and get dressed.' He didn't bark the words, but it was an order nonetheless.

She did as she was told, and when she was clothed he opened the door for her.

'But . . . but . . .' she stammered, at a loss as to what was expected of her.

'Don't forget your coat,' he said, 'it'll be getting cold outside.' He took her coat from the chaise longue, helped her on with it and thrust the straw boater into her hands.

'But what about our pastries?' She was in a state of utter confusion. 'What about the port wine?'

'Take them with you.' He picked up the unopened bottle of wine and the parcel of pastries wrapped in brown paper and loaded them into her arms. 'There you are. Off you go.' And he bundled her out onto the steps that led up to the street, closing the basement door behind her.

Edna Pusey was delighted to see young Mr Brereton at breakfast the following morning. What a pleasant surprise. He was never at breakfast on a Monday, his *piece of fluff* always staying over on a Sunday. She did hope it meant he'd given that awful common girl her walking orders. He deserved someone so much better.

James gave no further thought to Betsy, apart from ruing the fact he'd spent so much money on her. What a fool he'd been. He was now reduced to selling the fob watch and chain. And when the proceeds of the sale were gone, what then? He'd become accustomed to a finer life-style than could be provided by Clyde McTavish and the Great Western Hotel.

He sat on the chaise longue examining the watch in the light from the gas lamp on the wall behind him. He hadn't looked at it for months, having left it sitting in the locked deposit box at the bottom of his wardrobe, the box itself only visited when he was in need of a fresh supply of cash. Now he admired its rich, golden gleam, turning it over in his hands, feeling its weight, running the chain through his fingers. He knew very little about pocket watches, but this was surely a fine one, bound to fetch an excellent price. In fact it was such a fine watch he felt loath to part with it. He pictured himself in a perfectly cut three-piece suit, the chain of the pocket watch serving as centrepiece on the vest. And the vest would have cloth-covered buttons, hand-made, just like those on the vest Charles had been wearing.

The thought set him off on a new tangent, the watch and all it represented becoming strangely mesmeric. He could see the chain dangling from Charles' vest, he could see the vest's cloth-covered buttons, and above the vest and the shirt collar, he could see the purple-veined neck and the bloated face with its bulbous dead eyes.

As the watch continued to cast its spell, James found himself reliving every moment of that night. Every word, every image, every touch and sound returned to him with all the clarity of yesterday. The repulsiveness of the man he'd murdered . . .

'Take your clothes off, boy, show me the goods. Nice and slow now, I like a bit of a tease.'

The sight of the man waving his hideous erection . . .

'Come on, boy, get down here and give me your mouth.'

He could see his hands around the man's throat. He could feel his fingers closing, the grip becoming tighter and tighter. He could hear the guttural sounds of the man fighting for his life . . .

James was glad he'd murdered Charles. No, he corrected himself, not murder. Self-defence. Then he corrected him-self again. No, not self-defence. Execution! Yes, that was the right term. Odious creatures like Charles should be executed; he'd been doing the world a favour ridding it of a man like that. And there are so many like him, aren't there? He recoiled at the memory of Monty's Bar on that Sunday night, the two men kissing in a corner, others circling the room, hunting their choice among fellow degenerates.

He recalled how he'd initially felt sickened when he'd realised their intent. And he recalled how easily he'd persuaded himself nothing was wrong simply because of the money Monty had been paying him. But everything was wrong, wasn't it? He felt sickened all over again, remembering that night and those odious creatures. Like Charles, they should be exterminated. Such men didn't deserve to live . . .

And upon that instant the solution presented itself. There was money to be made from such men. What was it Charles had said when he'd virtually accused him of prostitution? *'You don't wander Hyde Park and the Domain at night selling your wares? Course you do, boy, I've seen you there.'*

Hyde Park and the Domain, James thought. He knew both well in the innocence of day. But it appeared these picturesque areas served an altogether different purpose at night.

Having made his decision, he returned the fob watch to the deposit box. No need to sell it. Not yet anyway. He would explore this new avenue of possibility first. If moneyed men like Charles cruised these areas in order to satisfy their sexual perversions then they deserved to be robbed.

James put the deposit box back in the wardrobe, placed his old kitbag on top and closed the door. It was only then that a thought occurred. He remembered the satisfaction – no, far more than that, the *enjoyment* – Charles' death had afforded him. Would he be driven to kill again? It was not his intention, but perhaps the role he was destined to play in the lives of these men was that of executioner.

CHAPTER FIVE

Discovering the rendezvous preferences of Sydney's homosexual society did not prove as easy as James had expected. His memory of Charles' accusatory taunt had led him to believe that if he openly paraded around Hyde Park and the Domain after dark he was bound to be accosted. But this was not so. After several nights' extensive and fruitless exploration he realised his expectations had been naive; that those seeking homosexual dalliances did not openly parade, rather they skulked about in the shadows. He changed his tack and before long chanced upon a popular spot where men 'loitered with intent'. Or so it appeared on this particular night.

It was well after midnight. He'd walked to Hyde Park from Surry Hills the moment the Great Western Hotel had closed and had been prowling its more shadowy recesses for over an hour. He was in an area on the College Street side of the park, leafy and well shaded from the nearby gas lamps and he halted when, up ahead, he saw a man lingering among the trees. The man was looking around as if searching for something or someone, which to James appeared most suspicious. He must surely be a deviant.

From where James stood in the shadows, the man had not seen him and he was about to make his presence known, but paused as he saw another man approaching from the opposite direction.

He edged further back into the shadows and watched as the two met and struck up a conversation. He could hear no more than the low murmur of their voices, but the night was clear and in the light of the moon he could see them, although not in detail, well enough. He noted they were standing closer together than was necessary, much closer than men would usually stand. He further noted that, like the homosexuals he'd seen in Monty's Bar, they appeared quite normal, which he found odd and somehow wrong. They shouldn't look normal.

Then barely a minute or so later the two turned and walked away together, cutting through the park in the direction of the city. Yes, James thought, this was definitely one of those places where men loitered, just as Charles had said they did.

He stepped out from the shadows and, hands in coat pockets, struck a casual pose, gazing around as if waiting for someone, or perhaps seeking someone, hoping in any event that he appeared to be offering an invitation.

It didn't take long.

'Hello there,' a voice said from behind him.

He turned. The man was middle-aged and well dressed, a tan-coloured three-piece suit and matching overcoat, but he was so extremely ordinary that James was surprised. He'd expected a face more florid, more dissipated, more like Charles'.

'Hello,' James said.

'Oh my goodness'—the man, too, appeared surprised—'you're very young.'

'I'm twenty,' James said, and he smiled invitingly. 'Are you seeking a good time?' He had no idea what he was expected to say in 'plying his trade', as Charles had put it, but it sounded right to him. 'If so I can certainly offer you one.'

'Ah.' Edwin Peabody, an accountant at the Sydney offices of Burns, Philp & Co, Limited, had indeed been hoping to make contact with one of his own kind and to enjoy a homoerotic encounter, but he hadn't been seeking a prostitute. The young man was so handsome though, and his smile so winning, the prospect was enticing. 'May I enquire,' he said hesitantly, 'your fee . . .?'

'Whatever you feel is a fair price,' James replied with another devastating smile.

'Well . . .' The answer had come as a huge surprise, and Edwin returned the smile. 'That is a most extraordinary response,' he said. He'd never been with a prostitute. He couldn't help feeling intrigued and he was certainly attracted. 'I promise I shall make it worth your while then,' he said and he proffered his hand. 'I'm Ed, by the way.' In his day-to-day existence no one ever called Edwin Peabody 'Ed', but he always adopted the diminutive when embarking upon an intimate liaison. He liked being on a first-name basis.

'Hello, Ed.' James automatically returned the handshake. The man's smile was so pleasant, so friendly, he was further taken aback. Everything about this man was wrong. He was too ordinary, too affable, too nice to be a deviant.

'Shall we go to my home or would you prefer an hotel?' Edwin asked, his voice also too pleasant, too affable, too nice.

'Whichever you wish,' James said briskly. His hand was being held onto just a little too long for his liking.

Edwin was loving the feel of the young man's hand, the grip so unexpectedly strong yet the skin so smooth and unspoiled. 'I think perhaps my home,' he said, 'more intimate, more personal. We can find a cab in Oxford Street.' He took James' hand in both of his now and, gazing down, stroked the back of it with his fingers, enjoying the silkiness. 'You have beautiful hands,' he murmured, 'truly beautiful.'

As he looked up and their eyes locked, James was repulsed by the naked desire he could see there. This man was a disgusting degenerate, no better than Charles. He locked his hands around Edwin's wrists and dragged him into the grove of trees, where he smashed the man's back hard up against a trunk then grasped him by the throat.

'You filthy pervert,' he hissed, 'I'll kill you!' Rage engulfed him. 'I'll fucking kill you, you sick bastard!'

Edwin was gasping, and in a state of profound shock. Speechless. Terrified. The young man's eyes were murderous. *Oh dear God,* he thought, *I'm about to die.*

He stammered incomprehensively, 'Don't . . . d . . . d . . . don't . . . don't . . .' He meant to say, 'Don't kill me.' He'd beg if he could. 'Don't kill me . . . don't kill me . . .' He'd beg from the very depths of his soul, but the words simply wouldn't come out. 'Don't . . . don't . . .' He felt the warmth of his urine trickling down his legs, and he started to cry. There were no words at all now, not even a stammer, just sobs of sheer terror.

The irrational surge of anger had passed and James released his hold on Edwin's neck to watch as he slithered down the trunk of the tree, a blubbering mess with legs no longer able to support his body. He could see the dark stain on the crotch of the man's trousers.

He's pissed himself, he thought. *He's pissed himself and he's pathetic and pitiful and contemptible. But he doesn't deserve to die.*

James was relieved to discover he was not driven to be this man's executioner, that the desire to kill had left him. But he had not forgotten his reason for embarking upon this current enterprise.

He squatted beside the wreck of a man. 'Give me your money,' he demanded, 'everything you have.'

'Oh . . . ah . . . yes, yes . . .' Edwin rediscovered his stammer and very quickly his voice. 'Here, here,' he gasped,

delving into his inside coat pocket for his money pouch
and into his jacket pocket for the coins he kept at the ready
for hansom cabs. 'Here, here, take it, take it,' he stuttered
and shovelled it all James' way, some coins spilling to the
ground.

James gathered the money, stood pocketing it, then
walked away without another word.

Edwin remained where he was, chest heaving with relief
that he was still alive. He watched the receding figure of
his would-be killer vanish into the gloom and vowed he
would never again wander Hyde Park at night. He didn't as
a rule. Normally he found his contacts at the Coffee Room
in the Imperial Arcade, a fashionable spot frequented by
discreet men, or else the Turkish Baths in lower Liverpool
Street, another safe meeting place. He wasn't sure why
he'd decided upon Hyde Park tonight, perhaps he'd fancied
an element of danger. The unknown and the unexpected
could be titillating. *Never again,* he vowed as he finally
found the strength to scrape himself up off the ground.
Never, never, never again!

James' haul that night was substantial. Fifteen pounds
of folding money in the pouch and ten shillings in coins.
He was pleased. He'd been right. There was a profit to be
made from these debauched men.

He took to regularly visiting the same area of Hyde
Park, and discovered also a popular corner of the Domain
where men 'loitered with intent'. He ascertained, too,
the favoured nights such men were on the hunt, which
strangely – to him – tended to be mid-week rather than
a Friday or Saturday. He didn't know why this might be,
but presumed it was possibly because there would be less
people around.

'Where've you been? I been waiting here all night.'

She hadn't, it was still night – four o'clock on a Thursday
morning, to be precise – but Betsy had been sitting on the

basement steps for a substantial length of time, certainly since the Great Western had closed.

She stood. 'You got another girl, haven't you?'

James was tired. It had been a long night and not a profitable one. He'd been approached by only two men over a whole four hours, neither of whom had appeared wealthy and he never wasted his energy on those without money, it wasn't worth the effort. He'd told both men to 'bugger off' in no uncertain terms, but one hadn't. One had placed a hand on his crotch instead, not threateningly, but invitingly, thereby enraging him to the point where he'd bashed the man senseless. His knuckles were bloodied and aching, and all he wanted to do was bathe his wounded hand and get some sleep before reporting for work.

'Go home, Betsy,' he said. This wasn't the first time she'd attempted to reignite their affair, accosting him in the street or knocking on the basement door, always with a plea, which he'd rejected in as reasonable a manner as possible. But this was the first time she'd lain in wait for him. Betsy was becoming decidedly wearisome.

'You have, haven't you, you got another girl.' Her tone, although accusatory, was also plaintive. She missed James. They'd had such good times together. And now she had no one. Just the drudgery of work and then upstairs to her horrible little room above the bakery. 'That's it, isn't it?' she demanded. 'You've found someone else.'

'Yes, that's it, I have,' James said brutally. 'I've found someone else. I've got another girl now, so go away, Betsy. Go away and leave me alone, do you hear?' He stamped past her down the steps, unlocked the basement door and slammed it behind him.

She stood gazing blankly at the door, knowing that beyond it was the pretty home she'd made for him, and for a brief time she'd hoped for herself. He'd changed, she thought. He wasn't at all the naive boy she'd first met.

'You're a hard man, James Brereton,' she yelled at the door, loud enough so she knew he would hear her. 'You're a hard, cruel man.'

Then Betsy Brown gathered her shawl around her and walked with all the dignity she could muster back up the street to the bakery and her room at the top of the stairs.

James hadn't wished to be brutal, but he knew it was the only way to rid himself of Betsy. Her words now seemed to him overly harsh. He did not see himself as a hard man at all. Nor a cruel man. If anything he saw himself as a just man. And this despite the life he was currently leading. He never robbed those who couldn't afford to be parted with the money they were carrying, and he was never unduly violent to those he *did* rob. Furthermore, he no longer had any wish to kill these men whom he'd come to view as weaklings, nor even to do them harm. Their sort deserved to be robbed, it was true, but they were not like Charles. They did not deserve to die.

The successful robberies James carried out were invariably conducted along the lines of his encounter with Edwin Peabody, the only difference being his temper remained in check and he made no murderous threats. He would charm his prospective 'client', then agree to accompany him to a hotel room, or on the odd occasion even to the man's home. But he never did. He always ensured the robbery took place in Hyde Park or the Domain.

'A slight change of plan, I'm afraid,' he would say, choosing a particularly secluded spot as the two of them set off from their initial rendezvous point. 'I won't be accompanying you after all.' He would draw to a halt, the man would stop beside him and, dropping all vestiges of charm, his voice and his eyes would signal a deadly intent. 'You'll give me your money instead,' he would say. Even without the murderous threat, it was imperative he instil fear. 'And I mean *all* your money. Right here and right now.'

His power, his purpose and his very intensity were such that few argued. Most were only too eager to make their escape, and those several who attempted any form of resistance soon acquiesced. A surprisingly strong hand to the neck and fingers that locked in a steel-like grip were a quick dissuader.

James' ploy proved so successful that he acquired more than enough funds to maintain the lifestyle to which he'd become accustomed, particularly now he was without the added expense of Betsy. He bought himself some fine new attire and joined a men's club in Oxford Street where, late on a Friday night and well into the wee hours, he happily lost more than he won at the poker table. Why should he not? He could afford to do so.

He considered leaving the employ of the Great Western Hotel and also moving to grander lodgings, but found himself loath to do either. He enjoyed the raucous cama- raderie of the Great Western and was very fond of his basement. So he continued, in essence, to lead a double life. On Fridays, after returning home from work to don his finery, he would pose as a gentleman at the Hampton Club. Here he would mingle with any number of Sydney's business elite; the Grenfell brothers who owned the city's finest emporium and others of their ilk; men who would never visit the bar of the Great Western, thereby offering no fear of discovery.

James was aware such men did not accept him as being of their class, but this was of no concern in the Hampton Club. So long as he had sufficient money to lose at the tables the men mingled with him pleasantly enough. And as they did, he studied them closely; their general behaviour, their manners and affectations, even their way of speaking, determined to discover how he might one day pass muster as a gentleman. It was an interesting exercise.

He entertained himself also on his jaunts to the park, dressing in his finer clothes and acting the role of a well-bred young man so that those who accosted him initially believed he was one of them. Their reaction upon discovering he expected to be paid for his services was always amusing; a mix of astonishment, disbelief, disapproval and more. But they never said no, did they? And then when they further discovered he was neither a well-bred young man, nor a prostitute, nor a sexual pervert, but simply after their money, their reaction was even more amusing.

James revelled in the game he was playing, and also in its profitability. Despite his losses at the poker table, the money in the deposit box that sat on the floor of the wardrobe was steadily mounting. And acquiring it was so simple! Not only were the men he robbed easily intimidated, there was no competition. His original assumption that male prostitutes would be regularly roaming these favoured paths had proved untrue. He'd encountered only one so far.

It had been just before Christmas, a lad of around his age who would have been good-looking were it not for an air of desperation. Watching from the shadows, James had sensed a 'neediness' about him, the way he appeared uncertain, insecure, and he'd wondered if the lad had been driven to seek a living in this sordid way through no fault of his own. A ghastly thought. He'd felt sorry for him and had been about to make his presence known. He would have struck up a conversation, made an enquiry, perhaps given the lad some money to tide him over. But the lad had seen him and, upon sizing him up as a competitor, had slunk away into the surrounding gloom.

Since then, James had encountered no other young man on his nightly prowls and, as a new year ushered in and the weeks passed, he decided that the male prostitutes to whom Charles had referred, if indeed there were any, must patrol different areas of Hyde Park and the Domain.

Which left him all the more surprised on that night in late February 1893. The night he met Ben.

The summer had been a particularly sultry one, with humidity levels higher than was customary for Sydney, and despite the lateness of the hour the night remained muggy. It was not long before James' birthday – he would turn eighteen in early March, only a week or so now – and he was in his regular Hyde Park haunt near College Street. He preferred the park to the Domain because there was more leafy coverage from where he could observe without being seen. Easier then to choose his target of preference. He had already let one potential victim pass by. Middle-aged, as was customary, but not wealthy enough, he'd decided, judging by the man's attire.

Barely a half an hour later, he saw another man approaching, and to his amazement this time a *young* man. A rather good-looking young man from what he could make out, and well dressed what's more.

James made no move, but watched, fascinated. The young man appeared only a few years older than him, around twenty or so, and he was walking unnecessarily slowly, looking about as if perhaps seeking something. Could he possibly be a prostitute? If so, he was a very well-dressed one. *But then so am I, aren't I?* James thought.

The young man passed him by where he stood unseen in the grove of trees, but didn't go far, turning to walk slowly back the way he'd come. *Yes,* James thought, *he's patrolling this well-known beat. He has to be a prostitute.*

Intrigued, he stepped out from the trees into the young man's path. 'Hello,' he said with a friendly smile.

'Oh.' The young man gave a gasp, momentarily startled, but recovered to return the smile. 'Hello there. You quite took me by surprise.'

Well spoken, too, James thought. *Not what you'd call a toff, but he could pass as a gentleman.*

'Sorry,' he said, adopting his own refined manner of speech, the one he'd been observing at the Hampton Club and practising of late, 'didn't mean to frighten you, old chap.'

The young man looked amused, which James found somehow irritating.

'What are you doing skulking around the park at this hour of the night?' he demanded with an air of pomposity.

'I might ask the same thing of you,' the young man replied, still amused.

'It's stifling indoors,' James said, 'I'm simply taking in the night air.'

'So am I. Why are you putting on that funny voice? It really doesn't work you know.'

James instantly deflated. Who did this bloke think he was!? But it appeared the young man intended no insult. Nor did he appear to be seeking an answer as he went on to introduce himself.

'I'm sort of looking around,' he said pleasantly. 'I'm from the country, just arrived in Sydney. The name's Ben.'

He proffered his hand, which James instinctively took while returning no name of his own.

'Hello,' he said, dropping the 'funny voice' before throwing out the challenge. 'Are you a prostitute?'

'Good grief, no.' Ben was plainly shocked. 'What on earth would make you think that?'

'You're very young.'

'So are you.' Then a brief pause while a thought occurred. 'Why,' he asked, 'are *you* a prostitute?'

James speedily reassessed the situation. 'Nope,' he replied glibly before changing the subject. 'What part of the country are you from?'

'A property not far from Goulburn.'

'Goulburn, eh?' A sage-like nod. 'Sheep country.'

'Yes,' Ben said eagerly, 'how did you know?'

'Oh I know quite a lot about sheep.' The Goulburn plains were renowned as excellent pasture lands, it was where some of the country's finest Merino wool was produced, James thought. Every shearer in Australia knew that.

Ben seemed to find his knowledge of sheep most interesting. 'Would you like to come back to my hotel for a drink?' he asked. 'I'm staying at the Metropole.'

He was being invited back 'for a drink', and to the Metropole no less. James was impressed. The Metropole was one of Sydney's grandest hotels, second only to the Australia. Ben was obviously wealthy. *Strange,* he thought, *that such a good-looking young bloke should be a pervert. But then perhaps not,* he corrected himself, remembering Monty's Bar. *They come in all varieties, don't they?*

'Why not,' he replied, 'sounds like a good idea to me.' Yes, he decided, he'd break his rule just this once and go to the hotel. Ben wouldn't carry all his cash around with him, there was bound to be money in his room. And if not, there'd quite likely be items worth stealing in a place like the Metropole.

'Excellent,' Ben said. 'Shall we walk? Bit late to find a cab and it's not that far.'

They set off along College Street, passing St Mary's Cathedral, its stonework gleaming gold in the light of the gas lamps, then down Macquarie Street where other glorious stone buildings sang of Sydney's past. And as they walked they chatted. Or Ben did, leading the conversation. James found himself drawn in despite any misgivings he may have had. The man was very easy company.

'So tell me,' Ben started out, 'how do you know so much about sheep?'

'My father was a shearer.'

'Really? Where?'

'Queensland. Longreach for the most part, Central Western region.'

'Ah . . .' Ben nodded knowingly. 'Barcaldine, home to the Shearers' Strike.'

'That's right. I was there. My father was killed in the strike.' James had blurted the words out before he knew it. He had no idea why, apart from the fact that perhaps for some reason he wished to impress. He chastised himself. He must not lose sight of the task ahead. 'A number of men were,' he added brusquely, 'although most of you lot down south don't know that.'

'Yes,' Ben said, feeling sympathetic, assuming the young man's brusqueness was due to raw emotion, 'it must have been tough up there.' He realised all of a sudden that the young man hadn't offered his name upon introduction. *How odd,* he thought. Under the circumstances, omission of a surname was expected, but a first name was surely essential. Even a first name of one's invention.

'By the way, what's your name?' he asked.

'James.' An alias didn't spring to mind and James didn't even hesitate. Where was the harm?

As they walked on they continued to talk, mainly about the sheep industry, and by the time they reached the Metropole they were chatting away like old friends. James even admitted to having been a shearer himself.

'Why did you give it up?'

'After Pa died there wasn't much left for me in Queensland so I came down here to Sydney.' *Damn, I said 'Pa' when I should have said 'my father'.* He gave a shrug. 'I wanted to see the big city.'

'Do you miss the country? I know I would. The smell of the bush, the wide open spaces . . .?' Ben left the question hanging.

It was something James had given no thought to for so long that he was caught out and answered honestly. 'Yes, I do,' he replied after a moment's reflection.

'Ah, here we are,' Ben announced. They'd reached the junction of Young, Bent and Phillip streets where the Metropole Hotel towered magnificently, six storeys high with frontages that looked out over all three streets.

'Come along.' Ben led the way briskly across the road. 'I'm on the second floor,' he said as they walked through the main doors.

James tried not to appear awe-struck by the mosaic-tiled floors and the ornate stained-glass windows as they crossed the massive foyer and started up the grand staircase. He was still playing nonchalant as Ben unlocked the door and turned on the light, which miraculously happened to be electric. Then he found himself ushered into a room more lavish than any he'd ever seen or even imagined. *Do people really live like this?*

'Brandy or whisky, which do you prefer?' Ben asked, crossing to the sideboard. 'I had both laid on for just such an occasion as this.'

Just such an occasion as what? James wondered. *What is it exactly you perverts get up to?* Recalling his sordid run-in with Charles, he preferred not to dwell upon the matter. 'I don't mind,' he said with a shrug. He rarely drank hard liquor. 'Whatever you're having.'

'Brandy it is then.'

As Ben poured two generous measures into the brandy balloons that sat beside the bottle, James assessed him. This was the first time he'd had a clear view of the man. Just as he'd thought, Ben was young, little more than twenty, and good-looking. Clean-shaven, a fine head of hair, as dark as he himself was fair, and his carriage was impressive. Here was a young man with style. James caught sight of his own reflection in the gilt-framed mirror that stood beside the wardrobe and automatically corrected his slouch, straightening his back, lifting his chin.

'Thank you,' he said accepting the drink that was handed him. But as he took the brandy balloon, Ben's hand lingered a little longer than was necessary and their fingers touched. *That was deliberate,* James thought, trying his hardest not to flinch and quickly withdrawing his hand.

'Take a seat.' Ben gestured to the elegant carved-wood sofa with buttoned upholstery in a delicate shade of apricot, and when James chose a matching hard-back chair instead he smiled regretfully.

'Cheers,' he said, clinking glasses and seating himself on the sofa. He took a swig of his drink, then leaned forward, placing his brandy balloon on the coffee table between them.

'You are not one of my persuasion, are you?' he asked.

'And what persuasion would that be?' For some unknown reason James found himself hedging. He knew he shouldn't. He knew that now he was here he should just get on with things. *Rob the bloke of his money and get out,* he told himself, but instead he studied his glass, buying time, and was about to take a sip of his brandy.

'Oh come along, James,' Ben said with a touch of impatience, 'you know very well what I mean. You're not homosexual.'

James was shocked, and again for some unknown reason. The word was jarring coming from this stylish young man whom he'd found so charming. How could Ben openly admit to being a pervert?

'No,' he admitted, putting the glass back on the table. 'No, I'm not.'

'Then why are you here?'

Ben's eyes were studying him astutely and James noticed what an arresting shade of blue they were. Not ice-blue like his, but a deep blue, almost purple. *How odd. People with dark hair usually have brown eyes, don't they?* But he didn't flinch this time, and he didn't draw away from the confrontation. This time he met Ben's gaze directly.

'I'm here to rob you,' he said.

There was a moment's pause as their eyes remained locked. Then Ben picked up his brandy balloon, leaned back in the sofa and laughed.

'Of course you are,' he said. He took a sip of the brandy and laughed again, self-deprecatingly this time. 'How silly of me not to have guessed.'

'Why should you have guessed?' James found the notion vaguely insulting.

'Because I knew there was something odd about you right from the start. Probably the funny voice that did it.'

James felt his anger on the rise. 'You're laughing at me,' he said dangerously. 'I wouldn't if I were you. That could get you into a whole lot of trouble.'

'I'm not laughing at you at all,' Ben said, 'I'm laughing at myself for being such a fool. Well come along then . . .' He delved a hand into his breast pocket and withdrew a leather money pouch, dumping it on the coffee table. 'Rob me.' He waved a hand about airily. 'Search the place if you like, see if there's any more cash lying around. That's what you came here for, isn't it?'

James was further angered. The man's tone was contemptuous and deeply offensive. How dare Ben attempt to humiliate him!

'And why *shouldn't* I rob you?' he barked, rising to his feet. 'Look at all this!' He strode about the room, scorning its opulence, then turned back to hurl abuse at Ben. 'Look at *you*! Living in the lap of luxury while others are starving. One of the *landed gentry*,' he sneered, rendering the term as repellent as he believed it to be. 'A filthy-rich fucking farmer who treats his shearers like scum and expects them to work for nothing. That's what the bloody strike was about! Don't you realise, man, that's what the bloody strike was *about*!'

Realising he'd worked himself into a lather, which wouldn't serve any purpose, James abruptly halted his tirade. *Just rob the bloke and get out of here,* he thought. He picked up the money pouch from the table and shoved it in his pocket. 'You wealthy bastards deserve to be robbed,' he said scathingly.

'I'm not wealthy, actually.' Ben had been lounging back in the sofa cradling his brandy balloon to his chest throughout the entire eruption. Now he leaned forward, elbows on knees, and quietly proceeded to explain. 'I suppose my father could be called wealthy, he's certainly successful. But like the rest of the country we're suffering dreadfully from this current drought, not to mention the depression. And as for *all this* as you say'—he waved his brandy balloon at the surrounding opulence—'it's only for show. And that includes the whisky and brandy I might add,' he said, taking a healthy swig as if to emphasise his point. 'They weren't laid on for you or any other assignation I might have made. They're here in order for me to fete the prospective clients my father has arranged for me to meet over the next several weeks. I'm in Sydney on business, you see. We need to keep the overseas buyers in the dark as much as possible – can't have them thinking the drought and the depression is unduly affecting us. Hence *all this.*'

Having stated his case, he leaned back once again and raised his glass in a salute. 'Oh do sit down, James,' he said. 'We were enjoying each other's company and having such pleasant chats.'

James' anger had abated, but he made no move.

'Please do,' Ben urged. 'I promise I shan't make any advances upon you,' he said with a smile. 'I wouldn't dare anyway. You're far too frightening.'

James sat.

'One other thing I simply have to set straight though,' Ben added. 'We treat our shearers well and we pay them according to their true worth. We always have.' Once again he raised his glass. 'Now come along, drink your brandy, we'll toast to a truce.'

'I don't like brandy.'

'Whisky then.' He rose from the sofa.

'I don't like whisky either.'

'Oh.' He sat back down. 'Then I must lay in something else for your next visit, mustn't I,' he said flippantly.

'Why did you choose the Hyde Park beat?'

The question was so confronting Ben was taken by surprise.

'I didn't know where else to go,' he admitted. 'I heard some derisive comments in a bar about "filthy homosexuals" cruising that particular area – "depraved degenerates who should all be exterminated" – you know, that sort of thing. So I thought I'd give it a try. I had no idea what to expect.' His smile was rueful. 'You can't imagine how happy I was when you happened along.' He took a final swig of his brandy, emptying the glass. 'I should have known better.'

'Yes, you should. Maybe next time you might try the Turkish baths in Liverpool Street.'

'What?' Ben had been about to rise in order to refill his glass, but instead stopped to gawk in amazement.

'I believe that's one of the spots where fashionable men like you meet.'

'How the devil would you know that?'

'I heard a bloke say it once.'

James vividly recalled the occasion. The man had been around fifty, well dressed and well spoken, obviously one of the upper class, but unlike most others of his ilk he hadn't become a gibbering mess upon realising he was being robbed. Far from it. He'd accused James of being 'a young wretch' and demanded he 'clear off'. It was only when he'd found himself bailed up against a tree with a hand at his throat that he'd accepted defeat, and even then he'd shown not the slightest sign of fear.

'Should have stuck to the Turkish baths in Liverpool Street,' he'd said disdainfully as he'd handed over his purse, 'you don't get any riff-raff in there.'

James had respected him for it. The bloke had guts. He'd even wondered briefly whether the man might report the robbery to the police. But no, he'd decided. No homosexual loitering in Hyde Park would risk reporting an attack – not even a bloke with this sort of guts. Which is what made the whole exercise so easy.

'Well, thank you for the information,' Ben said as he rose and crossed to the sideboard, 'I shall certainly bear the Turkish baths in mind.' He poured himself another brandy and returned to the sofa. 'Any *other* illicit meeting places you might know for those of my kind?' He smiled cheekily as he sat, enjoying the banter. This was fun.

'No,' James said, although in actual fact there *was* one. He could have said 'Monty's Bar in Woolloomooloo on a Sunday'. But he didn't. He didn't want to be reminded of *that* night. 'Why *are* you . . .?' He fumbled a little, not knowing why he should wish to pose the question, only that he found Ben so very interesting. 'Why *are* you . . .?' Another slightly awkward pause. 'Of your kind?' He opted tastefully for Ben's term.

'Homosexual, you mean?'

'Yes.'

'It's not a matter of choice, James. It's who I am.' Ben dropped the bantering tone. He could tell James was a country boy in every sense of the term, not only raised on the land, but still a boy, albeit a tough one. *You have an enquiring mind though, don't you, James?* he thought. *You really are interested in an answer. Very well then, I'll give you one.*

'I've known I was different from an early age,' he said, 'I suppose around twelve or so, but I didn't know why. Until boarding school, when I discovered with another boy just *how* I was different.'

He searched for the flicker of distaste he expected to see in James' eyes, but there was none. The focus remained absolute. Ben felt strangely gratified.

'We weren't just playing young boys' lewd games, I can assure you,' he said. 'My friend Alex had never known why he was different either, it was a great relief to us both.' He smiled fondly at the memory. 'Dear Alex, we shared so much. Right through high school, and nobody knew. First love is a wonderful thing.' Ben grinned disarmingly, the banter back in his voice. He was aware that, despite the flatteringly rapt attention, he wasn't altogether getting through. But he hadn't expected to. How could James possibly understand?

'Did you have a wonderful first love, James?' he asked.

'Nope.' Betsy couldn't really count as a wonderful first love, James supposed.

'What a pity. Perhaps you will one day soon, you're still very young. How old *are* you, may I ask?'

'I'll be eighteen next week.' The truth had popped out just like that, before he'd realised he'd said it, but what matter? Tonight seemed to be a night for truths and, besides, he'd never see the bloke again.

'Eighteen! Ah, then I insist,' Ben said, raising his glass, 'I absolutely *insist* you join me in a drink so we can toast your birthday.'

James eyed his brandy balloon warily, but even as he did Ben picked it up and thrust it at him.

'Eighteen is a milestone that must be saluted. Whether or not you enjoy a brandy, it's imperative we propose a toast.'

Glass now in hand, James was forced to join suit as Ben raised his glass.

'To the magical age of eighteen,' Ben proposed.

They clinked glasses and drank, James' eyes threatening to water from the fumes. He'd never drunk out of a brandy balloon before.

When the fieriness of the fumes and the burn of the liquor had died down he was left with an aftertaste quite different from the strong spirits he'd previously quaffed from small whisky glasses.

'It's not bad,' he said.

'Not bad!' Ben pretended outrage. 'It's the best! The finest cognac imported from France, I'll have you know.'

They talked. Over the next two brandies they talked about a lot of things, starting out with the fact that Ben was twenty-two and expected to take over the running of the family sheep property one day. Then they moved on to farming in general and then the second brandy led to introductions.

'Ben McKinnon by the way,' Ben said, offering his hand.

'James Brereton.'

They shook and dived straight back into conversation, still about sheep farming; the dire consequences of drought; the breeding of Merinos; then talk of shearing, which led to the discovery they shared a mutual admiration for Jack Howe.

'He's my hero,' James said. 'Greatest gun shearer of all time. Three hundred and twenty-one sheep in one day. Nobody's come near that!'

'He's everyone's hero,' Ben agreed. 'He set a record just last year with the new Wolseley shearing machine too. Dad was so impressed he's thinking of installing Wolseley machines in our shed and that's probably all because of Jack Howe.'

As they talked, James marvelled at how easy it was being in Ben's company, despite their very obvious differences. Ben wasn't at all uppity as he'd first appeared, but like any ordinary bloke you'd meet on a farm. *A bit more refined and he talks a bit better,* James thought, *but we're speaking the same language, aren't we?* The fact prompted him to ask a further question.

'How does everyone back home feel about you being . . . homosexual?' This time, his tongue loosened by the brandy, there was only the slightest hesitation.

'Oh dear God, they don't know,' Ben said, miming horror at the mere thought. 'Just imagine if they did. What do you think they'd do to me, all those workers on the farm? The labourers, the shed hands, the shearers . . . Being the boss's son wouldn't save me, they'd probably slay me alive. And if they didn't, Christ alone knows my father certainly would!'

James remembered that time when the rouseabout had been beaten up; the shed hands and shearers had set upon him with such a vengeance. 'He's a deviant, son,' George Wakefield had said, 'pay no heed, nothing to do with us.' He recalled how he and his father had just stood by and watched. *Yes,* he thought, *you're right, mate. Being the boss's son wouldn't save you.* He felt sorry for Ben.

Fifteen minutes later, as Ben rose to fetch the bottle for a fourth brandy, James also stood.

'No thanks,' he said, already feeling the effects of three generous serves, 'another one of those and I'll never get home.'

'You're quite welcome to stay here,' Ben suggested. 'The sofa would be comfortable enough. And you'd be quite safe,' he added with a smile.

'I know I would'—James returned the smile—'but no thanks anyway.' He took the money pouch from his pocket and tossed it onto the table. 'Thanks for the brandies,' he said.

'You sure you don't want to keep that?'

James wasn't sure whether the query was serious or whether Ben was joking, but his answer was genuine.

'I don't rob people I know.' Then he added a further word of advice. 'You should avoid Hyde Park at night, it's not safe.'

Ben threw back his head and gave a bark of laughter. 'Obviously,' he said. 'It paid off this time though, didn't it, I found a new friend.' His mood was suddenly sober and his gaze direct. 'I found someone I can trust with my secret, and that's very important to me. I *can* trust you, James, can't I?'

'Yes.' The reply came without a moment's hesitation. 'You can.'

An agreement rested between them. An agreement both recognised as a bond.

'So . . .' Ben smacked his hands together as a fresh idea occurred. 'I know absolutely no one here in Sydney – do you have a circle of friends I might meet? I have to admit I'm not all that attracted to the Turkish baths in Liverpool Street.'

James thought of the gang he mixed with at the Great Western Hotel. 'My circle of friends doesn't include any of your "persuasion",' he said.

'Oh you'd be surprised,' Ben replied with the suggestive raise of an eyebrow. 'We're everywhere, I can promise you.'

'Do you play poker?'

'Of course. Doesn't everyone?'

'I could take you to a gentlemen's club I go to now and then. Probably your sort of place, come to think of it. Quite a few toffs.'

'Splendid. Sounds ideal.'

'How about Friday night then? Around eleven?'

'I shall look forward to it. Very much.'

James told him the address of the Hampton Club in Oxford Street, Ben writing it down in the notepad that sat on the escritoire by the window, and they agreed to meet outside at eleven o'clock on Friday. Then . . .

'Good night, James.' Ben offered his hand.

'Night, Ben. See you Friday.'

They shook and only minutes later James found himself walking through the deserted streets on his way back to Surry Hills, pondering his newfound friend and the events of the night.

CHAPTER SIX

'A property near Goulburn?' Thaddeus Grenfell's eyes lit up. 'I say, you're not one of the *wool* McKinnons, are you?'

'Yes, sir. That I am.'

'Excellent.' Thaddeus exchanged a look with his brother Geoffrey, who was equally delighted. 'Thaddeus and Geoffrey Grenfell,' he said, leaning forward in his armchair and extending his hand. 'Good to meet you, lad, good to meet you.'

Both brothers shook Ben's hand effusively.

'Yes, indeed,' Geoffrey agreed, 'a great pleasure.'

The brothers were in their fifties, stylishly attired, as befitted men of their standing, Thaddeus tending to the portly with an abundance of greying facial hair, although well trimmed, Geoffrey the younger of the two, less portly and beardless, but with a lavish black moustache, equally well trimmed.

Standing by, James watched on, distinctly envious, but not in the least surprised. The Grenfell brothers had never greeted him with such enthusiasm. They would welcome him to the poker table, certainly, but with a manner always patronising, as if he should feel privileged merely being in their presence.

'Ah, here's young Brereton,' they'd say, 'we're a man short, do come join us, boy.' James loathed being called 'boy', particularly given his newly acquired status.

Their manner had changed, however, the moment he'd introduced them to his new friend.

'This is Benjamin McKinnon,' he'd said. 'Ben's a friend of mine from a family property near Goulburn . . .' He'd been about to go on and say, 'Ben, this is Thaddeus and Geoffrey Grenfell,' but the brothers hadn't given him a chance, ignoring him altogether.

'We've recently done business with your father,' Thaddeus said, leaning back expansively and puffing away at his cigar.

Neither brother had risen from his plush, leather armchair upon introduction, but Geoffrey now waved a welcoming hand.

'We're downing a quick brandy before going to the table, do join us.'

Ben and James exchanged a glance and sat in their own plush, leather armchairs. The lounge of the Hampton Club abounded with such, there was not a hard-back in sight.

Thaddeus drained his brandy balloon and signalled a waiter. 'What'll it be, lads, brandies all round?'

'Thank you sir, yes,' Ben said.

'None of this "sir" business, Ben,' Thaddeus protested, 'you can't play poker with a fellow who calls you "sir", what?'

The brothers shared a jovial laugh.

'And you, young James,' Thaddeus went on, 'a beer, I presume?'

'No, a brandy would be fine, thanks.'

'Ah.' Thaddeus raised an eyebrow, but made no comment; the boy normally drank beer. He held up a hand with four fingers extended and the approaching waiter gave a nod before disappearing. 'Yes,' he said, returning his attention to Ben, 'we delivered a glorious drawing-room suite of ebonised mahogany to Glenfinnan Station only last month . . .'

'Designed by Smee & Sons of Finsbury, London,' Geoffrey added, not to be outdone, 'finest retail cabinet-makers in the business.'

'They most certainly are,' Thaddeus agreed; the brothers always worked as a double act when spruiking the quality of their goods. 'Your father has impeccable taste, I must say.'

Of course, Ben thought, *the Grenfell Emporium.* When James had dragged him over to meet the men he'd simply said, 'Come on, I'll introduce you to a couple of toffs.' These were the Grenfell brothers who owned the emporium.

'Yes, that's right,' he replied, 'Dad's been doing a bit of renovating at Glenfinnan, he says it's time we spruced things. He's shortly to purchase my older sister, Adele, a dining-room suite as a wedding gift, so I'll wager you haven't heard the last from him.'

'Excellent news. We're here to serve, lad,' Thaddeus said with bonhomie, 'we're here to serve.' And he drained the last of his brandy just as the waiter arrived with four fresh balloons.

Holding their glasses aloft, James joined in the 'cheers' as they toasted one another, but when he'd taken a sip he glanced an unmistakeable message to Ben. *Not as good as your cognac at the Metropole,* his eyes said.

It was a winning night all round for young James Brereton. He came out on top at the poker table, not in a particularly dramatic way, but he outplayed the brothers. 'Luck of the draw,' he said modestly. And when they parted company in the early hours of the morning, the Grenfell brothers were referring to him as 'lad', which he considered a perfectly acceptable reference given his youth. He was aware he hadn't yet joined the ranks of Benjamin McKinnon and that he probably never would, but at least he was no longer 'boy'. He was also aware that he had the presence of Ben to thank for this fact.

Over the ensuing several weeks, the two became regulars at the Hampton Club, and elsewhere too, their friendship growing exponentially. Ben visited the Great Western Hotel on a number of occasions and was as welcomed by the locals at the bar as he had been by the members in the Hampton Club lounge. They'd even celebrated James' birthday at the Great Western, although they hadn't admitted to it being his eighteenth.

'A very happy birthday to my good mate, James,' Ben had rowdily toasted, and they'd all joined in.

James had been thankful Ben had made no mention of which *particular* birthday, Clyde and the bar's regulars believing he was in his twenties, but his warning glance hadn't proved necessary. Ben was canny enough to have sensed the lie.

The two had continued partying until late that night. 'It's not every day a bloke turns eighteen,' Ben had declared, and they'd progressed from the Great Western on to another rough-and-tumble bar in Darlinghurst where yet more birthday toasts were made, once again rowdily led by Ben.

James was lost in admiration of Ben's chameleon-like character. He envied the way his newfound friend fitted so seamlessly into every walk of society.

Ben had, in turn, been relieved to discover that James was legitimately employed, or so he'd humorously professed.

'So you don't earn your living solely by robbing poor, innocent homosexuals in Hyde Park,' he'd said. 'I must say that comes as a relief.'

James had had the grace to feel just a little guilty, particularly given his recent discovery that not all homosexual men were depraved monsters. He was learning a lot from Ben, whom he found not only a source of fascination, but a model upon which he might base himself.

When they were at the Hampton Club he tried to emulate Ben's manner, and in doing so developed a certain style of his own. His 'funny voice' attempt to sound upper class had been foolish, he realised, so he adopted instead an air of confidence, which proved most effective. He had, after all, never lacked confidence; it was just a matter of how to channel it socially.

Strangely enough, the one who benefitted most from this newly formed friendship was Ben McKinnon himself, or so he declared one night, and with disarming candour. He'd accompanied James back to the basement on a Wednesday, having called into the Great Western at around ten o'clock.

'Nowhere else to go,' he'd said when he'd turned up at the bar, 'just felt like a chat.'

James had thought how lonely Ben looked. Lonely and even a bit forlorn. 'Come back to my place,' he'd said, 'I'm only around the corner.'

Ben had never been to the basement, and James had wondered how he might react to a place he'd no doubt perceive as a hovel. But no matter. He'd grabbed a bottle of brandy from the stock behind the bar, making a note for Clyde who would take it off his wages at the end of the week, and shortly after closing time they'd walked out into the street.

Ben had shown no sign of surprise upon being ushered into the basement, although he must surely have felt a little disconcerted.

'Very cosy,' he'd remarked 'although the chaise longue seems a little out of place.'

'The choice of a girl I was seeing.'

'Ah yes.' His nod said it all. 'A girl, of course.'

James poured them both a brandy in the little squat glasses he kept on his desk. 'Sorry, no balloons,' he said as they sat at the small dining table.

They clinked and drank.

'I thought you didn't like this stuff,' Ben said.

'I'm working on acquiring a taste for it. Seems the right thing to do.'

'*De rigeur* you mean.' In response to his friend's blank look, Ben added with a whimsical smile, 'The fashionable choice.'

'Yes,' James agreed enthusiastically, 'that's exactly what I mean. De what?'

'*De rigeur.* It's French. Literally means "in strictness", but it's applied to etiquette.'

'Ah. Good. *De rigeur.*' James practised the sound, committing it to memory. A new term. Excellent.

Ben felt a wave of affection for his friend, as he had on a number of occasions recently. It was clear to him that James was working hard to improve himself, but he really didn't need to. Not in Ben's opinion, anyway. *You're pretty impressive as you are, my friend,* he thought.

'I have my last business meeting on Monday,' he said with what seemed a touch of regret, 'head back to Glenfinnan first thing Tuesday morning.'

'Is that why you look glum? Aren't you happy to be going home?'

'Oh yes, I've had enough of the big city, looking forward to the smell of the bush and all that.' Ben attempted to lounge back in his chair – which was difficult, it being a hard-back. *This place could really do with a couple of armchairs,* he thought. 'But I've very much enjoyed my Sydney sojourn. Far more than I'd expected to, I must say . . .'

James would like to have enquired about the precise meaning of 'sojourn', but didn't dare interrupt. Something was on Ben's mind, he looked very serious. And if Ben wanted to talk then James was more than prepared to listen.

'. . . And that has a great deal to do with you, James.'

Well, this was a surprise. 'In what way?'

'In a way I've never experienced before.' It was then Ben spoke with a candour that astonished. 'During the short time we've known each other, I've felt such a sense of freedom in your presence. Hard to explain, really, but when we're together I'm at ease. I'm comfortable being who I am with you. Can you understand that?'

'No. No I can't understand that at all.' James was utterly mystified. 'You're at ease with everyone,' he protested. 'You fit in wherever you are and whoever you're with. I've never known anyone who fits in as easily as you do . . .'

'It's always easy to fit in when deep down you know that you don't belong anywhere,' Ben replied, which only further mystified James. 'I've spent the whole of my life playing different roles, being what's expected of me. Of course it's easy, it's become second nature.' Having dismissed the matter as of no consequence, he took a sip of his brandy before continuing thoughtfully. 'You, on the other hand,' he said, 'you have a talent for just being you.'

James focused intently upon his friend. He was aware Ben intended no insult, but what on earth could he mean?

'Oh you're working on your social skills, trying to better yourself, I know that,' Ben went on, 'but it's who you *are* that is particularly striking, James. You're direct and you're honest.' He gave a droll smile. 'That is when you're not robbing people with a sexual preference that differs from the norm.' The smile quickly disappeared and he was once again in earnest. 'You find others of such inestimable interest that when you talk to them you *give* of yourself. You give of who you truly are. Do you understand what I'm getting at?'

James shook his head.

Ben laughed, and this time his manner was bordering on flirtatious. 'Of course you don't. Your being unaware of the effect you have on others is what makes you so frightfully attractive.' Then he continued in all seriousness. 'What I'm trying to say is, I'm glad we've come to know each other the way we have. I'm glad and I'm grateful. No one has accepted me as you have simply because I haven't allowed them to, I haven't been able to trust them. But you know me, James. You know the real me, just as I know the real you. And most important of all, I know I can trust you.'

'Yes,' James solemnly agreed. 'Oh yes, you can trust me all right.' *But you don't really know me, do you, Ben? What would you say if I told you I'd killed two men? What would you say if I told you I'd originally planned not only to rob homosexuals, but to execute them?*

But even as such thoughts crossed his mind, James realised Ben possibly *did* know the real him. Whoever that was. Somewhere between being James Wakefield and becoming James Brereton, he'd lost sight of exactly who he might be.

Ben swigged the last of his brandy and reverted to his customary flamboyant self. 'Drink up, man, you're sadly lagging.' He plonked his glass on the table and rose to fetch the bottle.

James obediently followed suit, wincing as he did at the burn of the liquor.

'Yes, it's the most awful second-rate stuff, isn't it,' Ben agreed, rejoining him. 'I'll bring you a bottle of cognac from the Metropole next time.' He filled their glasses, dumped the bottle on the table between them and continued without drawing breath. 'All of this introspection has delivered to me the obvious conclusion,' he said blithely, 'which is why I called around for a chat tonight. You need someone to take over your life, James. And I intend that someone to be me.'

'Eh?' James looked at him blankly.

'You don't plan to spend the whole of your life wandering around Hyde Park robbing people, do you?'

The question was facetious, but James answered in all honesty.

'Of course not. I don't do that anymore.' Which was the truth. He hadn't prowled Hyde Park since the night he'd met Ben.

'You can't live properly on the wage you get at the Great Western,' Ben went on, 'and despite your skill at the poker table, you can't rely on your winnings as a gambler.'

'That's true,' James admitted; he'd been digging into his savings of late.

'All of which points to just one thing. The obvious solution . . .' Ben halted, a pause for dramatic effect.

'Which is . . .?'

'You come to Glenfinnan and work on the land.'

The notion came as such a surprise James found himself stumped for an answer.

'You said you were a shearer, didn't you?' Ben urged. 'And a good shearer at that?'

'I did. And I am. Or I used to be.'

'It's hardly a skill one forgets.'

'But we're not even into winter yet. You won't need shearers till the spring.'

'So?' Ben wasn't about to drop the subject easily. 'There's always work to be done – new fencing, endless repairs, rabbiting . . . Good grief, most shearers go rabbiting during the off season. We'd find a job for you at Glenfinnan.'

From James' uncertain expression, Ben realised he was starting to sound pushy, perhaps even a little over-eager. Why *was* that? He only knew how much he longed to continue his friendship with James Brereton.

He downed his brandy in one hit. 'No other way to drink rubbish like this,' he said and rose languidly from the table. 'Do give the subject some thought, James. It's just an idea, but a good one I think.'

'Yes it is.' James also stood, although he left his brandy untouched. 'Thanks for the offer, mate. I'll certainly give it some thought in the spring.'

'Good.' Ben felt a pang of disappointment. *Not sooner?*
'You do that. Must be off now.' He proffered his hand and
they shook. 'See you at the club on Friday, yes?'

'Yep. See you Friday. 'Night, Ben.'

This particular Friday night at the Hampton Club offered
up something altogether different. An unexpected invitation. The catalyst had been Ben's casual mention to the
Grenfell brothers upon bidding them farewell that he was
returning to Glenfinnan the following Tuesday.

'Well then, dear me,' Thaddeus said after the briefest
glance to his brother, 'you must come to lunch on Sunday.
We insist, don't we, Geoffrey?'

'Indeed we do,' Geoffrey agreed. 'You simply must come
along.' There was the slightest hesitation before he turned
to James. 'Both of you,' he added, realising there was no
way out of including the young Brereton boy.

'We always do a family luncheon on a Sunday, often
including one or two special guests,' Thaddeus said expansively. 'Geoffrey and I take it in turns, it's become quite a
tradition, don't you know. We're at my house this Sunday.'
He produced a card from his vest pocket and presented it
to Ben. 'Wolseley Road, Point Piper, twelve o'clock sharp,
do hope you'll come.'

The assumption that young Ben McKinnon would jump
at such an invitation was obvious, but so too was the eagerness of the Grenfell brothers' offer. In their joint opinion
the link with young McKinnon was well worth nurturing.
They'd never met the lad's father – Alastair McKinnon had
ordered his new furnishings from a Smee & Sons catalogue
provided by the emporium – but the master of a property
as fine as Glenfinnan was bound to prove a highly valuable
customer.

'That's very kind of you, Thaddeus . . .' Ben wasn't particularly keen on the idea and as he pocketed the card was

about to offer his apologies and suggest 'perhaps another time', but James leapt in.

'Most kind indeed,' he said, 'we'd love to come.'

'We certainly would.' Ben picked up his cue seamlessly. 'Twelve o'clock, you say?'

'On the dot, lads,' Thaddeus replied, the brothers beaming benevolently, 'on the dot.'

'Why in the devil's name did you do that?' Ben muttered after they'd collected their overcoats and stepped out into the crisp, cold, darkness of Oxford Street. 'They're the most awful, pompous bores.'

'All right for you, *old man*,' James replied mockingly, 'you don't need their sort. Sadly, I do. For me they're a step up the social ladder, *don't you know*.'

Ben laughed. 'I get your drift. Very well, we'll turn up at Point Piper and put on *a jolly good show*.'

It was agreed Ben would collect James in a hansom cab at around a half past eleven.

'I shall make sure I hire a particularly smart one,' he promised.

'Good idea. See you Sunday then,' James said as they parted company.

'What a thrill. Can't wait.'

Edna Pusey had been keeping a lookout from the ground-floor front sitting-room window for some time. She'd made enquiries of Mr Brereton as she'd served his breakfast. She did so adore the way he always breakfasted on a Sunday these days, ever since he'd given that *piece of fluff* her walking orders.

'A heavenly morning outside, Mr Brereton,' she'd said, placing his eggs and bacon on the table.

'It certainly is, Mrs Pusey,' he'd agreed, 'a fine autumn day.'

'Do you have any plans, being a Sunday and such glorious weather?'

'I do, yes.' James had been delighted she'd asked. 'I'm to lunch with the Grenfell family in Point Piper.'

'The Grenfell brothers of the Grenfell Emporium?' Edna had been all but breathless at the thought.

'The very same.'

'Dear me, what a thrill.'

James smiled, recalling Ben's words.

'I'll fetch your toast.' And she'd bustled off.

Edna had been keeping an eye out for a good two hours. In fact she'd been drifting intermittently to the front window ever since he'd left the breakfast table. She watched now as a hansom cab pulled up outside. A very smart hansom cab too, with a neat little bay at the trot, not one of those drab cabs hauled by a nag that looked all but dead.

A dark-haired young man, stylishly dressed, alighted and made for the basement stairs, but before he could reach them Mr Brereton appeared, equally resplendent. Even more so in Edna's opinion, but then Edna had always nurtured special feelings for Mr Brereton.

What a fine young gentleman he is, to be sure, she thought as she watched the two greet each other effusively and climb into the cab. *Precisely the son I would have had should I have chosen motherhood.*

The driver gave a flick of his whip and the neat little bay set off at a trot.

'Crikey,' James said when close to a half an hour later the hansom cab pulled into the circular driveway of Thaddeus Grenfell's Georgian-style mansion. 'He calls it a house.'

'Yes, a bit on the grand side.' Ben had seen a number of houses just as grand; the Glenfinnan colonial-style homestead was equally grand and, in his opinion, far more elegant, but he didn't say so.

They stepped from the cab and Ben paid the driver
while James stood gawking at the massive two-storey
sandstone-brick home that would have stretched a full
two blocks wide in the overcrowded suburb of Surry
Hills. Slate-roofed and surrounded by grassy slopes and
formal landscaped gardens, its tiled front verandah and its
upstairs balcony were both delicately trimmed with railings of cast-iron lacework, relieving, although only a little,
the severe façade of the building.

'Ah, the lads have arrived.' Thaddeus himself appeared
on the verandah, closely followed by Geoffrey. 'Welcome,
welcome.'

After handshakes were shared all round, the brothers
ushered Ben and James into the main entrance hall.

James feigned nonchalance as they entered, but his eyes
missed nothing. The entrance hall was magnificent. An
ornately tiled floor; a high moulded ceiling; a broad central
oak staircase that led up to the first floor, and two double
cedar doors leading off either side. One of the sets of doors
to the right was open and voices could clearly be heard.

A servant stepped forward to take their coats and hats,
but as they were both hatless and, given the fine weather,
without overcoats his services were not needed, so he
stepped back again.

'The family is gathered in the drawing room,' Thaddeus
said, leading the way, 'we're having a drink before luncheon. Do come on through.'

He headed for the open doors to the right, Ben and
James following, with Geoffrey bringing up the rear.

'Our young friends have arrived,' he grandly announced
as they made their entrance.

The assembled guests were predominantly women, with
only one man present. The women numbered six in all,
four middle-aged and two of around twenty or so, each
fashionably dressed in the latest style – a high-necked

gown with slightly puffed shoulders and long sleeves, the older women favouring blacks and browns, the younger pastel shades. The general impression was that all of them shopped at the same place, which indeed they did; the Grenfell Emporium's fashion department was known to offer the very latest in *haute couture*.

Thaddeus made the introductions, starting with his wife, Amelia, a large woman with a wealth of over-coiffed grey hair that sat on top of her head like a well-mannered cat. Then there was Geoffrey's wife, Bernice, a smaller version of Amelia but with a coif less cat-like and wire-framed spectacles. There followed a third wife, Clementine, who Thaddeus announced was his younger brother's widow, and her pastel-clad daughters, Dora in lemon and Evelyn in lilac. Finally, he introduced the one couple who were not Grenfells.

'And this is Cecil and Millicent Sudbury,' he said of the pallid man in the well-cut grey suit and his plain little wife who appeared uncomfortably nervous. 'Cecil is our hard-working general manager at the Grenfell Emporium,' Thaddeus explained.

'How do you do, gentlemen,' Cecil said as he shook hands with the two younger men. None of the women had offered their gloved hands, but had simply given a nod upon introduction.

'A pleasure to meet you, Mr McKinnon,' Cecil went on, his handshake with Ben particularly fervent. 'I recently had the great honour of personally overseeing the delivery of a fine set of furniture to your father's property near Goulburn.'

Amelia Grenfell gave a moue of disapproval; poor form to discuss business at a family gathering. Her husband, Thaddeus, however, beamed. Cecil may have been over-doing things, but he knew his place, and that's what he was here for after all. Cecil had visited Grenfell Manor only several times in the past and only ever on business. His plain little wife had never once been invited; small wonder she looked nervous.

'How do you do, Mr Sudbury,' Ben replied with a pleasant smile.

James had been adding up who everyone was upon introduction, thankful that Sudbury was the only new name to memorise. All the ladies were either a Mrs or a Miss Grenfell. *How fortunate,* he thought. *And how very attractive Evelyn is in her pretty lilac gown.* He hoped he might be seated next to Evelyn at the luncheon table.

'Your father is obviously *aux fait* with the finest when it comes to furnishings . . .'

Cecil Sudbury's blatant sycophancy continued, Thaddeus beaming, Amelia glowering, and Ben's dutiful smile remaining firmly in place. Then as the cabinet-making skills of Smee & Sons of Finsbury, London came up for discussion, several others, disinterested, started quietly chatting among themselves, and James was free to survey his surrounds.

The drawing room, no less imposing than the rest of the house, boasted a magnificent marble fireplace and mantel, and above the mantel hung an original painting. A huge oil on canvas depicting an Australian landscape, it dominated the room as was clearly intended.

After accepting a glass from the tray of a passing waiter – sherry for the ladies and beer for the gentlemen – James found himself drifting towards the painting. He'd never seen a thing of such beauty, he hadn't even known such a thing could exist; that the world he knew so well could be so gloriously captured. He felt he could step into the very depths of the landscape. He could smell the lemony bite of the eucalypts, shafts of light shining between branches dappling the ground; he could hear the crackle beneath his boots as he walked through undergrowth so familiar; he could feel the warmth of the sun caressing his shoulders . . . The more he stared the more mesmerised he became, and the more mesmerised he became the more he longed to be back in the bushland of his childhood.

'It's beautiful, isn't it?' a voice said softly, and he turned to discover Evelyn in her pretty lilac gown standing beside him.

'Yes,' he agreed, 'it's very beautiful.'

'It's a McCubbin.'

'Really?' He had no idea what a McCubbin might be, but as it appeared something remarkable he reacted suitably impressed.

'That's right. Frederick McCubbin's become frightfully fashionable lately,' Evelyn went on, 'everyone's buying him up. Well, those who can afford him, anyway.' She gave a light laugh. 'Uncle Thaddeus is a collector of fine art. He's particularly proud of this piece.'

She beamed at the painting and James suspected she saw nothing there but its value, which he found disappointing.

'McCubbin is one of the leaders in the Australian Impressionism movement,' Evelyn said, turning her bright smile back to him. Evelyn was very proud of her knowledge of art. 'Uncle Thaddeus says it won't be long before the works of the Australian impressionists are more expensive than those of the realists, they're becoming so fashionable.'

James suddenly didn't care whether he was seated next to Evelyn at luncheon. She was pretty, but he had a feeling she wasn't really his type.

'Ah, young James, I see you're admiring the McCubbin, what?' Thaddeus had been delighted to note James' interest in the landscape. That's why it was there, in order to be admired.

'He's one of the leaders of the new Australian Impressionism movement, don't you know.'

'Yes,' James replied, 'so Miss Grenfell has been telling me.'

'He and Roberts and Streeton and Conder, absolute masters of the form, destined to set the world on fire. I have a truly marvellous collection. Must show you my library and art gallery after luncheon.'

'I shall look forward to that, Thaddeus.' These days James no longer felt the instinctive urge to respond with 'sir'. Thanks to his newly acquired social confidence, 'Thaddeus' tripped quite easily off the tongue. He returned his attention to the painting. 'This McCubbin piece is particularly beautiful,' he added, careful to choose the right words.

'Yes it is, isn't it?' Thaddeus smiled radiantly like a proud father.

Barely ten minutes later, luncheon was announced and they adjourned to the dining room, which proved even grander than the drawing room. A huge, crystal chandelier, candelabra-shaped wall lamps and a twelve-seater dining table elegantly set for eleven, but which, with extension added, comfortably accommodated twenty-four. And here, once again, was a giant marble fireplace with mantel where, once again above the mantel, an original painting dominated the room. Another massive oil on canvas, the painting this time was a portrait. A full-length portrait of three men standing side by side, three proud, confident men: the Grenfell brothers.

As the guests milled into the room, James drew to an instant halt, transfixed by the painting. In the middle stood Thaddeus, to his right Geoffrey, and to his left the youngest brother of the three, Charles. James found himself staring directly into the eyes of the man he'd killed. *So that man was Charles Grenfell,* he realised with a sense of shock that was confronting, yet surprisingly mild.

The gentlemen of the party were diligently pulling out chairs for the ladies to be seated, while two servants hovered nearby prepared to place napkins on laps, but Thaddeus ignored them all, joining James to beam once again with pride at the family portrait.

'Ah, I can tell you have the eye of a true art lover, James,' he said. 'It's a remarkable piece, isn't it? A new young portraitist, name of John Longstaff. Saw his work in Melbourne around seven years ago and so adored it I commissioned him to paint this. Paid a great deal more than its value at the time too I might add . . .'

James continued to stare dispassionately at the painting as Thaddeus raved on. *I know those eyes*, he thought. And he did. Even behind the proud, formal pose he could see the depravity that lurked within. He could feel the lust of the man who had attempted to degrade him in the vilest of ways. Now as he gazed at the image before him he could see those same eyes bulging with terror. He was so glad he'd killed Charles Grenfell.

'Yes, young Longstaff had just won the National Gallery of Victoria's first travelling scholarship, you see, and he needed extra money before taking off for Europe, so things worked out very nicely for all. He's since been exhibited in the Paris Salon and his portraits are proving hugely popular in London, so my eye for talent didn't let me down, what?' Thaddeus was positively preening at the thought. 'Marvellously lifelike, don't you think?'

'Yes, marvellously lifelike.'

'Please do sit, gentlemen.' Amelia's voice cut knife-like through the hiatus as, with the ladies now seated, the gentlemen continued to linger, waiting for their host to take his place at the head of the table.

'Yes, yes, of course, so sorry my dear,' Thaddeus said although he wasn't in the least sorry, 'just sharing fine art with a fellow enthusiast.' He flapped his hand at a central seat opposite the portrait. 'James, you sit there so you can admire the painting, there's a good lad,' he added approvingly.

Everyone took their places, James discovering he was seated beside Evelyn as he'd initially hoped he might be. Seated opposite was Ben, who raised a congratulatory eyebrow having observed his friend's early interest in the prettier of the two Grenfell girls. But James was now far more interested in the portrait.

Amelia's annoyance with her husband was not so much due to his lack of etiquette as to what she considered his complete lack of sensitivity. How dare Thaddeus expound upon the merits of the artist and the portrait to a perfect stranger while omitting any mention of the third brother depicted in the work, particularly given the presence of Charles' widow and daughters. It was not only insensitive, it was downright tasteless.

As the servants commenced pouring the wine – a chablis – and serving the soup – a cream of asparagus – she explained the tragic circumstances of her brother-in-law's death to the two guests at the table who had never known Charles.

'My husband's youngest brother, Charles, passed away last year,' she said with a sympathetic smile in the direction of Clementine, Evelyn and Dora. 'So unexpected. A heart attack.' She didn't even need to share a glance with Thaddeus, the story having become so well rehearsed it might as well have been the truth. 'A merciful way to go, perhaps, but so heartbreaking for the family.' Another smile to Clementine and her daughters. 'And the girls were of course both devastated. They still are to this very day.'

James was forced to divert his eyes from the portrait as beside him Evelyn turned to gaze soulfully at him.

'Yes, it was terrible,' she whispered, 'poor Daddy.'

Poor Daddy, indeed, James thought, but he nodded his sympathy to the girl before looking dutifully to the mother. 'How very sad for you, Mrs Grenfell,' he said, and because she was a pretty woman in a worn sort of way, he actually meant it. How hideous to be married to a man like Charles.

'Yes,' she said, 'it was most sad. Thank you for your sympathy, Mr Brereton.'

It hadn't been sad for Clementine at all. Charles' death had been a godsend. She'd longed to leave him for years, but how was a woman expected to support herself without a husband? The only difficulty had been the maintenance of her grieving widow performance, which had been necessary for the girls, who had never known their father to be the disgusting libertine he was. Even more necessary for the family, who would do anything rather than have the Grenfell name besmirched. God it was a relief to be rid of him.

Observing the go-ahead nod from his wife, Thaddeus made his customary toast to family and friends, and the luncheon was officially under way. The asparagus soup was complimented upon by Cedric Sudbury in an ingratiating manner, which Amelia found irksome, and as the conversation turned to mundane affairs, James continued to study the portrait. Or rather the one figure that was of particular interest.

His eyes were drawn to the heavy gold chain that dangled from Charles Grenfell's vest pocket, and to the fob watch the man held in his right hand, displaying it to the artist as if it were some sort of prize. *He's showing the piece off,* James thought, *rather odd. I wonder why?*

It was the very same watch that now rested in the deposit box at the bottom of James' wardrobe, and he remembered how, several times, he'd been tempted to wear it to the Hampton Club. He recalled how he'd even practised the flourish with which he would consult the timepiece in order to impress onlookers. He'd finally decided against it, however, telling himself it was probably a bit too showy for someone his age and that he might end up looking rather silly.

Thank God, he now thought, *a wise decision.* There were no personal engravings on the watch, it was true, but it was an extremely identifiable piece nonetheless, the brothers would certainly have recognised it.

The soup plates now cleared, the fillet of white fish arrived, and the conversation, particularly among the men, turned to politics. Still James said little, his attention remaining principally on the painting, despite the fact that Ben was darting him meaningful looks. Surely they were here because James wished to make an impression, Ben was thinking, at least that's what he'd said, hadn't he? Yet here he was, offering the occasional nod, a word now and then, before turning to stare distractedly at that awful smug portrait of the Grenfell brothers.

'We on the land have been equally hard-hit, wouldn't you agree, James?'

Finally, with the arrival of the lamb cutlets, Ben decided it was time to nudge his friend into action. The collapse of the Federal Bank in January had been discussed and the men were now in deep conversation about the effects of the ongoing depression, particularly upon city businesses.

'Oh?' Thaddeus was more than a tad surprised by the remark. What in heaven's name would the young Brereton boy know about those on the land?

'James and his family were also in the wool business,' Ben explained.

'Ah.' Thaddeus was most interested. *Well fancy that, who would have thought?*

'Yes, James' father is sadly no longer with us, having passed away several years ago,' Ben went on, 'but James himself knows a great deal about the sheep industry, don't you, James?'

Ben focused upon his lamb cutlets as if to emphasise the point and James, left to fend on his own, was finally dragged away from the painting and into the conversation.

'It's true, farmers are having a very hard time during the depression,' he said, 'especially given the complications brought on by the drought, what with the grasses dried up and feed being so expensive.'

Ben gave a nod of approval.

The day proceeded to drag on interminably. So enamoured was Thaddeus of young James Brereton's apparent devotion to fine art that following the luncheon, he insisted upon taking not only James and Ben, but the whole party including his family members – with the exception of Amelia, who steadfastly refused – upon a guided tour of every painting on display throughout the entire Grenfell mansion.

'What on earth were you playing at?' Ben queried several hours later as he collapsed theatrically on the chaise longue in the basement. 'All that ridiculous business about fine art. Surely that was going too far. Hardly necessary, I would have thought. Everyone but you and Thaddeus was bored witless.'

James fetched the bottle of second-rate brandy from the desk, sat himself down at the small dining table and poured two glasses. 'I killed Charles Grenfell,' he said.

'You what?'

The words had not slipped out accidentally. James had made a conscious decision that afternoon. He had decided he would tell Ben everything. And he did.

They sat together at the table and as they proceeded to demolish the cheap brandy he gave his friend a detailed account of all that had taken place that night in Woolloomooloo.

'Sort of explains things really, doesn't it?' Ben said after a lengthy pause.

James looked a query.

'Why you sought vengeance upon homosexuals.'

'Perhaps,' James replied with a shrug, 'in a way.'

'You poor boy.' Ben was not being facetious. His sympathy was genuine.

But James was not seeking sympathy. Nor even understanding. 'I killed the man who murdered my father too,' he said. 'It seems I'm quite adept at killing.'

Ben wasn't sure what to say. 'I suppose we all would be if we were driven to it,' he suggested.

'But would we all enjoy it, Ben?' There was a cold, hard edge to James' voice now. '*I* did. I enjoyed it very much.'

He drained the last of his brandy. By now the bottle was empty, but neither of them was the least bit drunk.

'So we really do know each other's secrets now, don't we?' James gave a wry smile. 'We know everything about each other down to the last sordid detail.'

'Yes, we do.' Ben returned the smile, equally wry. 'It takes a lot of trust to share secrets like ours.'

'It does at that.' James stood. 'We're out of brandy,' he said, 'let's find a pub that's open on Sundays.'

Ben rose wordlessly from his chair and they walked out the door.

'I've changed my mind, by the way,' James said as they set off up the basement stairs to the street.

'About what?'

'I won't wait until the spring to come to Glenfinnan. I'll tie things up here and join you in a month.' He paused briefly. 'That is if the offer still stands.'

'Oh the offer still stands all right.' Ben's reply was casual, but he could not have felt happier. The offer would still stand whether James had killed two men or twenty. They were friends for life.

'Good. I could do with a change.'

And together they walked off down Bourke Street.

PART TWO

CHAPTER SEVEN

Alastair McKinnon was fifty-five years old. He had been born in Australia, but was fiercely proud of his Scottish ancestry, his father Douglas having served with the British-led army of the Seventh Coalition, which had claimed victory at the Battle of Waterloo. This epic conflict had marked the end of the Napoleonic wars, and ten years later a grateful Britain had granted Douglas a soldier settlement – a gift of land on the opposite side of the world. Here, during the 1830s, he had taken a wife, Mary, much younger in years, and settled in the fertile plains near the fledgling township of Goulburn, calling his property Glenfinnan after his home town in the Highlands of Scotland. And it was here he had set out to found a farming dynasty destined to rank among the finest breeders of Merino sheep in the country.

Douglas and Mary were now long dead, but their son Alastair, the current McKinnon patriarch, was as driven as his father had been. Indeed, with greater knowledge and more sophisticated methodology to hand, Alastair had proved even more successful than his father in the breeding of both fine-woolled and strong-woolled sheep, the two favoured varieties of Merinos. Furthermore, he was intent upon imbuing a third generation of McKinnons with equal fervour and dedication.

The McKinnons, however, were not as successful in the breeding of their own kind as they were in the breeding of their sheep. Neither generation had been as fortunate as they might have wished in the production of male heirs. Mary had produced only one son, Alastair's birth having been followed by two daughters, and Alastair's wife, Grace, had in turn produced a similarly disappointing issue with regard to gender. First a daughter, Adele, then – cause for much celebration – a son, Benjamin, swiftly followed by several miscarriages and finally a second daughter, Jennifer, after which there were to be no more children.

The birth of Jennifer, or Jenna as she insisted upon being called from a very early age, had so weakened Grace's constitution that she was medically warned any further child-bearing attempt might result in her death. Grace, strong-willed and determined as she was, had been quite prepared to take the risk, but Alastair had not. He dearly loved his pretty, young wife.

As things turned out, Jenna's difficult birth had sadly contributed to her mother's early demise, nonetheless. Grace died in 1884, shortly before the child's tenth birthday. She had been just thirty-six years old.

Alastair never sought another wife. There were any number of women who would happily have taken up the mantle of Mistress of Glenfinnan, not only for the title and position it offered but for the acquisition of a strong, virile husband like Alastair McKinnon. But Alastair was simply not interested. Instead, he contented himself with just one son to carry his name on into the future. And what did it matter anyway, he decided. The Goulburn plains were peopled with many a McKinnon, if not by name, then by blood. Both his sisters had married locally, one a farmer and one a station manager, and the eldest of his two daughters was about to follow suit. Adele was engaged to the manager of Glenfinnan no less, and would shortly move into the station master's house up on the hill, a pleasant home, ready-built for a family. Her fiancé, Phillip Caton, was a fine sheepman – and cattleman too for that matter – skilled at his trade and already like a second son. They were neighbours the whole lot of them, living only several miles from one another, an extended family, and when Ben married he was bound to produce fine sons. Alastair McKinnon was content with his lot.

In the meantime, like his pioneering father before him, and like the son who was destined to follow his path, he devoted his life to the breeding of impeccable Merino stock. Unlike many a second-generation property owner who had been brought up in the comparative luxury of a successful pastoral enterprise, Alastair had no intention of resting on the laurels earned by his father. His work was ever-inventive, ever-evolving, and at times downright surprising.

'Well, well, that sure would be a decision that'd take the industry by surprise,' Phillip replied in response to Alastair's unexpected declaration.

The two were inspecting several prize rams in the home paddock not far from the Big House, Phillip's attention being particularly focused upon Sovereign Prince, a fine-woolled ram of Saxon blood.

'He's a beauty all right . . .' Leaning down, he parted the dense fleece with his fingers, exposing the depth of the fine, white wool, feeling the softness of its texture, examining the evenness of the crimps right up to the tips, admiring these and every other sign of purity. 'Our boy here'd be bound to win first prize.'

'But he won't, because he won't be shown,' Alastair said bluntly. 'I mean it, Phil. I'm done with showing sheep.' He crossed his sizeable arms over his sizeable chest and leaned back against the nearest fence post, defying disagreement.

A thickset man, ginger-haired and ginger-bearded, he could present a formidable figure, as he very well knew, and was not one to shy from confrontation. 'I've made up my mind, no more sheep shows for us, mate. Waste of time and they're irrelevant anyway. A prize-winning ram might look good, but that doesn't mean he's a top breeder. The whole thing's a load of bosh, as you very well know.'

Alastair was obviously prepared to do battle, but as usual, if it was an out-and-out fight he wanted he'd picked the wrong man. Phil Caton, laid-back, even-tempered and patient, was impossible to ruffle at the best of times. Which, as station owner and manager, made the two an oddly compatible pair.

The younger man straightened his gangly body. Everything about Phil appeared gangly and untidy, including the droopy forelock of his nondescript hair and his equally droopy, nondescript moustache. Although only in his early thirties, he was a rangy man, somehow colourless, and could have been any age. He gave the ram a pat on its massive backside and watched as it sauntered off haughtily to join the several other top-quality sheep, each of Saxon and Spanish bloodlines, that stood together in a placid row. Stud rams they might have been, but they appeared quite content in each other's company. *Funny that*, Phil thought. *Wouldn't be the same with cattle. You'd never get prime bulls behaving like that.*

'Bosh maybe, Boss,' he agreed mildly – to Phil, Alastair was invariably 'Boss' when they talked business, otherwise theirs was a first-name basis, the two were good friends – 'but you've got to admit that showing's a handy form of advertising. Buyers are impressed by prize-winning sheep, and Glenfinnan's carried off more First and Best Merino stud rams than just about any other breeder over the last ten years. Everyone'll be expecting us to show, particularly with Wagga Wagga coming up soon.' Phil really wasn't sure

Alastair's idea was a wise one. *We'd be cutting ourselves off altogether,* he thought, *opting out of the whole system of advertising, dangerous thing to do.* 'All the breeders show their prize-winning sheep at Wagga.'

But Alastair had given the matter a great deal of consideration. He resented the time wasted on preparing a ram for show; he resented the misconception of a good-looking ram's breeding value; and he resented above all the tricks used by some to disguise an animal's defects. He remembered how, on one occasion, the deception had been so obvious – to him anyway, if not to the judges – he'd suggested to the winning breeder they turn their rams out into a paddock for twelve months and re-compete the following year. The challenge had not been accepted, the breeder knowing full well that in twelve months his animal's sunken back, currently disguised by the cut of its wool, would have been plain for all to see.

'The whole thing's a waste of time,' he growled, 'particularly now the Vermonts have become fashionable.' *And therein,* he thought, *lies the major problem.* This was a subject that particularly irked Alastair. To him the Vermonts were the final straw. 'All the judges can see is that bloody great fleece, they're blind to the mess that lies underneath.'

Alastair McKinnon had refused to buy the American Vermont stud rams that had become extremely popular of late. Beneath the enormous fleece, the vast number of wrinkles on the animals' bodies were disastrous for local conditions, he maintained. The wrinkles rendered the animals not only difficult to shear but prone to fly strike, and fly strike was the Australian sheep farmers' curse.

'Many a good flock's been ruined by Vermonts,' he said, 'just goes to show what can happen when a fad gets out of hand.' He shook his head vehemently. 'I tell you right here and now, mate, I'm not risking my purebred bloodlines being presumed inferior to Vermonts just because judges and buyers can't see beyond a bloody great fleece.'

Phil smiled and raised a suggestive eyebrow. 'So we're talking about pride, are we?'

'Nah.' Alastair felt himself relax. Having made the radical decision to stop showing his sheep, he supposed he had rather been spoiling for a fight, or at least a disagreement, but Phil always managed to calm him down somehow. Even unwittingly, as he had just done. 'Quite the opposite, actually,' he said, 'my plan being we don't even *attempt* to win. Instead of focusing on *prizes*, we focus on *prices*. Do you get my drift?' The question was rhetorical and he sailed straight on. 'We know we breed the best stud rams and we know we sell the best quality wool – who needs a show ribbon to prove it? Waste of time and effort. Sales figures prove the point a whole lot better. And word gets around,' he added with a wink. '*There's* your advertising value.'

'Yes, I get your drift all right.' Phil glanced over at Sovereign Prince, still standing, ever-patient and docile, but posed like a champion nonetheless beside his equally placid mates. 'That fella there would fetch at least 500 guineas at the Sydney stud sale . . .' The two men shared a smile. 'And of course word would get around,' Phil added with a wink of his own.

'Come on up to the Big House,' Alastair said, 'time for morning tea.' He could see nineteen-year-old Jenna, who'd just bounded out of the main back door and across the verandah, skirts raised in the most unladylike manner, ginger hair flying, now headed down the slope like an unruly filly on her way to announce morning tea.

They closed the gate to the home paddock and set off towards Glenfinnan House where it stood in its attractive copse of trees and gardens five hundred yards or so away. A sprawling, two-storey colonial-style homestead, built of stone and surrounded on all sides by broad wooden verandahs and upstairs balconies, Glenfinnan House, always referred to simply as the Big House, was the largest structure that existed on the 30,000 acre estate. Among the many others were outbuildings of all varieties – stables and barns, the vast woolshed, the shearers' quarters, and dotted about the landscape of gentle slopes and open plains, workers' cottages and the homes of staff members. Nestled in the prettiest countryside and encircled by endless paddocks, the Glenfinnan property rather resembled an attractive village, particularly on festive occasions when public holidays were celebrated by staff and workers; or when the McKinnons held one of their garden parties, which were always well attended by members of the extended family and neighbouring farmers, all of whom considered it nothing to travel a good twenty miles in order to socialise.

'The flock wool samples Ben took to Sydney were well received,' Alastair said as the two men made their way up the slope towards the back verandah of the Big House, 'particularly given they were accompanied by the independent assessment reports from the Technological Museum. Ben tells me the overseas buyers were most impressed. I think with the current financial crisis they'd been expecting a big drop in both quantity and quality.'

Phil nodded approvingly. 'Yes, despite the drought, last year's clip was a pretty good one,' he said. 'So tell me, Alastair, how does Ben feel about the decision not to show? I take it he knows.'

'Tea's up,' Jenna yelled from twenty yards away, still barrelling her way towards them.

'Yep he knows, I told him last night.' Alastair's grin was confident. 'He got my drift too.'

'Difficult not to,' Phil agreed wryly, 'you're pretty persuasive. So that's it then. As of right now, big changes afoot at Glenfinnan, eh? No shows, starting with Wagga.'

'No Wagga Show?' Jenna skidded to a horrified halt beside them. 'What do you mean, no Wagga Show?'

As they continued on their way to the Big House, she skipped alongside the men demanding answers, even weaving from side to side as if trying to round them up while she fired off her questions. Her father always called her his kelpie daughter. And it was true, her nature was not unlike that of the working dogs on the property; intelligent, inquisitive, a ball of energy.

In both appearance and personality, Jenna took after her father. Ginger-haired, square jawed and obstinate, a force to be reckoned with at all times. Her older sister, Adele, and her brother, Benjamin, both bore very clearly the genes of their mother. Dark-haired and fine-boned, like Grace they were elegant. But, like Grace, they were also strong-willed and determined. There was no weak link in the McKinnon stock.

'It's all in the breeding,' Alastair was wont to say.

When they reached the house, Jenna bounded on ahead, past the cooking kitchen, which was separate from the main building in case of fire, and across the verandah, barging into the family breakfast room, the flywire door slapping shut behind her.

'Did you know we're not entering a ram in the Wagga Show?' she demanded of her brother, who was seated at the large, wooden table, sipping at the steaming mug of tea that had just been poured for him.

'Yep,' Ben replied, 'sure did.'

'Oh.' Their older sister, Adele, upon sighting her father and fiancé out on the verandah had already started pouring another mug, but now paused, she too finding the news most surprising. 'Really?'

As Phil opened the flywire door, her look to him was quizzical.

'Yes, really,' he said with a smile, 'just found out myself.'

'Good heavens above, why?'

Alastair and Phil plonked themselves down at the table and, while Adele poured everyone hefty mugs of tea, the whole argument for not showing Glenfinnan's stud rams was revisited.

The family – and more often than not senior working staff who were like family members anyway – always gathered in the huge breakfast room at the rear of the house where wooden benches flanked the central table and tea was served in mugs. If the McKinnons were entertaining guests, then they would be in the front drawing room where the furniture was mahogany and tea was served in cups and saucers of fine bone china. This practice was in no sense due to any form of snobbery, it was simply the way things were done. Their neighbours for miles around were exactly the same. Entertaining in style was an art form and a courtesy enjoyed by all.

Beth, the live-in cook and general housekeeper, appeared from the cooking kitchen out the back with a platter of scones freshly baked in the wood-fired oven. Cream was lifted from the icebox, homemade strawberry jam, already fetched from the pantry, was sitting on the table, and the feast began in earnest.

Bethany Hobson was a homely woman in her late forties whom Alastair had employed not long after Grace's death, finding himself unable to cope with the housekeeping duties his wife had so ably managed. There were two other live-in household staff – never referred to or treated in any way as servants – who had been retained well before Bethany's time. There was Mildred, now middle-aged but still known as Millie, a cheery woman who did the cleaning and laundry and helped in the kitchen, and there was her husband Boris Zladcov, a dour man of indeterminate European origin with a great knowledge and love of horses. Boris tended the garden and looked after the home

stables where the horses loved him as much as he loved
them. Over the years, Millie and Boris, and also Bethany,
had become a part of the family, although Bethany not
altogether in the way she may have wished, for there had
been a time when she had secretly dreamed of becoming
the second Mrs Alastair McKinnon. Those days were
past, however, the fantasy by now long-faded, and Beth
remained as she always had been and always would be, just
Beth. Fondly perceived as a somewhat maternal figure, she
was referred to by all, and at all times, as Beth, although if
the truth be known she actually preferred Bethany.

'Well I think it's a *terrible* decision,' Jenna declared,
having listened to every argument put forward for the
non-showing of stud rams. *'Ab-so-lute-ly terrible!'* She
repeated herself, emphasising every syllable just to ensure
they correctly read her passion. 'No Wagga Show! How
could you even *contemplate* such a thing?' She glared at
her father, Phil and her brother, accusing them all equally.
'The Wagga Show's the highlight of the year!'

'It doesn't mean we're not *going* to the Wagga Show,'
Ben said with a touch of exasperation. 'Hell, Jenna, of
course we'll still be going to the show. You'll still compete
in the gymkhana, we'll still go to all the sideshows like we
did when we were children, and we'll still do the rounds of
the livestock entries. We just won't be exhibiting our own,
that's all.'

'Oh.' Jenna realised she may have over-reacted a little, that
she may not have thought things through properly, which
was not unlike her, but she wasn't prepared to back down
altogether. 'Won't we look a bit stupid, doing the rounds of
the livestock when we don't have an entry ourselves?'

'Not at all,' Ben said, flashing a smile across the table
at his father, 'we'll be checking out the competition, and
while we are they'll be wondering why we're not competing. I reckon that'll rattle them quite a bit.' Ben thoroughly

approved of his father's decision. Furthermore, he thoroughly understood the reasoning behind it.

Alastair returned the smile. Father and son, although physically and temperamentally unalike, quite simply adored each other. To Ben, Alastair McKinnon was something of a hero, a man's man, respected by all who knew him; and rightly so in Ben's opinion. To Alastair, Ben was a son to be proud of – strong, good-looking and fiercely intelligent; the son other men envied and wished was their own.

'Ben's quite right, Jenna,' Alastair said. 'You listen to your brother, he's making a lot of sense.'

Jenna, who'd lost interest by now, happily dived a hand out to grab a second scone, which happened to be the last on the platter. Her major concern had been the gymkhana anyway. Horses were Jenna's true passion.

'Marvellous scones, Beth,' she said, ladling on the jam, 'any more hot ones left out there?'

'Of course there are, dear.' Bethany smiled obligingly, gathered up the empty platter and disappeared to fetch a fresh batch.

Alastair focused upon his eldest daughter as he boasted of Ben's successful visit to Sydney and the expected total value of the flock wool. Adele was always far more interested in the business side of things than flighty Jenna.

'So Phil and I were just saying,' he went on, 'that it seems the '92 clip will fetch a good price all round in both quantity and quality. Not at all bad for a drought year, not to mention a depression.'

'We might pay for it this year, though, if conditions remain the same,' Phil dourly remarked to the company in general. Phil always chose to burst a bubble he considered might be a little unrealistic. Catching a fond, but mildly reproachful glance from Adele, however, he decided to soften the blow. 'Just a reminder, that's all,' he added.

'Which is another reason we should give the Wolseley machines a go,' Ben said, referring once again to his father. 'If we're likely to have a thin year in production we should make up for it by leading the way in innovation.' This was another topic they'd discussed the previous night.

'Oh yes?' Phil instantly directed his attention to Alastair, having gathered there'd been further talk of the shearing machines between father and son.

'Yep, that's right,' Alastair said. 'Ben was telling me about this mate he met in Sydney, a shearer who worked up north with Jack Howe . . .'

The name received instant attention from all present, the women included, even Beth, who'd just returned with the fresh platter of scones. Everyone in the sheep industry knew of Jack Howe.

'And that got us both talking about the Wolseley machine,' Alastair continued before he was interrupted by his son.

'Everyone's talking about Howe's shearing record with the new machinery, Phil,' Ben said, eager to present the argument he'd put to his father the previous evening, 'and I think, given our reputation, we should be leading the way.'

Last night's discussion had actually started out with Ben singing the praises of his new friend James Brereton. He'd been paving the way for James' arrival at Glenfinnan.

'James has worked with Jack Howe, Dad,' he'd boasted, which had made the favourable impression intended, and only minutes later discussion had turned to the new Wolseley shearing machines.

The situation was now repeating itself.

'Well we've certainly been contemplating the shift to machinery,' Phil agreed, and they were off and running.

The Irishman, Frederick York Wolseley, had not been alone in his efforts to invent a sheep-shearing machine, but he had been the first to manufacture a commercially viable one. The Wolseley Sheep-Shearing Machine Company Limited had been established in Sydney in 1887 before transferring to England two years later. Australia, however, remained the birthplace of its invention, Wolseley being a great promoter of his machine, and Jack Howe remained its champion.

'Ever since Howe set the record last year,' Ben went on, 'rural newspapers all over the country have been publishing the tallies from sheds with Wolseley machines. To my mind it's high time we joined the fray.'

But there was no need for further salesmanship. Both Alastair and Phil could see the advantages.

'Good advertising, Boss, that sort of publicity,' Phil said with one of his quirky smiles.

'Too late to get fully set up for this year,' Alastair replied. He needed no convincing, his son's arguments having already paved the way. 'The conversion will take some time, we'll need to build a sizeable extension to the woolshed. But we can certainly get the ball rolling. I'll put an advance order in for the machines and we'll start on the extension right away. That'll make us well and truly ready for the '94 season.'

Ben was delighted by their joint reaction. 'We'll need extra workers to build the extension, Dad,' he said. 'Perfect timing for James to arrive.'

'Indeed,' Alastair agreed. 'I must say I'm rather looking forward to meeting your mate who's worked with Jack Howe. A bloke like that'll no doubt have some colourful stories to tell.'

'Yep. Bound to.'

Oh hell, Ben thought, *I'd better warn James I may have overplayed the Jack Howe hand a bit. I'd better warn him, too, that he's not to let anyone know he's only eighteen.*

*

James Brereton arrived at Glenfinnan barely a month later. Ben picked him up from Goulburn Railway Station in a neat little buggy drawn by a pretty grey pony called Tess.

'Bit swish,' James said as he hefted his suitcase and kitbag onto the buggy's rear luggage rack. 'I'd expected a dray.'

'No work dray for you, old man,' Ben replied with a grin and a flamboyant wave of his hand, 'I'm here to collect you in style.' He looked it too in his dapper, navy-blue blazer and matching cravat, which had been a deliberate choice. 'Actually,' he admitted as James climbed up to sit beside him, 'we've started building an extension to the woolshed and the drays are being put to use carting wood and trans-porting workers.'

'But I'm a worker.'

'Exactly. And when you're working you'll be transported by dray along with the other half dozen blokes. For now'— he gave a flick of the reins—'you're my guest.'

Tess set off at a smart pace, and during the half-hour drive to the property, Ben gave James a rundown on what to expect, starting immediately with the warnings.

'Right,' James briskly replied, 'I'm not eighteen, under-stood. I'm used to that. So let's make me twenty-two, same as you. And as for Jack Howe, that's simple enough. I didn't actually work with him, but my father did. And I *did* meet him. Pa introduced me to him, giant of a bloke.' James smiled with easy confidence. 'We can fudge that one, Ben, I'll just tell Pa's stories.'

'Excellent.' Ben smiled happily back at him. 'It's so good to see you, James. Really it is.' *It's far more than good, my friend,* he thought. *It's wonderful.*

They'd reached the outskirts of Goulburn by now.

'Much bigger town than I'd expected,' James said, having admired the stone buildings that lined the streets; some regal and gracious, others austere and purposeful, but all signalling a sense of permanence. 'An impressive town too,' he added.

'City, mate, city,' Ben replied in mock stern admonishment. 'Declared Australia's first inland city in 1863 by Queen Victoria herself. We locals are very proud of that fact.'

'City. Right. Sorry.' But James was no longer admiring the City of Goulburn as he looked ahead at the rolling plains. 'Good pasturelands,' he said. 'Even with the effects of the drought you can tell it's healthy countryside – or would be with a bit of rain.'

Already James was revelling in a sense of being back where he belonged. He hadn't realised how stifling Sydney had become to him. *This is where I need to be,* he thought, *out here on the land.* He felt somehow as if he was coming home.

The afternoon held a bite, winter would soon be upon them, but the weather was fine, the sky a vibrant blue, and as he breathed in the freshness of the air and smelt the lemony scent of the eucalypts he felt unbelievably happy.

Drinking in his surrounds, he was only vaguely aware of Ben rattling on about the work he'd be doing and the accommodation that would be provided. Something about bunking in with several other labourers in one of the workers' cottages for now, then into the shearers' quarters when the season began.

'It's all to do with this extension that we're building to the woolshed you see,' Ben now went on to explain. 'We're getting ready for next year when we switch over to the Wolseley machines. Which means you'll just be doing straight out labouring work for a while. Do hope you don't mind.'

Mind, James thought, *why on earth would I mind?* He longed to work hard. He longed to exercise muscles that had become slack, to feel the physical efforts of his labour,

to serve a purpose beyond handing beers over the counter
to drunks.

'I can't wait to go to work,' he said, 'and the harder the
better. Thanks for asking me out here, Ben.' His grin was
euphoric as he gazed about at the landscape. 'I love it already.'

Ben breathed a sigh of relief. He'd been wondering why
James was so quiet.

They didn't talk for quite some time after that, there
didn't seem any need. Then . . .

'Healthy stock,' James said as they passed paddocks
where flocks of sheep grazed on hay feed.

'Yep, they're ours,' Ben replied, 'we're on Glenfinnan
property now. They're in good nick all right, but we need
the grasslands back.'

Up ahead to the right, a solid, single-storey stone farm-
house with a broad front verandah sat on a small hill.
Nestled among a copse of autumnal-hued poplars, it was
most attractive.

'That's the homestead I take it,' James said admiringly.

'No, that's the Station Manager's house,' Ben explained,
'bloke called Phil Caton. Nice chap. He and my sister
Adele are getting married next month. She'll move in with
him then. They're doing the place up at the moment, new
furniture and all that.'

Ben continued to point out the various buildings they
passed; the woolshed where several labourers were hard
at work on the new construction; the sheep pens and
shearers' quarters nearby; the main stables and smithy's
workshop; the several workers' cottages bunched together,
and here and there the houses for staff. Finally he pointed
to the left where, up ahead, rows of conifers had been
planted as a windbreak.

'That's Glenfinnan House,' he said, and a minute or so
later they pulled off the dirt road into the conifer-lined
driveway that led to the Big House.

'Crikey,' James exclaimed, 'you didn't tell me it was like *this*!' He stared in wonder at the vast homestead sprawled elegantly among the informal gardens surrounding it. He'd never seen anything so grand.

Ben gave a hoot of delighted laughter. 'Oh come along now, James,' he said, 'you knew I was a toff. Good grief, you've called me one any number of times.'

'But *this* . . .' James was genuinely in awe. 'This is something else. This is truly beautiful.'

'Yes, it is rather, isn't it?' Ben didn't know why, but he found himself strangely gratified by the depth of James' reaction.

'Good grief, you're extraordinarily *young*,' Alastair McKinnon exclaimed in his customary blunt manner, looking James up and down as they shook hands on the back verandah. 'Ben led me to believe you'd be at least thirty, perhaps even closer to forty,' he said accusingly.

'No I didn't, Dad,' Ben countered, 'that was just your assumption.' His lie followed with the greatest of ease. 'James is twenty-two, same age as me.'

'Is that so? Really?' Alastair conducted an even more blatant examination. 'You certainly don't look it.'

'I know, sir.' James smiled apologetically. 'Your reaction is the one I usually get, I'm afraid. I've always looked younger than my years.' Which was true.

As Alastair's eyes met the steady, confident gaze of the young man whose handshake was surprisingly strong, he felt reassured. *But good God,* he thought, *the boy looks no more than seventeen.*

'And you worked up in Queensland with Jack Howe?' he queried, still with an air of disbelief.

'That's right, sir. I'd just turned sixteen when I started out as a shearer,' James replied, 'my father was an excellent teacher.' Which was also true.

'Come on in then, lads.' Alastair, realising he was being remiss keeping the two out on the verandah, ushered them into the kitchen. 'It's a long trip from Sydney and Beth's made us all some tea.'

Ben and James entered, seating themselves at the table while introductions were made to Beth, who poured mugs of tea all round before proceeding to cut thick slices from the pound cake she'd baked that morning.

'Welcome to Glenfinnan, James,' Alastair said, and from where he stood on the opposite side of the table, he raised his mug in a toast. Eager to get back to work, he hadn't sat. 'I hope you'll enjoy working here with us.'

'I know I shall, sir.' James returned the salute with his own mug. 'Thank you most sincerely for the offer. I cannot tell you how greatly I am obliged to you, Mr McKinnon.' His words could have sounded gushing, but they didn't, for the simple reason they were offered from the heart.

Ben looked from his friend to his father, loving the connection he could see there. Loving his father for agreeing to meet James on this personal level, loving James for his genuine show of respect and sincerity, loving everything about this moment.

Alastair downed his tea blisteringly hot, scalding his throat, but that was the way he liked it. Then grabbing two hefty slices of pound cake he headed for the door.

'Work calls,' he said. 'Ben will take you to your quarters and show you the ropes, James. I believe you're to dine here tonight with the family if that suits.'

James was more than taken aback by the welcome, he was amazed. He was only a worker after all. 'That would most certainly suit, sir,' he said, 'thank you very—'

But Alastair McKinnon was already out on the verandah. 'See you around seven then,' he called over his shoulder as the flywire door slapped shut behind him.

'Dinner with the family?' James queried to Ben in hushed tones, feeling a little self-conscious even in front of Beth.

'Yep.' Ben helped himself to a slice of pound cake and smiled cheerily. 'He knows you and I are great mates.'

It was late in the afternoon, approaching dusk, when Ben delivered James and his gear to the workers' cottage, which he was to be sharing with three other men who were labouring on the nearby woolshed extension.

After tying Tess and the buggy to the hitching rail, they walked inside. The men were not there, but Ben explained they were probably having tea in the shearers' quarters a ten-minute walk away.

'They mostly socialise there at the end of the day's work,' he explained as James heaved his suitcase onto one of the bunks in the small two-man bedroom. 'That's where all the meals are served. There's half a dozen blokes working on the extension and Dad's set up a cookhouse at the shearers' quarters.'

'And tonight I'm dining with the family,' James said. The prospect had been plaguing him ever since they'd left the Big House. Dinner in a home as grand as Glenfinnan House was bound to be formal.

'You are. By way of a welcome. As my friend.' Ben noticed the worried frown. 'Why? What's the matter?'

'I don't have anything to wear. Anything proper that is. I sold all my fancy clothes. Didn't think I'd need them out here.'

'Oh don't worry,' Ben said dismissively, 'dinner's an informal affair unless we have guests.' He grinned, seeing the humour in his remark. 'Which you are, naturally, but you don't qualify, if you know what I mean.'

James nodded. Yes, of course he knew, which didn't in the least solve the problem.

'There's nothing wrong with that lounge coat you're wearing,' Ben said encouragingly.

The remark cheered James no end. He'd chosen to travel in his one and only lounge coat because it was woollen and warm, but it could well serve as informal evening wear.

'I have a shirt with turn-up collar and a tie,' he suggested.

'Ideal,' Ben declared with a clap of his hands. 'Excellent, in fact. You'll be the best-dressed person at table.'

Frivolous though Ben's behaviour appeared, he was genuinely affected by James' admission to having sold his 'fancy clothes'. He would have presumed these had been packed in mothballs and stored away in Sydney for the resumption of the lifestyle James had been so bent upon pursuing.

Have you cut yourself off from that superficial world, James? he wondered. *If so, I'm glad. It doesn't suit you.* He hoped also, and fervently, that it meant James intended to stay for some time.

'It's a good half hour before we need to head back,' he said. 'You unpack your things and get yourself settled in. I'll wait outside and enjoy the view.'

Each of the workers' cottages, three in all and barely a hundred yards from one another, had a small front verandah overlooking the sheep pens, woolshed and shearers' quarters, which sat in the picturesque valley half a mile away.

'Take your time,' he called as he stepped outside.

James unpacked his suitcase, placing his clothes in the small chest of drawers and narrow wardrobe that were on his side of the room, empty and clearly allotted to him. He carefully spread out on the bunk his one good shirt with its turn-up collar, noting as he did that it should really have an iron applied to it, but deciding it would pass muster beneath the lounge coat.

Wrapped among his work clothes was the book of nursery rhymes he'd always kept, never wondering why he did, aside from the fact it was simply part of his life.

But looking at it now, here back in sheep country where he belonged, it evoked such memories.

He studied the cover: *Popular Nursery Tales and Rhymes*, then underneath, the words, '*With One Hundred and Seventy Illustrations*'. All he could see was George Wakefield seated on a log in front of a camp fire, somewhere, anywhere, entrancing him with stories of old. He opened the cover to the frontispiece, to the beautiful drawing of the mother gathering her children about her. The book was his father, and also his family; the family he'd never had. He would never part with it. He placed it in the top drawer of the chest.

He lifted out, too, his father's beautifully maintained blade shears, wrapped in kidskin and hopefully to be put to good use in the very near future. '*It's hardly a skill one forgets,*' Ben had said. James hoped this was true, it had been some time since he'd tested his shearing skills.

Then from the bottom of the suitcase, he lifted out his work boots and also the small wooden deposit box, the key to which lived on his person at all times, switched from pocket to pocket. He didn't open the box. He didn't need to. He knew exactly what was inside. Not a great deal of cash, for he'd spent most of his savings, but the gold fob watch and chain was there. Would it be safe? he wondered. Should he ask Ben? *No,* he told himself, *not necessary.*

His decision was not based upon secrecy. Far from it. He would happily have told Ben all about the watch and its having belonged to Charles Grenfell. He and Ben had no secrets from one another. *No,* he thought, *workers don't steal from their room-mates. A bit of cash lying around perhaps, but certainly not a locked deposit box.* He placed it at the bottom of the wardrobe beneath his kitbag.

After changing into his shirt and tie, he buffed his boots with the special cloth he kept for the purpose. He was proud of his boots, which were eminently respectable;

every man needed a good pair of boots. Then he joined Ben on the verandah.

'Ready to go,' he said.

Back at the stables of the Big House, as they alighted from the buggy, the hunched figure of Boris Zladcov stepped out of the gloom. Ben made the introductions and the two men shook hands.

'Boris is part of the family,' he explained, 'although in truth we don't matter to him at all. The horses are his real family, just as he's theirs.'

Boris gave a grunt, and as if to emphasise the point Tess nuzzled her head into his shoulder.

Leaving the stableman to his duties, Ben led the way to the rear of the house. 'He's actually a good bloke, our Boris,' he said as they went, 'just doesn't know how to smile – leaves all the niceties to his wife.'

They freshened up in the washhouse, which was adjacent to the cooking kitchen. Here water was pumped directly from the nearby dam to the household tank for domestic use. After splashing his face with freezing cold water and drying off with one of the fresh towels that sat on the bench, Ben raked his fingers through his crop of black hair and struck up a pose.

'See?' he said. 'That's all I'm doing. I shan't even change. That's how casual we're going to be.'

James was aware the statement was made to put him at ease. But why bother? he wondered. Ben was impeccably tailored in his neat navy-blue blazer and matching cravat. And his hair looked perfectly in place.

As things turned out, there was no real cause for worry. Certainly dinner was held in the spacious dining room of the Big House at a ten-seater mahogany table set for six (with its full extension added the table could seat twenty), but the atmosphere was indeed casual and the dress informal.

Well, more or less, James thought, taking in the men's lounge coats and cravats and the women's pretty day dresses with puffy leg-of-mutton sleeves. Informal in style, yes, but all well cut and of fine fabric. *The McKinnons are hardly a family short of funds,* he thought wryly.

Alastair McKinnon himself set the tone of the evening with a warm and hearty welcome.

'This is Ben's young friend, James Brereton, who is to be working with us,' he said as they gathered about the table. Then he made the introductions all round. His eldest daughter, Adele and her fiancée, Phillip Caton who was Station Manager – James shared a handshake with Phil; his youngest daughter, Jennifer, 'known to one and all as Jenna,' he swiftly added, aware she was about to interrupt; and then he went on to introduce those whom James took to be staff, but who were obviously treated more or less as members of the family. James found the fact a little surprising.

'. . . And this is Beth, whom you've already met briefly and who looks after us all so well,' Alastair said, 'ably assisted by Millie . . .'

Beth and Millie, who were standing beside the servery counter gave nods and smiles and cheery 'hellos'.

'You'll have met Millie's husband, Boris, at the stables,' Alastair said, and that completed the introductions.

'Sit everyone, sit,' he jovially commanded, seating himself at the head of the table, and they all did as they were told while Millie started pouring drinks from the servery – a choice of beer or cider, red wine to follow with the main course – and Beth returned to the kitchen to fetch the large tureen of soup, which was to be served at table.

James was further surprised when, upon Beth's reappearance, the tureen was positioned before Adele, who proceeded to ladle generous servings into the stack of bowls Millie placed on the table beside her. At which point both staff disappeared and the family members were left to look after themselves, steaming bowls of vegetable soup being passed from one to another.

Yep, they're casual all right, James thought, *just like an ordinary family.* Not that he knew what that was. He'd never been part of an ordinary family, or any other sort of family for that matter.

As the evening progressed he realised the McKinnons actually *were* everything an ordinary family was presumed to be. *Although with a bit more money and style than most,* he thought, noting as Beth placed the leg of lamb before Alastair that the platter it sat on was silver, and as Millie positioned the dishes of vegetables in the centre of the table for family members to help themselves that the dishes were of the finest bone china.

The staff once again disappeared, and as Alastair carved the lamb and plates were passed around, the conversation turned to the forthcoming wedding, which was only three weeks away.

'Adele's having the final fitting for her wedding gown tomorrow,' Jenna announced to James. 'She's employed a dressmaker in Goulburn rather than choose a designer gown from one of the overseas fashion catalogues. Which means my sister's not only beautiful, but a practical woman, devoid of pretension,' she added with pride. 'All McKinnon women are like that.' Jenna flicked her ginger hair over her shoulder, hoping her brother's friend found her as attractive as she found him.

'Of course I employed a local woman,' Adele said lightly. Her comment directed to James, she was aware her younger sister was showing off in order to impress. 'Who needs lace and frippery? A waste of money, if you ask me.' She gave a toss of her head and smiled at her gangly fiancé, who did his best to disguise his feelings, but with little success. The normally undemonstrative Phil Caton was bursting with pride and had been for the past six months ever since they'd announced their engagement. What had he done to deserve a woman like this?

'I didn't even look at the Grenfell catalogue Phil gave me,' Adele said as she reached for the bowl of potatoes.

'And so you shouldn't, I quite agree,' Ben interjected. Aware that the mention of the name Grenfell had garnered James' instant attention, he gave a cheeky grin to the table in general. 'That's why I told Dad to order your wedding present directly from Smee & Sons of Finsbury, London rather than from the catalogue provided by the Grenfell Emporium.'

Ben wasn't giving away any secrets. The eight-seater oak dining-room suite had come up for much discussion. Adele had been adamant she wanted no larger than an eight-seater. 'Elegant, but practical,' she'd said. It was due to arrive in seven weeks, just a month after the wedding and, furthermore, it was to be delivered from the docks of Sydney to Glenfinnan by a privately hired transport service.

Ben's cheeky grin was directed to the assembled company, but it was purely for James' benefit. 'Cut out the middle man, I say. Who needs the Grenfells?'

The two shared a smile that carried a wealth of secrets.

'Now, anyone for red wine?' Changing the subject, Ben jumped to his feet and picked up one of the two bottles that sat on the servery counter. 'We have an excellent shiraz to hand,' he said, holding it aloft.

Again to James' surprise, the family was left to serve themselves, Ben pouring fresh glasses for those who wanted wine and refilling the glasses of those who wished to remain with their earlier preference.

'Beth, Millie and Boris take their meals together in their own dining room after we've been looked after,' he explained in an aside, aware of his friend's puzzlement. 'Dad's a bit of a stickler about staff not being treated like servants.'

James nodded. Yes, he'd gathered that. He gazed about at the sibling camaraderie, and at the obvious bond between father and offspring. How he would love to be part of a family like this.

'So, James,' Alastair said, having saluted the table with his glass of shiraz, 'I believe you may be able to regale us with stories of Jack Howe. You worked with him in Queensland, did you not?'

'I did, sir, yes, although my father worked with him far longer than I.' James intended to keep as close to the truth as possible. 'My father died several years ago, but he worked a great deal with Jack and they became good mates.' Which was not altogether true, but to James, as he continued, it seemed to be.

'Oh I tell you,' he went on, shaking his head admiringly, 'Jack Howe in motion is a wonder to behold. You wouldn't believe a man could be that big and that strong. He stands well over six feet tall, as powerful as a bull, and with hands the size of these dinner plates. No shearer can match him. Never could and never will. Although many have tried, and many more will no doubt follow.'

James laughed. He was relaxed now, enjoying himself. While talking of his boyhood hero, all he could see and hear was George Wakefield. George Wakefield telling stories of Jack Howe to his son. James was becoming his father.

'And a more good-natured man than Jack you're never likely to meet,' he continued. 'You should just see him, the other shearers doing all they can to distract him, jumping on his back, tickling him, pulling at his hair. But Jack never loses his temper. Never for one second. He just swats them off like flies and keeps on working.'

James had never seen such a sight himself, but hearing George now, he could swear that he had. And just like his father, he was keeping the gathering thoroughly entertained. They were hanging on his every word. One among them in particular.

Jenna McKinnon had been attracted to James Brereton the moment she'd laid eyes on him. What woman wouldn't be? *So this is Ben's new best mate from Sydney,* she'd thought. *God, he's good-looking.*

Now, watching him in full flow, animated, spellbinding even, she was more than attracted. Here was a man she wanted to know. Here was a man she was *determined* to know.

CHAPTER EIGHT

James revelled in his labours, just as he'd known he would. Within barely a week he could feel his body responding to the physical demands made upon it. After the initial stiffening of muscles, which had grown slack from non-use, he felt himself becoming stronger by the day and rejoiced in the sensation. He even resented the morning and afternoon smoko breaks Phil Caton called, when the labourers would lounge around over mugs of tea in the gathering area outside the nearby shearers' quarters; he'd far rather have gone on working. But he joined the others, knowing it would create ill will if he didn't.

He got on well with Rufus, the man who shared his bunk room; given their proximity, they were civil and respectful to one another. He got on well enough, too, with the other workers in general, although he noted there was neither the camaraderie nor the competitiveness that existed between shearers. These men were a different breed, he decided.

It didn't really help that they knew he was good friends with the boss's son, and also, it would appear, with the boss's younger daughter. Jenna, for some strange reason, had taken to turning up now and then around smoko time when he was free for a chat. He wished she wouldn't. After a cheery 'hello' to the other workers she would corner him, edging him aside, and there was no getting away. Aware of looks cast in their direction, he would avert his eyes as she talked, nodding occasionally and adding a comment, not wishing to be hurtful, but hopefully displaying to the others this was none of his doing. He rather regretted the fact he didn't smoke. In assiduously avoiding her gaze he could have concentrated on rolling a cigarette or tamping a pipe.

Not that Jenna appeared remotely perturbed by his lack of attention. If anything it only made her all the more talkative. About everything and nothing. The weather, her horses, the Wagga Show and the gymkhana events. She seemed to him a very confident and uninhibited young woman, which he would normally have found enjoyable, but aware as he was of the distance her presence created between him and the other men, he felt uncomfortable in her company and heard barely a word she said.

Until one day, on the fourth of her impromptu visits to the shearing shed . . .

'But of course I'm the black sheep of the family,' she blithely remarked, 'always have been . . .'

Black sheep. Now here was a term of interest. He turned to her.

'Black sheep? Why do you say that?'

Jenna was thrilled. He'd finally appeared to notice her. Desperate as always to impress, she'd been waxing on about her sister Adele and the impending wedding. 'Less than a fortnight away now and you're sure to be invited, being a close friend of Ben's,' she'd said. 'I do hope you'll come. It may well be a stuffy affair, but there'll be a lovely party afterwards with lots of dancing. Personally I'd have chosen something a little more original than the staid old church wedding, but of course I'm the black sheep of the family, always have been . . .' And that's when, at last, she'd garnered his attention.

'Black sheep? Why do you say that?' He'd turned to her, his focus absolute.

Jenna continued seamlessly without missing a beat, but her pulse was racing. Here was the breakthrough she'd been seeking.

'Because I'm the one who defies convention,' she said with a characteristic toss of her head, setting her ginger hair into a shimmer that somehow reminded James of the way Red Nell used to flick her head in careless disdain, setting her chestnut mane all a shiver.

How interesting, he thought, and for the first time he noticed the colour of Jenna's eyes. Were they green, or were they hazel? Or were they a mixture of both? They seemed to change colour even as he studied them. Another source of interest. He'd presumed all ginger-haired people had blue eyes. Certainly the ones he'd met had, and he'd worked with any number of ginger and red-haired men up north. Always called 'Red' or 'Ginger', the younger ones with freckles, the older ones blistered and sun-damaged. *But every single one of them had blue eyes, didn't they?*

The intensity of his gaze was sending shivers through Jenna. He clearly found her fascinating and was waiting for her to go on. God, he was attractive.

'You must surely have noticed how conventional our family is, James,' she said with a carefree laugh that she hoped he found captivating. 'Even boringly so.'

His eyes remained fixed upon hers, still intrigued by the changing colours. No, he hadn't found the family conventional, although he wouldn't know what a conventional family was. He'd loved the way they'd cleared the table themselves after dinner, stacking everything in the kitchen to be tended to the following morning, the women even disposing of the scraps and placing foods in the pantry and meat safe. Ben had told him it was the customary procedure when they weren't entertaining guests. Did other wealthy people who had servants (servants they referred to as *'staff'* what's more) do that? he'd wondered.

The Grenfells certainly wouldn't, would they? And he hadn't found the McKinnons in the least boring. Far from it. He'd found them enviable, each and every one. So enviable that he'd longed to be part of such a family.

Emboldened by his silence and convinced he was awaiting further explanation, Jenna was more than happy to oblige.

'Adele has always been the perfect daughter,' she went on, 'whereas I've tended to be something of a rebel. Probably due to being spoilt as the youngest,' she admitted with a self-effacing shrug. 'But Adele took on the duties of a farmer's wife at a very early age after our mother died. That is until Dad hired Beth as a housekeeper when he felt it became too much. And as for Ben . . .'

She gave another toss of her head, and James was once again visited by an image of Red Nell's mane.

'Well never was there a truer farmer's son than Ben!' Jenna struck a pose, hand to heart, enjoying her performance and the attention it was receiving. 'My dear brother, the heir apparent, is nobly prepared to take over the reins as the future patriarch of the McKinnon dynasty,' she declared dramatically, 'and like his father and his grandfather before him he will do the name proud.' Then she dropped the act and grinned cheekily. 'I ask you now, James, can one get any more conventional than that? Adele and Ben fit the pattern perfectly. But somehow I don't. I don't conform to type, you see. I'm forced to admit – and unashamedly I might add – that I have no idea where I sit in the scheme of things. Which,' she concluded with a ring of triumph, 'makes me the black sheep of the family.'

James' views differed altogether. Jenna knew so little about her brother. *If it's simply a matter of conforming to type,* he thought, *then the black sheep in this family is surely Ben.*

'There's nothing wrong with being a black sheep,' he said, his smile fondly indulgent. Although a year younger than Jenna, he felt a great deal older. The way she was showing off in order to impress him was so childlike. 'A black sheep can be the most valuable of all, Jenna.'

She stared back at him, mystified. What on earth did *that* mean?

'But then again, a black sheep can also be of the least value,' he added enigmatically. 'It all depends on the way you look at things.'

Her utter confusion amused him as he'd intended it should. Perhaps one day he would show her the book of nursery tales. Perhaps he would explain to her the true meaning of 'Baa Baa Black Sheep'. His father's explanation all those years ago remained etched in his mind. But George Wakefield having been his whole world, virtually every word the man had uttered remained etched in his mind.

'Smoko's over, mate.' It was Rufus. The other workers were already walking off. A most unusual scenario; James was always the one leading the way.

'Nice talking to you, Jenna,' he said and he left her to join the others.

'Yes. Bye, James,' she called after him. She had no idea what his allusion to black sheep could possibly have meant. But no matter. The smile had won her. And, oh, the mischievous light in those piercing blue eyes . . .

Young Jenna McKinnon was convinced then and there that she'd fallen in love. Just like that. In an instant. They said it could happen, didn't they?

Jenna's prediction about the wedding proved correct. The following week, James received an official, gilt-edged invitation to the nuptials of Adele McKinnon and Phillip Caton to be held at St Peter and Paul's Cathedral, 42 Verner Street, Goulburn. The envelope had been slipped under the front door of the cottage and was discovered by

Rufus when they returned from work. *'James Brereton, Esq'* it read in copperplate, gold lettering.

'Pretty bloody fancy,' Rufus scoffed, handing it to him.

James wondered who might be responsible for his inclusion at such an auspicious event – his good friend, Ben or Ben's sister, Jenna?

He asked Ben outright at the family stables that Saturday as they prepared for their early-morning ride. The two rode together regularly during the weekend when the workers would go into town to get drunk on a Saturday, leaving Sunday to nurse hangovers. James preferred his weekend rides with Ben.

'It was Jenna's idea,' Ben replied airily, tightening the girth on Baron, a feisty black gelding who loved to race, 'hadn't even occurred to me, to be honest. Although I was certainly going to ask you to the reception back here at the Big House. Bound to be a slap-up affair. Nothing formal, no sit-down dinner, Adele didn't want that, just a big party for friends and neighbours. We're renowned for our parties, you know.'

'Thank you,' James said tightly, 'I would like to come to the party. But I couldn't possibly attend the wedding.' He focused upon saddling Bella, the statuesque bay Ben had allotted him. He and the mare had already developed a strong relationship. Bella had taken to him instantly, as he had to her. James had a way with horses.

'Why ever not?' Ben asked in all innocence.

'It wouldn't be right. For God's sake, I'm a worker, Ben, not part of your family or one of your family's fancy friends.'

'Of course you are. You're *my* friend—'

'You know what I mean,' James interrupted with a touch of impatience, and Bella snorted as he gave an extra strong tug on the girth. 'I'm not one of the landed gentry.'

Ben realised in that instant that James really *did* want to attend the wedding. *But of course,* he recalled, *James always wanted to move up in the world, he'd be bound to view this as a step in the right direction.* Not for one second was Ben critical of the fact. To the contrary, he would do all he could to assist his friend's aspirations.

'You will come, James,' he said as he mounted Baron, wheeling him on the spot, the gelding keen to take off. 'You will come as a favour to me.'

James mounted Bella, the mare equally keen, the race between both riders and horses a favourite pastime for all. He was about to protest further, but Ben wouldn't hear a word. Not now, anyway.

'We'll talk about it when we get to the quarry,' he said and with a touch of his heels, Baron was away, Bella following in quick pursuit. The two miles across the plains from the homestead to the stone quarry was their regular race track.

Ben proved the winner this morning.

'Not fair,' James said as they dismounted at the grove of trees that marked the end of the course, beyond which the ground became rocky. 'It wasn't a legal start.'

'I had to shut you up somehow,' Ben replied good-naturedly.

Loosening the girths, they left the horses grazing among the trees and walked up to the top of the ridge, not bothering to tether the animals in the sure knowledge that Baron and Bella would never stray.

As was customary at the conclusion of a race, they sat together on the large flat rock overlooking the old stone quarry far below. Ben had said it was a favourite spot of his for watching a sunset fan out across the breadth of the valley. It had become a favourite spot for the two of them now, a secluded place where no one else went, a place they considered their own.

'Convict teams used to work this quarry,' Ben had explained the first time he'd brought James to the site. 'There's a well down there, see?' He'd pointed to the circle of roughly hewn rocks topped with a sheet of rusted corrugated iron, which sat at the bottom of the ridge not far from where their horses were grazing. 'Convicts built that. Dad's been meaning to fill it in, but never got around to it. I've always thought what a bloody good place to hide a body.'

'I must remember that,' James had said.

'Yes. Would have come in handy for the disposal of Charles Grenfell,' Ben had replied, and they'd smiled, both aware of the trust between them and the bond they shared.

Ben gathered his coat tightly about him to ward off the chill wind. The morning was clear and the view was pretty, but up here on the ridge the bite of winter was fierce.

'Please come to the wedding, James,' he said. 'I'd really like you to, and I know Jenna would too.'

No reply.

'Personally, I think she's smitten with you.'

Still no reply.

He's looking a bit sullen, Ben thought. 'Ah, now there's an idea,' he said brightly, determined to joke his friend out of whatever mood had beset him, 'we could marry you and Jenna off. You two could give birth to the next generation of McKinnons and save me the trouble of having to procreate.'

Yet again, no answer.

Ben dropped the frivolous tone. 'Do come to the wedding, James,' he said. 'Please. I really want you to. We all do. The whole family.'

'I don't have the right clothes,' James replied, still not meeting Ben's eyes but looking out over the valley.

Ben didn't let himself smile, although he wanted to. *This is going to be easy after all,* he thought. 'You can borrow some of mine, we're about the same size.'

'No thank you. I can buy my own. I do have money, you know.'

'Of course you do.' *And of course you also have pride,* Ben thought, once again stifling a smile. 'Right'—he jumped to his feet—'decision made. We'll buy you some new clothes this very morning. Come on,' he urged, 'we're going into town.'

'You mean city.'

'What?'

'You told me I wasn't to call Goulburn a town.' James gave a sheepish smile as he stood. He knew he'd been easily bought, that Ben had seen right through his protestations and feigned reluctance.

'Don't be ridiculous. Everyone calls it a town.'

They rode back to Glenfinnan, stopping off at the workers' cottage where James collected his stash of money from the deposit box in his wardrobe. Rufus and the other two men were lounging about on the front verandah having a smoke. With the boss's permission, the workers would drive one of the drays into Goulburn later in the day.

Rufus tipped the brim of his hat respectfully to the boss's son, but the other two didn't bother. Instead, they gave James a baleful look. They didn't approve of the special standing he appeared to have with the McKinnon family.

Ben and James rode their horses directly into town.

'Quicker than harnessing up Tess and the buggy,' Ben said, 'and Lockie will package the stuff so we can carry it.'

Lockwoods in Auburn Street was Goulburn's only clothing store that offered anything sartorial, the other outlets supplying more along the lines of informal and practical attire together with work wear. The proprietor, Lockie, was an amiable Londoner with a knowledge of fashion, and his wife, Dora, a former factory seamstress, was a talented dressmaker. Both were well known to the McKinnons.

It had been Dora who had made Adele's wedding gown – exactly along the lines Adele had requested, simple and elegant. 'Every stitch personally hand-sewn,' had been Lockie's proud boast.

'Perhaps not quite as fine a purchase as you may have made in the fashion department of the Grenfell Emporium,' Ben said flippantly as James paraded before him in a charcoal tailcoat and trousers offset by a light-grey waistcoat, 'but it does the trick.' *It certainly does,* he thought admiringly. *You are devastatingly handsome, my friend.*

James also bought a new shirt with stand-up collar and a black bow tie, Lockie obligingly packing everything into a bag with a strap that could be slung across the shoulder and a half an hour later they were on their way home.

'Mission accomplished,' Ben announced triumphantly.

The following Saturday morning saw the two preparing themselves for the wedding, which was to take place at noon, Ben having insisted James join him at the Big House so they could dress together.

'The men will rib you without mercy if they see you formally frocked up,' he said, which they both knew to be true.

They stood side by side in his bedroom, examining their images in the large gilt-framed mirror.

'Excellent,' Ben declared, 'although you could do with a top hat. We both could.'

'What?'

'A top hat, old man. Imperative for a wedding.'

'Why didn't you tell me?' James was horrified. A top hat, of course; he'd look completely wrong without one.

'Why bother? I have two of the damn things.' Ben strode to his wardrobe, flung open the doors and after ferreting about in the hat rack produced two top hats. 'The grey or the black?' he asked, twirling one in each hand.

James pointed to the grey.

'Good choice,' Ben said.

They donned their respective headwear and once again checked the mirror.

'What a couple of dandies, eh?'

'Yes.' James gazed at his image. He'd never worn a top hat before. 'Yes, you're right,' he agreed. 'We're a pair of toffs all right.' He wondered what in the world his father might think.

The Big House had been a sea of activity throughout the morning in preparation for the party that would follow mid-afternoon and no doubt proceed on into the night. The furniture in the larger of the two drawing rooms, which was reserved for formal occasions and most particularly for parties, had been totally re-arranged. Bulkier pieces – sideboards, tables and armchairs – had been removed altogether, along with rugs, exposing the polished wooden floor with its parquet borders. The French upright piano, which normally lived in the family sitting room, had been placed in one corner, and hard-back chairs, stools and small coffee tables positioned against the walls, leaving the entire central space clear to serve as a dance floor. It looked for all the world like a ballroom, and would serve as such. Adele and Jenna were both proficient on the piano, with any number of cousins more than happy to follow suit or to join in on violin, guitar or harmonica. Family parties were always a musical affair.

The formal dining room had also undergone a major change. The twenty-seater table was extended to its full capacity, but the chairs had been removed and these, too, placed against the walls with small coffee tables set here and there beside them. The dining was to be buffet style, guests helping themselves while waiters circulated serving drinks. Those guests, presumably the elderly or infirm, who wished for more comfort would be encouraged to adjourn to the family sitting room where several dining tables had been set up. The two rooms adjoined each other and with the large twin doors that linked them opened wide, they formed an excellent all-round entertaining area, which was the intention of their design.

Most of the work had been done by the suppliers and caterers Alastair had hired. Teams of workers had arrived early, turning the entire household upside down, the kitchen and breakfast room taken over altogether for food preparation and storage. But the family was accustomed to such mayhem. Glenfinnan House had seen many a large party in the past. None of equal import to this one, however, none offering such cause for celebration. Family and friends from the surrounding region would gather to toast the marriage of Alastair McKinnon's eldest daughter. This was to be a grand occasion.

As noon approached, a bevy of horse-drawn vehicles pulled up either directly outside St Peter and Paul's Cathedral in Goulburn or several blocks away at the nearby livery stables. People alighted in droves from coaches and carriages, from traps, buggies and sulkies, from carts and wagons, some leaving their coachman or driver to look after their vehicles, others depositing them in the care of the stables and walking to the Cathedral.

The McKinnons cleverly managed a mixture of both. The household staff being considered members of the family, Beth, Millie and Boris were all invited to the wedding. Their services were not required even for the party that would follow, everything having been left in the hands of the caterers. It was common knowledge, however, that nothing would stop Beth and Millie from overseeing the proceedings back at the Big House, just as it was common knowledge that nothing would allow Boris to leave his precious horses in the sole care of the lads at the local livery stables. After the family members had alighted outside the cathedral, Boris would personally oversee the delivery of each McKinnon vehicle and, far more importantly, each McKinnon animal, to the stables where he would stay and tend to them. The task had not been allotted him, it was his choice and his alone. Boris had not the least desire to attend the church service, vastly preferring the company of horses to people.

Ben and James were the only ones to differ from the plan, Ben announcing he would drive the two of them in the buggy directly to the stables where they would leave both the buggy and Tess to await Boris' tender care while they walked to the cathedral.

They enjoyed the drive into town, despite the drab greyness of the day.

'You'd think with this amount of cloud it might rain, wouldn't you?' Ben complained, looking up at the lowering sky. 'Adele wouldn't mind in the least if it pelted down on her big day. Neither would Phil. They'd probably consider it the best wedding gift they could possibly ask for.'

Apart from his brief trip to Lockwoods in order to buy clothes, this was to be James' first visit to Goulburn since his arrival in the area, his only view of the city having been during the drive from the railway station. He was looking forward to seeing some of the fine buildings he'd glimpsed.

'You'll find the cathedral pretty impressive,' Ben said. 'Traditional gothic design, but built from local greenstone that's found in very limited quantities around here so it's certainly what you'd call unique. Frightfully imposing of course,' he added with a wry smile, 'typically Catholic.'

Tess trotted on for a further several minutes, the men remaining silent, before Ben continued.

'Not that we're particularly Catholic ourselves,' he said, 'but my mother was, so we were more or less brought up that way. Dad never goes to mass, never attends confession, never even steps inside a church. He never did, mind you, which I remember didn't seem to overly bother Mum. But she made sure I was sent to St Patrick's College, which is a highly respectable day and boarding school for good Catholic boys.' Ben smiled reminiscently. 'Dear old St Pat's.' His smile broadened into a grin and he raised a suggestive eyebrow. 'Fond memories indeed. For me anyway. Others may differ.'

The cathedral proved as impressive as Ben had promised. On approach, James gazed in awe at the intricate stonework of its giant tower, such a strange shade of green-grey, its slate roof of deep purple, its narrow, arched windows ornately framed in contrasting stone. And when they entered, the inside was equally spectacular. Broad aisles bordered by moulded columns led to arches, which in turn led to small chapels on either side, and overhead the vast arched wooden ceiling was divided into bays, spandrels of timber resting on columns. He'd never seen such magnificence.

In contrast to the grandeur of the surrounds, the ceremony itself proved comparatively modest, just as Adele had wished it to be. All eyes watched admiringly as she walked down the aisle on the arm of her father. She looked extraordinarily lovely. Tall, elegant, her dark hair piled high displaying the beauty of her neck, the clear lines of her simple-cut gown emphasising the slenderness of her body and the grace of her carriage.

Alastair McKinnon was beaming right and left to the gathered congregation, making no attempt whatsoever to disguise his unashamed pride, while at the other end of the aisle, Phil Caton's eyes never once left his approaching wife-to-be. Jaw agape, he was gawking adoringly as if he couldn't believe his luck, which was the absolute truth. Beside Phil stood Ben, who was to play the role of best man, Phil having no family of his own. Dark-haired like his sister and graceful of carriage, Ben also was elegant. It was obvious the siblings had been similarly blessed.

Observing the scene as it unfolded, James was once again struck by the contradictory nature of the McKinnons. Here was a family with wealth to spare and with looks that could only be the result of good breeding. They were refined, stylish, like well-bred racehorses, and by all appearances decidedly upper class. *But they're not really, are they?* he thought. *There's something quite ordinary about them. They're solid, down-to-earth, no airs and graces . . .* The contradiction was attractive. *And they're all like that,* he thought, *the whole damn lot of them.*

James had met the entire extended family during the brief mingling that had taken place outside the cathedral, Ben introducing him to Alastair's two younger sisters, Adriana and Alexandra, together with their husbands and respective offspring.

'And this is my veritable sea of cousins,' he'd said, before proceeding to introduce each and every one.

James couldn't for the life of him remember their names, but he was aware of one blatantly obvious factor; the use of abbreviations, or the lack thereof. There was a Victoria and an Elizabeth, he recalled, but they were not a 'Vic' or a 'Liz'. Nor were the other girls' names abbreviated. The boys' names however were. All of them. There was a Colin who was 'Col' and a William who was 'Will', and so it went on, he couldn't remember the rest. He commented upon this fact to Ben as they entered the cathedral.

'Of course,' Ben said, 'like working dogs. The boys are always reduced to one syllable. Easier to command that way.'

Yes, James decided, it made sense. Sheep dogs were often allowed personal names, but when working they were always one syllable. *Funny though,* he thought, *nobody calls Alastair McKinnon 'Al'.* He wondered whether they ever had.

Following the ceremony, there was further mingling outside the cathedral and James tried to memorise the cousins' names, nine in all, some in their twenties, some still teenagers, but with little success. There was one name, however, that struck a chord.

'Hello, Alex.'

Ben had shepherded him over to greet a young man standing beside a middle-aged couple, both of whom were busily congratulating the newlyweds.

The young man turned, a pleasant-faced fellow in his early twenties.

'I'd like you to meet James Brereton,' Ben said, 'a very good friend of mine.'

James could have sworn he heard the slightest emphasis on *very good.*

'James, this is Alexander Oakley.'

As they shook hands and exchanged how-do-you-dos, James was aware Alexander Oakley was avoiding his eyes. But Alexander Oakley was also avoiding Ben's eyes. And James knew why. This was *the* Alex, he thought. The Alex from St Patrick's College days, and Ben's emphasis on *very good* had been deliberate. Why? What was his intention?

It was impossible to tell as Ben carried on expansively. 'Haven't seen you for such a long time, Alex, how have you been?'

'Very well, thank you. Lovely ceremony.'

'Yes, yes, quite lovely . . .'

Ben was about to continue, but the middle-aged couple, who happened to be Alex's parents, had completed their congratulations and it was now up to Alex to offer his. He turned away, clearly thankful for the change of direction and Ben introduced James to the Oakleys Senior.

'Mr and Mrs Oakley are well-known property owners in the region,' he explained, 'and long-time family friends. Alex and I went to boarding school together,' he loudly added, ensuring Alex, who had kissed Adele's cheek and was now shaking Phil's hand, could hear. 'Will you be coming back to the Big House for the party?' he asked.

'We will most certainly, Ben,' Reginald Oakley replied, 'but we won't stay long. We like to get home before dark, don't we, dear?'

His wife, Phyllis, nodded. 'We do, yes.' She smiled. 'But I must say, I'm very much looking forward to a bit of a "do".'

At that point, Alex turned to his parents, having completed his congratulations, and Ben once again dived in.

'How about you, Alex? Will you be coming back to the Big House for the party?'

'I'm afraid not,' Alex replied stiffly. 'Celia's expecting in one month and I don't like to leave her alone any longer than necessary.'

'Ah, yes.' Ben thumped the pummel of his hand against his forehead in a melodramatic gesture of exasperation. 'Of course. I'd heard and I'd completely forgotten. Do forgive me. Your first, isn't it?'

Alex nodded.

'Marvellous news.' Ben flashed a beatific smile at James as if sharing happiness all round, then back to Alex. 'Praying for a son, no doubt.'

'Of course.' Alex's discomfort was by now painfully obvious. 'Well, I must be off. Nice to see you, Ben.' And he was gone.

Ben and James made their own departure barely ten minutes later, but James waited until they'd collected Tess and the buggy from the livery stables before confronting Ben. He was mystified, and also annoyed. He'd actually felt sorry for Alex.

'Why did you do that?' he demanded when they'd left the heavy traffic behind them and were on the outskirts of town.

'Do what?'

'Confront Alex the way you did.'

Ben feigned innocence. 'And what way would that be?'

This only annoyed James further. 'Inferring I was your "special friend" for a start,' he snapped. 'What the hell was *that* supposed to mean?'

'But it's the truth. You're my friend and you're special.'

'Oh for Christ's sake, Ben, stop treating me like a fool.' James was angry now. 'What the hell were you playing at? Why did you do it?'

A pause. And then the truth. 'I wanted to see him squirm.'

Taken by surprise, James was lost for an answer.

'Yes, it was probably a bit cruel of me to humiliate him like that,' Ben admitted. 'I was a bit cruel to you too,' he added with an apologetic smile. 'You do realise that he'll presume we're lovers.'

'I gathered that was your intention,' James said tightly. 'Why?'

'I suppose I'm cross with him for having thrown in the sponge the way he has,' Ben admitted. 'Not that I'll have any alternative myself,' he added with a careless shrug. 'I'll have to marry some poor unsuspecting girl, hopefully manage to sire an heir or two, or maybe three, and then spend the rest of my life living a lie.' His attempt at nonchalance was starting to sound bitter. 'Ah well.' Another careless shrug. 'I intend to sow my wild oats in the meantime.' He grinned devilishly. 'My meetings with agents and buyers were so successful Dad assures me there'll be many more trips to Sydney. I won't be short of opportunities.'

They lapsed into silence for the rest of the drive back to Glenfinnan.

*

The party was in full swing. People had gorged themselves on the generous buffet that seemed never-ending, every empty platter instantly replaced. Glasses had been constantly refilled, speeches made – although upon Adele's orders only brief ones – and any number of toasts raised to the happy couple. Now came the time for dancing, and the many cousins happily provided the music. The aunts too. Adriana and Alexandra were both proficient on the piano, as were all McKinnon women, and with Elizabeth's violin, Will's guitar and Col's harmonica, the mix was, as always, excellent.

Jenna was teaching James to dance, and James, having downed enough beer to lose his inhibitions, was very much enjoying the experience.

So was Jenna. She was glad they were not performing the old-fashioned quadrilles she'd learned at school, but rather those dances requiring couples to embrace. So much more intimate, and she adored the feel of his arm about her.

'You should hold me a little closer, James,' she suggested, 'it's easier to coordinate our movements that way.'

James did as he was told. He was proving an apt enough pupil, quickly learning to distinguish the difference between a waltz and a polka, and he took to the galop with ease. The galop was the simplest of the closed-couple dances, the two-step requiring a good deal more expertise.

'Oops, sorry,' he said as his two-step once again went awry and he trod on her toes. But Jenna didn't mind in the least.

Ben had not taken to the dance floor, although he was an excellent dancer and very much enjoyed dancing. He hadn't been in the mood. After imbibing more than his share of both champagne and beer, he'd purloined a bottle of cognac from the liquor cabinet and gone out to the verandah on the western side of the house, the one which the bedrooms opened onto and where family members often sat to watch the sunset. Here, despite the bitter cold, he sat alone, drinking far too much and feeling morose. Glib as his conversation with James had been during the drive home, his meeting with Alex had re-opened old wounds. He could think of nothing but Alex now. Or rather the relationship they'd had. The closeness of it. The physical and emotional intimacy and far, far more. The way they'd bared their souls to one another. The relief they'd discovered in sharing their past and the agony of their respective youths. Able finally to be who they truly were, revealing themselves for the first time in their lives. No one had known him as Alex had. And no one had known Alex as he had. Little wonder he felt betrayed. And yet he couldn't blame Alex. He had no right. But he was now reminded of how bleak his own future appeared.

Flippant though he'd sounded, he'd been honest with James. He was destined to follow the same path as Alex. To marry some poor young woman who believed he loved her, to sire her children, and probably cheat on her in order to satisfy his sexual urges.

A sordid life, he thought, downing another hefty gulp of cognac. He was swigging directly from the bottle now, couldn't be bothered pouring the stuff into a glass. Jesus Christ, all he wanted was someone with whom to share his life, someone with whom he could be honest, who accepted him exactly as he was. Someone who loved him, for God's sake, was that too much to ask?

'So there you are.' James appeared. Unable to find Ben, he'd walked around the side of the house, puzzled that his friend had chosen to desert the festivities. 'I was wondering where you'd got to.'

He stepped up onto the verandah and sat in one of the wicker chairs, studying Ben in the approaching gloom. He could see Ben was unhappy, slumped forward as he was, elbows on knees, the empty glass lying on its side by his feet, the bottle of brandy dangling from his hand. *And he's drunk what's more,* James thought, *very, very drunk.*

'What's up, mate?'

Ben stared back at him blearily. Here was the one person who knew his secret, the one person to whom he could speak openly. And so he did, the words pouring out.

'I don't want to be anything other than what I am, James, you understand that, don't you?' His voice was slurred. 'I don't want to have to live a lie. I don't want to have to pretend I'm someone I'm not for the rest of my life. I want what I had with Alex. We loved each other, Alex and me. What's so wrong with that? Come on now, you tell me, what so bloody wrong with that?' He was waving the bottle around and it suddenly left his hand to fly through the air before coming to land on the verandah and skitter across the floorboards, fortunately without breaking.

James picked it up and stood it against one of the posts, looking about as he did, checking there was no one around who might have heard Ben's rant. They were safe, the place was deserted.

'Come on mate, you've had enough.' He hoisted Ben to his feet, half carrying, half dragging him towards the nearest door, which he knew led to his bedroom. 'Time to sleep it off.'

'Why?' Ben waved an arm about drunkenly. 'It's not bedtime, it's not even dark yet.'

'It will be soon. Come on now.' James opened the door. 'We're putting you to bed.'

'You coming with me?' A wan but hopeful smile. 'That'd be nice.'

Inside, James dumped him on the bed and took off his boots, Ben still rambling on.

'You should stay here, you know. I mean that, I really do. It's a Saturday night, the men'll be drunk when they get back from town. They'll probably bash you up when they see you in your fancy clothes.' His voice was starting to fade a little. 'You should stay here, James. Really you should. You should stay here with me . . .'

James pulled the coverlet over him and crept from the bedroom. Behind him, he could hear Ben gently snoring.

Many guests had already left, intent upon getting home before darkness set in, but others were happy to stay, making the all-too-familiar trip back to their properties in the light of the lamps that hung from their vehicles. James accepted the offer of a lift from Adriana and her husband, Rob, together with their two youngest children, teenagers who still lived at home. The elder three had long since married and moved out, although they remained in the area. It seemed all those of McKinnon blood did.

'We go right past the workers' cottages,' Adriana insisted, 'no trouble at all, and there's plenty of room in the wagon.'

It was ten o'clock when they dropped him at the turn-off that led to the cottages. He thanked them and made his way up the hill. Even from a distance he could hear the men carousing. They'd come back from town drunk, returned the dray to the work stables and were now getting stuck into the grog they'd brought home with them. It was a Saturday night after all. James hoped there wouldn't be trouble as Ben had predicted there might. He didn't feel like a fight, and he certainly didn't want to risk his new clothes being damaged.

He was thankful to discover the men were gathered in one of the other cottages, and that his was deserted, for the moment anyway. He lit one of the kerosene lamps and took it into his bedroom where he quickly undressed. He would fold up his new clothes and pack them away in the bottom of his wardrobe where they would remain well out of sight, giving the men no cause to jeer.

He donned the warm undergarments he wore to bed and proceeded with great care to fold the clothes, but as he bent down to remove his kitbag and place them into the wardrobe, he noticed something missing.

The deposit box. It was gone.

He didn't even bother searching Rufus' wardrobe or chest of drawers. He was sure Rufus wouldn't have stolen it, and even if he had he certainly wouldn't leave it in the room where it could be so easily discovered.

James sat on the bed, pondering the situation. Should he go to the cottage where the men were carousing right now and confront them? Unwise in their drunken condition, he decided. But he would certainly confront Rufus in the morning. Rufus, sharing their twin bunk room as he did, was the only one who could have known about the deposit box.

Of one thing James was certain. Come what may, he must get Charles Grenfell's gold fob watch back.

CHAPTER NINE

Rufus was fast asleep on his bunk when James awoke. Lying on his back and snoring loudly, the man hadn't even bothered to undress but was fully clothed with the exception of his boots, which he'd had enough sense to remove before passing out.

The usual Saturday night, James thought. The others would all be in the same condition, sleeping off the effects of the grog, and probably wouldn't awaken until mid-morning.

James wasn't prepared to wait that long.

He poured cold water from the jug into the basin on the washstand, washed and dried his face, quickly dressed and then took action.

'Hey, Rufus!' He bent down and, grabbing the man by the shoulders, shook him roughly. 'Hey, Rufus, wake up,' he said loudly.

The snoring came to an abrupt halt and Rufus gave a startled snort, but he didn't wake up. Instead he muttered something and rolled over onto his side facing the wall.

James would have none of it.

'I said wake up!' he yelled, dragging on the man's shoulders so roughly that Rufus rolled back onto his other side and nearly fell off the bed.

He was well and truly awake now and, albeit befuddled, in a state of panic.

'What? What's the matter? What's happening?' Slinging his legs over the side of the bunk, he sat bolt upright and looked about in wide-eyed alarm.

'I have to talk to you,' James said urgently.

'You have to *talk* to me!' The man's disbelief was comical. 'Shit, I thought the place was on fire or something. For Christ's sake, go away and leave me alone . . .'

He was about to slump back, but James plonked himself down on the bunk and, once again grabbing both shoulders, turned Rufus to face him.

'I said *we need to talk,*' he repeated, and this time his tone was fierce.

Rufus stared back blearily, recognising the urgency in the boy's eyes. Over twice James' age, his beard already flecked with grey, Rufus always thought of James as a boy. So did the others, all of whom derided him behind his back. But none would have openly confronted young James Brereton, recognising a power behind the youthful façade. The boy was strong and fit, not one to be easily overcome in a physical challenge.

'Talk about what?' Rufus queried sulkily.

'That.' James pointed to the open door of his wardrobe. 'I had a small wooden deposit box stashed in that cupboard.' As his eyes bored into Rufus' seeking any sign of guilt, he was rewarded with a flash of something. If not guilt, then at least recognition. 'It's gone,' he said accusingly.

'I didn't take it.'

'But you told the others about it, am I right?'

'Yeah,' Rufus admitted after a pause. He had the grace to look a little shamefaced. 'But I didn't think any of the blokes would nick it. They were just talking about you being a bit of a toady that's all, sucking up to the boss, pretending to be something you're not . . .' He gave an offhand shrug, searching for the right words, on the defensive now as James' eyes continued to bore into his. 'The way you're best mates with the boss's son, cosying up to his sister, you know how it is . . .'

No, James didn't 'know how it is', but his eyes said, *go on.*

'Well, I told them you had a fancy deposit box kept under lock and key, like one of those rich geezers. I made a joke. Said, "Christ knows what he's got in there, probably Queen Victoria's crown bloody jewels . . ." Just having fun, you know. Didn't mean any harm.'

Rufus was becoming a little disconcerted. The ice-blue eyes drilling into his were somehow unnerving. 'I didn't think anyone would steal the thing, James, truly I didn't,' he said in all honesty. 'You do believe me, don't you?'

'Yes,' James finally replied, 'I believe you. Do you have any idea which one of them it was?'

Rufus could have hazarded a guess, but wasn't prepared to risk it, convinced the others might turn on him if he did. Personally, he would have put his money on Dunk, who was particularly scathing of James. Thomas 'Dunk' Dunkley had had it in for the boy right from the start. 'Who does he think he is?' Dunk would say. 'Sucking up to the boss the way he does, working extra hard just to make the rest of us look bad. Reckons he's better than us, that's what it is.' Dunk, a tough, embittered man in his mid-forties, was very good at stirring up the others, all seven of whom now bore a grudge against James Brereton, although they probably wouldn't have known precisely why.

Rufus recalled, too, how when they'd been at the pub in Goulburn the previous afternoon Dunk had carried on about James being a guest at the McKinnon wedding. 'Strutting about like a right toff at this very minute, I'll bet,' Dunk had sneered. 'Should be taken down a peg or two that one. Young bastard needs to be taught a lesson.' *Perhaps this was Dunk's 'lesson'*, Rufus thought. *Perhaps*

when they'd returned from the pub and got into the grog,
Dunk had snuck over here and nicked the box.

'Nup, wouldn't know.' He shook his head in answer to
James' query. 'Couldn't say who.'

James sensed Rufus had his definite suspicions, but
wasn't about to rat on a fellow worker, which was understandable, he supposed. In any event, nothing was to be
gained by pushing the man further.

He stood, contemplating his next course of action, but his
thoughts were interrupted by a loud pounding on the cottage
door and a voice calling, 'You in there, James?' It was Ben.

He walked from the room and behind him Rufus
slumped back on the bunk. As James crossed to the front
door, the pounding continued and he wondered whether
it might awaken the other two workers who shared the
cottage. If this was the case then he would confront them.
But there was not a sound from the other bunk room and
the door remained firmly closed.

He opened the front door of the cottage to discover Ben
standing on the small verandah, Baron and Bella tied up at
the hitching rail behind him.

'I've come to collect you for our morning ride,' Ben said
brightly. He was fresh-faced and eager, the drunkenness of
the previous afternoon having had little after-effect, or so
it seemed.

'I thought you'd be sleeping things off,' James said.

Ben vaguely remembered having been maudlin in the
drink and probably saying more than he should have,
but he didn't really care. James could be trusted with anything he may have blurted out.

'Nope. As you can see, bright as a button. You ready
to go?'

But his friend appeared uncertain, which surprised Ben,
who'd expected him to embrace the opportunity; James
always loved their morning rides.

'What's up?' he queried. 'Something wrong?'

James came to an instant decision. The men wouldn't resurface until at least mid-morning. As there seemed little point in attempting to rouse them before then, he would share his dilemma with Ben.

'Tell you all about it when we get to the quarry,' he said and stepped out onto the verandah, closing the cottage door behind him.

It was James who won the race this morning, but only by the merest margin, no more than a yard or so.

'I'd call it half a body length,' he declared as they left the horses at the creek and wandered up the rocky ridge to the top of the stone quarry.

'So tell me,' Ben urged when they were seated on the rock overlooking the valley. 'What's happened?'

James told him of the locked deposit box and its over-night disappearance.

'Bit naive of you to have kept it there in the first place,' Ben said with a distinct lack of sympathy. 'You should have given it to me to look after at the Big House.'

'Perhaps,' James acknowledged. 'That thought did occur. But I've never known workmates to steal from one another. A bit of cash lying around maybe, but not an item of obvious value like this.'

'These are not the sort of men you're accustomed to working with, James,' Ben said. 'These are not shearers. These are desperate men lining up for whatever work they can get in the midst of a depression. There's no honour among such men, certainly not during times like these.'

'Yes,' James agreed wryly, 'I've gathered that.'

'So how much money was in the box? How much have you lost?'

'It's not the money. There wasn't a lot there anyway, no more than twenty quid. It's the watch.' And he proceeded to tell Ben all about Charles Grenfell's gold fob watch and chain.

'He was wearing it the night I killed him,' he said, feeling oddly detached as he recalled that night. 'It was in his vest pocket and I took it from his body. Went through all his other pockets too, took his money as well.'

'You never told me about the watch.' Ben's response was also detached, but for purely practical reasons.

'I didn't think it necessary.'

'Are there any distinguishing marks on it? Any—'

'No,' James interrupted briskly, 'no carved initials, no identification as such, but the Grenfell brothers would certainly recognise it if they saw it. Good God, it's even in that portrait of the three of them. The huge one hanging on the dining-room wall, remember? Charles Grenfell's showing it off as if it's some sort of trophy.'

'Yes. Yes, of course I remember.' Ben also remembered James' fascination with the portrait, the way he couldn't seem to take his eyes off it. *Hardly surprising given the circumstances*, he thought. *Until then he hadn't known the man he'd killed was Charles Grenfell.*

'So you think the box was stolen some time yesterday,' he said.

'Definitely. It was there when I lifted out my clothes for the wedding – just before you picked me up in the buggy.'

'And it was locked, you say?'

'Yep, I've got the key right here.' James dived a hand inside his flannel coat, unbuttoned the upper pocket of his work shirt and produced the key. 'I carry it with me always.'

'I wonder if the thief's discovered what's inside,' Ben said thoughtfully, 'whether he's managed to break the box open.'

'It's pretty damn solid. He'd need to take to it with an axe.'

'Then that's our first step. We go to the shearers' quarters.' Ben stood and made his announcement with an air of triumph. 'There's a chopping block and a wood heap out the back that supplies the shearers' kitchen stove. A couple of axes can always be found there. That's where our man would head.'

They rode back and as the workers' cottages came into view, Ben, who was busily concocting a plan, wondered how long it would be before the men roused themselves for breakfast. When they did, they'd be hungry and would head straight to the shearers' quarters.

'Nah mate, not for a while yet, it's only nine o'clock,' Ricky, the cook, assured him upon enquiry. 'The boys won't be here before ten at the least, more likely half past, always the same after a Saturday on the turps.'

James nodded. He could have told Ben that.

'I'll ring the tucker bell at ten though,' Ricky went on, 'just to give 'em a reminder.'

Ricky Biggins, referred to by the men simply as 'Cookie', was another employee who'd become rather like family to the McKinnons. Employed by Alastair on a regular yearly basis, Ricky and his wife, Rosie, a tough, wiry couple now in their fifties, would settle into the same workers' cottage every shearing season. In the earlier days they'd had their two children with them, but both had since grown up and moved on, possibly thankful to escape the life their parents so thoroughly embraced. Ricky and Rosie Biggins were shearers' cooks. And when it wasn't the shearing season, they put themselves out for hire as cooks for workers wherever workers' cooks were needed. They were good at their job and loved their itinerant lifestyle.

In the kitchen, Rosie had kindled the stove's wood fire, which was now burning steadily, the huge kettle sitting on the stovetop being slowly brought to the boil, frypans and saucepans at the ready, while in the covered area outside,

Ricky was setting up one of several tables that stood with benches either side. Bowls for porridge, plates for bacon and eggs, jugs of milk, tubs with lashings of lard and a central basket loaded with damper. A longer table, which was benchless and ran at a right angle to the others, acted as a servery and was set up with ladles, egg slices, serving forks and the cutlery the men would collect when they queued up for their food.

'Hey, Ricky, did any of the men take an axe from the wood heap yesterday?' Ben asked.

'What for?' Ricky didn't even look up from his work. 'To chop firewood?' He gave a wry harrumph. 'Not bloody likely, me and Rosie do that. The blokes never lend a hand, not their job, they reckon.'

'So you don't know if someone borrowed an axe?'

That caught Ricky's attention. 'Dunno, we didn't need to chop wood yesterday, had a good supply ready done.' He straightened up and looked Ben in the eye. 'If someone borrowed one of my axes, they'd better have put it back in its bloody place. Rosie and me keep both well sharpened and under cover in the tool shed. You go check for yourself, Ben,' he suggested, 'and you let me know.'

Then as Ben started to leave he called after him, 'If one of them axes is missing there'll be hell to pay, I can tell you.'

Ben and James walked around to the rear of the building where ready-cut firewood was neatly stacked against the wall and a chopping block stood next to a pile of uncut logs. They didn't bother checking the nearby tool shed. There was no need. Lying beside the chopping block was an axe.

'He didn't even put it back where he found it,' Ben said. 'Pretty careless.'

James knelt to examine the chopping block. 'And this sure as hell hasn't come from firewood,' he said, holding up one of the highly polished slivers that lay there. He stood,

looking about, eyes searching for the giveaway evidence.
'I'd say the bloke was drunk when he did this. Must have
been after they got back from the pub. And I'd say he probably chucked the box away once he'd taken what was in it.
What do you reckon?'

'Yep.' Ben nodded. 'Like I said, pretty careless.'

Splitting up, they set out on a search of the immediate
area and in no time at all made the discovery. Or Ben did.
Halfway between the shearers' quarters and the cottages,
there it was. Lying among a colourful clump of hakea
wattle shrubs golden with winter blossom.

'Is this it?' he asked, rejoining James and holding up the
shattered box, which was all but cleaved in two.

'It is,' James said, taking it from him. 'I wonder if the
watch survived.'

'We'll soon find out,' Ben promised ominously. 'We'll
wait until they're gathered together for breakfast and
we'll confront them, the whole damn lot of them.'

James agreed, and with their plan now in place, they
returned to the shearers' quarters where Ricky was
angered to hear that one of his precious axes had been left
out in the open all night.

'When I find out who it was I'll have his guts for garters,'
he growled.

'Kettle's boiling,' Rosie announced and five minutes later
she served Ben and James tin mugs of steaming hot tea.

They took their mugs over to where they'd left Baron
and Bella happily grazing a hundred yards or so away.
They'd already watered their horses and loosened the
girths. Then, settling themselves on the ground beside a
black box eucalypt, they leaned back against its trunk and
prepared to wait.

At ten o'clock on the dot, the tucker bell sounded.

It didn't take long for the men to appear. Hungry and
hungover they emerged from their cottages, setting off

in dribs and drabs down the slope towards the shearers' quarters.

By ten thirty all seven of them were there, queuing up with their bowls at the table where Ricky was serving the porridge and Rosie pouring the tea. They didn't notice the two men sitting in the shade cast by the low-slung branches of the black box tree. Even the horses, saddled and peacefully grazing, received no comment; Cookie and Rosie had horses.

Ben and James waited until the workers were seated at the table digging into their porridge, then, as Rosie disappeared into the kitchen to start on the bacon and eggs, they made their appearance. They crossed the hundred yards or so and strode together up to the servery table where they dumped their tin mugs and turned to face the men, James with the deposit box under one arm.

'I have an announcement to make,' Ben loudly declared.

The men looked up from their bowls to stare balefully at him. *How dare the boss's prick of a son interrupt their Sunday breakfast!* their eyes said. *What right did he have?*

But two sets of eyes had noted the box tucked under James Brereton's left arm.

So he found it, Rufus thought and he couldn't help his eyes flickering to Dunk, who was sitting at the end of the bench opposite him.

You bastard, Brereton, Dunk thought. *You just had to run off and report this, didn't you? Run off and report it to your best mate, the fucking boss's fucking son. You slimy, toady young bastard!*

Ben took the box from James and held it up. 'This deposit box was taken from James Brereton's cupboard yesterday,' he announced. 'As you can see, it's been smashed open and the contents stolen. I want the culprit to admit to the crime here and now, and return those contents.'

A pause ensued. But it was a pause that spoke multitudes. A pause that told the whole story. For the men, every one of them, had instantly guessed who the culprit was, and they couldn't help themselves, surreptitious glances cast in Dunk's direction, eyes flickering briefly to see what his reaction might be. And Dunk himself, glaring directly at Ben. Then turning to glare at the table in general, angry, defiant, his eyes saying, *If you don't stand by me then fuck the whole lot of you.*

Ben slammed down the box on the servery table and strode over to Dunk. 'It was you, wasn't it?' he said accusingly.

'I'm not admitting to a thing,' Dunk replied with bravado. He was not easily frightened, and certainly not by the pretty-boy son of the boss, who'd probably never done a day's work in his life. 'You got no right accusing me, sonny. You got no right accusing *any* of us.' He waved a hand at the table as if the insult had been directed at all of them, then pointed to the box. 'That thing could have been nicked by anyone. A drifter, a passer-by, probably one of them black bastards that nick the eggs from the chook pen.'

'But it wasn't, was it,' Ben demanded, 'it was nicked by you!' With both hands, he grabbed the man by the lapels of his coat and dragged him to his feet. 'There was money and a gold watch in that box. You'll give them back. Right now!'

'Get your mitts off me, you little shit.' Dunk was outraged. How dare this young upstart lay a finger on him! He balled his right hand into a fist and landed a blow to the solar plexus.

Winded, Ben released his grip to stagger back a pace or two and Dunk followed up with another punch. He didn't in the least care that this was the boss's son, he refused to be intimidated by a useless pretty boy.

But Ben was far from useless. And Dunk's presumption that he'd never done a day's work in his life was far from the truth. Despite his impeccable good looks, Benjamin McKinnon was a farmer's son, born and bred to work, and his body, although slim, was taut and well muscled.

Ben returned a crippling punch of his own and the fight was on.

Drawn by the ruckus, Rosie had come out from the kitchen and was standing beside Ricky.

'Take Ben's horse,' he muttered to her, gesturing at Baron, they both knew the animal well, 'go to the Big House and fetch the boss.'

Rosie sprinted over to Baron, tightened the girth, and barely minutes later was off at full gallop.

Having recovered from their initial shock that Dunk had had the temerity to take a punch at the boss's son, the men were now enjoying the fight. A fight was always good entertainment and they were egging on Dunk, aware that he'd get the sack for sure, but not really caring. It wasn't often you got to see a punch-up between a worker and one of the bosses.

James' initial reaction had been to spring to his friend's aid, but upon witnessing the speed and efficiency of Ben's response he was aware Ben didn't need his assistance and wouldn't thank him for it. Ben had assumed this fight as his.

Dunk was taken aback. The pretty boy could fight. The pretty boy was fast too, dancing and dodging around so he couldn't land a punch. *Stay still, you bastard,* his mind yelled. But the pretty boy wouldn't, and Dunk was getting tired. *Only one thing for it, got to slow him down, got to take him by surprise.*

He chose his moment with care then kicked out viciously, aiming for the pretty boy's crotch, his boot landing right on target. *Cop that,* he thought as Ben dropped to the ground, clutching his groin.

With the pretty boy on his knees, Dunk closed in for the finish. A kick to the head, then when the prick was lying in the dirt a couple to the ribs and the fight would be over. But he was suddenly whirled about and found himself facing James Brereton. Hands once again clutched the lapels of his coat and before he knew it he was tugged sharply forward, a skull making connection with his face. He heard his nose crunch and, like the pretty boy, he sank to his knees.

James helped up Ben and sat him on the end of the bench to recover. 'You've got to learn to fight dirty, mate,' he muttered. Then he looked down at the man with the pulped nose and the bloodied face. 'Get up and empty your pockets, Dunk,' he ordered.

But Dunk appeared not to hear. And perhaps in all honesty he didn't. His ears were ringing, he couldn't see properly and he was decidedly dizzy.

James hauled him to his feet where he stood swaying unsteadily, trying to clear his head. *What had just happened? Had he been head-butted?*

'I said empty your pockets,' James repeated.

Dunk stared dully back at him. *Yes, that's what had happened. The boy had head-butted him.*

'Go to hell,' he growled through gritted teeth that seemed to ache.

James dragged Dunk's coat off him, a mid-length sack-like flannel coat. The man would surely have slept in his clothes last night, like most of the men did when they'd passed out from the grog. Dunk would have been wearing this coat when he'd smashed open the box with the axe. It would have been perfectly natural to have pocketed its contents.

The theory proved right. Delving his hands into the coat's pockets, James discovered the roll of treasury notes, around twenty pounds in all, still tied with string. Dunk hadn't even counted the amount yet. And here, too, was the solid gold fob watch and chain.

'It survived,' he said, passing the piece to Ben who had by now recovered himself.

Ben examined the watch, which was sturdy and undamaged. Then he stood and held it up for all to see, the richness of its gold gleaming in the wintry mid-morning sun.

'This is the property of James Brereton,' he declared. He looked scathingly at Dunk. 'This man has stolen this watch and will be dealt with accordingly.'

Dunk's head had cleared enough for him to respond, and he did so with vigour. 'Oh is that so?' he snarled, planting his feet wide in order to anchor himself and maintain his balance. 'And just who did I steal it from? You tell me that.'

The remark was bewildering and no answer was forthcoming, but the men, porridge forgotten, were paying rapt attention, every single one of them.

'A thief,' Dunk announced triumphantly, 'that's who. I've only stolen back what was already stolen. Where would this boy get a solid gold watch and chain like that?'

Again, no one had an answer, but glances were exchanged between the men. What Dunk was saying rang true.

Sensing the men were with him, Dunk continued in the same vein. 'Brereton's been pretending he's something he's not right from the start. Pretending he's better than us. And why do you think that is?'

Once again no one answered, but the question had been rhetorical anyway. Dunk was doing what Dunk did best. Whipping up resentment in his fellow workers, spreading ill will in order to gain an advantage. Thomas Dunkley was the most cunning of men.

'Right from the start we've seen how he's wormed his way into the boss's family, haven't we? We've all seen that. Best mates with the boss's son, cosying up to the boss's daughter, play-acting like he's one of the upper classes,

when we all know he's not. We all know he's a common
worker just like the rest of us. So what's his game, eh?'

Mutters were going about the table. The men were
getting riled, Dunk could tell. He had them well and truly
on his side now.

He turned to Ben. 'You and your folk might be wise
to take note,' he said with a smugly unpleasant smile.
'Brereton probably wormed his way into some other rich
sod's family in order to steal that watch you've got right
there.' He gestured at the piece Ben still held in his hand.
'And who knows what else besides. You want to look out,
mate.'

Ben was so enraged he might well have attacked the man
had James not stopped him.

'Don't,' James muttered, 'he's egging you on. It's what
he's after.'

'I'll tell you something else too, sonny. Might be a good
idea to warn your dad. That's what I'd do if I were you.
Yeah.' Dunk nodded sagely. Despite his aching face he
was enjoying himself. 'I'd warn your daddy that this "best
mate" of yours is nothing more than a common thief.'

As if on cue, there was a pounding of hooves and twenty
yards from the shearers' quarters two horses pulled up in a
cloud of dust. Alastair McKinnon had arrived.

He and Rosie dismounted and Alastair left the horses in
her care as he strode up to his son.

'What's going on here?' he demanded. 'Rosie told me
there was a fight between you and one of the workers.' He
looked from Ben to the man with the bloodied face and the
obviously broken nose. He'd been outraged to hear such a
thing had happened, but was pleased to see that at least his
son had won.

Ben decided to keep things simple. 'This man stole this
watch from James,' he said, handing the fob watch and
chain to his father.

Alastair looked at the watch in his hand, feeling the weight of it, a heavy piece, obviously of great value. Then he looked at the man accused of the theft. 'Is this true? Did you steal this watch?'

Dunk knew he didn't stand a chance with the boss, but he sure as hell wasn't going down without taking the Brereton boy with him. 'As I was just saying to the others, sir, I was only stealing back what had already been stolen. This boy is a thief. That watch isn't his. Never was—'

'Your name?' Alastair barked an interruption. He didn't know the workers' names. That was the Station Manager's area, Phil Caton was overseeing the woolshed extension.

'Thomas Dunkley, sir.'

'You are dismissed, Mr Dunkley. We do not suffer thievery at Glenfinnan. You will pack your belongings and leave today. A dray will be arranged to take you to the railway station.'

'Very good, sir. But in lieu of notice . . .'

'And you should count yourself fortunate that I will not report this episode to the police.' Alastair turned to his son. 'I'll see you and James back at the Big House,' he said, 'and bring this with you.' He returned the fob watch and chain to Ben and strode off to where Rosie was minding his horse.

Dunk felt a wave of satisfaction as he watched Ben and James walk away to collect their horses. *You're in trouble, boy,* he thought. *You're in really big trouble.* He resumed his position at the table. He'd finish his breakfast before he left.

'Shall I put the eggs and bacon on now?' Rosie asked, joining Ricky at the servery.

'Yes, love,' he replied. 'Sooner the better, porridge has gone cold.'

Ben and James were silent during the short ride to the Big House, which they did not turn into a race, but took at a slow trot. Before they'd mounted their horses Ben had tried to return the watch to James, but he'd refused to take it.

'No, your father wants to discuss this, you hold on to it for now.' And as they rode, James wondered what story he could possibly come up with that might satisfy Alastair McKinnon.

For some strange reason, Ben wasn't at all worried. He saw no need to be. James was such a fine young man that his father surely could not suspect him of any nefarious deed. Ben's mind was actually somewhere else altogether, straying distractedly along a more romantic path.

He'd enjoyed going into battle on James' behalf, and he would have proved victorious had his opponent not reverted to dirty tactics. He'd also enjoyed the way James had leapt to his defence. They'd made a fine team. Facing their enemy together like a pair of Spartan soldiers, each man protecting his lover. *If only it were true,* he thought wistfully. *If only the two of us could travel through life like that.* God how he loved James!

'I have no wish to cast suspicion upon you, James,' Alastair said, approaching the subject with something he hoped was discretion, although discretion was not his strongest suit. 'But I am interested to know how you come to have such a valuable item in your possession.'

They were seated in the breakfast room, the gold watch and chain sitting on the big wooden table before them.

Ben stared back, appalled. How could his father possibly say such a thing? He might as well have openly accused James of theft.

'It was a gift, sir,' James said awkwardly. He'd not been able to come up with a specific plan and now paused, not knowing how to go on.

In that instant, however, Ben did. And he voiced himself defiantly, as if Alastair McKinnon had had no right to ask such a question. 'It belonged to his father.' Ben's tone carried all the accusation he intended it should. 'James' father was killed in Barcaldine during the shearing strike; that watch is very precious to him.'

'I see.' Alastair was feeling decidedly uncomfortable and his son wasn't helping. He liked James and was not enjoying this confrontation, but he needed to know. The lad's father had been a shearer. How could a shearer own such a watch? 'A gift, you say?'

'Yes, that's right, sir.' Ben's words had inspired James. 'A gift to my father,' he said, the image of George Wakefield springing immediately to mind. 'When he was little more than a lad, my father saved a man's life. Rescued him from drowning in a flash river flood.' This had been one of George's many stories and, as James went on, he omitted the dramatic embellishments, which were not necessary, but added a few of his own, which served his purpose. 'The man my father saved was his boss, a wealthy farmer, and the boss gifted him that watch.'

It might have been George himself talking as James continued to channel his father. 'Pa never wore it,' he said, 'but he kept it tucked away, treasuring it for the whole of his life. Then of course when he died, it came to me. And I, too, keep it tucked away. As a memory of my father more than anything else. I would never sell it. And like Pa, I would never wear it. It's far too valuable.'

'I see,' Alastair said once again, now feeling more uncomfortable than ever. He pushed the watch across the table to James. 'Well, young man, I suggest you keep it tucked away somewhere safer,' he said.

'Yes sir, I shall. Thank you, Mr McKinnon.'

'I'll look after it for you if you like,' Ben offered as all three men stood. 'I have a valuables box, which is kept under lock and key. It'll be perfectly safe here at the Big House.'

'Thanks, Ben.' James handed him the watch. 'That's an excellent idea.'

'Come on, we'll stow it away, then go for a ride. My turn to beat you this time.'

They walked from the breakfast room, Alastair watching them go. So the gold watch and chain had belonged to the boy's dead father, he thought. How very embarrassing.

CHAPTER TEN

Several weeks later, the woolshed's extension was finally completed. The work required had been extensive. A huge new area had been built onto the rear of the shed in order to accommodate the ten stands of Wolseley shearing machines, which were to be installed the following year, together with a whole new board and pens, doubling the size of the original shed.

The job now done, the workers took their leave. James was thankful to see them go. He'd become more alienated than ever from the men these days, despite Dunk's departure. Or perhaps *because* of Dunk's departure and the events that had led up to it, he couldn't be sure. But the resentment Dunk had stirred up among the men remained palpable. Even Rufus, with whom he'd previously shared an amiable enough relationship, seemed hostile. It would be a relief to have the cottage to himself.

As had been arranged, he was to stay on at Glenfinnan working as a general farmhand until the commencement of the shearing season. This was less than two months away now, and on the Saturday morning when the men were collected in the dray that was to take them to the railway station – Boris in the driver's seat – his conspicuous absence was loudly commented upon. Loudly enough for him to hear even through the cottage door, which Rufus had just closed behind him as he left with his suitcase and kitbag.

'Funny how some blokes have things so easy, isn't it?'

'Well he's best mates with the boss's son, isn't he?'

'Pretty much best mates with the boss's daughter too.' A suggestive remark followed by lewd chuckles.

'Yep, sure knows which side his bread's buttered on that one.'

Then the sound of the dray setting off down the track.

Little wonder James hadn't come outside to wave them goodbye.

Ricky and Rosie Biggins were also staying on for the season, when they would take up their duty as shearers' cooks. Over the ensuing month or so they were to fill in for Boris and Millie who would take their annual holidays. Boris, who loathed being parted from his horses, never wanted to go on holiday, but Millie had elderly parents in Brisbane and insisted upon visiting them once a year.

James was to take his meals with Ricky and Rosie at their workers' cottage, so it was a convenient arrangement all round. The three of them would breakfast very early and Rosie would pack him a lunch to take to work, more often than not thick slices of damper stuffed with cold roast lamb and homemade pickles. Then at night he would rejoin them for dinner.

On Sundays, though, there was the weekly meal with the McKinnons. The family always had a roast dinner on Sundays, always lamb, and although it was called a roast 'dinner', always served at lunchtime.

James was a regular guest at the Sunday lunch, which was a casual affair, served up in the breakfast room. Ben had insisted he join them after their morning ride, and as the weeks had passed it had become a ritual. A ritual that Jenna very much enjoyed. She would brazenly flirt with James at every opportunity that presented itself.

Jenna McKinnon remained in hot pursuit of James Brereton. In fact these days Jenna's pursuit was hotter than

ever. The flames that had been fanned during the party at
the Big House continued to burn, and ever more brightly.
The feel of his arm about her as she'd taught him to dance,
the closeness of their bodies, the touch of his cheek against
hers as she'd gaily demanded he hold her even closer.
'Closer, James, closer,' she'd urged, 'it's easier to coordinate
our movements that way.' Innocent though she may have
sounded, to Jenna the experience had been highly sexual.
She was unashamedly in love with James Brereton, and
had now determined he was not only the man to whom she
would surrender her virginity, but the man she would marry.
She'd said as much to both her brother and her father when
each had taken her aside to offer advice in his specific way.

'For God's sake leave the poor bloke alone,' Ben had
said, 'can't you see you're embarrassing him?'

'No I'm not,' she'd responded, 'he likes it. He finds me
attractive. I'm going to marry him.'

Ben had later informed James of the exchange.

'You don't stand a chance in hell, mate,' he'd said jokingly. 'When Jenna sets her mind on something, she gets
it, believe me.'

They'd shared a laugh at Jenna's expense, but there had
been some truth in what she'd said. James *did* enjoy the
way Jenna flirted with him, and he *did* find her attractive,
but he was self-conscious when they were in the presence
of her father, whom he sensed did not at all approve. His
assumption was quite right.

'I would prefer it, Jenna,' Alastair had said when he'd
taken his daughter aside, 'if you would temper your behaviour in the company of young James.'

'In what way, Daddy?' she'd enquired.

'The way you toy with him, my dear . . .' Alastair had
felt awkward. This sort of advice should surely come from
a mother. 'It's not altogether proper. A little unseemly, if
you know what I mean.'

'No I don't, I'm afraid. I don't know at all what you mean.' Jenna had appeared genuinely bewildered. 'I'm only displaying my affection for James, Daddy. I'm going to marry him, you see.'

'Ah.' Alastair had been left in a state of bewilderment himself. Was she being serious, or was she out to make mischief? Jenna was such a wilful girl, it was often so difficult to tell. But he worried nonetheless. Was this just a passing, girlish infatuation or had she really set her sights on young James Brereton? If the latter, then he would far rather she hadn't. They knew nothing of the lad's family, for a start. Where had he come from? And from what sort of stock? In Alastair's firm opinion, breeding was the all-important factor, be it applied to sheep or to people. His views had nothing to do with snobbery or where a person sat in the social scale, but everything to do with solid, reliable stock. *Bloodlines,* he thought, *that's what counts. Good-quality breeding.*

He did so wish Jenna would find a local boy, one whose family he knew, one with a bloodline he recognised.

James threw himself into his new labours with zeal, just as he had in the building of the shed extension, enjoying the physical exertion while preparing his body for the rigours of shearing. And given the maintenance required at Glenfinnan there was plenty of work to be had, in particular the constant reparation of fencing. With over eighty paddocks on the property, the task of repairing not only the fences, but also the wire netting set in place as protection against rabbits, was endless. And then there was always the problem of the rabbits themselves.

'Rabbiting' was an ongoing chore for farmers throughout the entire region. The eradication of the pests that were devouring the grasslands essential for the grazing of sheep had been a problem for Australian farmers for the past thirty years. And all because of one man.

In 1859, newly arrived settler Thomas Austin had imported twenty-four wild rabbits from his family's property in western England to his estate roughly forty kilometres west of Geelong in Victoria. He had introduced the rabbits to his new home for the purposes of 'sport', but his sport had proved costly, for this particular breed of rabbits, caught in the wild, had adapted with ease to the local conditions, proliferating in untold numbers.

Previous to Austin's importations, the rabbits that had found their way to Australia – including the five that arrived with the First Fleet in 1788 – had been domestic animals, proving little threat. Thomas Austin's rabbits were a different breed altogether. These twenty-four wild-caught animals were of a genetic strain predisposed to become successful invaders, and would prove the fastest colonisation rate ever recorded for an introduced mammal.

Within three years of their importation 'Austin rabbits', as they had quickly become known, were the farmers' curse, multiplying by the thousands to form a 'grey blanket' that continued to spread and wreak havoc across the land.

'Look at the bastards, will you,' Alastair cursed, 'farmers' bloody scourge.' He pointed at the distant hill-side, which in the dusk light appeared to be moving, but was an optical illusion. The 'grey blanket' was moving, not the hill. 'Bloody Austin rabbits!'

On the Glenfinnan property itself the rabbit population was, for the most part, kept under control with the digging out of burrows and the placement of wire netting, but 'rabbiting' remained essential and was a regular practice, particularly during the non-shearing season.

Jenna enjoyed rabbiting. She always had. Even as a ten-year-old she'd never been squeamish about bashing a rabbit over the head with a hefty stick, although her choice of weapon had occasioned some family dispute in the early days.

'You will *stop* nicking my cricket bat, Jenna,' her thirteen-year-old brother had raged, as yet again he'd wiped the blood from his prized bat. 'If I catch you one more time . . . !'

Alastair had fashioned a special club for Jenna after that, loving his little girl's guts and the fact she never flinched at the brutality required when rabbiting. Neither did she flinch at the duty of skinning and gutting rabbits. Over the years she'd even made an art of producing the perfect pelt. Rabbit pelts, well cut and well treated, could be sold, and she was always proud of the quality of hers.

These days Jenna loved rabbiting more than ever, but not for the chase, nor for the pride in a successful hunt, nor even for the collection of pelts. These days she loved rabbiting because, more often than not, she would be in the company of James Brereton.

'Get in there, Trev,' she yelled boisterously, 'get after him boy!' And Trevor, the little black-and-white fox terrier, disappeared down the burrow, a flurry of dirt following. Trev loved digging as much as he loved the thrill of the chase. He rarely came out the other end of a burrow, but a rabbit did, sometimes quite a number of rabbits, while Trev remained busily digging. And when they appeared, Gloria the whippet-cross would be on sentry duty, tense, eagle-eyed and ready to spring into action. Bert the beagle would also be standing by, but Bert was getting on a bit and speed was not his specialty anyway.

Unlike the property's working dogs – kelpies and border collies bred specifically for the mustering of sheep – rabbiting dogs came in various breeds that served various purposes. Foxies were favoured for their size and ability to scamper through rock crevices, hollow logs and the like, greyhounds and whippets chosen for their speed across

open spaces, and beagles valued for their highly developed
sense of smell.

Bert, despite his advancing years, could still happily scent
out rabbit burrows from vast distances, although at the
age of ten, it was presumed he wouldn't last much longer.
Fortunately the McKinnons, who bred all their own dogs,
selecting which of the litter to keep and giving away the
rest, already had two of Bert's highly capable offspring fully
trained, but old Bert remained Jenna's personal favourite.

The moment the rabbits were flushed from the burrow,
mayhem ensued. Gloria took only seconds to claim her first
victim, but she never harmed the animal, simply downing
it and holding on. Gloria didn't enjoy killing. But, Jenna
did. Jenna, trusty club in hand, was there in an instant,
leaving Gloria free to take off in pursuit of her next quarry.

James and Ben would be there too, digging in alongside
Trev and bashing at any rabbits that emerged with their
spades, a messy and gruesome business, but an essential
one. Personally they both found a great deal more fun in a
hunt at dusk, picking off rabbits with their new American
lever-action Winchester rifles as the 'grey blanket' moved
across a deserted hillside, but the digging out and clearing
of burrows on the Glenfinnan property itself was of far
greater importance.

If the number of burrows appeared to be increasing, as
was sometimes the case after the shearing season when
less attention had been paid to the problem, then the rabbiting forays became more intense. A greater number of
dogs were employed, there were more people and more
clubs, more blood and more gore. But for the moment, the
team consisted of Jenna, Ben, Jenna's three favourite dogs,
and Ben's best friend, James Brereton. Jenna, who couldn't
have been happier, threw herself into her love of rabbiting
with all the gusto she'd displayed as a ten-year-old, but
these days with far more finesse.

James watched her admiringly. The efficiency with which she disposed of a rabbit fascinated him. Very little blood and gore came into play when Jenna wielded her club. A quick grab of the animal's ears, a brief whack to the back of its head and she was onto the next one. Both he and Ben were far messier.

There was a great deal about Jenna that fascinated James. The image of her in her practical men's overalls dealing out lethal blows was so at odds with the twirling of her skirts and the coquettish games she played. And yet perhaps not, he told himself, remembering the night of the dance just the previous Saturday. Jenna's coquetry could be as bold and forthright as her expertise in the killing of rabbits.

'Don't you think it's time you kissed me?' she'd demanded as she'd brazenly fronted him, looking most fetching in the wattle-shaded taffeta gown that so complemented the ginger of her hair.

'Why?' He'd been nonplussed.

'Because you want to . . .' A pause, the hazel-green eyes challenging him. Then, 'And because I want you to.'

A further pause as he contemplated the challenge. Would he, or wouldn't he? He knew that he shouldn't.

The dance had been Jenna's idea from the outset.

'We'll go the three of us,' she'd announced to her brother in that bossy way of hers, 'you, me and James. It's at the town hall next Saturday, bound to be a grand affair, everyone'll be there.'

So they'd gone. Naturally. Jenna always got her way.

And she'd been right. It *had* been a grand affair. The town hall itself was grand. An imposing structure with a red-brick façade, small curved iron lace balcony and Dutch gable, it stood in Auburn Street beside the equally imposing post office, starkly white in contrast, with a majestic clock tower that dominated the surrounds. Two of

Goulburn's proudest buildings. And Goulburn had many proud buildings.

James had thoroughly enjoyed himself. Any inhibitions he may have harboured about mingling in social echelons above his level had quickly disappeared. The rowdier and more ill-kempt of the farm workers were not in attendance, it was true, preferring the many pubs Goulburn had to offer on a Saturday night, but any number of familiar faces were present. There were members of the extended McKinnon clan, cousins aplenty, and neighbours too, many of whom he'd met at Glenfinnan. This was the middle-class farming society that abounded in these parts, a society that James was rapidly coming to view as his own.

He'd danced the night away, mainly with Jenna, who'd barely let him out of her sight, and who'd glared dagger-like at her cousin Victoria when Victoria had had the temerity to dive in and claim him for the 'ladies choice' quadrille. In fact James had escaped Jenna for little over an hour the entire evening, and then not by choice, for he'd been very much enjoying both her company and the dancing, but upon the insistence of Ben.

'Let's go to Mandelsons,' Ben urged. 'I need a rest, a beer and some male conversation.' Ben, highly popular with the ladies as always, professed he was not only 'all danced out', but 'all talked out'. 'Too much girlish chat,' he said, 'and, besides, the punch they're serving here is as weak as piss.'

So they'd walked around the corner and along to Mandelsons, a stylish hotel where the upstairs accommodation offered an elegant balcony overlooking the broad avenue of Clinton Street, and where a downstairs bar attracted the serious drinking man.

Jenna had tried to accompany them, but Ben would have none of it. 'We need a bit of men's time, Jenna,' he said, waving her away, 'give poor James a rest for God's sake. I'll get him back to you in an hour, I promise.'

Jenna had stomped off in a sulk. 'All right,' she'd called over her shoulder. 'One hour. I'll be waiting.'

The bar was alive with masculinity; the smell of beer and cigars, the rowdy laughs of men mildly under the influence of alcohol and determined to become more so, some already visibly drunk. But to James it didn't appear a troublesome place, the drinkers simply bent on having a good time. There were even quite a few men in evening dress, they too having sought escape from the dance.

They bought their beers and joined forces with a group seated in the corner, some of whom Ben knew, together with several newcomers to town. Introductions were made, and within only minutes they were caught up in the joys of mateship and camaraderie.

Three beers and one hour later, James was ready to return to the dance. But Ben was not.

'No, you go on ahead, mate,' he said, waving the freshly poured beer he'd just accepted, James having refused the last round. 'I'll join up with you in a half an hour or so.' He raised his glass in a toast to Matthew, the man who'd bought the round. 'Too much female chat back there,' he added with a laugh, 'I'll stay here with the boys for a while.'

James returned to the town hall where, as she'd promised she would be, Jenna was waiting. But Jenna was not just 'waiting'. She'd set up watch outside in the street with the intent to ambush. And ambush she did.

James was so taken by surprise when she stepped out from the shadows at the side of the building to confront him that he actually gasped.

'It's been over an hour,' she said accusingly, 'you're late.' Then she grasped his hand and guided him back into the shadows. 'Don't you think it's time you kissed me?'

'Why?'

'Because you want to . . . And because I want you to.'

Would he? A pause. He knew he shouldn't.

But he did.

And the way she returned the kiss had left nothing in doubt. He'd intended a modest kiss, certainly to start with, his lips gently parted and non-threatening as he had no wish to frighten her. But Jenna had other ideas. The moment their mouths touched, she opened hers to him, forcing his lips further apart, her tongue darting here and there, shamelessly exploring him. Then her arms were around him and she was thrusting her groin against his in such a wanton fashion he couldn't help but feel his body respond. *This can't be happening,* he thought. *She's a virgin, she has to be!* Her blatant lust was unbelievably confronting.

It had been a long time since James had been with a woman and his arousal was instant. He returned the kiss with equal passion, but even as he did he tried to create some distance between their bodies in order to avoid direct contact below the waist, aware that despite the taffeta gown and petticoats she must surely be aware of his rampant erection. But if she was, it didn't appear to have any adverse effect upon her. Quite the opposite. The harder he became the more strongly she clutched him and the more fiercely she thrust herself at him. *We might as well be fucking right here in the street,* he thought.

Finally, he broke away and they stood staring at each other, both breathing heavily. He was the one who finally broke eye contact.

'I'm sorry,' he said, gazing at the ground.

'I'm not,' she replied. Then she gaily tucked her arm through his. 'Let's return to the dance,' she suggested and they stepped out from the shadows.

They walked back up the half dozen steps and into the town hall arm in arm, James willing his erection to disappear every step of the way.

The evening's merriment was in full swing and they took to the dance floor as if nothing had happened. But they both knew something had. Jenna was relishing every moment, her behaviour becoming more and more provocative. She teased and flirted outrageously, doing her best to make their contact as intimate as possible during the closed-couple dances.

'I do so love the quick-step, don't you?' she murmured, pressing herself against him. And all the while she taunted him with her smile. *We have a secret, don't we, James? she was saying. We both know you want me. You'd like to take me, right here and now, wouldn't you?*

He would, it was true. He'd never seen or thought of Jenna this way before. He'd never considered her beautiful. Interesting, yes; attractive, perhaps, although Adele was the true beauty of the family. But at this moment Jenna was far more than beautiful, she was the most desirable woman he'd ever encountered. A seductress. A siren. He was tortured with lust. Every time their bodies came into close contact he felt a quiver run through him like an electrical current.

Finally, he was forced to call a halt.

'Let's have some punch, shall we,' he suggested. There'd been far too many closed-couple dances in a row and he couldn't take any more. 'It'll be time to go home soon anyway.' He wondered distractedly what was taking Ben so long and whether perhaps he should return to Mandelsons and find him. They'd agreed to fetch the buggy from the stables at ten o'clock.

But only minutes later, while the two of them stood at the punch table, glasses in hand, Ben arrived.

'It's time to go home,' he said tersely.

'But it's only twenty to ten,' Jenna countered rebelliously, glancing at the clock on the wall, 'and I haven't
finished my punch.'

'I said it's time to go home,' Ben repeated. He took the
glass from her, plonked it onto the table and turned to
leave.

He's angry, James thought, *he's very, very angry. What
happened back there?*

Ben's mood remained dark during the drive home. James
could clearly see the hard, set line of his mouth in the light
cast by the buggy's lantern that swayed on its peg. He
knew better than to make any enquiry in Jenna's presence,
however. Ben would no doubt tell him tomorrow after
their Sunday horse race. That is, if he wished to do so. The
stone quarry was where they shared their secrets. And if
Ben had no wish to tell him, then that would be all right
too. A friendship like theirs made no demands.

In the meantime, the blackness of Ben's mood was
proving a suitable distraction from the wriggling of
Jenna's body as she cosied up beside him, chatting away
animatedly.

They dropped him at the turn-off to the cottage.

'Do you want me to bring Bella around tomorrow?' Ben
asked. They were the first words he'd spoken throughout
the entire drive.

'No, no, I'll meet you at the stables.' James enjoyed
the brisk half hour's walk to the Big House where they'd
saddle up the horses together. 'Around nine?'

Ben nodded and gave a flick of the reins.

'Good night, James,' Jenna turned and called after him
as Tess trotted on. 'I loved dancing with you. We must do
it more often. I'd like that.'

'Good night, Jenna,' he called back to her.

*

The following morning, Ben was the clear winner in their race to the quarry, but he'd ridden like a madman, urging Baron on at a dangerously frantic pace, and James had felt neither the urge nor the need to compete at such a level.

'Do you want to tell me?' he asked when they'd left their horses grazing near the old convict well and were sitting on the rock overlooking the valley and the stone quarry below.

'Tell you what?' Ben's eyes remained fixed ahead.

'Why you're so angry.' There was no response, so James gave a careless shrug. 'Don't tell me if you don't want to, but something happened last night and you're still angry about it, so if it helps to talk . . .'

He left the offer hanging and waited. Ben finally turned to him.

'You're right, I *am* angry. I'm angry about everything. About who I am. The injustice of it all. The pretence. The whole fucking thing!' There was fury in the way he spat out the words.

'Why don't you just tell me what happened.'

'You wouldn't understand.' Ben's tone was dismissive. 'You couldn't possibly understand.'

'Why not try me and find out?' James sat patiently, elbows on knees, once again waiting and watching as if he had all day, which he did, and was quite prepared to listen.

Ben took a deep breath, preparing himself and when he'd calmed down he began. 'You remember Matthew from the bar at Mandelsons last night?'

'Of course I do, nice bloke.'

'Yes, I thought so too. I hadn't met him or his mates before. They're from out of town.'

'I gathered that.'

'He got pretty drunk after you left – seemed he couldn't really handle his liquor – but I liked him nonetheless, we got on very well.'

James said nothing, waiting to see where this was leading, although he had a vague suspicion he might know.

'He liked me too, I could tell. He liked me a lot. A bit too much as things turned out,' Ben said. 'When I went to the privy out the back of the hotel he followed me. I suppose he thought I wanted him to. Anyway, he tried to kiss me.'

Ben had turned to James and was studying him closely, searching for the sign of revulsion he thought he might see, but there was none. Only avid interest.

'As I said, Matthew was drunk,' he went on, 'perhaps deliberately so. Perhaps he'd been working up the courage to make a move like that. And as he made to kiss me he ran his fingers down my arms, sort of checking me out.'

'What did you do?'

'I belted him.' In recalling the moment, Ben saw the man's eyes, the hope there instantly turning to terror. 'I belted him as hard as I could. Not just the once, either. I bashed him up and left him puking in the courtyard. Then I went back into the bar and told the two blokes he was with that their mate was a pervert and they should go and get him and take him back to wherever he came from. I said he didn't belong in this town.'

'Why did you do that?' James was surprised. He hadn't expected the story to turn out this way.

'I can't afford to have people see me for who I am.' Ben, too, seemed surprised. Surprised and even outraged that James felt the need to ask such a question. 'How had Matthew recognised me as one of his kind, James?' he demanded. 'How could he possibly have known without my sending any form of signal?'

It was a question James was incapable of answering and he would have been the least qualified person to do so, he thought. In general company there was never a thing about Ben that would suggest homosexuality.

'I don't know,' he replied. 'But you said you liked one another, I suppose Matthew sensed some form of connection.' He instantly recognised his response had not been in the least helpful, but there was something else he found of far greater interest, and he couldn't resist asking. 'Did you beat the bloke up purely to prevent others guessing the truth, Ben? Is that really all it was? Or did you find him in some way offensive?'

'Of course I didn't find him offensive! I didn't find him in any way offensive, far from it!' The question had been asked in complete innocence, but Ben seemed about to explode with frustration. He gave an exasperated gesture of surrender. 'God almighty, I *longed* for him to kiss me. When he touched me my whole body quivered. I *wanted* him! Can't you understand that?'

'Yes.' James nodded, Ben's exasperation having had not the least effect upon him. He found the whole episode intensely interesting. 'Oh yes, I can understand that all right,' he replied, remembering how he'd been aquiver with desire himself just the previous night. 'I suppose lust is lust in any form, really,' he said thoughtfully.

'Which is why I had to bash Matthew up, don't you see?'

'Yes, I suppose so.' That part James couldn't really see at all, but he experienced a surge of sympathy nonetheless. Sympathy for both Ben and for Matthew. 'What a pity. That's rather sad.'

Ben had felt a sense of relief in letting the truth pour out, even though he hadn't achieved any answers. And unburdening himself to James without receiving any form of judgement or even criticism, he'd once again been grateful for the friendship they shared. The fact that James seemed able to divorce himself from the revulsion others might feel at the mere thought of homosexuality remained a constant source of amazement to him. But then James Brereton was a rare creature.

The Sunday lunch later that day had progressed much as normal, although Jenna had been more flirtatious than ever in her attentions to James, fluttering giddily about him, touching him unnecessarily as she regaled everyone with the fact that the two of them had barely left the dance floor on Saturday.

'James dances divinely,' she said, enraptured, 'you should have seen us. What a figure we cut.'

Adele and Phil Caton had been present, and Adele, always serene, always unruffled, had finally voiced her disapproval, albeit mildly, of her younger sister's behaviour. Perhaps being the only other female present she'd considered it her duty to do so.

'Oh do leave poor James alone, dear,' she'd said gently, 'you're making him feel most uncomfortable.'

Adele was quite right. James was squirming in his chair, aware of the disapproving looks from Alastair McKinnon, who appeared somehow to think he might be encouraging Jenna's behaviour. Which he was not. Jenna was no doubt reliving the previous night's lustful experience, but he was most certainly not. He didn't find her in the least attractive at this moment; to the contrary, he found her girlishness intensely irritating.

Jenna sulked at Adele's admonishment, retreating briefly into herself, which was a relief to all, and the conversation turned from the dance at the town hall to things more general, principally the approach of the shearing season.

Then Ben made his unexpected announcement.

'I've decided to go to Sydney next weekend,' he said, 'just for a few days, maybe a week. I'll catch the train on Friday. I intend to get the trip out of the way well before the start of the shearing season,' he assured his father, and also Phil Caton.

He'd obviously made his plans, which rather took the others by surprise.

'Why do you want to go to Sydney?' Alastair asked, his tone inferring why would *anyone* want to go to Sydney, which was the general opinion around the table.

'I need to buy some new clothes.'

'What, for the *shearing* season?' Jenna scoffed. She'd emerged from her sulk and was on the attack now in her typically confronting manner.

'Some new *dress* clothes, Jenna,' Ben replied calmly. 'The outfit I wore to the dance last night was a little on the tattered side I thought.'

'What's wrong with Lockies?' his father enquired.

'I'm after something finer, Dad. I intend to visit the fashion department at the Grenfell Emporium. They have the very best quality there.'

'You can order from their catalogue,' Jenna retorted, being deliberately argumentative. 'You don't have to go to Sydney to buy stuff from Grenfell's. Everyone knows that . . .'

'I *want* to go to Sydney,' Ben snapped, his tone calling a halt to any further conversation on the matter. 'I *want* to go to Sydney and I *shall* go to Sydney.'

The family accepted his decision, quaint though they found his reasoning. Only James knew exactly why Ben wanted to go.

The following week it was back to business as usual: the mending of fences, the replacement of wire netting, and, of course, rabbiting.

James watched Jenna in her overalls, which despite the brutality of the exercise remained virtually blood-free; she would wear a butcher's apron for the skinning and gutting process the following day. Her total focus and efficiency in the dispatching of rabbits had always been admirable, but was now more interesting than ever as he relived their lustful exchange just the previous Saturday. She was such a mix of contradictions. So blunt, so forthright, and yet so girlish, sometimes irritatingly so, but the desire he'd felt that night remained strongly etched in his mind. He must take care not to become aroused with her again. There were brothels in Goulburn if he needed a woman; he would pay a visit to town next weekend, he decided. What a pity Ben couldn't seek a similar release for his pent-up sexual frustration.

James worried for his friend. Recalling the circumstances of their first meeting, he hoped Ben would be safe in whatever nefarious search he conducted around the parks and streets of Sydney.

Sydney could be such a dangerous place.

Any fears James may have held proved totally unfounded, however, when Ben returned elated.

He'd been gone a whole ten days, and he regaled his experiences – an edited version only – to the family with his customary insouciance, the debonair Ben McKinnon so attractive to all.

'I had the grandest time, I must say. I really don't know why you lot prefer to avoid the social whirl of Sydney. I find it most stimulating.' He'd been to the Hampton Club any number of times, he told them. 'It's where the who's who of Sydney gather,' he'd said. And he'd dined with the Grenfells in Point Piper. 'Even went sailing on Sydney Harbour,' he boasted, 'they have a friend with a yacht. Now that really was an experience.'

But privately with James, seated together in the workers' cottage sharing a beer, Ben's elation hit new heights and for quite a different reason.

'Monty's Bar at the Crown and Anchor in Woolloomooloo on a Sunday night,' he triumphantly announced. 'You were quite right, James, that's the place for men like me.'

James found the news daunting. Monty's Bar at the Crown and Anchor held distinctly unpleasant memories.

'I didn't recommend you go to Monty's,' he said.

'No of course you didn't, but you remember when you told me all about Charles Grenfell and "that night",' he said meaningfully.

'Yes.'

'Well I must say you painted Monty's most colourfully, I couldn't wait to visit the place. It sounded far more attractive than the Turkish baths in Liverpool Street. And I met a very pleasant fellow. As it turned out, a fellow in circumstances not unlike mine,' he added.

Ben recalled the instant sense of abandonment he'd felt upon entering Monty's Bar. He couldn't believe what he was seeing. Two men, seated side by side in a booth by the frosted windows, were openly kissing. Others were leaning closely together conversing in a way far too intimate to be considered normal. Others appeared to be circling the room, on the hunt, just as James had said they were 'that night'. Ben had decided to do the same.

He'd bought himself a beer and wandered about looking others over, knowing he was being looked over himself and with a great deal of interest. There were ageing Romeos, tawdry old men seeking the company of pretty boys, a number of whom were working the floor or serving behind the bar. One or two of the Romeos had given him the eye, which he'd ignored. There were attractive men too, and he spoke to several before making his choice. Or perhaps it was Peter who had made the choice, who could tell? But their eyes had locked in that special way, and they'd remained locked for too long, the signal had been clear.

'Peter was from out of town,' he went on, 'somewhere in the country, I didn't ask where; he was seeking anonymity, just like me. We didn't even bother sharing surnames.' Upon reflection Ben rather wished they had, and he had a feeling Peter might have wished the same. But it would have been foolish, they'd both known that. 'We saw each other any number of times over the following week, it was all very liberating.'

He leaned back in his chair and gazed thoughtfully at the half-finished beer he held in his hand. 'So liberating in fact that I've settled on a long-term plan.'

'Oh?'

'There'll be many trips to Sydney from now on. Dad was so pleased with the results of my meetings with the overseas buyers, he'll be only too happy for me to take care of that side of the business. He loathes going to Sydney, so does Phil for that matter.' Ben smiled cheekily. 'Monty's Bar can become a regular haunt of mine. Very convenient all round.'

James scowled. 'I wouldn't advise that Ben. Woolloomooloo is a very rough area.'

'I'm not interested in your advice, James. You don't suffer the same problem I do.' Ben's tone was not rude, just stating a case that was not open for discussion. He'd made his decision. 'I told you I intended to sow my wild oats before settling down and living the tedious lie demanded of me. Do you remember that?'

'Of course I do.'

'So this is my long-term plan.' Ben swigged back the rest of his beer. 'I'm shortly to turn twenty-three,' he said, slamming his glass down on the table by way of emphasis. 'I shall marry when I'm twenty-eight years of age,' he announced triumphantly. 'That gives me exactly five years!'

His handsome face broke into a grin that was utterly engaging, but which did not for one moment allay James' concern. In his opinion Ben was courting disaster. But he shrugged. This was, after all, none of his business.

CHAPTER ELEVEN

Ben had not been alone in the sating of his frustrated sexual desires. James, having recognised his own need, had visited a brothel in Goulburn as planned. More than one brothel, in fact. He'd decided to make a weekend of it. Stabling his horse (and Bella had by now become 'his horse', personally gifted to him by Ben) he'd stayed in town on the Friday and Saturday night, visiting each of Goulburn's brothels in turn. Goulburn had only two brothels, or so he'd been told upon enquiry – two brothels that were considered efficiently run, vaguely discreet, and hopefully clean, that is. God only knew how many pimps and whores might have been conducting profitable businesses in the seedier parts of town. Even so, upon his return to Glenfinnan on the Sunday, he hoped he hadn't contracted any of the dreaded forms of sexual diseases he'd read about.

His experience had not been in any way erotic, a simple 'servicing', no more, but he was glad to have assuaged his lust and now felt safe in the knowledge that Jenna's attentions, no matter how forward they might prove to be, would not result in the fearful arousal he'd experienced on the night of the dance.

He could not have anticipated, however, the lengths to which Jenna might go.

*

There was a tap on his door. It was nine o'clock on a Saturday night. He'd been reading in the light of the kerosene lamp as he often did, sitting at the small wooden table hunched over the latest book he'd borrowed from the copious collection they had at the Big House. He very much enjoyed reading. He was shortly to go to bed and wondered who it might be tapping on his door at this hour. Ben, no doubt, probably with a bottle of cognac and a desire to chat – this had happened a number of times in the past.

Crossing to the door, he wondered what exactly Ben might feel the need to chat *about*. It was usually something plaguing his mind. The busyness that lay ahead with the start of the season perhaps? The arrival of the shearers next week would certainly rule out any visits to Sydney, and for quite some time. Ben would enjoy pouring out his frustration, venting his wrath at the injustice of life as they got steadily drunk together. And James would enjoy being the sounding board for all Ben was unable to say out loud to others. That's what friends were for.

He opened the door. Jenna stood there.

'You'll be moving into the shearers' quarters when the men arrive next week, won't you?' It wasn't really a question at all, nor even a statement, but more an accusation that she barked at him.

'That's right.' He was confused. Of course he'd be moving into the shearers' quarters. He'd be one of them, working together as a team, as brothers, as competitors, the way shearers always did. He'd hardly distance himself from them by remaining in the cottage.

'This might be our last chance then,' she said, 'for a while anyway.'

She barged past him and into the cottage, leaving him standing there in the open doorway, his frame silhouetted in the light from the kerosene lamp.

He turned to confront her. How dare she? How dare she place him in such a position! She must leave immediately! But to his absolute horror he discovered she was already in a state of undress. She was wearing a loose, ankle-length skirt designed for riding, together with a long-sleeved blouse, and the top three buttons of the blouse were unfastened, displaying the fact that she wore no undergarment. He could clearly make out the swell of her breasts.

'Close the door, James,' she said.

He did. Very quickly. Good God, who might have seen her arrive? Ricky and Rosie from their cottage further up the hill? Where had she tethered Misty? Jenna McKinnon's stylish, black-maned, black-tailed grey mare was known by all. He must get rid of her as quickly as possible. She could cost him his job. Alastair McKinnon would surely fire him on even the slightest suspicion.

'Stop that, Jenna,' he ordered, 'stop that.'

She'd undone the remaining front buttons of the blouse and was now unfastening those on the cuffs of its sleeves. He cursed her. Oh shit! She could probably be seen through the window.

He dived forward, intending to turn off the kerosene lamp that sat on the table.

'No, no,' she said with gentle urgency, 'leave it, I beg you. Just the curtains will do.' And she crossed to the window, drawing the curtains herself, before turning back to him and letting the blouse drop to the floor.

She stood before him, half naked, and despite his burgeoning sense of panic he couldn't fail to admire the perfect mounds of her breasts with their small, pink nipples, already hardened and inviting. He'd never seen breasts so beautifully formed.

'Jenna, stop it,' he once again ordered, 'you mustn't. We can't.'

But her voice remained gently reassuring as she answered the panicked questions circling his mind.

'No one saw me, James.' Her hands were behind her back now, unfastening the waistband of her skirt. 'Misty is tethered among the trees out the back. No one knows I'm here.'

Then the skirt dropped to join the blouse on the floor and she was altogether naked, wearing no undergarments of any description. Jenna had come well prepared.

She stepped over the threshold of the skirt that encircled her and as she stood brazenly offering herself, James was lost in admiration. Her body was glorious. Animal-like and healthy, everything about her so elegant, the golden thatch at her groin matching the ginger of her hair, legs strong, but slender and well formed, the legs of a race horse. How could he have known she would be this beautiful? And the overall image was so extraordinarily erotic, perhaps because she was still wearing her riding boots. Was she aware of that?

She was. Very slowly she walked the several paces between them.

'I think we should take these off, don't you?' she said, and putting her arms around his neck, she rested her weight on one leg, wrapped the other around him and rubbed her booted foot against the back of his calf.

He wasn't actually sure whether she was referring to her boots or to his clothes, but it didn't matter. He was lost. Barely a minute later they were in the little bedroom and on his bunk, divested of both boots and clothes.

Jenna had planned her seduction to the very last detail. She'd been living this moment in her mind for a long time. Perhaps even years. Preparing herself for the loss of her virginity, practising with any number of local boys, teasing them, leading them on, but always opting out at the last moment, saving herself for the right man. And James was the right man. She would give herself to him wholeheart-edly. She didn't even care if she got pregnant. To the contrary, she welcomed the idea. He'd have to marry her then, wouldn't he?

She was moist and welcoming as he entered her, but within only seconds James became aware of a barrier to his thrusts, and he felt her involuntarily stiffen from the pain.

Oh hell, he realised, *she's a virgin.* He'd initially assumed she would be, despite her overtly sexual behaviour at the dance, but given this wanton offering up of her body, the notion had somehow escaped him. In truth, he'd been so confronted and so immediately aroused, the thought hadn't even crossed his mind.

James had never encountered a virgin. The several whores he'd slept with and Betsy from the bakery had all been women of experience. He stopped thrusting immedi-ately and was about to withdraw, but she wouldn't let him.

'No, no,' she hissed, wrapping her legs around him and locking him there. 'Break me, James, break me.'

And then it was Jenna doing the thrusting. Bucking like a wild pony, grunting from the pain but urging him on. And finally he was through, past the barrier and deep, deep inside her.

Jenna thrilled to the experience, ignoring the pain that still dully persisted, more an ache and an irritation now. She'd finally lost her virginity, and to the man she'd chosen, no less. James Brereton belonged to her from this moment on.

As she felt him approach his climax, she clung to him fiercely, willing him to stay inside her, but at the last moment he broke free.

'Oh,' she said like a disappointed child, as she sat up and watched him spill himself onto the bloodied sheet, 'I wish you hadn't done that.'

'Why for Christ's sake?' he panted, slumping back on the narrow bunk. 'You don't want to get pregnant, do you?'

'Yes, I do actually.' She slumped back beside him.

He stared at her, dumbfounded.

'To you anyway,' she explained. Then she followed up her outrageous comment with an even bolder statement. 'You see, I want to marry you, James.'

'Ah.' He wasn't sure what to say by way of reply. He recalled she'd made the same statement to her brother, or so Ben had told him, and they'd shared a laugh together. 'You don't stand a chance in hell, mate,' Ben had said, 'when Jenna sets her mind on something, she gets it, believe me.'

Well not this time, James told himself. *I'm not going to lose the best job I'm ever likely to have because the boss's spoilt daughter has a crush on me.*

'I don't think your father would approve, Jenna,' he said, rising to his feet and reaching for the clothes he'd flung on top of the chest of drawers. 'I don't think Alastair McKinnon views me as son-in-law material.'

'We'll see about that.' Jenna flung her legs over the side of the bed, pulled on her boots and stood. She started stripping the soiled linen from the bunk. 'I'll take this home and launder it myself,' she said, rolling the sheet into a ball and tucking it under her arm before marching off naked into the living room where her skirt and blouse remained strewn on the floor.

He followed her, watching as she dressed, still mesmerised by the elegance of her body, so different from the blowsy, bosomy women he'd known.

'I'll bring fresh linen around tomorrow,' she said when she was fully clothed and ready to go, the sheet once again tucked under her arm. 'I'll arrive around the same time, shall I?' It wasn't a question, and even if it had been she didn't wait for an answer as she crossed to where he stood.

'We might as well make the most of the few days we have left, James.'

She turned her face up to his and he found himself automatically bending to kiss her. Then quickly and quietly she slipped out the door.

She visited him two more times that week and, despite the danger she represented, James was unable to resist.

He was thankful, perhaps even grateful, when the shearers arrived and he shifted into their quarters. At last the temptation was gone, the threat no longer existed. He could now sink all his energy into achieving his ultimate goal, the goal he'd set for himself ever since his arrival at Glenfinnan.

James was aware he would be starting out as a total newcomer, a man employed simply upon the recommendation of the boss's son, but come the end of the season his aim was to be a gun shearer, one capable of shearing a sheep within only minutes. Perhaps accomplished enough even to compete for the status of ringer. The term was not official, but the ringer was recognised as the fastest shearer in the shed, the man whose daily tally outmatched all others.

He knew he was setting himself a task that was nigh on impossible, for there would doubtless be several gun shearers in the six-man team employed at Glenfinnan. Alastair McKinnon was known to be a fair employer who treated his men well, a farmer who adhered to the list of workers' rights set out by the recently formed Shearers' Union. The gun shearers who were only too happy to work at Glenfinnan would be in hot competition to claim the top tally. But James was nonetheless determined, spurred on as he was by his childhood dream to emulate the legendary Jack Howe.

He remembered how his father had laughed when he'd made that boast. 'You'll have to muscle up a bit boy,' George Wakefield had said.

But he *had* muscled up, hadn't he? He was by now far stronger and far fitter than his father had been. And he'd prove it what's more. He'd prove his true worth to George Wakefield. Strange, he often thought, how his father never seemed very far away.

The new home he now shared with the raucous, tough-talking, heavy-drinking shearers was a radical change after the solitude of the cottage, but it proved a welcome distraction from Jenna, who as the nights passed rarely entered his mind. He knew he didn't love her, that she'd been a brief sexual obsession, no more, and that if he paid the occasional visit to the brothels in Goulburn on a Saturday night the problem would be solved.

However, there remained the Sunday lunches to contend with. He and Ben still went for their morning ride and Ben still insisted he stay for the roast dinner at the Big House, which as always he very much enjoyed. The shearers would be nursing their Saturday-night hangovers back at the quarters anyway – there was little camaraderie to be found there on a Sunday.

Jenna continued to flirt with him throughout lunch as she always had, but there was a subtle difference now. Her flirtatiousness was neither as girlish nor as skittish as it had been. There was a womanliness about her that, to James, was all too readable. He wondered if anyone else could see it. Her sister, Adele, surely, with the intuition shared by women? Her father, whose disapproval had always been so obvious, surely he sensed a difference in his daughter? But for all the furtive glances James cast around the table, searching for signs, nothing was revealed. No one appeared to be paying her the least attention. Jenna was just being Jenna.

There was one, however, who *had* noticed a behavioural difference. Although not in Jenna.

'Have you and my sister been making the beast with two backs by any chance, James?' Ben asked flippantly.

Following lunch Ben had suggested the two of them take a bottle of cognac and have a wander around the garden, which was in full spring bloom. They were currently seated in an arbour overhung with lilac wisteria blossom, looking out at the rose beds amass with a miscellany of vibrant colour. Boris' intricate irrigation system worked wonders, although no one knew exactly how.

'What?' James started guiltily. He didn't understand the phrase, but Ben's quizzical expression and the mere mention of 'you and my sister' was enough to set his heart racing. 'What do you mean?' He tried, unsuccessfully, to sound innocent.

'Shakespeare, old man,' Ben said with a careless wave of his hand. 'Iago in *Othello*. "Making the beast with two backs". The Bard is referring to sex.'

James stared at him blankly. *Oh God, Ben knows,* he thought.

'Are you and Jenna fucking, is what I'm asking,' Ben went on with a touch of exasperation at his friend's apparent lack of understanding.

'Um . . .' James felt himself flush. 'Not anymore. We did. Briefly. Three times. But no more than that, and I can promise it won't happen again.'

He took Ben's silence as the rightful censure of a brother's horrified outrage at the defilement of his sister and felt doubly guilty.

'I'm sorry, Ben, really I am. I don't know what came over me. She just . . .' He halted. It wasn't right for him to lay any of the blame on Jenna, he should have practised greater control that first night when she'd visited him at the cottage. 'I don't know what to say. I just . . .' What *was* there he could say? He'd robbed the girl of her virginity. He'd had no right to do such an unforgiveable thing. 'I understand how angry you must be seeing the way she's changed. I can see it myself, it's so readable. And I feel so—'

'Rubbish,' Ben interrupted briskly, 'she hasn't changed at all. Jenna's been so longing to lose her virginity she's been in heat for years. *You're* the one who's readable, James.'

'Really?'

'Of course. You've been waving your guilt about like a banner. I'm amazed I'm the only one of the family who's noticed.'

James was struck speechless. As so often in the past, Ben had taken him completely by surprise.

'Oh my dear friend,' Ben picked up the bottle that sat beside the garden bench and replenished his glass, 'duplicity really is not your strongest point, is it?' He laughed and waved the bottle invitingly. 'Come along now, drink up and let's talk. You need some serious counsel.'

James obediently drained his glass.

'I really do think you should go ahead and marry her, James,' Ben went on, doling out a liberal serve of cognac. 'It's what she's been after right from the start, don't you remember I told you so?'

'Yes. And she told me so herself.'

'So there you are then!' A triumphant declaration. 'Do as she wants. Put a ring on her finger and make the girl happy.'

'But . . .' Accustomed though he was to Ben's flippancy, the conversation seemed to James altogether too frivolous; they were talking about the man's sister for God's sake. 'But . . .' He found himself on the verge of stuttering as he sought a reply. 'But . . . your father would never approve the match . . .'

'Given time he would. Dad likes you well enough and he's seen what a hard worker you are. Besides, Jenna will wear him down eventually, you can be sure of that.'

'But . . . I don't love her, Ben.' James halted, he hadn't meant to sound insulting. 'I mean I like her, of course, I like her a great deal, and I find her devilishly attractive, but I'm not *in love* with her if you know what I mean. Surely—'

'Oh you silly, naive boy,' Ben scoffed, 'what's love got to do with marriage?' He gave a bark of laughter and took a swig of his cognac. 'We'll both marry girls we don't love – another of life's tribulations we'll share.' Then he grinned wickedly. 'At least you'll be able to enjoy sex with yours. And in the meantime . . .' He raised his glass in salutation. 'We'll have become family. Bonded through marriage. How glorious!' He clinked his glass against James' and downed the rest of his cognac, not bothered in the least that his toast was not returned. *Oh my dearest James,* he thought, *if we can't be lovers, then we shall become brothers.* The prospect filled Ben with untold joy.

Despite the blithe approach to his sister's future, Ben had unwittingly struck a serious chord in James' mind. And with the use of just one word. Family.

James recalled with great clarity that first evening he'd spent at Glenfinnan, the meal shared in the formal dining room of the Big House. A lamb roast, unsurprisingly; the McKinnons were very fond of their lamb roasts. The room itself had been formal; the furnishings, the broad mahogany table and settings, right down to the silver platter and fine bone china, but the company had been far from formal. The company had been warm, loving, inviting, all the things he'd never known in his life. He remembered the longing he'd felt as he'd gazed about, observing the bond between siblings and patriarch. *How I would love to be part of a family like this.* That was what he'd thought.

Could such a thing actually come to pass? he now wondered. Was it possible he could be accepted as a member of the McKinnon clan? Could he really become a link in the chain of such a dynasty?

To James the prospect seemed beyond belief, but Ben was grinning at him with such supreme confidence that he found himself unable to dismiss the idea, his mind whirling with possibilities. He could learn to love Jenna, that part would be easy, but he would have to prove himself to her father, which would present a far greater problem. Alastair McKinnon considered him inferior stock, of this much James was sure. *It's all in the breeding,* he could hear Alastair say. Here was the problem he would need to overcome.

He raised his glass and returned Ben's smile. 'I agree it would be nice to be brothers-in-law,' he said pleasantly and left the conversation there. Time would prove whether or not such a thing was possible. But he now had a goal. He would keep Jenna at arm's length, there must be no further physical contact between them that might arouse suspicion. And in the meantime he would do everything within his power, everything humanly possible, to elevate his status in the eyes of the Glenfinnan patriarch. This was his plan.

Ben wisely pushed no further, aware he'd planted the seed that was now successfully germinating.

James assumed the fresh goal he'd set himself would assist his personal ambition. The quickest way to earn Alastair McKinnon's respect would surely be to prove himself the fastest shearer on the team. With this in mind, the following day he attacked his work with renewed vigour, speed now of the essence. The decision proved catastrophic.

'You're going too hard, James,' Phil Caton said quietly, having taken him aside during the first of the half-hour smoko breaks, which the shearers took every two hours. 'You're rushing things, mate, you're snagging them too much. Young Ned's doing the same thing,' he added, referring to the other younger member of the team. 'If you keep this up I'll have to lay the two of you off when we start on the rams tomorrow. Can't run the risk of damaging the big fellas.'

'Oh. Right. Sorry, Phil. I'll slow down, take things nice and steady, I promise.'

James felt mortified as he watched Phil cross over to Ned for a few quiet words obviously along similar lines. Ned was an inexperienced shearer and it showed. How humiliating that he should be assumed in the same category. He knew he'd nicked his sheep, and any number of times, but in picking up his pace he'd lost his rhythm. Momentarily anyway. He would have found it again given a bit more time. The lesson was a salutary one though as he recalled his father's instruction.

'Nice and steady does it, son,' George had said over and over, demonstrating the action with his perfectly maintained blade shears – the same blade shears James was currently using, maintained in the same perfect condition. 'Just like this, see? Nice and steady, all in the rhythm it is. Listen to the click of the blades and lose yourself to the rhythm. Like this, see? You get to the end of your line and then you're back to the beginning, following the next line in the very same way.' George's voice had become a chant, keeping time with the action of his forearm, and his wrist, and his hand, and the progression of the blades as he'd painstakingly taught his boy how to be a shearer.

The bell sounded, smoko was over. For the rest of the day, James adhered to the words and the rhythm as he worked, aware that Phil Caton was observing every sheep shorn by every shearer present as he chalked up the tallies on the board for all to see. Speed could come later, he told himself, there would be time to prove his worth.

The following day poor young Ned was laid off, reduced to the duties of shed hand, at least until they'd finished shearing the highly valuable rams. He'd be given another chance when they resumed work on the general flock. But James, to his intense relief, was saved a similar mortification; the rams were considered safe in his hands.

Weeks passed and the days melded repetitively into one
another, days of utter chaos, or so it seemed in the shearing
shed. Here the air was rank with the stench of lanolin and
sweat as unprotesting sheep were dragged across greasy
floorboards. Here strong men laboured endlessly, bare-
footed boys scampered about with brooms, fleeces were
flung high in the air with reckless abandon, and workers
could be seen jumping up and down atop wool bins. To the
uninitiated the shearing shed was a madhouse. But there
was order to the chaos. Everything had a purpose. Far
from being a madhouse, the shearing shed was run with
clockwork-like precision.

The eight-hour day commenced at half past seven in the
morning when the shearers would be at their 'stands' on
the shearing board, awaiting the bell to be sounded by Phil
Caton, the overseer. Upon the bell's sounding each shearer
dives into the interior catching pen where the sheep are
corralled, drags an animal back to his stand and the work
commences. He removes the belly wool first, which is
separated from the main fleece by an attendant shed hand
or rouseabout while the sheep is still being shorn. When
the animal is completely shorn, the shearer bundles it out
through a chute in the wall to the exterior counting pen
and returns for his next sheep. Should he be a gun shearer,
the entire process might be accomplished in as little as two
to three minutes. A gun shearer could shear two hundred
sheep a day.

In the meantime, the rouseabouts are kept constantly
busy. The fleece is taken to the other end of the shed where
it must be thrown high, clean side facing down, to land on
a wool table consisting of slats that form a grid through
which the short pieces of wool, or *locks*, and debris can
fall to the floor. The fleece is then *skirted* to remove unde-
sirable parts, after which it is classed by the overseer who
regularly takes samples, before being rolled up and placed

in the appropriate wool bin. When the bin is full its contents are pressed and baled, the bales ready to be identified with the name of the station and its owner. In this case the identification will read 'Glenfinnan, McKinnon,' a name highly respected throughout the entire wool industry. The bales are then stored, awaiting transportation to Sydney for auction or for further transport overseas.

James kept his eye on the tally board, as all the shearers did. He refused to be daunted by the fact he was regularly coming in fourth on the six-man team; two were gun shearers after all. Gouldy and Batts were already well into the 190 or so sheep a day; it'd be a battle to see who would get to the 200 mark first as the race intensified. But then Dave Gould and Don Batts, hardened men of around forty, were well known in the trade, their leading status expected. James doubted he would achieve ringer position with those two on the team, but he was sure he could overtake Dobson, the man third on the tally board. The two beneath him, young Ned and old Paddy presented no competition, Ned inexperienced and Paddy well past his prime.

Nice and steady does it, he kept telling himself as he stuck to the rhythm he'd adopted. But the rhythm was gradually increasing in speed. Without losing a beat he was becoming faster, and his numbers were beginning to show on the tally board.

Not only was the work relentless, it was exhausting, pushing a man's body to its limits. Shearing was no job for the faint-hearted. Backs ached, joints throbbed, muscles spasmed. The half-hour smoko breaks, far from being a luxury, were essential as bodies threatened to seize up altogether. At the end of the work day they massaged their wrists and their hands to ease the pain; at the end of the week their arm felt it might drop off and they were all but hobbling as they left the shed. Each night after dinner they sat out on the communal verandah of the quarters

knocking back beers or swigging from the bottle of rum
that was passed around, sharing stories and reminis-
cences, telling lewd jokes. But it wasn't long before they
collapsed on their bunks in the row of tiny rooms they
shared, two men to a room, sleep overwhelming them.
And the weekend was spent getting drunk. Shearers were
always heavy drinkers. You didn't notice the pain when
you were drunk.

Saturdays they'd clean themselves up, attempting to wash
away the stench of lanolin that had permeated the very
pores of their skin. Then they'd go into town where they'd
spend their time drinking and gambling and womanising
before carting fresh grog back to the station, stocking up
for the following week and partying on further.

Sundays were always hungover, but more often than not
started out with good intention; the scrubbing of work
clothes that were putrid, the all-important cleaning of
equipment – a shearer's blades were tended to with infinite
care – but more often than not, Sundays, too, ended up on
the grog before an early night in preparation for another
week's hard slog.

James had no trouble at all socialising with the shearers.
He and Ned being the two youngest by far – Ned had just
turned twenty – shared a room. But James found, strangely
enough, that he had more in common with the older
members of the team. Hard-living, tough-talking as they
were, he knew these men. They were no different from the
Queensland shearers, an honest breed deep down. There
was a recognition, a code of ethics shared among them,
unlike the disparate, fractious labourers he'd worked with
on the shed extension.

He was aware nonetheless that he must not risk alienat-
ing them by being too familiar with the McKinnon family.
A distance must always be maintained between farmer and
shearers who, although reliant upon one another, were on

many an occasion avowed enemies. James' experience of the Queensland shearers' strike had taught him that much.

Bearing this in mind, he now eschewed the Sunday family lunches at the Big House, although he still occasionally went for a morning ride with Ben; back at the quarters the men would be sleeping off their hangovers anyway, no one would miss him.

Ben always invited him to the Big House for lunch, but when James declined he clearly understood the reason.

'Yes,' he'd say reluctantly, 'probably wise under the circumstances. Pity about that.'

There was another reason why avoiding the family lunches was a wise move, James had decided – it helped distance him from Jenna. Her family may not as yet have noticed a difference in her behaviour, but he found the intimacy she displayed in his presence profoundly confronting.

So he devoted himself to a shearer's life; endless, grinding work, aching muscles, drunkenness and the occasional visit to a brothel on a Saturday night. But his body was young and strong, he could withstand the pace. And in the shed as he slowly increased his rhythm he watched his numbers creep up the tally board. He was above Dobson now, and by a good three sheep a day.

'Phil told me you're doing remarkably well,' Ben said as they left their horses grazing and walked up to the rock at the top of the ridge.

'Did he really?' *Unusual,* James thought, *out of keeping for Phil, surely.* 'How come he told you that?'

'Because I asked him,' Ben shamelessly admitted. 'He reckons you have the makings of a gun shearer. Says you're working so hard it's possible you might even reach 200 a day by the end of the season.'

'That is my intention,' James replied a little stiffly as they sat. He didn't turn to look at Ben, but focused on the valley instead. He considered it the height of cheek that Ben should check on his progress.

'Oh for goodness sake, James, stop being stuffy,' Ben said dismissively, aware of his friend's displeasure. 'I wanted to know how you're faring, what's wrong with that? And come on now, admit it, you must be delighted to hear Phil thinks of you so highly.'

James *was* delighted. The notion Phil Caton considered him gun shearer potential was nothing short of thrilling. But he wasn't about to admit that.

'I would rather not be checked up on as if I'm a novice, Ben; it's insulting. I'm an experienced shearer, just as I told you.' He really *was* sounding stuffy now, and he knew it, but he was part of a professional six-man team and was not about to be treated like a child.

Ben was forced to take the matter seriously, or at least appear to. 'I wasn't to know that though, was I?' He studied his friend for a moment, allowing James time to absorb the comment. 'I had only your word, didn't I, James? And you were employed purely because I vouch-safed your credentials. I believe this justifies my enquiry.'

James felt instantly guilty. Ben was, of course, quite right. 'Yes,' he said, 'it does. I'm sorry, mate, I'm really—'

But Ben brushed the topic aside, 'No matter, no matter . . .' he said. It was immaterial to him anyway; he'd made enquiries of Phil right from the start and had been only too relieved to discover James' qualifica-tions were bona fide. He turned as he heard the trot of approaching hooves. 'Oh dear, we have company.' He was irritated that someone should intrude upon their special place.

James, too, turned and they both watched as Jenna brought Misty to a halt beside the old convict well.

'Hello, you two,' she called up to them as she dis-mounted. 'I thought I might find you here.'

They called back their hellos, Ben's irritation now annoyance, and watched further as she loosened Misty's girth, preparing to leave the animal with Bella and Baron who were patiently grazing. It was obviously her intention to join the two of them on the ridge.

'Shall I disappear and leave you alone with her?' Ben murmured.

'I'd rather you didn't,' James replied.

Jenna was by now marching up the rise to meet them.

'I want to talk to James,' she announced upon arrival. 'Alone,' she added with a telling nod to her brother.

'I do believe I've received my orders,' Ben said apologetically as he stood. 'Good luck, old man,' he added and set off down the rocky slope to collect Baron.

Jenna plonked herself beside James. 'You've been avoiding me, haven't you,' she said accusingly, without even waiting until her brother was out of earshot.

'No. I've been working.'

'Not during the weekends. You could have seen me then. You don't even come to Sunday lunch anymore. Why?' Jenna was at her belligerent best.

'Not a good idea for a shearer to fraternise too much with the farmer and his family, Jenna,' he explained patiently. 'The others in the team might disapprove, particularly if they're union men. At least that's the way things are in Queensland.' He was quite sure the situation was the same in New South Wales – wasn't she aware of this fact?

But if she was, the matter appeared of no interest to her.

'You're avoiding me, I can tell, and I want to know why. Are you frightened of my father? Of what he might do if he were to find out about us?'

'I know exactly what your father would do if he were to find out about us, Jenna. He would dismiss me on the spot. Or else he would shoot me. Both courses of action would be quite understandable.' James looked directly into her eyes. 'Which is why we must give him nothing to "find out",' he added meaningfully.

Below them they heard the clatter of hooves on hardened ground as Ben set off at a modest trot. He would urge Baron into a canter and probably a gallop when he reached softer ground. Ben liked to ride hard.

Up on the ridge, Jenna and James paid no heed to his departure. Their eyes locked and she met the intensity of his gaze as she offered up a challenge of her own.

'Do you really think we can call a halt to what we've started, James?' She rested a hand upon his thigh, the light pressure of her fingers, the warmth she created producing a familiar frisson, the very touch of her was enough. 'Do you really believe this is possible?' The hand moved just a little, becoming a caress.

But James steeled himself. 'Yes,' he said, 'we can. And we must. That is if you wish to achieve what you want. Or rather what you claim you want.'

'And that is . . .?'

Upon her query the ice-blue eyes that most found unsettling drilled into hers, and there was a pause before he answered. He was testing her.

'You said you wanted to marry me.'

But her gaze did not falter; it took a great deal to unsettle Jenna. And very slowly she smiled. Then she broke the moment altogether, threw back her head and laughed.

'Why James,' she said, 'am I to take this as a proposal?'

He found her response jarring and her laughter irritating. The touch of her hand on his thigh was no longer enticing. How dare she make fun of him! Had she been baiting him? She and her brother Ben, his best friend, had they both been baiting him? Treating him like the gullible idiot they believed him to be? Was the whole suggestion he might become a part of this family a joke to them?

He stood. 'I fail to see the humour,' he replied coldly.
'I had presumed you were serious.'

Realising she'd offended him Jenna jumped to her feet,
horrified. 'But I was,' she said desperately, 'I *was* serious!
I *am* serious, James, I swear! I want to marry you more
than anything in the world. I've loved you from the
moment we first met.' She was clinging to him now, her
face upturned to his, begging him to kiss her.

So he did. Her reaction, overly dramatic though it was,
having reassured him, he put his arms around her and
kissed her gently, aware it was the right thing to do.

She nestled into his embrace. 'Oh my darling, we belong
together. I love you, and I know you love me . . .'

I don't, he thought, but he caressed her anyway, his
action immediately interpreted by Jenna as an invitation.

'Make love to me, James,' she urged, thrusting herself at
him. 'Please,' she pleaded, her breath hot against his neck,
'please, please. Make love to me. Right here, right now.
Make love to me, James.'

He was strangely unmoved and the answer came easily.
'No, Jenna,' he said. 'We won't make love again until we're
married.'

She stared back at him, barely daring to believe her
girlish wish could come true. She'd fantasised about him
for so long, made her outlandish remarks about marrying
him, but she'd been flaunting her rebellious nature, as she
had for the whole of her young life. Was this now really
possible? Did he really wish to make her his wife?

Then James sat her down and told her of his intention.
They would wait until well after the shearing season before
they approached her father, he said.

'I'm nobody now, don't you see? I need to prove my
worth to your father, and that's exactly what I shall do.
We must wait, Jenna. We must bide our time.'

She breathlessly agreed, happy, excited. He loved her, and her longed-for dream was about to be realised.

James was happy too. Things seemed much simpler now. They would work together as a team, he and Jenna.

CHAPTER TWELVE

With the shearing season drawing to an end James pushed himself harder and harder, his eyes regularly flickering to the tally board like a hawk eyeing its prey, waiting for the magic 200 to appear beside his name.

Gouldy was out-and-out favourite to claim the title of ringer, shearing in excess of 200 every single day, but Batts was lagging behind, not up to his usual form, or so they said. Batts couldn't seem to get above 197. James determined to place himself second in the race and to hit 200, to prove himself not only a gun shearer, but second to the best.

As things turned out, he proved neither. He hit 198, ahead of Batts, then Batts in a frantic last-ditch stand reached 201, proving he hadn't altogether lost his touch. And then, it seemed overnight, the catching pen was empty. The season was over, the last sheep sheared, and after a final, raucous, drunken night in town, the team dispersed to go their separate ways. All except James that is. James had by now become a fixture and would stay on as one of the many regular station hands employed at Glenfinnan. Until the following year when he would once again join up with the team to become a shearer.

'Next year, mate.' Phil Caton was conciliatory, and also complimentary. 'You'll hit 200 next year, James, you did an excellent job. You're a damn good shearer, son.'

Phil's words were a salve to James, who was deeply disappointed with the outcome. But he realised he'd been unrealistic in his expectations. It took time to become a gun shearer, most would never make the grade no matter how hard they tried. And if Phil considered him capable of doing so next year, then that would surely be proof enough of his worth for Alastair McKinnon; Alastair very much respected Phil Caton's opinion.

James decided now would be the right time to approach the man with the formal request he might court his daughter. Jenna agreed, but had another idea. She would make the first approach herself, she said, in order to pave the way.

'Daddy's putty in my hands,' she assured him with confidence. 'Besides, I told him ages ago that I wanted to marry you.'

James was shocked. She'd said as much to her brother, that he knew, but to *Alastair McKinnon*?

'What did your father say?'

'He didn't believe me. Or else he thought I was joking,' Jenna replied airily, 'hard to tell. He'll know I'm serious this time though,' she added, 'I'll make sure of that, my darling, I can promise you.'

'What the hell are you thinking, Jenna?' Alastair exploded. 'For God's sake, the boy's a bloody *shearer*!'

'Yes, and a very good one at that,' Jenna said haughtily, 'Phil believes so anyway, which surely means something.'

'Good, bad or indifferent, it doesn't stop him being a *shearer*!'

Deep down, Alastair McKinnon could not deny his innate disapproval of shearers, much as he might respect the work of those truly skilled in the trade. A Jack Howe, for instance, one had to admire a man like that. But the general run-of-the-mill shearer? A rough-and-tumble lot, ill-bred, uncouth, one of the crosses a farmer had to bear.

At least in Alastair's opinion. And in the opinion of many others. A case of 'us and them' existed in most farmers when it came down to shearers. Essential though they were to one other, they were different breeds altogether.

James was not to know that for all the work he'd put into achieving status as a shearer he'd unwittingly fallen a notch or so in Alastair's estimation. He might have been safer had he remained a farmhand. Now, not only did he have no recognisable bloodline that met with the patriarch's approval, he was one of the lowliest of breeds.

Alastair remained adamant in the confrontation with his daughter. 'Now you listen to me, Jenna, I won't have it, you hear? No daughter of mine marries a bloody *shearer*!'

Jenna remained equally adamant. 'This one does.' She refused to budge. 'I love him, Daddy, and I intend to marry him, with or without your approval.'

They'd reached a stalemate. Alastair was finally forced to at least give young James Brereton an audience and allow him to state his intentions. Which, he had to admit, the boy did with distinction.

'I wish to court Jenna, sir,' James said, standing stiffly to attention in Alastair's office and delivering his speech word for word and exactly the way Ben had coached him. 'With your permission, of course. We've developed a deep fondness for one another, Jenna and I, which I believe . . .' He paused. '*Over time . . .*' he stressed, 'could prove grounds for a successful marriage.'

Where on earth had the boy learned to talk like this? Alastair wondered. He was not only impressed, but to a certain extent appeased. At this stage the boy was seeking no more than the permission to court his daughter, and the phrase 'over time' was promising. James was not wishing to rush into things the way young people did these days (indeed the way Jenna would if she could) but was willing to wait and to woo, seeking the approval not only of his

intended, but also her family. Alastair liked the sound of
that. Jenna professed to love the boy, yes, but she might
well be romanticising her feelings – James was, after all,
extremely good-looking – and if it were to prove a mere
case of infatuation then time would sort things out.

'Very well, James,' he agreed, 'you have permission to
court my daughter. Observing every propriety of course,'
he added.

'Of course, sir, this is totally understood. Ben is quite
prepared to act as chaperone.' Ben had told James to add
that bit. Ben had also told him to stress the 'over time'
factor.

'The old man will hope it's just a passing phase Jenna
will grow out of,' he'd said.

'Good, good,' Alastair agreed. *Yes, I like the sound of
that too,* he thought, *only right Ben should keep an eye
on his young sister.*

The interview over, James nodded respectfully and left
the office.

Alastair couldn't help but admit that he actually liked
young James Brereton. *There's something impressive about
the boy,* he thought, as he watched the door close gently
behind him. If the worst came to the worst he supposed he
could suffer James as a son-in-law. Although if this were to
prove the case they'd have to find him a position of some
seeming importance at Glenfinnan, he certainly couldn't
remain a shearer.

Christmas was approaching and with it came the parties.
Glenfinnan and many neighbouring properties in the area
were known for their social festivities at this time of the
year. Garden parties, dinners and dances abounded and
the threesome of James, Jenna and Ben were seen regularly in attendance. It soon became apparent that young
James Brereton was courting Jenna McKinnon and that

her brother Ben was acting as chaperone. There were some who didn't altogether approve of the match, particularly those who had hoped their sons might become suitors to the younger McKinnon daughter. A number of eligible bachelors had experienced fleeting promises; indeed Jenna had been known to tease and flirt outrageously, but no relationship of any serious intent had resulted. Many a matron agreed it was most disappointing. And now this rank outsider had appeared from nowhere and bagged the prize, it would seem. Quite a bit of tut-tutting went on here and there.

The family, however, approved of James Brereton. Adriana and Alexandra, Alastair McKinnon's two younger sisters and their respective families – 'the sea of cousins' to whom Ben constantly referred – all liked James. It was true, they knew nothing of his background, but that didn't bother them enough to close ranks. The McKinnon line could do with an injection of fresh blood, the sisters agreed, both practical women. And if their brother Alastair appeared a little wary of his daughter's choice – well that was just Alastair being an over-protective father wasn't it?

The parties spilled into the new year, even while work continued as usual; a property like Glenfinnan didn't run itself. But the arrival of 1894 was cause for much celebration, particularly as this was the year the Wolseley shearing machines were to be installed. Glenfinnan was all set to move with the times.

As was his custom, Alastair had sent samples of wool from his latest clip to the Technological Museum in Sydney, inviting a report from them. He placed great importance upon these independent assessments, and the report returned to him was glowing:

'. . . *it would be difficult to select from any flock wool carrying such commanding length and pronounced character . . . staples well built, uniform and compact from base to the close tip . . . structure very pronounced, the crimp being even and true right throughout . . . a breeder's wool suitable for the manufacturer also . . .'*

For selling purposes no report could have been better.

In February, Alastair once again deputised his son to take the flock samples to Sydney, together with the museum's report. Ben was to impress the overseas buyers as he had so successfully the previous year. He had been booked into the Metropole for two weeks, his father told him.

The anonymity of Sydney beckoned, and Ben couldn't wait.

He said as much to James as they shared a beer on the back verandah of the Big House. 'My dose of freedom at long last.' He gave a theatrical sigh. 'Sheer heaven.' Then leaning back in his wicker chair he became reminiscent. 'We met this same time last year,' he said. 'Do you remember? That night in the park?'

'How could I forget?' James looked out to where Boris was tending the vegetable garden, and then to the vista stretching endlessly beyond. *Where would I be now if it weren't for Ben?* he wondered. It was difficult to believe how incredibly his life had changed since that night they'd met.

'I'll give everyone at the Hampton Club your regards, shall I?' Ben queried, raising an eyebrow. 'And perhaps also at Monty's?' he added with a devilish grin.

'You just take care, mate,' James sounded a warning. 'Don't go doing anything stupid like picking up blokes in the park.'

'Oh dear me,' Ben said and he laughed out loud, 'that was my lucky night.'

James joined in the laughter. 'Mine too,' he agreed.

A week later, on a Saturday, Ben left for Sydney and two days after that the Wolseley machines arrived, all ready for instalment, although this would take some time. Glenfinnan was a hive of activity.

Since the end of the shearing season James had been once more ensconced in one of the workers' cottages, this time sharing with another station hand, a pleasant young fellow around his age called Len. The son of a local family, Len had been working at Glenfinnan for a year or so.

The fact that James now shared a cottage proved no discouragement to Jenna, who turned up on his doorstep the very day after Ben left, prepared to take advantage of her brother's absence.

'It's Sunday. I thought you might like to go for a ride,' she said, and there was something very suggestive in the way she said it. At least James thought so. Jenna was extremely readable.

'No thank you, my love,' he replied. He'd taken to calling her 'my love' these days, knowing how much she liked it. 'I'm off for a walk instead.'

'I'll come with you then.'

The invitation in her eyes was unmistakable. He shook his head.

'I'll see you at lunch this afternoon,' he said. Now her suitor, he was naturally attending the Sunday luncheons at the Big House again.

Jenna peered through the open door to the cottage's tiny living room, which appeared remarkably empty and silent.

'Are you alone?' She knew he shared the cottage with another worker although she wasn't sure which one, there were any number of workers.

'Yes,' he admitted, 'Len goes to church on Sunday mornings.'

'Ah.' She smiled. Yes, she knew Len. Len was a nice boy. A local, and a devout Catholic – as was his whole family – of course he'd be at church. She appeared about to step inside.

'No, Jenna,' James said, barring her way. 'You must go.'

'You don't really mean that, do you?' Again the smile, now unashamedly seductive.

'You must go,' he repeated and he glanced at Misty. The mare was tied up to the hitching rail right in front of the cottage. A complete giveaway.

'I can tether her in the trees out the back,' Jenna suggested.

But James would have no bar of it. 'Go, Jenna. Go *right now*!'

He and Ben had agreed about the danger of indiscretion. Ben had been most insistent. 'Sex before marriage?' he'd said. 'Dad would kill you.'

Jenna pouted sulkily. She didn't look at all pretty when she sulked, he thought, she just looked bad-tempered. Which made her easily resistible. But he kissed her anyway. A chaste kiss that did not overstep the bounds of propriety should anyone have been watching.

'Not until we're married,' he whispered, 'remember?'

She flounced off across the verandah and down the steps and when she'd mounted Misty and was about to leave, he called out to her.

'I'll see you at lunch, my love.'

Ben was due to return to Glenfinnan at the end of February. 'In time for your birthday,' he'd said to James before he left. 'We'll have a huge celebration.' James would turn nineteen in early March, although as far as others were concerned he would be twenty-three.

But Ben did not return to Glenfinnan at the end of February, and there was no celebration, huge or otherwise, for James' birthday.

Benjamin McKinnon, sole male heir to the Glenfinnan Estate, was found dead in the backstreets of Sydney. He'd been murdered. Bashed to death. His body discovered by wharf workers early on a Monday morning in the dockside area of Woolloomooloo.

A terrible, tragic, senseless crime, all agreed. A robbery,

obviously, but surely the culprit or culprits hadn't needed to kill him. Couldn't they just have taken his money instead of murdering him, and in such a brutal manner? Why? everyone wondered. Why?

James was the only one who knew the truth. This had been no robbery. Ben hadn't been killed for his money. He may have made the mistake of picking the wrong man or he may have been set upon by those who detested his kind, but Ben had been killed simply for being who he was.

James wondered whether or not he should feel guilty. It was he, after all, who had told Ben of Monty's Bar in Woolloomooloo. But no, he decided, Ben had made his own choices in life. James absolved himself of all guilt, but he mourned the loss of his friend nonetheless. The one and only true friend he'd ever had, he realised. He would miss Ben.

The members of the McKinnon family grieved deeply, and in their own specific ways. Adele wept for the brother whom she'd loved so dearly. She wept too for the shocking injustice dealt him, so young, so vibrant, so much life left to live. And she wept also for the family's loss, deprived of the son destined to inherit the vast McKinnon estate. It all seemed so shockingly unfair.

Jenna didn't weep. Jenna raged. She'd always admired the way Ben had straddled both worlds – the rural and the urban – with such apparent ease. She didn't anymore. She hated Sydney; that wretched, heartless city had robbed her of the brother she loved. That city had deprived her family of its rightful son and heir, wiping him out brutally, meaninglessly. Jenna hated Sydney with a passion.

As Adele wept and Jenna raged, James kept his reaction very much to himself.

He saddled up Bella and rode out to the stone quarry where he walked to the top of the ridge. And as he sat on the large flat rock overlooking the valley, Ben was with

him. He could hear Ben's voice. All the secrets they'd
shared. Nothing had been sacred. The realisation came to
him then that he'd loved Ben. That apart from his father,
George Wakefield, Ben was the only person he had ever
loved, or quite possibly ever would – a pure love. A love for
the brother he'd never had.

Young Ben McKinnon's body was brought back to
Goulburn where he was buried at Mortis Street Cemetery.
It was here his mother Grace, and also his grandparents,
Douglas and Mary, were interred.

Everyone was in a state of shock. The extended McKinnon
family, the neighbouring farmers, the citizens of Goulburn
itself. How could such a thing have happened to one of
their own?

As for Alastair McKinnon . . . Alastair was devastated,
in a state of such anguish and despair many thought he
may never recover. His sisters and their families rallied
about him, Phil Caton took over all aspects of farm management, but as the months progressed Alastair remained
a broken man, consumed by the burden of his grief.

It was his daughter, Jenna, who finally made the breakthrough. Urged on by her selfishness perhaps, who could
tell, but nobody minded, because selfish or otherwise, her
ploy worked.

'I intend to be married by early spring, Daddy,' she said
firmly, not a request, but a statement. 'Before the start of
the shearing season.'

It was July now, nearly five months since her brother's
death, and Jenna considered it high time she move on with
her life.

Alastair stared back at her dully, disinterested. They
were in his office. The accountant, who lived with his
family in one of the property's staff houses, had just delivered a pile of paperwork for checking, as he did monthly,

but these days Alastair would simply hand it over to Phil. He couldn't be bothered doing anything.

'James and I have a proposition to put to you,' Jenna went on. 'May I bring him in? He's waiting outside.'

'Yes, of course,' Alastair replied. *If you must,* he thought. Frankly, he didn't care. Let Jenna marry the Brereton boy, it meant nothing to him now. Why should it? Just another one of the girls marrying into another family. With the death of his beloved son and heir the McKinnon name was gone forever. Alastair's whole world had changed irrevocably.

Jenna crossed to the door and ushered James inside.

'Good morning, sir,' James said as he crossed to the desk where the man seated on the other side appeared so much older and smaller than he had five months ago.

'May we sit, Daddy?'

'Yes, yes, do.' Alastair waved a careless hand at the hard-back chairs opposite him and the two of them sat.

'James has something he'd like to say to you.'

Jenna smiled encouragement at James, who proceeded to outline the plan they'd discussed.

'If Jenna and I are to wed before the spring, sir . . .' He started a little hesitantly, unsure of the reaction that might follow. 'As I believe she has told you she wishes . . .'

Alastair's tired nod said, *Yes, yes, get on with it.*

'If that is to be the case,' James continued, 'then I wish you to know I would be quite happy for her to continue carrying the McKinnon name.'

Alastair stared blankly back at him. *What is the boy actually saying?* he wondered.

'Our family name would officially become Brereton-McKinnon,' James explained, 'but we would be known as McKinnons, I've assured Jenna of that.'

Alastair still appeared unable to comprehend his point, so Jenna burst in eagerly.

'Don't you see, Daddy,' she said, barely able to contain her excitement, 'the family name will be preserved. Our children and our children's children will bear the name *McKinnon*. Your grandchildren will be McKinnons, Daddy. Your grand*sons*,' she went on emphatically, 'because there *will* be sons, I can promise you. The name will live on, don't you see? The McKinnon dynasty will survive.'

Her words finally sank in, and Alastair turned to James, his expression a mix of disbelief and wonderment.

'You would do this?' he said. 'You would forgo your family name and take that of another?'

'I would, sir.' James smiled lovingly at Jenna. 'For my wife's sake. If this is what Jenna wishes, then I am prepared to do so.'

On a personal level, James didn't really care, he'd never been a Brereton anyway. Perhaps if he still bore the name Wakefield, things might be different. *Yes, he thought, things would certainly be different. How proud George would be to see his name linked to that of a family like this!* But as such a thing was impossible, James had been more than happy to agree to Jenna's suggestion.

'It's the only way to drag Daddy out of the depths of his depression,' she'd urged. 'The McKinnon name must be preserved and we're the only ones who can do it. Furthermore, my darling, I can promise you that upon our doing so he will bless our marriage.'

It appeared Jenna had been right on both counts. This was the breakthrough her father had needed. And the marriage was certainly blessed.

'I am beholden to you, James,' Alastair said. *That a man should do such a thing,* he thought, *forsake his name for the love of his wife.* Any doubts Alastair may have had about the match vanished in an instant. Here indeed was a worthy husband for his daughter. A man prepared to sacrifice his family name in order to preserve that of another? Unbelievable! Alastair's gratitude knew no bounds.

The rest of the family, too, was grateful, every single one of them only too thankful to have their patriarch returned to them. Adriana and Alexandra had worried for their brother's very sanity. They'd been informed by their nieces that Alastair was so consumed by grief he hadn't even allowed anyone into Ben's room to sort through his belongings. For five long months the door had remained closed, the room left exactly as it had been the day Ben had left for Sydney.

Alastair continued to refuse all help with his son's belongings, but his refusal was now healthy.

'No, thank you,' he said once again to his daughters. Adele and Jenna had both offered many times to take on the task. 'I shall do so myself.'

The door was finally opened and Alastair entered the realm of his son. He closed the door behind him and stayed for some time. Several days, in fact, leaving to sleep in his own room at night, but returning intermittently throughout the mornings and afternoons that followed, always closing the door, often staying for hours. No one knew whether he was sorting through Ben's belongings or whether he was just soaking up the presence of his son.

Around a week later, however, following luncheon on Sunday, he asked James to join him in his office.

'If you wouldn't mind coming with me, James,' he said, 'I have something of yours I wish to return.'

It was the gold fob watch and chain.

As soon as they entered the office Alastair crossed straight to where it sat on his desk, glinting in the afternoon's wintry light that shone through the bay windows.

'I'm sorry I didn't return your father's watch to you sooner,' he said, picking it up. 'It was in Ben's valuables box. He'd put it there for safe-keeping.'

'Yes, I know he had, sir,' James replied, 'I was with him when he did so.'

'It's a valuable piece, James,' Alastair said. 'Would you like me to lock it away in the safe here at the Big House?'

'No, thank you all the same, sir. I'm in trustworthy company now, and I think I'd rather have it with me.'

'Of course. It's only right a son would wish to have his father's watch close by him at all times, a symbol of family and a tie with the past.' He handed the piece to James. 'Take care, my boy, keep it safe.'

James looked down at the watch and chain he'd stolen from the body of Charles Grenfell. The story pleased him. He liked to think of the watch having belonged to his father.

'Thank you, sir, I shall,' he said, and he slipped it into his pocket.

The wedding was low-key, held at St Peter and Paul's Cathedral as were all McKinnon weddings, but a modest affair, restrained and befitting a family who had lost a son six months earlier. Jenna didn't care, she hadn't wanted anything showy, although she did miss the grand, flam-boyant party that would normally have followed; she would have liked to have danced the night away. There was still a party, nonetheless. The extended family gathered back at the Big House for supper where they toasted the happy couple and speeches were made. After which Jenna and James departed for the attractive staff cottage that had been assigned to them now they were man and wife, and which befitted James' new status as Deputy Station Manager, a position created solely for him.

There was no honeymoon. With the shearing season looming, time did not allow for one, but Jenna didn't care about that either. She had James all to herself and nothing else mattered.

'You said not until we're married, remember . . .' she'd whispered in his ear the first night when she'd insisted he carry her over the threshold. 'Well we're married now, James. We're married, my darling, and you're all mine.'

Jenna was insatiable that night and throughout the nights that followed, which did not in the least bother James, who was more than capable of meeting her demands. Theirs was a highly sexually charged relationship, which they both agreed made excellent grounds upon which to base a marriage.

The Wolseley machines proved successful from the outset, mainly because Phil Caton had selected his now extended, ten-man shearing team with care, ensuring he contracted those experienced with the equipment, which was new to many.

Gouldy was back for the '94 season, and so was Batts. Gouldy, in particular, was as skilled with machine-operated handpieces as he was with blade shears.

Before the arrival of the team, James had personally trialled one of the handpieces, Phil watching on as he sheared a sheep. He'd never in his life used machine shears and didn't know quite what to expect, but he'd thrilled to the efficiency of the power-driven handpiece, which was linked by a shaft to the equipment overhead. A toothed blade, known as a 'cutter' travelled back and forth across the face of a comb as the shearer steadily guided the hand-piece through the base of the wool.

Following the curve of the sheep's body, the rhythm came instinctively to James, and he heard his father's voice . . . *'Nice and steady does it, son. You get to the end of your line, then you're back to the beginning, following the next one in the very same way . . .'* The handpiece automatically became an extension of his forearm and his wrist, even more so than the blade shears had. *I was born for this machinery,* he thought.

'You're a natural, James,' Phil said admiringly, 'you really haven't used a handpiece before?'

'Nup.'

'Well you're a bloody natural, mate, that's what you are. Pity we can't put you on the team.'

James thought so too. He longed to be here in the shed, competing with the others, testing his skills against the best. But this was not to be. Alastair McKinnon, with his daughter now wed, was more adamant than ever.

'No son-in-law of mine is going to be a shearer,' he'd declared.

James had resigned himself to the loss of his long-held ambition to emulate the great Jack Howe. But he told himself, realistically, such a thing would never have happened anyway; there would only ever be one Jack Howe. Besides, he'd come up in the world, hadn't he? And to a level undreamt of. He was one of the hierarchy at Glenfinnan, and a McKinnon no less. You didn't get much higher than that.

But throughout the season, in his position as overseer, marking up the tally board and checking the work of each shearer, he envied the men. Watching them, sweat pouring from brows, backs aching with fatigue, muscles threatening to seize up as they raced against the clock in a bid to earn the title of ringer, he longed to be one of them.

Jenna gave birth the following year, virtually nine months to the day after their wedding. Joshua Douglas Brereton-McKinnon was born on Saturday, 15 June 1895.

'Why Joshua?' James queried. He'd presumed she'd favour Douglas as a Christian name. Being the name of her grandfather, they'd chosen it in order to please Alastair, but she'd said she didn't much like 'Douglas'.

'We'll make that the middle name instead, shall we,' she suggested, 'middle names always tend to disappear. I like Joshua.'

'But why?'

The name Joshua seemed to have appeared from nowhere, but Jenna remained resolute in her choice.

'Because it's a powerful name,' she insisted, 'it's the name of a leader, and our son will be a leader. Joshua was the successor to Moses, you know,' she said with an air of superiority. Then in typical Jenna fashion, she added, 'Besides, I like Joshua. And Josh for short, I particularly like Josh.'

'Very well, my love.' James laughed. 'Joshua it is. Josh for short.' He didn't care what the child was called.

James hadn't even cared that the child was a boy. The child was healthy, that's all that mattered. And he was now a father. A man with a family of his own. He was twenty years old and there would be more children. Many more. He would father his own dynasty, just as Alastair had.

In his state of euphoria, James may not have cared whether or not his firstborn was a son, but there was one who did.

Alastair embraced the birth of his grandson with a euphoria that quite possibly outmatched that of James. The McKinnon name, synonymous with the breeding of the finest wool, had survived with integrity and honour for three generations and was now about to embark upon a fourth. The future was in safe hands.

PART THREE

CHAPTER THIRTEEN

Jenna's choice of name for her son proved most apt. Joshua was a born leader, the first true signs of his leadership capabilities becoming evident at a remarkably early age. By the time he was three he was leading his cousins, Zachary and Samuel into all sorts of trouble, and yet Zac and Sam were six months his senior.

Adele had given birth to her sturdy, healthy, non-identical twin boys in January 1895, much to her husband's absolute delight, the normally contained, unflappable Phil Caton proclaiming to all and sundry, and at the top of his voice, that he was the proudest man on earth.

Growing up together at Glenfinnan, their mothers being sisters, their fathers working side by side, the cousins were destined to be close, but from their earliest days Josh was the undisputed leader, just as he was with Adele's further two children, a girl and another boy. Just as he was, too, with his siblings who arrived in the several years that followed, Edward James Brereton-McKinnon born in early 1897 and his little sister, Emily Jane in late 1898.

Jenna and James were rewarded for their production of healthy progeny by a deeply grateful Alastair McKinnon, who insisted they move into the Big House.

'This is your rightful home,' he declared. 'The Big House belongs to the next generation. There is no point in my rattling around here on my own; all I need is one of the smaller bedrooms and my office. Besides, I want my family nearby; I want to watch the little ones grow up.'

The new arrangement worked beautifully. Alastair remained at the helm of Glenfinnan, but James and Jenna were now master and mistress of the Big House, their children the next generation of McKinnons.

Adele, far from bearing a grudge or viewing her younger sister's elevated status with envy, was deeply grateful to both Jenna and James. Her own husband could never have borne such a burden. She would never have wished it upon him. She and Phil were very happy in their house up on the hill, and she treasured the friendship shared between her offspring and those of her sister.

Physically, Josh and Ted took after their father, fair-haired, piercingly blue-eyed and auguring to be tall. Emily, ginger-haired and hazel-eyed, was very much Jenna, but prettier, her face fine-boned without the square McKinnon jaw.

James adored being a father. He embraced every aspect of parenthood, loving his children with a passion and spoiling them shamelessly, more so with each passing year as he observed their emerging personalities.

Determined to become a hero to his children the same way his father had been to him, he entertained them with George Wakefield's fanciful tales, building a 'Brereton' family history that they could inherit along with that of the McKinnons'. He showed them the gold fob watch and chain and regaled them with Grandfather George's heroic rescue of the rich farmer who had awarded it to him. And recalling his own childhood delight, he read to them from his well-worn copy of *Popular Nursery Tales and Rhymes*, unveiling to them the true background behind the apparently harmless children's stories. And just as he had been, they were fascinated.

'Mary, Mary, Quite Contrary' . . . 'Goosey, Goosey Gander' . . . 'Georgie Porgie' . . . 'Jack Sprat' . . . On and on the list went, and the more gruesome, the more political, the more greedy and opportunistic the true meanings he revealed, the more the children loved them. Particularly Josh, and not just because Josh was the eldest, but because Josh was exceedingly clever.

When the boy was six, James tested him with 'Baa Baa Black Sheep', just the way George had tested *him* when he was six, and Josh passed with flying colours.

'The value of the black sheep's wool when it goes to market,' the boy said thoughtfully upon being challenged, 'would depend upon what the people want to buy.' Then the answer appeared to come to him. 'I'd be the "master", Dad,' he triumphantly declared, 'I'd be the King, and I'd *tell* the people what they want to buy.'

Seeing so much of his own answer in the boy's response, James could not have been more gratified. 'You're right, son,' he said, and remembering George's words he quoted his father. 'People are like sheep. They need a leader.'

Then Josh went one step further. 'No,' he disagreed, 'sheep don't need a leader. Sheep need to be bullied.' Josh was thinking of the musters and the dogs, the way the collies and kelpies nipped at the sheep's heels and sometimes even jumped across the sheep's backs, herding them along. 'Sheep don't follow, Dad,' he insisted. 'Sheep get driven.' Josh was already wondering whether, if people were like sheep as his dad had just said, they too needed to be driven rather than led. The notion was interesting.

'Baa Baa Black Sheep' made an indelible impression upon Josh, just as it had upon his father.

James tried hard not to let it show, but Josh was his undeniable favourite. Two years later, when he tried the same test on six-year-old Edward, the results differed hugely. Young Ted didn't appear interested in the market and the value of the black sheep's wool. All Ted could think of was 'the little boy' and the way he'd been cheated by the 'master' and the 'dame'.

'That's not fair,' he said, affronted, 'the poor farmer! He works hard the whole season and then the King and the Church take all his profit? That's theft, Dad. That's downright robbery.'

Dear, sweet-natured Ted, James thought fondly, *he really doesn't see the overall picture the way Josh does.*

As for little Emily Jane, no test was applied, no test considered necessary, her future being thoroughly assured. Pretty as a picture, little Emily Jane was bound to break hearts one day, men would vie for her hand.

Like her brothers, Emily found the nursery rhymes entertaining, but she didn't much care for those that had a political background; power, greed and opportunism held no interest for her. She far preferred the gruesome stories, the ones that spoke of torture and beheadings and the killing of priests by throwing them down stairs. She thought these were awfully funny and would break into the prettiest peals of little-girl laughter. And the more she laughed the more James embellished the stories. He doted on his daughter.

As time passed, Jenna couldn't help feeling somewhat piqued by her husband's devotion to their children. James paid more attention to them than he did to her these days. The highly sexual relationship they'd shared was no longer what it had been. She assumed this was normal, the natural progression that occurred when parenthood took over, but wasn't it the mother's libido that was supposed to wane rather than the father's?

It was true, James was not as sexually driven as he had been in the early days of their marriage, but he did not consider himself entirely to blame. Jenna didn't appear to have noticed the changes time and childbirth had wrought upon her. The once glorious body had thickened and the once pert breasts now sagged a little. She was on the cusp of thirty yet she might have been forty. When she tried to seduce him with the girlish flirtation of old she appeared to him ludicrous. Aware she was frustrated, he performed his conjugal duties now and then, in order to avoid her ill-temper, but he no longer found her arousing. He was faithful to her though. A loyal husband, he didn't seek satisfaction elsewhere. If the truth be known, he didn't really need to. Sex no longer seemed of any great importance. Given the constant work required of him in the running of Glenfinnan and the delightful distraction of his children, life was full.

Alastair McKinnon died in 1904. He was sixty-six years old, and would no doubt have lived quite a deal longer had it not been for the loss of his son. But he was not the physically robust man of previous years. Ben's death a decade earlier had taken its toll.

He died content, however, in the knowledge that the McKinnon name was flourishing, and that all thanks for its preservation were due to James Brereton. During his final days, he ensured James was aware of his gratitude, but he ensured also that his son-in-law was reminded of the legacy bestowed upon him.

'Not long to go now, James,' he said one Sunday afternoon when James visited the bedroom where he'd languished for the past month, his needs regularly attended to by the ever-loyal Beth and Millie. 'Only a few weeks I'd say, perhaps less. Who can tell?'

James had pulled up a chair and was seated next to the bed, nine-year-old Josh standing beside him. During the week, Josh and Ted attended boarding school at St Patrick's College in Goulburn, but they came home for the weekends, collected each Friday late-afternoon by Boris and returned early each Monday morning.

James always brought Josh along on his Sunday visits to Alastair's bedside, not only because Josh was Alastair's favourite grandchild, but because, for some unknown reason, Josh simply loved visiting the old man. While his brother Ted and his cousins Zac and Sam were off playing and relishing the freedom of Sunday, Josh preferred the company of a dying old man. Most strange, but he seemed to find Alastair a source of great fascination.

'Sit, boy, sit,' Alastair ordered, patting the counterpane with a fragile, purple-veined hand.

Josh obeyed, plonking himself on the bed and briefly studying the hand that seemed to him claw-like and somehow non-human. That's what happened to the hands of people who were dying, he supposed. Josh found the changes he regularly observed in the old man riveting, like watching fruit rotting on the vine. Life withering away before his very eyes. Death was so interesting.

Alastair smiled. The intelligence in the boy's gaze as he studied his hand was indisputable.

Josh looked up, his eyes meeting those of the old man and he returned the smile, happily, invitingly, ever eager to make contact.

Alastair, as usual, was won. The boy's charm and personality was as engaging as his intelligence. *Young Josh McKinnon is destined for great things,* he thought.

To Alastair, his grandchildren were always McKinnons, the Brereton appendage seeming to have become lost along the way. As was the case, he'd been pleased to note, with most of the locals in the area, all of whom referred to Jenna's offspring simply as 'the McKinnon children'.

He returned his attention to James. He'd decided today would be the day he'd make his speech, the one he'd been preparing for some time, brief, but to the point. Even if he did manage to last a few more weeks, who knew when he might turn into a dithering mess. His memory had been wandering a great deal of late; best to play things safe.

'You are aware of my gratitude, aren't you, James.' He didn't wait for a reply; he hadn't been posing a question. 'I owe you a great debt for preserving my family's name and before I depart this world, I wish to thank you with all my heart.'

'I'm honoured to be a part of your family, Alastair,' James replied with utter sincerity, 'and I thank you in turn for the privilege.'

It was every bit the response Alastair might have wished for.

'I need say no more than that then. I had prepared quite a deal more, I might add, but it's obviously not necessary.' He held out the same withered hand that had so fascinated his grandson and the two men shook. Then, as they released their hold, Alastair added his reminder of the legacy James had inherited.

'Our family is in your hands now, James, and in the hands of your sons . . .' He turned to look at Josh. 'Your sons whom I know will go on to honour our name.'

He and the boy once again shared a special smile.

Then Josh offered his own hand, and he and his grandfather shook, the action not only delighting Alastair, but confirming his belief in the future.

Yes, he thought, *things are sadly not as I'd planned them to be, but at least I am free to die without worry.*

Josh had wanted to experience the feel of the claw-like, non-human hand, and he wasn't disappointed. *Yes,* he thought, *this is just the way the hand of a dying man should feel.*

He saw his grandfather only one more time after that. The following Sunday. But they didn't speak. The old man was sleeping and it was decided not to wake him.

Alastair died less than a week later. He was buried at Mortis Street Cemetery. The brand-new Goulburn General Cemetery had opened that very same year and Mortis Street had now been officially closed for burials, but exceptions were made for family members. Which meant that Alastair McKinnon was able to be interred alongside his wife, Grace and his son, Benjamin. It seemed to many the end of an era all round.

There was no denying the fact that Josh McKinnon was a precocious boy, gifted from the outset with intelligence and talents well beyond his years. By the age of ten he was already an accomplished horseman and an excellent marksman with both rifle and handgun. But by the time he'd reached twelve it was his academic abilities that most impressed his teacher at St Patrick's College.

'Joshua is a brilliant student, Mr Brereton-McKinnon,' James was informed by Leonard Crompton, Josh's teacher, who also happened to be the newly appointed deputy headmaster.

Leonard Crompton was not a local but had arrived at St Patrick's fresh from Sydney just one year previous. He did not therefore see Josh as a local would, as the eldest son of the McKinnon clan destined to take over the reign of Glenfinnan. Rather he saw Josh as one of the most promising pupils he'd ever encountered and one who should be encouraged to pursue a life in the world of academia.

'Your boy's secondary education,' Leonard continued, 'will be of the greatest importance if he is to achieve the academic qualifications of which he is more than capable.'

Leonard did not intend to cast aspersions upon the teaching staff of St Patrick's, but he was aware they were accustomed to tutoring the sons of farmers who would not be encouraged to go on to university, but would return to work on their families' properties. He was also convinced his colleagues failed to recognise the intellectual capacity of young Joshua, which was unique in a place like Goulburn. It was, therefore, his bounden duty to point this gifted child in the right direction.

Leonard Crompton considered himself a dedicated teacher rather than the self-opinionated snob that deep down he was.

'What would you suggest then, Mr Crompton?'

'Sydney Grammar School.' Leonard's response fired back bullet-like; his *alma mater* was where the boy belonged.

It took no time at all for him to convince James.

That same night, however, when James brought up the subject with his wife as they prepared for bed, Jenna was not so easy to convince.

'Sydney!' The very thought appalled her. 'Why Sydney?'

'Because we want the best,' James replied. 'We *need* the best. Josh *deserves* the best.'

'What's wrong with St Pat's?' Jenna demanded. 'It's the best school in Goulburn!'

'And Sydney Grammar is the best school in Australia,' he countered, a direct quote from Leonard.

'What,' she scoffed, 'just because Josh's *teacher* went there?' Jenna was unreservedly scathing of Leonard Crompton. 'Who does the man think he is? Besides,' she added, clinching the argument, at least in her eyes, 'Sydney Grammar is non-denominational, I want him to attend a Catholic school.' Jenna, a non-believer like her father, didn't actually care whether or not the school of choice was Catholic, she simply would not allow her son to be sent away to Sydney, which she considered a loathsome place.

'If Sydney Grammar was good enough for Australia's first Prime Minister,' James announced, once again quoting Leonard and with a pomposity not dissimilar, 'then it's good enough for Josh.'

Leonard had driven the point home with considerable force, citing the creation of the Federal government just six years previously. 'The Commonwealth of Australia's first Prime Minister, Edmund Barton, was a Sydney Grammar student,' he'd announced. 'Such is the calibre of education afforded those who display true potential.' Then he'd added with import, 'Those like your son,' appearing to imply Josh was prime ministerial material.

Little wonder James had been impressed. Leonard had even gone on to supply the necessary contact regarding reputable lodgings for Josh.

'Where my own nephew is lodging,' he'd boasted as he'd written down the name and address on a notepad. 'My brother's boy, Harold, is attending Sydney Grammar. There you are,' he'd said, tearing off the page and handing it to James. 'Potts Point. Impeccable household, tantamount to a guardianship arrangement no less, and within easy walking distance of Sydney Grammar.'

Leonard had appeared to have all the answers. James had been so impressed that he was now determined to impress in equal measure upon his wife the importance of their eldest son's education.

Over the ensuing days, or rather the nights when he returned home after a heavy day's work, he eventually wore her down. Or that is, he and Josh did. When the possibility had been mentioned to Josh he'd been excited beyond measure; he longed to go to Sydney. Jenna couldn't fight them both.

She demanded a solid promise of James, however: that he would personally investigate all aspects of Josh's accommodation. She must know everything about the people and the household involved. He was to make a trip to Sydney within the next week or so and report back on the 'guardianship arrangement' of which Leonard Crompton had been so boastful.

'If there appears anything remotely lacking in competence, I will not have it, James,' she said. 'I will not have my son running rife in Sydney without adequate supervision. Don't forget, it was Sydney that killed my brother,' she warned him, her tone condemnatory.

'Of course, my love, of course. I promise you I shall assure everything is in order.'

James found himself very much looking forward to Sydney. A brief trip only, that is. Good God, he certainly wouldn't want to live there! But he realised it was a whole fourteen years since he'd been a part of the vast, bustling city that was Sydney. He'd not returned once since those days, which now seemed a lifetime ago. He would enjoy revisiting a few of his old haunts.

He caught the train a fortnight later, and upon his arrival booked himself into the Metropole Hotel.

Well, well, look at you, he thought, catching sight of his image in one of the mirrors as he strode across the mosaic-tiled floor of the main foyer. He was looking most dapper, a smart three-piece suit, the chain of the fob watch dangling from his vest. He wore the watch quite often these days, whenever he and Jenna went into town for a dance, or a dinner, or an official function at the town hall, any occasion that called for a little formality. He would make a habit of taking it from his vest pocket now and then in order to check the time, always – of course – when in company, the whole point being to put it out there on show.

He climbed the grand staircase to the second floor, the bellboy following with his suitcase. He unlocked the door to his room and entered, switching on the electric light, the wall brackets springing to life. *Magic!* The bellboy deposited his suitcase, nodded subserviently, and left. James gazed about, marvelling at the opulence that surrounded him, again catching sight of himself in a mirror. *Well, well, look at you,* he thought. *Here you are back at the Metropole where it all started. Who would have believed any of this possible?*

He could see Ben lounging back on the sofa right there. A different sofa this time, not an apricot shade, but just as elegant. He could see Ben over there by the sideboard, pouring cognac into a brandy balloon. He could see Ben leaning forward across the coffee table, glass raised in a toast.

'To the magical age of eighteen.'

He could hear Ben's voice and the clink of their glasses; he could see Ben's eyes as they met his across the rim of their brandy balloons; he could smell the fumes and taste the burn of his first sip of cognac . . . He was surrounded by yesteryear.

Throughout the whole of the following day, James continued to see Ben. Even when he paid a visit to Sydney Grammar School to enrol Josh – having written in advance for an appointment – there was Ben.

Sydney Grammar School was in College Street, opposite Hyde Park. A magnificent sandstone building designed by the colonial architect, James Barnet, as central to the cultural focus of Sydney Town. But James wasn't looking at the 'Big School' building, as it was known, he was staring across College Street at the park. It was right there, in that very clearing, that he'd first met Ben.

After completing his son's enrolment, James didn't visit Potts Point to check on the lodgings where it was suggested Josh be housed, deciding his inspection could wait until tomorrow. If the household appeared unsuitable he would find another in any event and Jenna would be none the wiser. Instead, he revisited the past as he'd promised himself he would.

He walked along the old familiar route of Oxford Street, turning into Bourke, amazed that things hadn't changed all that much really, everything remained recognisable to him. He popped into the Great Western Hotel, only to discover it was no longer the Great Western but the Hopetoun, renamed in 1901 as a tribute to John Hope, 7th Earl of Hopetoun, who'd been created Australia's first Governor-General. At least that's what he was told upon enquiry.

Clyde was no longer the hotel's publican and James didn't recognise the worker behind the bar. Nor did he recognise any of the locals who were currently drinking there, but the atmosphere was very much the same. He ate a lunch of bread, cheese and pickles, drank a pint of beer and once again saw Ben, mingling with ease the way Ben had among the rough, working-class men who frequented the Great Western and other such pubs that abounded in Surry Hills.

He left and wandered along Bourke Street to the bigger terrace houses, the ones with basements.

That one had been his, he thought, that one there in need of a coat of paint, looking even shabbier than it had in those days, but otherwise much the same. That had been his basement. He could picture Ben there too, on the other side of that door at the bottom of the steps, the pair of them sharing cheap brandy. 'Next time I'm bringing cognac,' he could hear Ben say.

That night he visited the Hampton Club, where normally he would have worn his fob watch and chain, a place like the Hampton Club being the perfect venue for such accoutrements. He decided against it, however. Not that anyone would see the watch itself, tucked away in his vest pocket, but what if someone were to ask the time when he was in the presence of the Grenfell brothers? That wouldn't do at all.

He'd fully expected to see the Grenfells and was quite prepared to join them for a game of poker; he would have

liked the opportunity to drop a casual mention of his
new position in society. But the Grenfells were not there.
Probably because it wasn't a Friday.

Ben was there though. Ben was at the poker table. And
he was in the lounge downing a cognac. And he was at the
bar having a beer.

Oh Christ, James thought, *you're everywhere, Ben.
You're bloody well everywhere!*

The following day, James got down to the business of his
son's lodgings. The address Leonard Crompton had given
him was in Victoria Street, Potts Point, and he walked
there from the Metropole. A very pleasant walk through
Hyde Park, first down and then up the hill of William
Street and into the broad, leafy avenue of Victoria.

He discovered the house to be quite grand. Built of
sandstone and freestanding among its many conjoined
neighbours, it featured a far wider frontage than those of
the terraces, with a central front door, bay windows either
side, and a verandah that stretched the whole width. It
stood two storeys high with an upstairs balcony displaying
the customary decorative iron lacework that was so fashionable, and built on a hill as it was, also boasted a large
basement with a courtyard and a door that led in from the
narrow lane on one side. The house was set back from
the street, the attractive moulded gate of its iron-railing
fence invitingly open, a short path leading up to the front
door, flanked by pretty flower beds.

James studied the house approvingly. It was certainly
large enough to accommodate a number of young students,
he thought.

He walked through the gate, along the path, up the two
steps to the verandah and rapped three times with the
heavy brass lion's head door knocker. Then he stood back
and waited.

The woman who answered the door was elderly, late sixties, possibly even seventy, but by no means infirm. Her appearance was stern if anything; rigid-backed, white-haired, a face more masculine than feminine; the sort of woman who would frighten young boys, there was something military about her. *Most promising,* James thought.

'Miss Allbright?' he queried.

'That is correct.' Her voice, too, had a military edge.

'I'm James Brereton-McKinnon.'

'Ah, yes,'—she thrust out her hand—'Mr Crompton wrote informing me you were likely to call upon us.' The handshake, although bony, was as firm as any man's. 'Do come in.'

She stood aside, he entered and she closed the front door behind them.

He was standing in a hallway with a door either side, ahead to the right a staircase that led to the upper floors, to the left a passage that led to the rest of the ground floor. He briefly noted that the hall rug was not of the finest quality, but hardy; that the railings of the staircase were well designed and of good, solid blackwood; and that the wall-bracketed lighting fixtures were not particularly ornate, but serviceable. The house itself would once have been a handsome dwelling, but the décor and fittings were sadly lacking any personal flair. This was a house converted to serve a practical purpose.

Miss Allbright picked up a bell that sat on the hall table and rang it sharply, startling him considerably and allowing him no time for further assessment.

'Follow me.' Putting down the bell, she marched through the open door to the right and he trailed obediently after her into a front room that reflected the character he'd already observed. A room that should have been impressive, high moulded ceiling, decorative cornices, pretty bay

windows looking out to the street, but with furnishings
no more than functional, furnishings that might even be
termed 'cheap' – James had come to recognise true quality
furniture. The large desk that dominated the room, the
Carver that sat behind it, the several hard-back chairs lined
up in front as if arranged for an interview, all were of pine.
Here, too, the rug was hardy, and the drapes either side of
the windows were not plush velvet, but heavy-duty cotton,
everything intended again to be purely functional.

'Do please sit, Mr Brereton-McKinnon.'

Seating herself behind the desk, Miss Allbright gestured
to one of the hard-back chairs and he sat as she continued
seamlessly.

'Mr Crompton mentioned you might wish to book your
son in with us,' she said, 'his nephew Harold is one of our
student lodgers, you know.'

'Yes, so he told me.' Even as James was wondering
who the 'us' might be, two more elderly women appeared
at the open office door, having been summoned, it would
seem, by the bell. He guessed them to be in their early to
mid-sixties, a good deal prettier than Miss Allbright and
strangely similar to one another. He wondered whether
they might be sisters.

The women entered the room, closing the door behind
them, and he rose to his feet.

'May I introduce Mrs Adcock and Mrs Muldoon,'
Miss Allbright announced. 'Ladies, this is Mr
Brereton-McKinnon.'

Handshakes and 'how-do-you-dos' were shared and,
upon a gesture from Miss Allbright, all three of them sat
in the hard-back chairs facing the desk.

No one uttered a word – it was obvious to James that
no one was expected to – as Miss Allbright took up a pen
and opened the large, ledger-like book that sat on the desk
before her.

'You are most fortunate, Mr Brereton-McKinnon, for we do have a vacancy at the moment. Just the one. We accommodate twelve students here at Allbright House and there are presently eleven. Your timing is perfect. May I have your son's details?'

James was taken aback. Surely he should be given a tour of 'Allbright House' (he hadn't seen the name displayed out the front) before they got down to business. But he was apparently so privileged to be allotted lodging here for his son that he found himself automatically answering the questions she fired at him. Josh's name? Age? Medical condition? Any chronic allergies that might require dietary attention?

'Mrs Adcock is a retired nurse,' Miss Allbright explained, 'the health of our boys is of paramount importance at all times.'

The list continued. Finally she closed the book.

'Well that seems to have completed the formalities,' she said, and then she went on to explain the cost of the lodgings per school term, with enquiries as to whether Josh would be going home for holidays, and whether he would require a daily lunch packed for him, which she strongly recommended he should.

'We have an excellent cook and kitchen assistant,' she said. 'A growing boy's diet demands full attention.'

The interview, if such it could be termed, appeared to have come to an end, and apart from responding to Miss Allbright's rapid-fire questions, James had uttered not a word of his own. No input had been invited of him. Nor of the Mesdames Adcock and Muldoon, for that matter, other than nods of agreement now and then.

James was satisfied with the costs, substantial as they were. However, there was one matter he felt should be brought up for discussion.

'Mr Crompton did mention a "guardianship" factor,' he said. 'Given my son's youth and the fact that he will not have yet turned thirteen years of age when he joins you early next year . . .'

'Yes, yes of course,' Miss Allbright briskly replied, 'we ladies take on all aspects of guardianship.' She looked to her colleagues, who nodded effusively. 'Not in the official legal sense, you understand, we are not an adoption agency.' An intended witticism, her smile was brittle. 'But we care very much for our boys, devoting our personal attention to each and every one. We like to think we provide them with no less than *three* mothers, don't we ladies?'

Further smiles were shared all round.

'Now,' she continued as she rose to her feet, 'I presume you'll be wanting to take a look at your son's future home.'

He stood, nonplussed by the speed of events. 'Yes. Thank you.'

A brief tour of Allbright House ensued, personally conducted by Miss Albright while the mesdames excused themselves to return to their chores various.

First the kitchen and dining room at the rear of the ground floor. A servery one end, a long wooden table, benches either side, austere but spotlessly clean. He was then taken directly upstairs, the remainder of the ground floor housing the women's quarters, which were naturally off limits. Upstairs, two dormitories, four boys to a room, two twin bunks in each, upper and lower. A shared wash-room and lavatory. Then straight down to the basement. There, one dormitory, another two twin bunks. Next door, the common room where the lads could all study together before bed time, or quietly pursue leisure activities. 'Jigsaw puzzles and the like,' he was told, 'nothing noisy.' A further washroom and toilet. And out the back, the house built on a hill as it was, the basement led to a courtyard surrounded by a high stone wall.

During the tour, which was conducted at lightning speed, they came upon a worker here and there – a kitchenhand

chopping vegetables for the evening stew, a maid cleaning the basement bathroom, the mesdames themselves
hanging linen on the clothes line in the courtyard, but no
sign of any lodgers. Being mid-morning and mid-term the
place was deserted, the boys all at school, but James was
astounded at how neat and tidy everything was, including
the dormitories. There was no evidence at all of boisterous,
messy young lads. He commented upon the fact.

'Yes, we don't allow slovenliness at Allbright House,'
came the stern reply.

Twenty minutes later he was out in the street wondering how everything had happened so quickly. Wondering
also about the very militant Miss Allbright and the Mesdames Adcock and Muldoon, who looked so like sisters.
Were they?

All three were sisters, actually. Daughters of a military man. It had been the idea of the eldest, Prudence, to
convert the old family home to a lodging house for young
male students. Those who attended Sydney Grammar
School within easy walking distance; those who were the
sons of wealthy, successful men. It would give her two
younger widowed sisters something to do with their lives
and hopefully earn them all a decent living. Her sisters'
husbands had been spineless, useless men, leaving their
wives with nothing. So unlike the father whom Prudence
Allbright had idolised and emulated the whole of her life.
Had Prudence been born a male, as she heartily wished she
had, she would have joined the army.

Satisfied that his mission had been successfully accomplished, James returned to Glenfinnan. He'd enjoyed his
trip to Sydney, brief though it was, and looked forward
to repeating the experience early the following year when
he would bring Josh to the city. Sydney was certainly
stimulating. But for a short visit only, he reminded himself.
Glenfinnan was where he truly belonged. No, more than

that. Far more than that. Glenfinnan was his life, the very
air that he breathed.

James remained determined to fulfil his obligation to
Alastair McKinnon. At thirty-two years of age he was now
patriarch of Glenfinnan, responsible for the future of the
McKinnon family and the honour of their name.

With this responsibility uppermost in mind, he had
taken Phil Caton on as his partner right from the start.
The quality of Glenfinnan wool had to be maintained at
all costs.

'I'll be relying on your knowledge and expertise Phil,'
he'd insisted. 'Hell, what do I know about breeding, I'm a
bloody shearer! I need more than a Station Manager, mate,
I need a partner who really knows the ropes.'

Phil had agreed. They'd hired a new Station Manager
and it was Phil who had, from that day on, looked after
all aspects of breeding management that had once been
Alastair's domain, the only part irksome to him being the
necessary trips to Sydney his seniority now demanded.

The decision had proved a wise one. Glenfinnan wool
still bore the McKinnon brand. They hadn't even changed
the stencils they used to stamp the bales, which read *Glenfinnan, McKinnon.* And the reports that arrived from
independent assessors remained as glowing as they had
been in Alastair's day. An account published in one of the
chief pastoral journals in that very year of 1907 was proof
of the fact.

'. . . *the McKinnon breed favours a bold type of sheep
with good heavy necks free from body wrinkles. Stud rams
of this type cut 28 pounds of wool for twelve months'
growth and stud ewes of similar type 18 pounds, whole
flocks of three-year-old wethers averaging 14 pounds
9 ounces. McKinnon remains a credit to the country,
doing much to advance the standard of the pure Merino
sheep of Australia . . .'*

It appeared at times as if Alastair were still alive, which very much pleased James, being indisputable proof that he was fulfilling his promise to the old man.

In the meantime, with a business manager, accountant and secretary looking after the financial side of things, he was free to bask in his position as one of the landed gentry, a fact which never ceased to amaze and delight him. *Well, well,* he would think, *who would have believed this possible?*

James' life certainly bore all the trappings of wealth. Far more so than Alastair's had. More servants were employed at the Big House these days, although they were never referred to as 'servants', but 'staff', just as Alastair himself had decreed. Millie and Boris were still there, but Beth had retired to live with her sister in Adelaide, and a new couple, Maude and Wallace Briggs, pleasant middle-aged Lancastrians, had joined the ranks of live-in domestic help. Maude was employed as housekeeper and cook, and Wallace principally as chauffeur, although in truth he served a far broader purpose. Being a qualified mechanic, Wallace was responsible not only for the upkeep of James' recently acquired motor vehicles but the steam-driven shearing machines, now numbering fourteen, and also the carbide plant at the rear of the garden, which provided gas lighting for the Big House.

There were other domestic workers, all of whom lived in nearby staff houses and who arrived on a daily basis to tend to the general cleaning and laundry. There was also a full-time gardener responsible for the upkeep of the attractively designed informal front gardens and flower beds, together with the maintenance and re-planting of the ever-expanding vegetable plots and the pruning and harvesting of the fruit trees and vines that supplied the entire fresh produce required at the Big House.

This left Boris free of his former gardening duties and able to devote himself exclusively to equine affairs, which was essential these days given the extension to the stables, the acquisition of purebred horses and the hiring of two new stablehands to serve under his management.

James did not view the employment of extra staff as excessive in any way, considering the added expenditure perfectly valid. A property like Glenfinnan required a great deal of upkeep. Besides, he didn't laze away his time, he still worked daily alongside his farmhands, relishing the physical labour, and he and Jenna did after all have three young children to rear.

Jenna, too, welcomed the extra staff, particularly once her children had grown well past the toddler stage. With so many ready people on hand to keep an eye on the youngsters she had all the time in the world to devote to her horses. A staunch member of the Tirranna Picnic Race Club, Jenna devoted herself not only to her horses and to the club, but to picnic racing in general, a sport of tremendous importance throughout the entire region. Country folk travelled long distances to attend and compete their animals at the annual race meetings that were a township's pride and joy.

The Tirranna Picnic Race Club was something of an institution, having been established by local landowners in 1855 at a property just outside Goulburn. When the City of Goulburn's railway had officially opened in 1869, making the Tirranna Picnic Races accessible to Sydney racing enthusiasts, it had soon become known that the track was one of the best in the colony. As a consequence, the annual meet at Tirranna had attracted major interest, receiving regular reportage in the Sydney press, including coverage of the fashions of the day as socialites and those of influence from all walks of life poured into Goulburn by train for one of the events of the season.

With the turn of the century and the federation of the colonies that had ensued the following year, the Tirranna

Picnic Races had retained its popularity, particularly among country communities. People flocked from far and wide to the meet that extended over two days with a huge formal ball to follow. This was the social event of the rural calendar year, and especially for the local property owners of significance, those who pitted their horses against one another in a bid for superiority.

Jenna Brereton-McKinnon considered the Tirranna Picnic Races her personal triumph. And she had every right to do so. A McKinnon-bred horse had won the main race no less than twice over the past four years, claiming the 18-carat-gold Tirranna Picnic Race Club Challenge Cup for Glenfinnan. Jenna was now fervently dedicated to the breeding of race horses. A very expensive hobby.

James was proud of his wife's wins at Tirranna and happy to allow the considerable financial outlay required for the breeding of horses, all of which was excellent for the image of Glenfinnan. He did not personally involve himself in horse racing, however, his interest now lying in motor vehicles, which were surely destined to become the mode of transport for the future.

He'd had a sizeable garage built at the rear of the house in 1905 when he'd acquired his first car, a Swift Tourer, which had taken some time to master. 'A little more complicated than a horse,' he'd said to Jenna. But with excellent tuition from the then newly employed Wallace Briggs he'd learned to tame the beast. Now, two years later, he'd acquired a second car, another Swift, which Wallace had assured him was an excellent make of vehicle. A four-seater with a convertible soft top and powered by a four-cylinder engine, it was an elegant car, and James had now come to feel comfortable at the wheel.

The children, all three, adored motor cars. When the boys came home from St Patrick's College at the week-ends, Sundays were always spent careering around the dirt

tracks of Glenfinnan and out onto the main road, the boys
in the back seat, Emily beside James up the front screaming, 'Faster, Daddy, faster,' at the top of her voice.

Ted, like Emily, was interested primarily in speed and
the faster the better, but Josh professed an interest in learning how to drive, so now and then James would take him
out on his own to give him a lesson. It was uncanny how
quickly the boy picked up the knack.

'You're better at this than I was,' he'd admitted when
they'd first started on the lessons. *Astounding,* he thought.
But then it wasn't really, was it? Josh proved himself pretty
astounding at just about everything he attempted.

Josh made no reply, but returned the compliment with a
dazzling smile, his charm nothing short of astounding too.

There was one aspect of himself James recognised in
Josh. Not the boy's innate talents, nor his charm, but the
interest he displayed in everything and everyone about
him. Josh focused upon things and people with immense
intensity, and always had from a very early age. Did this
perhaps explain his talents? It certainly explained why
people were drawn to him.

James remembered his father saying much the same
thing of him when he was a boy. 'You're a smart lad,
James,' he recalled George Wakefield saying, 'and you're
mature beyond your years. That's what attracts people to
you, son.' *Interesting,* he thought.

The rest of the year fled past and as 1908 dawned,
the time approached when Josh was due to go to Sydney
Grammar. His excitement knew no bounds. He was literally counting the days.

'I wish I was coming with you.' Eleven-year-old Ted was
hugely envious.

'Yeah, me too,' Josh replied sympathetically. He felt sorry
for his little brother. Ted wasn't a very good student, he'd
never get sent to Sydney Grammar. Not that he was dumb

or anything, but Teddy was a bit of a plodder, he wouldn't really amount to much. Like most farmers' sons, Teddy was destined to work on the farm. Josh had other plans.

The boys' cousins, twins Zac and Sam who'd already turned thirteen, were equally envious. 'Wish *we* were going to Sydney,' they grumbled.

But to Josh's mind the same applied to them, they were farm boys at heart. Sydney wouldn't serve them any purpose, they'd just come running back to Glenfinnan and lead the lives fate intended they should. Fate intended a different life for Josh. He wasn't sure what it was yet, but Sydney would be the start of it.

'Yeah, I wish we were all going together,' he said, and he gave a grin that was pure mischief, 'we'd sure as hell cause some trouble, eh?' He didn't for one minute wish they were all going together, he knew he'd be much better off on his own, but he loved his little brother and his cousins. They were good mates. Always had been, always would be.

Wallace drove James and Josh to the station on the Friday, Jenna coming along too in order to farewell her son. Ted and Emily weren't allowed.

'No room,' James said.

As she said her goodbyes, Jenna refused to be cloying. She was not that sort of mother. But she did gather her son to her in a quick, fierce embrace.

'You look after yourself now, Josh,' she ordered.

'Course I will, Mum.' Josh returned the hug and stepped aboard the train to join his father, who was standing at the open door.

A look was exchanged between James and Jenna. He knew how she worried and he returned her query with a confident nod that said, *He'll be fine, I'll make sure of it, I promise.*

Then the door was closed, father and son seated themselves in a carriage, and James leaned from the open window.

'See you in a few days, my love,' he called as the train slowly started to chug its way out of the station.

'See you in three months, Mum,' Josh called, waving excitedly.

James didn't stay on in Sydney for the several extra days he'd intended. There didn't seem any point. After the physical enrolment at Sydney Grammar that same day, where new students were welcomed by the headmaster, introduced to their form master and shown where they were to report the following Monday, James took the boy directly to his lodgings in Potts Point. Here he introduced him to Miss Allbright and the Mesdames Adcock and Muldoon, all of whom were lined up in the front office.

'Welcome to Allbright House, Joshua,' Prudence said.

'He prefers *Josh* actually,' James jumped straight in.

The look Prudence returned was withering. 'The other boys are welcome to adopt the diminutive, Mr Brereton-McKinnon,' she said icily. '*We* shall not.'

Josh was quick to calm the ruffled waters. 'I don't mind, Dad,' he said, and he treated Miss Allbright to a smile that was nothing short of charismatic. 'I like Joshua, actually.'

Prudence gave a terse nod to show she wasn't won quite that easily.

Ten minutes later, as James bade his son farewell, the ladies having left them alone briefly in order to do so, he suggested his plan of action.

'I'm staying on in Sydney for a few days, Josh,' he said. 'I'll call back here, see how you're settling in, we could perhaps have lunch together, and on Monday I'll walk to school with you . . .'

'I'd much rather you didn't, Dad,' Josh replied. 'It'd look as if I'm being mollycoddled. I'll find my way to school with the other boys, and I'll settle in here just fine.'

James understood implicitly. Yes, the boy was right, he thought, it would look like mollycoddling. They shook hands and walked together out into the hall where Miss Allbright was waiting to show Josh upstairs to his dormitory.

'See you in three months, Dad,' Josh said.

'Yep, see you back home, son.'

Josh was asserting his independence, there was no doubt about that. He'd even insisted upon catching the train back to Goulburn on his own when the term was up.

James decided not to stay on in Sydney, much as he'd looked forward to doing so, he'd enjoyed his previous trip. But if he was to be of no assistance to his son it now seemed somehow pointless.

He booked into the Metropole overnight and caught the train back the very next day, little knowing the impact Josh's sojourn in Sydney was to have on his life.

CHAPTER FOURTEEN

It was a crisp Saturday morning in late April when James drove into Goulburn to collect Josh from the railway station. Ted and Emily had insisted upon coming too, so Jenna had graciously declined in order to allow room for them.

'Far too cramped with three in the back,' she'd said, 'I'll welcome him when he gets home. Besides,' she'd added, 'the caterers will be setting up for tomorrow.' A garden party was arranged for Sunday, a typically grand Glenfinnan affair with the entire extended family, any number of neighbours and the hard-working staff, all of whom had been given the day off. Such parties were not unusual, particularly during the racing season, but Jenna had deliberately planned this one to coincide with Josh's homecoming.

The siblings' reunion was raucous from the moment Josh stepped off the train, Emily squealing and jumping up and down, Ted firing questions. 'Is Sydney Harbour as big as they say it is? Did you get to ride on a tram?'

Yes, Josh replied, Sydney Harbour was enormous, and yes, he'd ridden on a tram. 'Tons of times,' he boasted, 'there's lots of them.'

James finally interrupted. 'Let's talk about it during the drive,' he said, picking up Josh's suitcase and shepherding them out of the railway station. 'We want to be home in time for lunch.'

They piled into the car, Josh in the front, Ted and Emily in the back and the chatter continued, although mainly from Josh as, swivelled around in his seat, he enthralled his brother and sister with accounts of Sydney.

'I've done lots of exploring during the weekends,' he told them. 'You can walk to the harbour from where I'm staying in Potts Point. You go down the hill to Elizabeth Bay and you can walk all along the foreshore. It's really beautiful. And you can catch a tram to just about anywhere from Potts Point. My favourite tram's the one that goes to Bondi Beach, you can walk all around the cliffs there and the views are spectacular . . .'

James interrupted. *Is this degree of freedom just a little too much,* he wondered. 'Does Miss Allbright approve of this "exploring" of yours?' he asked. 'It sounds a bit dangerous to me, gallivanting about like that all on your own.'

'Oh we're not allowed to go out on our own,' Josh was quick to reassure his father. 'Not we youngest ones anyway. We have to at least be in pairs, but the five of us younger blokes usually go out together.' They did too, and they went wherever Josh wished to go. It was always Josh who led the troops, the others simply following along. 'Miss Allbright is insistent we look after one another,' he said. 'She's a very strict disciplinarian.'

'Yes, I had a feeling she might be.' James smiled. 'A bit of a martinet I would think. I hope you don't cause her any trouble.'

'No, I'm no trouble to her, Dad, she likes me.' Josh returned the smile. Of course Miss Allbright liked him. He was her favourite, because she knew he looked after the other boys.

Josh had quickly learned how to play Miss Allbright. Charm didn't win her the way it did the other two old ladies. Nor did subservience for that matter, she didn't want a lackey or a toady. She wanted a boy with leadership qualities, one she could trust. And Josh had made sure he fitted the bill.

'Miss Allbright and I get on really well,' he said, and having successfully appeased any worries his father might have had, he returned his attention to his audience in the back seat.

'I tell you what though, Teddy, the best place of all is Speakers Corner at the Domain on Sundays.' A shake of his head in wonderment as he addressed his brother directly, aware that Ted in particular would love this part. 'Speakers Corner is really something! The Butler Stairs are just along the street from Allbright House, you see, and they go right down the hill. They're huge and they're steep – one hundred and three steps in all, I've counted them – and if you go down them you can cut through Woolloomooloo at the bottom and then you're up the hill into Hyde Park . . .'

At the mention of Woolloomooloo and Hyde Park, James was on instant alert.

'. . . All sorts of speakers gather there to rant about their causes,' Josh went on, 'and the people you see, the things you hear. It's called freedom of speech, Teddy! True democracy!' Josh was firing himself up, just the way the speakers did, and Teddy was hanging on his every word.

James couldn't help interrupting once again. 'Woolloomooloo and Hyde Park can be unsavoury places, Josh,' he said. 'I trust you boys keep well clear of these areas after dark?'

Josh gave a hoot of laughter as if the mere suggestion was ludicrous. 'Crikey, Dad, we don't go *anywhere* after dark. Allbright House is a *prison* at night. Those old ladies are gaolers, I tell you. Every door to the outside world is locked.' He cast a humorous look to his brother and sister and pulled a silly face for their amusement. 'The old ladies keep us under lock and key after dark for fear we might turn into the murderous thugs that deep down they believe we truly are.'

Ted and Emily both laughed, Josh could be so funny.

Josh was gratified by the reaction. He would tell Teddy later that he *did* go out after dark. That he'd learned how to scale the basement's courtyard wall. That he'd swapped places with one of the boys in the downstairs dormitory in order to do so. He would tell Teddy how everyone had thought him so kind to offer Gordon his upstairs bunk, the upstairs dormitories being considered superior with their rear-balcony views across Woolloomooloo. So much more attractive than the walled-in claustrophobic courtyard the basement offered. But you couldn't escape from a two-storey-high balcony, could you? You could escape over an eight-foot-high wall though, once you'd fretted away at the chips and niches in the old stonework.

Josh loved roaming the streets of Sydney at night. He always took care to keep out of sight, but that made things even more exciting. Skulking about in the shadows, watching people who had no idea they were being watched, one got to see so much more. He would tell Teddy all of this later, and Teddy as always would be spellbound.

'So how do you get on with the other boys at Allbright House?' James asked, relieved to hear the old ladies were such successful gaolers, although in the case of Miss Allbright not particularly surprised.

'We get on really well, Dad,' Josh replied. 'Us younger ones anyway, there's four other blokes my age and we're good mates. The older boys don't tend to pay us all that much attention.' *Well they don't anymore, do they,* Josh thought. They had to begin with though. The older boys had set out to bully the new arrivals simply as a matter of course, but it hadn't worked.

'And Harold Crompton?' James was interested to hear about Leonard Crompton's nephew. 'How do you get on with Harold? What's he like?'

Josh decided to tell the truth. Harold had been the ringleader, after all. Harold was a bastard. 'He's fifteen, one of the older boys, and I don't like him.'

'Oh? Why's that?'

'He's a bully.'

'Really?' James was surprised to hear it. A well-bred upper-class boy like Harold Crompton? 'He tried to bully you, did he?'

'He tried to bully all of us younger ones who'd just arrived.'

'And what did you do?'

'I belted him. Twice.' Josh flashed a triumphant grin at his father. 'Just like you taught me, Dad.' He held up his right hand, fist firmly clenched. 'Once to the solar plexus, then to the jaw. Hurt my knuckles, but he went down like a sack of potatoes. Chipped a tooth too.'

James laughed. With pride, certainly. And, although he didn't quite know why, he rather liked the idea of Leonard Crompton's nephew getting a hiding. 'Good for you, son.'

'He didn't come back at any of us after that. Stopped picking on the younger blokes altogether. Harold Crompton's like all bullies. He's really a coward underneath.'

James felt a further rush of pride at the maturity of his son's assessment. 'I'd have to agree with you there, Josh. Bullies and cowards go hand in hand. And what about your schoolmates? Have you made good friends with the boys at school?'

'Oh yes, school's easy.' Josh gave a careless shrug. Everything about school was easy. The studies that he breezed through, the sports he excelled at, the friendships he made being a gregarious boy to whom others gravitated.

'I must say I'm really pleased with your term report,' James said, 'and so is your mother; she's as pleased as punch.'

The term report from Sydney Grammar had been glowing. Josh had quickly established himself as a star student, academically gifted, physically talented and popular with his fellow students. Not only had he achieved excellent marks in all subjects, but the teachers considered him obedient and personable. There really wasn't much more one could ask for, James and Jenna had agreed.

'We're both very proud of you, Josh.'

'Thanks Dad.' Josh considered he'd met all requirements of the questionnaire and as he'd lost the interest of his audience in the back seat, Ted and Emily now simply enjoying the drive, he decided this was the right time to introduce the topic uppermost in his mind. The matter of the librarian.

'Hey, Dad,' he said, 'there's someone I want you to meet in Sydney. Well, actually, there's someone who wants to meet *you*.'

'Oh yes?'

'She's the librarian at the Free Public Library in Bent Street, I go there now and then to study. We got talking the day I signed up for my membership and she was very keen to know more about me.'

James was intrigued. *She?* Surely Josh was a bit young to be interested in girls. And a librarian would hardly be a girl anyway. The boy was looking a little out of his age range, wasn't he?

'Why would your librarian want to meet me, son?'

'Because we have the same name. She's a Brereton like us. And guess what, Dad,' Josh continued eagerly, 'she comes from Queensland. I told her you came from Queensland too, and she's awfully keen to know if we're related.'

'I see.' *A Brereton. And from Queensland.* James was not unduly alarmed, but his mind was sifting through the facts. Could the librarian possibly be Harriet Brereton? Too much of a coincidence, surely. 'Is she old, this librarian?' he asked. Harriet would certainly be old by now.

'No, no, she's young,' Josh replied, 'and she's pretty too.' Josh had certainly noticed how pretty Miss Brereton was. He'd soon be thirteen and he was noticing girls quite a bit lately, women too for that matter. The young ones who were pretty, anyway. 'Miss Brereton's awfully keen to meet you, Dad. Will you come to Sydney with me when I go back next term? I promised I'd introduce you to her.'

Why not, James thought, *where's the harm?* 'Of course I'll come, Josh. I shall look forward to meeting her, it'll be fun.'

The weather stayed pleasantly fine for the garden party the following day. There must have been a hundred or more guests and at least half of them, it seemed, were of McKinnon blood. The families of Alastair's sisters Adriana and Alexandra had swollen immeasurably in numbers as their collective nine children had married and given birth to a new generation. Furthermore, they'd married locally, settling on the Goulburn plains as McKinnons did. With the addition of Adele, her husband Phil Caton and brood of four there was McKinnon blood aplenty, all would agree. But only one family present bore the McKinnon name.

James and Jenna stood on the front verandah, master and mistress of the Big House, and as they welcomed each new arrival James basked in the knowledge that it was he who was now the true patriarch of this dynasty.

Several generations being present among both family and neighbours, guests tended to group themselves according to age. The elderly were respectfully acknowledged then left to sit gossiping among themselves at the tables set

out on the surrounding verandahs, waiters hovering over
them with drinks and canapes. The middle-aged wandered
about the gardens, glasses in hand, women admiring one
another, or pretending to, as they paraded their fashionable gowns and bonnets, men energetically discussing the
business of farming, the current market and the general
news of the day. Young mothers with babies and toddlers
sat together on blankets overseeing child-minding duties
while the older children, free to roam at will, made their
own social choices, also according to age. Those older and
on the cusp of maturity tended towards flirtation, while
for those less mature, competition was the order of the
day, and the youngest ones simply threw themselves whole-
heartedly into raucous play.

Josh was tempted to flirt with one of his distant cousins,
Mary Louise. She was the youngest of Adriana's grand-
daughters who had, all of a sudden at the age of thirteen,
become frightfully pretty. And she had budding breasts.
Josh had of late been finding breasts distractingly attractive.
But when Zac and Sam produced the well-worn fifty-foot
length of rope and started rounding up a tug-o-war team he
changed his mind. He and Teddy would lead the other team,
he declared, eight to a side, and they would win.

They didn't, which Josh accepted in his customary good-
natured fashion, but after the tug-o-war came the races,
which he organised himself between all the boys roughly
his age. The races were followed by long jumps and then
arm-wrestling, and he managed to win most events, for he
was not only athletically talented, but very competitive.
By now, Mary Louise had ceased to exist.

Later, as the adults were served from the buffet stands
on the verandahs, taking their meals to the many tables
set up here and there, and as the children sprawled out on
the picnic rugs provided, Josh, Ted, Zac and Sam found a
space of their own well away from the others.

Leaning up against the walls of the wash house, they scoffed back their chicken sandwiches in thick, crusty bread and their homemade, oven-baked sausage rolls with tomato chutney. Maude Briggs had refused to allow the caterers carte blanche. As a cook, and an English cook at that, she was inordinately proud of, and eminently famous for, her sausage rolls. And no one made tomato chutney quite like Maude's.

The boys had shooed away the company of their siblings, little Emily Jane and the twins' younger sister, Mathilda and their baby brother, seven-year-old Thomas, all of whom had tried to join them. The four were a world unto themselves. Having grown up so closely and being of a similar age, they were really more like brothers than cousins. And there was a particular reason why they sought their privacy today. Josh had stories to tell.

As they sat devouring Maude's sausage rolls, he told them all about his true adventures in Sydney, how he'd scaled the courtyard's wall and roamed the streets, particularly on a Saturday night. He held nothing back. Teddy was not the only one with whom Josh shared everything.

'I know where the prostitutes ply their trade,' he said. 'I've watched them in Darlinghurst, that's a suburb not far from where I'm lodging. Crikey, you should just see them, they're bold as brass! The way they strut their wares. The low-cut blouses, you can see just about everything. And the way they jiggle their breasts.' He imitated the action, thrusting out his chest and wriggling it comically from side to side, aware the others were riveted. Then he told them the part he knew would truly impress. 'I even met one of them once.'

'You met a prostitute?' Ted queried, jaw agape.

'Yep. It was early in the evening, and she was on her own. She'd only just taken up her spot.' Josh was milking the story for all it was worth, enjoying every moment. 'She works the corner of Palmer Street, I'd seen her there before.

Anyway, she noticed me hanging around in the shadows and walked right up to me. Asked me what I was doing, accused me of spying on her.'

'What did you do?' Teddy again, still agape.

'Said I just liked to look at her 'cos I thought she was pretty.'

Zac burst out laughing. 'Geez, I bet that won her over.'

'It did. And I tell you what,' Josh went on in earnest, 'I wasn't lying, she really *is* pretty. Much younger than the other ones. She's my favourite.'

'So what did she say?' Zac asked. Gosh, how he wished he had adventures like this. He envied Josh. If he'd been confronted by a courtyard wall he would have found a way to scale it too.

'She told me to come back in five years.' The remark raised a laugh from them all. Then Josh added, 'And she told me to be careful. Said I could find myself in trouble sneaking around the streets at night.'

'She's right.' Sam's was the voice of reason, as it so often was. Sam was the sensible one of the twins. Gangly like their father and very obviously brothers, the two were non-identical in both appearance and nature, Zac adventurous and prone to take chances, Sam not timid, but practical, tending more to restraint. 'It's a dangerous thing you're doing, Josh,' he advised in all seriousness, 'you want to watch out. Everyone says Sydney's a really tough place.'

'Yeah, yeah.' Josh gave an easy shrug. 'I can look after myself.' He was showing off, certainly, but he loved impressing the others. It gave him great joy to entertain them the way he did. Particularly Teddy, knowing how Teddy just idolised his big brother.

The school holidays flew by, seeming like days rather than weeks, and before they knew it the second term was upon them. Time for Josh to return to Sydney. And as James had promised, time for him to accompany his son in order to meet the young librarian who was so keen to discover whether or not they were related.

On the Sunday morning, as he sat watching the country-side whizz by through the train carriage's window, James wondered about Josh's 'Miss Brereton'. He was not in the least perturbed. No one would ever suspect he had adopted the name, that he was not and never had been a Brereton. Why should they? There could be many Breretons in the world, this was simply a matter of coincidence, no more. But he still wondered what she would be like, this librarian.

'Dad, may I introduce Miss Brereton. Miss Brereton, this is my father, James Brereton-McKinnon.'

It was lunchtime the following day, Monday. The three of them were standing in the foyer of the Free Public Library on the corner of Bent and Macquarie streets and Josh's introduction was made with all the impressive formality he intended. He felt proud introducing these two; his father the fine gentleman in a smart three-piece suit, heavy gold watch chain dangling from vest pocket, and Miss Brereton as pretty as a picture. Josh had to admit he had a distinct crush on Miss Brereton and it was certainly his wish to impress her.

'How do you do, Miss Brereton.' James extended his hand. *So this is the librarian,* he thought. Josh had said she was young and he'd been right, she couldn't have been more than twenty, if that. Josh had also said she was pretty, but she was far more than pretty. This young woman was devastatingly attractive. Fair hair tied up in a chignon, the bluest of eyes that danced, and from what he could make out beneath the modesty of her dress, a body that might well be perfect.

'How do you do, Mr Brereton-McKinnon.'

Her handshake was firm, James liked that, and her smile was warm, he liked that too.

'I've looked forward to meeting you,' she said. 'Josh has spoken so much about you. I believe you come from Queensland?'

'Yes, that's correct, it's where I grew up,' he replied.

She seemed quite prepared to stand there talking, but James had a far better idea.

'Would you care for a spot of lunch?' he suggested. 'I'm staying nearby at the Metropole Hotel, and Josh and I thought we'd have a quick bite there before he needs to get back to school. He's halfway through his lunch break and we don't have much time.'

'Oh dear me, the Metropole . . .'

He very much liked the way she made no attempt to disguise the fact she was a little awe-struck by the Metropole Hotel. *How beguiling,* he thought.

'That would be lovely,' she said, 'I happen to have just started on a lunch break myself.'

'Yes, we'd hoped that might be the case.'

It was only a five-minute walk to the Metropole, and upon their arrival they settled themselves at a window table overlooking the passing parade of Phillip Street. James ordered drinks and a platter of mixed sandwiches for three, which they agreed given the limitations of a lunch break would be the quickest option, and then the conversation began, Miss Brereton keen to lead the way.

'As Josh may have mentioned, Mr Brereton-McKinnon,' she said, 'I'm interested to discover whether we may be related. I have no family, you see, my parents are both dead, and I've never before met someone with the same name. Josh told me you're a Brereton and that the McKinnon part of your name comes from your wife's family.' She flashed a glance at Josh, hoping she wasn't getting the boy into trouble, but Josh just returned a breezy smile.

'That's correct.' James was quick to put her at her ease. 'Where in Queensland do you come from, may I ask?'

'The Central Western region,' he replied, 'Longreach, Aramac, Barcaldine. Sheep country. My father was a shearer and we travelled around a lot.'

'I come from the same region,' she said eagerly. 'I grew up at Bowen Downs Station. Or rather at an outstation of Bowen Downs. There are many outstations. As you probably know, Bowen Downs is enormous.'

James found the excitement in her smile thoroughly engaging. 'Yes, indeed, massive,' he agreed, 'and hugely successful. They run cattle as well as sheep.'

'That's right . . .'

She was about to go on, but was interrupted by the arrival of the sandwiches, cut neatly into quarters and set out on a large silver platter, and also the drinks, two orange juices and a glass of beer for James. But as soon as the waiter had departed she continued, her eagerness unabated.

'So as we come from the same region it is possible we may be related, do you not think?' she asked hopefully. 'Do you have any other relatives in Central Queensland, or elsewhere for that matter, through which we may discover some link?'

Josh, who'd said nothing throughout the entire conversation, was already digging hungrily into the sandwiches, downing each one in two bites, but he'd been following their every word and continued to do so, eyes darting from Miss Brereton to his father, hoping against hope that they might be related.

'I'm sorry to be a disappointment, Miss Brereton,' James said, 'but I can offer you no help at all. Although I grew up in Queensland, I was born in England. I came out to Australia with my father as a very young boy, and I have no knowledge of any living relatives. My mother died in childbirth so I have no memory of her, and my father was killed during the Queensland shearing riots when I was sixteen years old.'

James always stuck to the truth. He'd made a habit of doing so over the years, embellishing his background with George Wakefield's fanciful stories it was true, but adhering to the basic facts, the only outright lie being his name.

'I really can't see how we could be related, I'm afraid,' he concluded apologetically.

'Oh. What a pity.'

Her disappointment was palpable, and so was Josh's. He knew the whole story of his father's background, but had hoped they might discover some link, he would so like to have been related to Miss Brereton. He grabbed a fifth sandwich and pushed the platter in her direction.

'These are awfully good,' he said.

'Thank you, Josh.' She smiled her pretty smile and placed a ham sandwich on her side plate.

Josh swigged back the remainder of his orange juice. 'What time is it, Dad?' he asked.

James took the fob watch from his vest pocket and checked the dial. 'A quarter to two.'

'Oh heck, I have to go.' Josh hastily stood, then remembered his manners. 'If you will excuse me please, Miss Brereton.' Once again he adopted the formal approach, even adding a deferential bow of his head.

'Of course,' she replied, 'you mustn't be late for school.'

'They won't mind if I tell them I've been to the library,' he said. 'Study and all that, you know.'

His response was so unashamedly cheeky that she laughed.

James found her laugh beautiful. The sound of it, and the look of it too. He wanted her to laugh again.

'Goodbye son,' he said. 'I'll be staying on in the city for a few days. I'm aware you don't want any "mollycoddling",' he added humorously, 'but you know where to find me should you wish.' He turned to Miss Brereton. 'I take

it you don't have to flee also? I do hope not, you haven't
eaten a thing.'

'No, no, I have another half hour yet.'

'Excellent.' James lifted three of the small, quartered
sandwiches onto his side plate and sat back, prepared to
enjoy himself.

Josh wished he could stay, but leaving the two of them
relishing each other's company he felt so proud to have set
the wheels in motion.

'He's a fine boy, your son, Mr Brereton-McKinnon,' she
said as she watched him go.

'Thank you. Yes, I tend to agree.' James bit into his
chicken sandwich and munched away for a moment or so.
'He's right, they're delicious,' he said as she started on her
choice of ham. 'It's a bit of a mouthful really, isn't it?'

She looked a query and he smiled.

'Not the sandwich,' he said, 'the name. Brereton-
McKinnon, bit much don't you think? I'd far prefer you
called me James.' He hoped she didn't consider him too
forward.

She didn't. 'Very well, James. And I'm Cordelia.'

'Ah. Unusual. I've never met a Cordelia.'

'Oh no one calls me Cordelia, I'm Delia for short,' she
said, reaching for a second sandwich, chicken this time.
'You're right, these are delicious.'

She had a healthy appetite. He liked that.

'Cordelia's from *King Lear*,' she explained, 'my mother
was a great fan of William Shakespeare and *King Lear* was
her favourite.'

He nodded as if he understood, although he had no idea
who King Lear might be. Not that it mattered. He loved
the way she managed to eat and talk and look beautiful all
at the same time.

'Cordelia's the nice one,' she went on, 'Mum always said
any mother who called her daughter Goneril or Regan
deserved to be shot.'

She laughed, so he laughed with her, still not understanding the reference, but delighting in the bonhomie.

'So which should I call you,' he asked, starting on his ham sandwich, 'Cordelia or Delia?'

'Oh Delia. Most definitely Delia. Mum was the only person who insisted upon Cordelia. She said as I'd been named after King Lear's only decent daughter it was sacrilegious to shorten it. But she didn't really mind at all, she was only joking.'

'Your mother sounds like a humorous woman.' James would rather they got away from King Lear before she discovered his ignorance.

'Yes, I suppose she could be.' Delia nodded thoughtfully as she helped herself to a third sandwich, telling herself they were only small after all. 'At least she could be with me, humorous and warm, we were very close. But I think I was the only one who ever really knew her. Other children found her a remote sort of figure. She was very strict with her pupils.'

'Pupils? She was a schoolteacher then?'

'Yes, that's right.'

'What was her name?' *It's not possible surely,* he thought.

'Harriet.'

Harriet Brereton. James could see her as clearly as if it were yesterday, the prim, little bespectacled school mistress with whom he'd lodged in Aramac. The woman he'd wished might be his mother. How she'd pushed him away when as a little boy he'd tried to cuddle up to her. Yes, she was certainly a remote figure. But it hadn't stopped him admiring her, had it? It hadn't stopped him adopting her name.

'Which do you prefer,' he asked, 'the ham or the chicken?'

'I like this one best, actually,' Delia said, peeling back the bread to look at the filling. 'It's cheese, cheddar I think, but with some delicious sort of pickle or gherkin.'

'Ah. I must try one then, mustn't I?' He took a cheese sandwich from the platter and placed it on his side plate, but he was no longer remotely interested in sandwiches. 'I'm intrigued,' he said casually, leaning in to study her with renewed interest, 'what on earth was a school-teacher doing at Bowen Downs Station?' *So this is Harriet Brereton's daughter.* He could think of nothing else. *How fascinating.*

'My mother had been a teacher at the school in Aramac . . .'

Yes, I know that.

'She was offered a position with a couple who ran one of the major outstations at Bowen Downs. They had three young children of school age and needed a governess, so she was ably qualified.'

I thought only the wealthier landowners employed governesses . . .

'My father died when I was little, and my mother found it convenient being able to work in a private home while raising a child.'

Ah, that explains it. Harriet Brereton would have worked principally for her keep, like many employees in remote outposts.

'I grew up with the Macreadys, a devoutly Christian family, my mother was indispensable to them. I never really got to know the children, who were much older than me, but when the whole family moved from Queensland to Sydney to look after Mrs Macready's aged parents, we moved with them, my mother still in their employ.'

James was spellbound by Delia's story, which to him did not add up at all. Yet she didn't appear to be lying.

'So you don't remember your father?' he asked.

'No, sadly. I was only a baby when Albert Brereton died. He was a foreman at Aramac Station. Life was very hard for my mother after he'd gone.'

'Yes, I can imagine it would be.' *But Harriet Brereton was a widow when I knew her as a boy,* James thought, *and a childless widow at that. Yet upon giving birth later in life she retained her previous husband's name, which can mean only one thing. Although Delia is convinced Albert Brereton was her father, she must have been born out of wedlock. How very interesting.*

Delia was starting to feel self-conscious, and also unnerved, caught in his gaze as she was. The intensity of those ice-blue eyes focused solely upon her. No one had ever looked at her this way. It was as if he found her mesmerising.

He did.

She tried her best to break the spell.

'You haven't finished your sandwiches,' she said, indicating the two quarters that sat on his side plate.

The distraction didn't work.

'Actually, I'm thinking of ordering another beer,' he said, his eyes not leaving hers for a second. 'Would you care for another orange juice? Or perhaps a beer yourself? Or perhaps a glass of wine?'

She gave a light laugh. At least it was meant to be a light laugh, but instead it sounded a little shaky. 'Why don't I be wicked and join you in a beer,' she said.

'Why don't you do that, Delia?'

They shared a smile and he signalled the waiter.

He could tell he'd unnerved her, and he could tell that she liked it. She liked it very much. She was attracted to him, he was sure. If he took her upstairs right now could he have her, he wondered? He certainly wanted to; the thought was nothing short of thrilling.

James' libido had been dormant for so long he'd forgotten what lust felt like. But he was aroused now. As they sat there together, the two of them in the Metropole Hotel eating assorted sandwiches, he desperately wanted Harriet Brereton's daughter.

If he were to bring about such a happening it would need
to be planned with care though. She was at least ten years
his junior, probably a virgin, and he was a respectable,
married man with a family. If anything were to come of
this he would need to practise discretion.

The beers arrived and they chatted away amicably.
Where did she live? he asked. In a nearby lodging house for
young ladies, she replied. *That wouldn't do*, he thought.
His room at the Metropole wouldn't do either. He was
known here and staff would talk. He would need to find a
more convenient location.

They talked of her job at the library, which she very
much enjoyed. How long had she worked there? he asked.
Well over a year now, throughout her mother's illness, she
said.

'I spent every moment I could nursing Mum at the end.
She died six months ago. Cancer.'

'How sad.'

'Yes, it was.' Then all of a sudden the realisation. 'Oh my
goodness, what time is it?'

He consulted his fob watch. 'Half past two.'

'Dear me, I must run,' she said, rising from the table,
'I'm going to be late as it is. Thank you so much, James,
I've had a wonderful time.'

'Shall we repeat the experience tomorrow?' he suggested
as he stood. 'Why don't we meet here at the Metropole,
same time, same place? I could even reserve this same
table.'

'Yes.' She flushed with pleasure, both surprised and
overwhelmed by the offer. 'That would be lovely.'

Then she was gone and he settled back with his beer. He
wouldn't attempt the seduction tomorrow, of course, far
too presumptuous. But he would prime her further, and
if all appeared promising he would make the appropriate
plans for his next visit to Sydney.

Lunch the following day was equally enjoyable. Assorted sandwiches again, he suggested. Being the quickest choice it would allow them time for a walk in the park, the weather was so pleasant for late autumn.

'And I see you have a coat with you to ward off the chill,' he said.

'An excellent idea,' she agreed.

As before, their talk over lunch was casual, amicable, but Delia felt herself strangely unsettled, something even akin to a mild state of panic. A walk in the park? It was as if he were courting her. And those eyes, his focus so intense. He couldn't by any chance be attempting to seduce her, could he?

She quickly realised he was. During their walk in Hyde Park, the way he tucked her arm into his was more than protective, more than gentlemanly, it was suggestive, intimate, as if they were lovers. She found it exciting, nonetheless. Exciting and familiar. She had felt this way before, but had not expected to repeat the experience; she had no wish to be placed in the path of sexual temptation. The episode was becoming distinctly unsettling.

They talked of the weather as they walked, and the beauty of the park, and the beauty of Sydney in general.

'Such a big, rough, dirty city,' he said, 'but with some areas of such beauty if you know where to look. I'm a great admirer of beauty.'

They weren't really talking of the city at all as he guided her to a quiet nook among the trees where no one could see them. Then he drew her to him and kissed her. Not threateningly, but so invitingly she couldn't help but respond. And when they parted there was no mistaking their mutual desire.

'I would like to know you better, Delia,' he said, his eyes locking with hers, 'a great deal better. Would you let me?'

She could do no more than nod. She wanted him as much as he wanted her.

'Tomorrow?' He murmured the query as he bent his lips
to her neck. 'I could arrange a suitable place which would
be discreet. You could stay the night with me. No one
would know. Shall I meet you at the library after work?'

She nodded again. 'Yes,' she whispered. And again they
kissed.

James hadn't thought for one minute things would be
this simple. The conquest appeared instantly within his
grasp. *How surprising*, he thought. For one he presumed
to be a virgin and therefore naive, she was very easily
seduced. He wouldn't even need to plan another trip to
Sydney.

He walked her back to the library.

'I shall see you tomorrow for a late afternoon tea, Delia,'
he said as they stood outside the main doors, his tone jovial
for the benefit of any passers-by. 'What time do you finish
work?'

'At a half past four.'

'Excellent, excellent, I shall be waiting.' He sounded
positively avuncular.

She tried to match the performance. 'I look forward to
it, James,' she said, fighting to contain the tremor in her
voice. 'Thank you for a very pleasant lunch.'

James' presumption was incorrect. Twenty-year-old
Delia Brereton was not a virgin. Nor was she naive enough
to believe their assignation would be anything other than a
one-night affair. She had been a sexually awakened young
woman for some time. James was not the only one whose
lust was now aroused.

Delia had been engaged just the previous year, to a
young man with whom she'd been desperately in love.
They'd planned a modest wedding, just a visit to the city's
registry office; with her mother so gravely ill there was
no point, they'd agreed, in arranging anything lavish. But
their mutual passion had driven them to become lovers

well before they'd taken their vows. *What difference would a few months make?* she'd asked herself; they loved each other.

It had made all the difference in the world. There'd been no wedding. After a three-month passionate affair, her young fiancé had disappeared. She'd been left to believe, and rightly so, that he'd only proposed in order to bed her.

Heartbroken, she'd sobbed her story out to her mother who'd been surprisingly understanding and sympathetic, while at the same time tough, as Harriet Brereton always was.

'Some men are like that, Delia,' she'd said. 'Pay no heed to the Macreadys and their Christian beliefs, you are not to blame for having put your trust in a man.' And then she'd told her daughter her own story, the story that Delia had sworn to take to her grave.

'It's not altogether unattractive,' James said, ushering her into the tiny front room of the little one-storey terrace house in Francis Street, just a block from Hyde Park. 'I've rented it for the next several days of my stay in Sydney.' The hint being that they might even repeat the experience should she wish to do so.

He'd gone to quite a deal of trouble finding the right place via an agent who dealt in inner-city real estate and the expense had been considerable, but he felt it was worth every penny. He didn't want to frighten her off.

'It's very pretty,' she said, gazing around, pleasantly surprised. She'd expected to be taken to a dingy boarding house where rooms were rented out nightly for nefarious purposes. She even had a heavy scarf draped around her shoulders with which she'd intended to cover her face in the presumption she'd be assumed a prostitute.

'Yes, it is, isn't it?' Gratified by her reaction, he too gazed around, congratulating himself on his foresight. 'It's one of the old workers' cottages, and the owners, whoever they may be, have done an excellent job doing it up for the rental market. Let me show you the kitchen.'

The two of them might have been a newly married couple inspecting a house with a view to purchase. But they weren't. He was pleased to note that the reticule she carried was a little larger than the normal drawstring handbag women tended to favour. She had come prepared to stay the night. Excellent.

They walked through to the kitchen where a bottle of wine and two glasses sat on the small wooden table.

'I thought you might like a glass of Sauterne,' he said, 'most refreshing.'

'Perhaps after I've seen the rest of the house?' Her eyes were suggesting something else altogether.

'Of course. Let me show you the bedroom.'

He led the way through to one of the two poky bedrooms, which was all but dark in the gloom of late afternoon. Pallid autumn light filtered through the tiny window that looked out to the rear of the house and a small squalid backyard. He drew the curtain across the window, but not before turning on the gas lamp in the wall bracket.

'I hope you don't mind if we leave the lamp on,' he said. He so wanted to see her body.

'I don't mind at all,' she said. She'd already divested herself of her coat and scarf, which were draped over the one and only chair in the room, and was now in the throes of undoing the buttons at the throat of her high-necked blouse. She and her fiancé had always liked to watch one another undress.

James read the message loud and clear, surprised to discover she was so bold. Hardly the behaviour of a virgin, he thought, but then perhaps he'd been wrong in his assumption.

He took the fob watch from his vest pocket and placed it on the bedside table. Then he dropped his coat to the floor. Then his jacket. Then his vest. But his eyes never once left her, watching her every action, mesmerised. He could tell she enjoyed him watching.

And then she was naked. Standing before him, unashamed in all her glory. For she was indeed glorious. The perfection of her body reminded him of his wife's body when Jenna had been young. But Delia Brereton was far more beautiful. *You are the most glorious creature imaginable,* he thought.

She had been awaiting his judgement and was not disappointed. She sought adoration and needed to be glorified. Her body was her gift. Her fiancé had looked at her in exactly this way, overwhelming her with his love, and it had always excited her. She unpinned her hair, the fairest of curls dropping to bare shoulders, and crossed to him.

Their lovemaking was fervent and their passion uninhibited as they fed one another's hunger. Both were re-awakened, both transported, James more strongly aroused than he could ever remember, Delia revisited by a craving she'd never expected to know again.

They brought each other to mutual climax, crying out together, fused as one, forgetting any safety precaution they might normally have taken. He did not withdraw, she did not twist herself free.

They lay side by side, panting for breath, both taken aback by the experience.

When they'd finally recovered he propped on one elbow to look at her. He smiled as he gently brushed a curl damp with sweat from her brow. 'We mustn't let that happen again, must we?'

She looked a query.

'We must take care next time,' he said. 'We must not risk a pregnancy.'

They both knew this was not destined to be a one-night experience. Nor two nights, nor even three.

He extended his stay in Sydney, remaining in the city for a whole week, and every single night they met at the little cottage in Francis Street.

They were obsessed with each other by now, and openly discussed their future. He knew he did not love her, that his wife and his family would always take precedence, but he knew also that he could not revert to the lacklustre, virtually sexless life to which he'd become accustomed. Having been so re-awakened he wondered how he'd ever allowed himself to accept such an existence.

Delia's feelings were far more complex. She was forced to admit to herself she was in love with James Brereton, but she resolved not to tell him so. He was a married man with children, she had no rights to him. She believed, deep down, that he loved her just as she did him, but she had no expectations beyond that of being his mistress, a situation she was prepared to accept.

James was brimming with enthusiasm as he spoke of the arrangements he would set in place. He would of course take a long-term lease on the little house. She would be able to move in and make it a home. He would come to Sydney on a regular basis. Once a month, possibly more, for he would take over the business aspects of Glenfinnan, which were normally the province of his partner, Phil Caton. There were endless responsibilities associated with such a position, he told her; the wool samples that needed to go to the Technological Museum, the meetings with overseas buyers, the auctions and God knows what else.

'My partner will be only too happy,' he went on, realising as he quoted his list that these were the duties Ben had looked forward to as valid reasons to visit Sydney all those years ago. He was seeking his own reasons now, wasn't he? And for the same purpose. Sexual satisfaction.

'Phil Caton can't abide the city,' he assured her with a smile, 'he hates having to come to Sydney.' Everything was going to be so easy.

They had formed a tryst. All was in place. They could talk as lovers now. And they did.

'Tell me about your childhood,' she said on their last evening together as they lay naked in each other's arms, the blanket pulled cosily up around their chins, the lamp still burning in its wall bracket. 'What sort of little boy were you?'

'A lonely little boy,' he replied, caressing her shoulder. 'Just me and my pa camping out during the shearing season. Then we'd move into some town or other during the off season so he could find work. When I got older and went to school Pa found me lodgings with a widow in Aramac. I missed him when he went off shearing on his own. He was all I had in the world.'

'Aramac?' She smiled, her face lighting up with pleasure. 'That's where my mother once taught.'

'Yes, so you said.' He no longer thought of Harriet Brereton. The fact that Delia was her daughter had ceased to be of any interest. God she was beautiful when she smiled.

'What a pity you didn't meet her. She was a wonderful woman, my mother.'

He nodded. The nakedness of her body against his was tantalising. It was barely an hour since they'd made love, but he could feel the familiar stirring of desire, and his hand found its way to her breast.

But she remained thoughtful, still pondering the past. 'We were both lonely children, weren't we? My mother, too, was all I had in the world. I loved her dearly, and I miss her still.'

Delia was aware of his hand on her breast, but thoughts of her mother aroused in her the strongest desire to share with him the secret she'd sworn to take to the grave. James would pass no judgement upon her, and to share the truth of her mother's past would be a measure of her love. It would create a bond between them.

'I want to tell you something, James,' she said and she sat up, leaning back against the bed head.

Realising the seriousness of her intent James sat up also and gave her his full attention.

'What is it, my darling?'

'An admission my mother made on her deathbed. I swore I'd tell no one, but I wish to tell you.'

He waited.

'Albert Brereton was not my father . . .'

He'd known that. What matter that she was born out of wedlock? It meant nothing.

'My father was a man called George Wakefield.'

Delia's thoughts were so fixed upon her mother she didn't notice in the gloom of the night and the hazy light cast by the gas lamp, the expression of horrified disbelief on James' face.

'They were secret lovers for some time,' she went on, 'but he left her when she discovered she was pregnant. A cruel man. He just walked away and she never saw him again.'

She turned to him, aglow with relief at having divulged the truth of her past. They shared something special now.

He stared back at her with a rising sense of revulsion. He knew every word she said was true. That day he and his father had abruptly left Aramac. That day his father had bought him his first horse, Barnaby. He hadn't gone to school that day. They'd simply ridden out of town, never to return.

He continued to stare, her beauty now suddenly and strangely hideous to him. How could he not have seen it before? Those vivid blue eyes. They were the eyes of his father. No, worse. They were his eyes. This was his sister. He had slept with his sister.

She could tell he was moved by her revelation, and the thought pleased her. 'I have told no one of this, James,' she whispered, nestling her head into his shoulder, her arm resting upon his chest. 'It's our very own secret. No one but you knows the truth.'

And no one must ever know, he thought.

'Rest, Delia,' he murmured, 'go to sleep now. There's a good girl. Go to sleep now.'

They snuggled down together under the blankets, she wondering at his change of heart. Why did he not wish to make love again? But no matter. She was perfectly happy resting in his arms.

James lay silently gazing up at the ceiling, listening to her breathing.

No one must ever know, he thought. *If you were to pose a risk to me, Delia, I would have to kill you. And I don't want to do that. It wouldn't be at all right to kill one's own sister.*

The irony did not escape him. As a lonely little boy how he would have loved to have had a sister. And now here she was. His own blood. And she could threaten his entire existence.

An hour later, when he was assured she was sleeping soundly, he crept out into the night.

CHAPTER FIFTEEN

Upon his return to Glenfinnan, James put aside all thoughts of Delia, which for some strange reason he found surprisingly easy. He had no sister. He had never had a sister. Delia Brereton simply did not exist.

He did not allow himself, either, to dwell upon what he had perceived as the reawakening of his sexual drive. His diminished libido of late had been entirely of his own making, he told himself. He'd become bored, lazy, satisfied to dawdle complacently into middle-age. He was thirty-three years old, for God's sake! He was in the prime of his life. Jenna was a fine, strong woman who'd borne him fine, strong children; she deserved a better husband.

'I missed you,' he said the very night of his return. And they made love the way they had in the earlier days of their marriage, vigorously, the way Jenna liked it.

He'd been gone for little more than a week and Jenna wondered why he should have so missed her. She wondered, also, whether perhaps something may have happened in the city to so revitalise her husband. But she wisely refrained from posing any questions, happily accepting instead the new status quo.

A month passed. And then a further month. And James had all but forgotten the entire episode of Harriet Brereton's daughter, Cordelia. Until a letter arrived. A local letter, its postmark showing it had been sent from Goulburn.

'Who on earth would be sending you a letter from town?' Jenna queried as she sifted through the mail that Emily had delivered to the breakfast table. On a Saturday morning, ten-year-old Emily always rode her pony to Glenfinnan's letterbox that stood at the corner of the main road a half a mile from the Big House. It was her favourite duty.

'No idea.' James was equally intrigued. No one posted letters locally. They rode or they drove vehicles of some description, either horse-drawn or motorised – mostly the former – to each other's property, even if they lived miles apart. Visits to one another for whatever purpose deemed necessary; the announcement of a birth, the sad news of a death, the official invitation to a christening or funeral or simply a party, presented the opportunity to socialise, which was neighbourly. No one stopped work during the shearing season, but it was otherwise presumed one would call a halt for an hour or so with the offer to 'come on up to the house for a cup of tea'.

'Most odd,' he remarked, taking the letter Jenna passed him and examining the postmark. He turned it over and on the back of the sealed envelope read the handwritten name 'Cordelia Johnson'. *Cordelia?*

'Business,' he said flippantly, setting it aside. 'Phil's domain, not mine, I'll drop it over to him this afternoon. Thank you, Millie.' He smiled at Millie as she placed his plate of fried eggs and lamb chops before him. He always enjoyed a hearty breakfast. They all did. Jenna, Ted and Emily were already tucking into their sausages and eggs. James preferred chops to sausages himself, which took a little longer to cook.

He ate slowly, methodically, mopping up the juices with thick slices of toast and when he'd finished he picked up the letter, collecting also the several others Jenna had sifted through that clearly related to business.

'I'll look at these in my office,' he said, and taking his mug of tea with him he disappeared upstairs, as he usually did, leaving the family to clear away the breakfast table.

He sat at his desk and ripped open the envelope. Her handwriting was neat and precise, just as one would expect of a librarian, he supposed. The context of the letter, too, was direct and to the point. At least it started out as such. The tone changed somewhat towards the end though. He did not like what he read at the end of the letter.

Dear James,

I am in Goulburn. As you will have noted from the back of this envelope, I have taken on an assumed name so as not to arouse interest or invite query. I am aware of just how famous the name Brereton is in these parts. I have leased a little worker's cottage in Australia Street – not unlike the little cottage so special to us in Francis Street, remember?

I can only presume your disappearance without a word was born of your fear our relationship might be discovered, that you worried the regular trips to Sydney you'd planned might arouse suspicion and that you had second thoughts. But I must assure you, James, I wish to cause no damage to your marriage and your family. I am quite prepared to move to Goulburn, which is why I have leased the cottage, and to adopt the plan we set out in such detail, you and I. Trips into the township from your property would raise no questions, which will surely allay your fears.

I make no claim upon you and I pose no threat to you. I wish no more than to be your mistress, James, for you must know that I love you. I love you with all my heart.

It is imperative I see you as soon as possible. You must come to me here in ustralia Street, number 26, where I shall be waiting. If u do not call upon me within one

week of receipt of this letter, I will not answer for the consequences. Please, James, please, I beg of you. I simply have to see you. I am desperate. My love for you makes me so.
Delia

She wrote that she posed no threat, yet in the last paragraph she said she would not answer for the consequences should he fail to call on her. *That is surely a threat,* he told himself. It meant, presumably, that she would call upon him herself – here at Glenfinnan.

James did not like the tone of the letter one bit. He sat back in his office chair, read it again and then burned it, watching the paper flicker briefly in the grate of the fireplace. *Delia Brereton may well have signed her own death warrant,* he thought. Must he really be forced to take such action? He did not relish the prospect. He thought of the girl's beauty. Her youth. *My own sister.* It didn't seem right at all.

'I think I'll head into town tonight,' he told Jenna the following afternoon. 'One of the boys said there's a poker game going at the club.'

'On a Sunday?' she queried.

He shrugged. 'A Sunday's as good as any other day.'

'Oh dear me, you'll answer for that at the pearly gates,' she said with a dire shake of her head, 'gambling on the Lord's day.'

They shared a good-natured laugh. Jenna had not one shred of religiosity in her being, although when it was convenient she pretended she had. Furthermore, she knew he gambled only moderately, so never minded in the least if he decided to join a poker game.

In fact, James thought, as he drove off to town in the early evening, Jenna was so trusting it would have been very easy to conduct an affair right under her nose.

Goulburn was quiet on a Sunday night. He parked near the railway station where there were several other cars, so his vehicle didn't look too out of place, and walked the several blocks to Australia Street. A narrow road lined with tiny single-storey workers' cottages, it ran just one short block between the major streets of Auburn and Bourke, and when he came to a halt before number 26 all was dark and deserted. Not a soul in sight. *Good,* he thought.

Curtains were drawn over the front windows of the house, but he could see a faint glow shining from within.

He knocked. The door opened. And there she stood in the shaft of light cast by a kerosene lamp that sat on the table in the small front room.

He stepped quickly inside, and she closed the door just as quickly behind him. Then she turned, her face alight with the pure joy of seeing him.

She made as if to move into the embrace she expected, but he held up a hand in warning and she halted abruptly. More than the hand, it was the look in his eyes that issued the true warning. She waited, confused.

'You should not have come here, Delia,' he said, his voice, ice, sounding the strongest warning of all. 'You are never to see me or contact me again. Do you understand?'

'No. No I don't understand.' She shook her head, more than confused, in a state of bewilderment bordering on panic, tears already starting to form. 'I don't understand at all. I haven't understood from the moment you left. You disappeared without a word, after we had made such plans. Why?' she begged. 'We are meant to be together. We are lovers, James. I love you with all my heart, and I know you love me . . .'

'We are not lovers.' His voice cut knife-like through her pleas. He had no option, he knew, but to tell her the truth. 'We are not meant to be together, Delia, we never were. I do not love you, and you are not to love me.'

'But . . . but . . . why do you . . .' She was stammering, barely able to speak, her tears now freely flowing. What did he mean? What was happening?

He grabbed her roughly by the arm, picked up the kerosene lamp with his other hand and looked around the room. 'A mirror,' he said, 'is there a mirror?'

She nodded and led the way through to the bedroom where, above the washstand in the corner, a mirror hung on the wall.

He all but dragged her to it and holding the lamp high forced her to gaze at their images.

'Look,' he demanded, 'look there and tell me what you see.'

'I see you, James.'

'No, no,' he snapped, 'look at the two of us. Do you not see the likeness?'

But Delia did not look at herself, she had no wish to do so. She could see nothing but him, the man she loved.

'I see only you, James,' she said, her eyes not leaving his image, 'I see only my lover.'

'No you don't. You see your brother.'

He studied her reflection closely, waiting for her reaction, wondering what it might be. But apart from the flicker of her eyes from his image to hers and then back again, there appeared nothing. She seemed unable to comprehend what he was saying. So he told her his story. Succinctly, harshly, skipping all detail.

'George Wakefield was my father,' he said. 'I adopted the name Brereton when I was sixteen in order to escape the law.' Then ignoring the images in the mirror he turned to fling the truth directly at her. 'You are my sister. Do you understand me, Delia?' It sprang from him like a form of accusation. 'We are brother and sister, you and I.'

Oh dear God, it can't be, she thought, her eyes still trained on their reflections. She could discern the likeness with shocking clarity now and the Christian teachings of her childhood called judgement upon her. *You are damned,* her mind screamed. *You have committed a mortal sin.*

'We will never see each other again, Delia.' Realising, by the horror of her reaction, that she accepted the truth and understood they could never be lovers, James felt a sense of relief. It appeared she would not pursue him. He would therefore not need to kill her. But she had to be warned, nonetheless.

'You must understand,' he explained, his voice a little less harsh, but still businesslike, still the voice of authority, 'that my original identity must be revealed to no one. I was born James Brereton and I married into the McKinnon family. This is who I was and who I have become. I have a family of my own now, and they must never know of my falsehood.'

She remained staring into the mirror, barely hearing him, still struck dumb by the revelation.

He placed the kerosene lamp on the washstand and taking her by the shoulders turned her to him, their faces only inches apart. 'Should you even think of betraying my identity, I would not hesitate to kill you, Delia,' he said.

There was no mistaking the intent in his eyes and in his voice. She was confronted by a man more than capable of killing, and she knew it.

'You do understand that, don't you?' He insisted upon an answer.

'Yes,' she whispered.

'Good.' He leaned his face down to hers and kissed her chastely on the lips, the kiss of a brother. 'What a pity it has come to this. I would have liked to have had a sister.'

He left, and she heard the front door quietly close behind him.

She stood there for some time, sickened in the knowledge that she had slept with her brother, but sickened far further by the knowledge that she still loved him. The touch of his lips on hers, chaste as the kiss had been, had aroused in her a longing, and she knew, God help her, that she would continue to love him for the rest of her life.

Two weeks later, it was the end of second term and Josh returned from Sydney for the holidays, James picking him up at the railway station. The reunion was as exuberant as ever, Ted and Emily having accompanied their father for the drive. The moment Josh stepped from the train onto the platform he was besieged by his siblings and James had to hustle them along to the waiting vehicle.

Rugged up against the cold, for it was a blustery day in late August, Ted and Emily piled into the back seat while Josh, as usual, sat in the front with his father.

'I don't suppose you heard about Miss Brereton, Dad?' he asked as the car pulled out from the station.

'No,' James replied, keeping his eyes firmly fixed on the road. 'Why? What should I know about Miss Brereton?'

'She's dead.' Josh pulled a folded-up newspaper from the pocket of his overcoat. 'There was a bit about it in the *Sydney Morning Herald,* I brought a copy home for you, didn't think it would have been reported in the *Goulburn Post.*'

'No, I didn't see anything,' James said. 'That's very sad. How did she die?' *And why was it reported in the newspaper?* he wondered.

'It happened ten days ago. Her body was discovered on the rocks at Bondi Beach, they don't know whether it was an accident or suicide.' Josh started to riffle through the pages of the newspaper. 'Do you want me to read it out to you?'

'No, no,' James said, 'I'll have a read of it when we get home. That's sad to hear indeed. A nice young woman like Miss Brereton. What a terrible thing to happen.'

It appeared the end of the discussion between father and son, but Josh, keen to impress Ted and Emily with his personal views, swivelled around to face the back seat.

'I'll bet it was suicide,' he said. 'She went off the rocks on the northern side of the bay. That's where the cliffs are *really* tall and steep. If you wanted to make sure you killed yourself and didn't just end up with a busted leg, that's where you'd go I reckon.'

Ted and Emily were, as always, impressed. To think Josh had known someone who'd committed suicide!

'What was she like?' Ted asked.

'Oh she was really nice,' Josh replied, 'awfully pretty too. Wouldn't have thought she was the suicidal type myself, but then you never can tell, can you? Or so they say. I knew her quite well. Used to see her now and then at the library. Dad and I even had lunch with her once, didn't we, Dad?'

'Yes, we did.' James was surprised. Josh was showing off, which was not unusual, but he'd have thought the boy would be a little more upset by the death of the young woman he'd appeared to so deeply admire. *Ah well,* he thought, *he's very young. Boys that age are mercurial, they go with the ebb and flow of the tide. Something else is now obviously of greater importance than his Miss Brereton.*

James wondered briefly whether the object of Josh's interest might be a girl but decided not to ask. That would be intrusive.

Something else was most certainly of greater importance to Josh than Miss Brereton, and even the dramatic details of Miss Brereton's death. This was something he couldn't wait to share with Ted. And with Zac and Sam too, of course. He had really big news for the boys this time. He would announce to them that Josh Brereton-McKinnon was no longer a virgin! That he had lost his virginity barely six weeks after his thirteenth birthday what's more! He was very proud of that fact.

'What's your name, boy?' she'd asked as she knelt in front of him, washing his genitals with a flannel that she kept dipping into the basin of water on the floor beside her.

'Josh,' he said, feeling painfully self-conscious. He'd never been examined like this before and found the situation most confronting. Humiliating too. He doubted whether he'd be able to get an erection, which was a possibility that hadn't once crossed his mind. Over the past several months, just thinking about doing it had made him hard. The older boys were always talking about girls and furtively passing around pictures that left little to the imagination. He'd determined to become the first of the younger ones to lose his virginity. But it wasn't going to happen at this rate, he thought, gazing down at his limp penis, which having already been washed, she was holding to one side as she applied the flannel to his balls.

'Josh, I like that. Short for Joshua, is it?'

'Yes.'

'Nice.' She looked up at him and smiled. 'I'm Carmelita.'

He'd been pleased to discover the young prostitute was as pretty close up as she had been standing on the gloomy corner of Palmer Street. She had a full-lipped mouth, which although unfashionable and considered common, was most inviting, and sandy-coloured hair that fell untamed to her shoulders – there was something wild about her. She seemed nice too, although he didn't believe for one minute her name was Carmelita. She had an English accent of some sort, he didn't know from where, but she sounded a bit like the Lockwoods who owned the clothing shop in Auburn Street and they were from London.

Josh had put aside his weekly allowances and fronted up to the girl openly on a Friday night.

'Is it five years already?' she'd asked with a cheeky smile.
'Yep.'

She'd laughed. 'Come along with you now, boy, how old
are you?'

'Fifteen.'

He was tall for his age and she'd believed him. Or if
not, she'd pretended to. And he had the money to pay, so
who cared? He'd paid for a full hour what's more, not just
a quickie. She'd rightly guessed him to be a virgin who
wanted to learn.

Carmelita knew the boy was squirming with embar-
rassment.

'All done.' She rose to her feet, dumping the flannel into
the basin that was tucked under her arm. 'A good wash
is necessary, you know,' she said, flashing him another
friendly smile to put him at his ease. 'I'm very particular
about cleanliness, and you'll be thankful that I am. You
won't catch the pox from *me*, lovey. I keep myself clean.
Not like some of the others, I can tell you.'

Josh cast a dubious glance at the bowl. The water had
been barely lukewarm and looked a little cloudy, he wondered how often she changed it. The flannel looked a bit on
the grubby side too. He hadn't thought of the pox. Should
he worry?

She returned the basin to the washstand from where
she'd fetched it and, due process completed, sashayed over
to him, undoing the buttons of her low-cut blouse beneath
which she clearly wore no underwear.

'Now, let's get started, shall we?'

When they arrived back from the railway station there
was a spread laid out for them in the kitchen, including
a large bowl of Maude's homemade sausage rolls. As the
children tucked in with gusto, Jenna demanded of her
son all the news from school, adding her congratulations

on yet another term that had resulted in excellent reports from his teachers. Josh answered everything dutifully, but as soon as possible he made good his escape, employing all his customary cheek and charm.

After scoffing his fair share of sausage rolls, he politely excused himself from the table, Jenna presuming he was paying a visit to the lavatory, only to re-appear a moment later, soccer ball in hand.

'Hey, Mum, would you mind awfully if Ted and I go and kick the ball around with Zac and Sam?' he asked. 'I haven't seen them for so long and there's tons of stuff to catch up on.'

Jenna laughed. She found the way the four of them were so inseparable thoroughly endearing. Why on earth would the boy want to talk to his mother about his school results when he could kick a football around with his brother and cousins?

'Of course, darling, off you go.'

Ted was up from the table like a shot. Josh had tales to tell.

'Me too,' Emily squealed and jumped to her feet. But her brothers were already out the back door. She had no hope of catching up with them. And even if she did they'd only send her home. She sat sulkily back down in her chair and grabbed another sausage roll.

The boys didn't kick the soccer ball around. The four of them huddled out of the wind behind the tractor shed at the rear of the Catons' house, Ted, Zac and Sam listening spellbound as Josh told his story.

'Turned out her name wasn't really Carmelita at all,' Josh said triumphantly, 'she just uses that name with the punters to sound exotic. She told me I could call her Lilly.'

Although he was showing off and enjoying every minute, Josh had in fact been truthful. He'd admitted to the utter humiliation of the washing procedure.

'She told me it was to save me getting the pox,' he said, 'but my dick was as limp as a dead fish, I was sure I wouldn't be able to do anything.'

He'd admitted also to the poor performance that had followed.

'She got me worked up all right, though,' he said, 'which I have to admit wasn't difficult because she's very good at her job.'

They'd all listened in silence as he described her body and what she did with it, and the feel of her mouth around him. They were rendered breathless by the images he painted.

'But when we got around to actually doing it I was hopeless,' he said, 'it was all over in a second, I just couldn't help myself.' His grin, however, was one of pure elation. 'I tell you what, though. The feel of the inside of her was bloody incredible. Everything you could've imagined and more. Much, much more.'

He delivered this particular announcement directly to Zac, who had listened throughout, slack-jawed with envy.

'But the *second* time,' Josh went on, relishing the moment, for here lay the true victory, 'the *second* time was something else! I'd booked her for a whole hour, see, and we talked in between. That's when she told me to call her Lilly. She was really nice. She taught me how to go slower and . . .' He shook his head, still lost in wonderment, unable to find the words to do justice to his experience. 'Well . . .' He shrugged. There was simply nothing more to say.

A pause followed as the others absorbed all he'd told them, their imaginations working overtime. The reactions of all three boys were varied.

Young Ted was in total awe of his brother for taking on something as adult as sex. But that was Josh for you, wasn't it? Josh was always way ahead of everyone else.

Ted was happy to bide his time and see what eventuated. Sex wasn't of great personal interest to him yet. Good to know what to expect though, he told himself.

Zac, however, had been living every moment of Josh's experience. Zac was aching to lose his virginity.

'You lucky bastard,' he said when he finally found his voice. 'I'm going to save up and go to a brothel. I know where there's one in town.'

Sam had found the story as stimulating as Zac had, but although he felt a certain degree of envy he was a little more circumspect.

'I'm not sure if that'd be wise,' he advised his brother.

'Why not?'

'How long ago did this happen, Josh?'

'Just over a week ago now. Why?'

'I dunno if I'm right, but I heard somewhere that the pox can take a little while to show.' He saw the flash of concern in Josh's eyes. 'Oh I'm sure you'll be fine,' he said reassuringly, 'I wouldn't worry too much.' His hearty smile to the others signalled there was strength in numbers. 'Let's all keep our fingers crossed, eh.'

Josh remembered the less-than-lukewarm basin of cloudy water and the none-too-clean looking flannel. He started to feel anxious.

After finishing a leisurely lunch, James retired to his office, taking the copy of the *Sydney Morning Herald* Josh had left for him on the kitchen table.

Seated at his desk, he sifted through its pages and found the small paragraph hidden away at the bottom of page three.

TRAGIC DISCOVERY AT BONDI BEACH, the heading read.

In the early hours of Sunday morning, local resident and rock fisherman, Mr Ronald Fitzgerald, discovered the

body of a young woman at the base of the cliffs on the
northern side of the bay.

Mr Fitzgerald immediately reported his find to the police
who, upon investigation, have proved the identity of the
woman to be twenty-year-old Miss Cordelia Brereton.

Miss Brereton, who appears to have no family, served as
librarian at the Free Public Library in the City of Sydney.

Police have announced that it is unknown whether this
tragic event is the result of an accident or suicide.

There it was. No more than that. James folded the newspaper and put it to one side.

Sad, he thought as he leaned back in his chair and gazed
out the window at the surrounding countryside, lush from
recent rain. *Sad, but for the best.*

He was relieved by the knowledge there was now no fear
of discovery, that this 'tragic event' had put an end to a
potential ongoing threat, but he was saddened nonetheless.
Poor Delia.

He dumped the newspaper into the wastepaper bin beside
his desk and sprang to his feet. There was work to be done.
A great deal of work. The shearing season would be upon
them in just over a month.

The muster was about to commence when the school
holidays came to an end and Josh was to return to Sydney.
Much as he adored Sydney, he was loath to go. The muster,
when the flocks were brought in for shearing, was always
his favourite time of the year. During the weekends when
he'd been home from St Patrick's College he'd loved nothing
more than being out there rounding up the sheep with the
men, and proving into the bargain that he could ride a
horse as well as, if not better than, any of the farmhands.

But times had changed. He was a Sydney Grammar
School student now and destined for bigger things.

Although scion of a wealthy sheep station owner, had he stayed in Goulburn, upon leaving school he might have remained little more than a glorified farmhand, at least until the death of his father when he would be destined to take over the reins of Glenfinnan. That day would come, but in the meantime Josh had other plans.

Strangely enough, his plans did not include university and the pursuit of an academic career as envisaged by his mentor from St Patrick's, the singularly self-opinionated Leonard Crompton. Josh had not the least ambition to prove himself *intellectually* superior. Just superior would do. His sole aim was to become rich and powerful. The two were synonymous, he knew, the acquisition of wealth automatically leading to power, and Sydney Grammar had much to offer in this regard. His focus would remain principally upon mathematics, the marketplace, business structure and anything relating to economics – literature and the arts be hanged. But there was the added factor that sons of business titans attended Sydney Grammar. Excellent future connections. *Who needs university?* he told himself. He had everything mapped out. He would be well on the road to success by the age of seventeen.

Despite the disappointment of not taking part in the muster, Josh headed back to Sydney and the final term of 1908 breathing a sigh of relief. His cousin Sam's warning had worried him. But he'd proved lucky. He hadn't caught a dose of the pox. He decided not to repeat the experience with Lilly, however. Just in case.

The whole of Glenfinnan was engulfed by the shearing season with the one exception of Jenna. Jenna's energies were concentrated upon the Tirranna Races, which were to take place early in the new year. Or, rather, her energies were concentrated upon Ebony Lass, the five-year-old mare she was convinced would bring home the Tirranna Picnic Race Club Challenge Cup for Glenfinnan.

As in previous years, she was a woman obsessed. Up at dawn each day to attend the mare's training sessions, she and trainer Patrick Hill were in endless discussion, and she shared every single development with James.

'We shaved another two seconds off this morning,' she said excitedly when he arrived home weary after a long day's work, 'and young Barney weighs a good half stone more than the jockey will.' Barney was the strapper. They hadn't as yet contracted the jockey, but the weight stipulations were finite. 'Pat's as sure as I am she can win.'

'That's excellent news, my love.' He smiled, despite his weariness. He was genuinely fond of Jenna and liked to see her happy. She was attractive, too, when she was happy, he thought. Certainly, her body was more along the 'buxom' lines these days, but what was wrong with that? She was a strong, good-looking woman and he was glad she was his wife. Their sex life had improved tremendously of late.

'You do know what this means, don't you?' she demanded. 'If we win a third time we get to keep the cup in perpetuity. The club will have to have another one made for next year. And the thing's 18-carat gold!' Her laughter, although girlish in its excitement, held a distinct ring of triumph. 'You do *know* that, James, don't you?'

He joined in her laughter. 'Yes of course I know that!' Just as he knew that the fact the cup was 18-carat gold and worth a substantial amount was utterly immaterial to her. 'You'll be a legend, Jenna, and I'll be so proud of you,' he said. 'You'll be right up there with David Innes Watt.'

During the years 1895 to 1906, horses bred and trained by David Innes Watt had won the Challenge Cup no less than three times, creating the precedent Jenna had been chasing for the past several years. Being awarded the cup in perpetuity was part and parcel of her obsession.

'No, no,' she declared with vehemence. '*Glenfinnan* will be right up there! *Glenfinnan* and Ebony Lass, James! A *McKinnon*-bred horse!'

'You're quite right, my love,' he agreed, dropping all vestige of banter, '*Glenfinnan* and *McKinnon*. Just as it should be. Just as it always shall be.'

And he kissed her. There were times when he even felt he loved Jenna.

Despite it being the second week in January, when the heat might have been unbearable, the first day of the races could not have dawned finer.

'The weather gods have been kind to you, my love,' James jovially remarked as they pulled up at the race track in the Swift convertible. They'd travelled with the soft top down, exposing them not only to the elements but for all to see, which, being the master and mistress of Glenfinnan, he'd considered only right. Most racegoers arrived by train, travelling the five and a half miles from Goulburn along the Cooma line. The McKinnon children themselves had caught the train, Wallace Briggs driving them to the station in James' other Swift vehicle that very morning.

Josh, Ted and Emily were already there, waiting at the entrance to the race course as their parents' vehicle pulled up. Driving had taken longer than the train trip, but James believed it worth the effort as he assisted Jenna from the passenger's seat.

'You look beautiful, my love,' he said. And she did, he thought, as she tossed the travelling scarf that had kept her bonnet in place back into the car and raised the pretty yellow parasol that matched her full-length skirt, lacy blouse and bolero to perfection. With her coppery hair, yellow had always been Jenna's colour.

'Thank you, my darling.' She smiled and took his arm. The remark pleased her, he'd been so amiable of late, but she didn't really care whether or not she looked beautiful. Everything except the Challenge Cup was immaterial to Jenna, even her husband's admiration. 'Let's hope the weather gods are as kind to us tomorrow,' she said.

The weather remained exceptionally pleasant, particularly for January when the midsummer conditions could have been uncomfortable, and the day passed most pleasurably for all.

The enclosure, as always, was picturesque, with open-fronted tents where trestle tables were set up providing all forms of delicacies and refreshments available for picnic luncheons; the Tirranna Race Club Committee was renowned for putting on a good show. Dotted here and there also were a number of gunyahs, Aboriginal-style bush huts fashioned out of branches and covered with bark. The practice had been adopted some time back, no one could remember exactly by whom, but the result was most colourful. Various club members, those of particular status that is, built the gunyahs and placed a sign above displaying the name of their property. Right near the entrance to the enclosure one of the largest of the gunyahs bore the name *GLENFINNAN*. Jenna always made it her personal responsibility to oversee the building of the McKinnon gunyah.

The track itself was splendid and the number in attendance most impressive, burgeoning by the hour as yet more racegoers arrived by train. Women paraded in their prettiest afternoon dresses, which reached nearly to the ground, allowing their neat high-buttoned shoes to show. Bonnets and flamboyant hats with feathers were hugely on display as was the variety of men's headwear, from the straw hats of farmers to the derbies of the middle class to the silk top hats of the rich. The Tirranna Picnic Races were for everyone.

James wore a top hat befitting his standing in society, but not wishing to appear ostentatious he had ensured it was modest in height and of a casual grey. The choice had been wise, he looked extremely stylish.

As planned, he and Jenna did not stay for the whole day. They made their social connections, mingling with fellow property owners and any number of dignitaries from Sydney, which James considered most valuable; they studied the horses in the mounting yard, which was of far greater interest to Jenna; and they watched the morning's races. But after a light picnic lunch, they returned to Glenfinnan, leaving the children with strict instructions to catch the five o'clock train back to Goulburn where Wallace would collect them. The big day was reserved for tomorrow when the main event, the Tirranna Picnic Race Club Challenge Cup, would be run in the afternoon.

The second day of the meet dawned equally fine, and this time when James and Jenna pulled up at the race track in the Swift convertible, Phil and Adele Caton were seated behind them. The McKinnon children had once again arrived earlier, having caught the train, and with them were the four Caton offspring, even the youngest, seven-year-old Tom, who had been entrusted to the care of his older siblings, Zac and Sam. They were all there at the entrance waiting to greet their parents. The entire Glenfinnan family had arrived in force to cheer Ebony Lass on to victory.

Adele, who was to turn thirty-nine later that same year, remained as beautiful as ever, the birth of four children having done little to ravage her looks. Heads turned in admiration as she mingled here and there, greeting people with her easy charm, hand linked through the arm of her gangly husband who looked as awkward as he felt. Phil Caton loved nothing more than to watch fine-bred race horses in action, but he did so hate the social aspect of functions as grand as this. He dreaded to think of the ball that would follow that night. But he would attend, of course, for Adele's sake.

Jenna disappeared for most of the day, spending her time with Pat Hill the trainer, Barney the strapper and Ebony Lass. She didn't even emerge to join the family for a picnic lunch. But shortly before the cup was to be run, they all met up at the mounting yard where they watched the horses and jockeys parade for the masses.

'Isn't she magnificent,' Jenna said, eyes trained on the black mare dancing about the yard, signalling she couldn't wait to get out there on the track. 'Ebony Lass just loves to run!'

'Yep,' Phil Caton agreed, 'she's a beauty all right.'

They repaired to their seats in the front row of the grandstand, and twenty minutes later, the starter's gun sounded. The race was on.

The Challenge Cup was run over one and a half miles. There were seven contenders and Ebony Lass got off to an excellent start.

For the first half of the race she ran neck to neck with two others, vying for the lead. It was to be a tight battle.

They were well past the one-mile mark when Jenna leapt to her feet. The black mare now led by two full body lengths. It appeared she had the race all but won.

'Go, Ebony Lass!' Jenna screamed at the top of her voice.

The children too, all seven of them, jumped up and down, screaming along with her. 'Go, Ebony Lass!' they yelled. 'Go, Ebony Lass!'

But even as the mare seemed on the verge of victory, a large bay gelding placed fourth in the field broke away from the others and in a burst of power sprinted for the finish line, devouring with each stride the distance between him and Ebony Lass.

The mare gamely battled on, maintaining her pace, but she'd given her all, there was nothing more left to give. And just yards from the finish line, the bay overtook her to win by a good half-body length. A decisive victory.

There was a collective groan from the children, but Jenna said nothing. She just plonked herself down in her seat, accepting the commiseration of the others with surprisingly good humour. Or so James thought.

'My, my, what a shame,' from Adele, 'she was so close.'

'Bad luck, Jenna,' from Phil Caton, 'she fought a great battle, just pipped at the finish.'

'Oh well, Phil,' Jenna replied with a shrug, 'that's the way things go.'

'I'm so sorry, my love,' James murmured, 'I know how much this meant to you.' *Why isn't she angry?* he wondered.

'We'll hire the jockey who rode the bay next year,' she replied, 'it was the jockey who won the race.'

She caught Pat's eye, and received a nod of acknowledgement. They both knew she was right. Furthermore, they both knew the jockey. She and Pat knew all the jockeys. And young Greg Pullen had paced his mount to perfection.

'Well said, Jenna.' James admired her show of sportsmanship, he'd expected her to throw a tantrum, or to sulk at the very least. 'There's always next year.'

'Yes, there is, my darling.' Her reply was feisty, the true Jenna of old. 'There will *always* be next year.' She grinned defiantly. 'I *will* win the cup a third time you know, I can promise you that!'

'Of course you will.' He loved her positivity.

An hour later, when she took him aside to tell him her news he loved her even more.

'I had anticipated celebrating two major events today,' she said as they stood in the large refreshments tent sipping chilled glasses of beer poured straight from the keg.

'Oh yes?' he queried.

'The Challenge Cup of course,' she said, 'but that's not to be.'

'And?' he prompted as she paused.

'And the baby,' she announced. 'I'm pregnant.'

James stared at her in sheer amazement. She was thirty-four years old. It had been ten years since the birth of Emily. He had presumed her child-bearing days were over.

Jenna threw back her head and laughed so loudly and energetically she spilled some beer from her glass. 'Oh my goodness . . .' She stepped quickly aside to avoid staining her dress, and others in the refreshment tent turned to stare at her, but she didn't stop giggling. 'You should just see the look on your face!'

'Well you have to admit it's a bit of a surprise.'

'Yes it is, isn't it,' she agreed. 'Are you glad?'

He took the glass from her and placed it together with his on the trestle table beside them. 'I'm far more than glad, my love,' he said, gathering her in his arms and gazing into those startlingly green-hazel eyes of hers. 'I'm the happiest man in the world.' He kissed her gently. 'Who needs a cup,' he said as their lips parted, 'you've given me the greatest prize of all.'

'It's the reward you get for being a loving husband,' she said saucily, but they both knew there was a ring of truth to the remark. Their sex life, which had been in the doldrums for years, had of late become reinvigorated. Surely this was the result.

James wondered vaguely whether he should thank Delia Brereton.

CHAPTER SIXTEEN

The two-day meet of the Tirranna Picnic Races was such a major event that it was only right the culminating ball on the Sunday night, which was held in the pavilion of the Goulburn Showground in order to accommodate the numbers, should be a spectacular affair. And it was.

The evening was well under way when James, Jenna, Adele and Phil arrived. Fashionably late, upon Jenna's insistence.

'The vulgar arrive early,' Jenna had said, 'and the overly eager arrive on time.'

'Quite.' Adele had instantly agreed.

The four of them had shared a bottle of champagne at the Big House before driving into Goulburn. Dom Pérignon. 'Only the best,' James had remarked as they toasted the news. 'To the forthcoming Brereton-McKinnon addition,' he proclaimed.

Jenna had been quite happy for him to announce her pregnancy. 'As you so rightly remarked, my darling,' she'd said, 'it's even better news than a third Challenge Cup win.'

Adele embraced her sister in the most heartfelt manner. 'Oh my dear, I'm so happy for you.'

By the time they arrived at the ball they were in the highest of spirits and prepared to thoroughly enjoy themselves, with the exception of Phil who would have preferred to stay home. But, for Adele's sake, he put on a brave face.

The pavilion, normally a cavernous and rather drab hall, was bedecked to gaudy perfection. Red, white and blue bunting hung from the ceiling, walls were draped with sparkly tinsel and baubles, and huge tubs of floral decorations sat in every corner pretending to elegance, but still somehow managing to look as gaudy as the rest, the object of the exercise being to create an air of festivity.

At the far end, a platform had been erected as a stage upon which a twelve-piece band played with verve, while the centre of the hall was kept clear as a dance floor. Around the peripheries were chairs for the elderly and those who preferred to remain spectators, together with small side tables upon which to rest glasses. Near the main entrance, on either side, were refreshment counters; to the left, one for drinks, mainly beer, cider and apple juice; to the right, one for delicacies which could be eaten daintily in the fingers, thereby minimising the staining of ladies' gloves.

A waltz had just started, 'The Blue Danube' no less, as James, Jenna, Adele and Phil entered, leaving their hats and wraps with the attendant manning the cloakroom set up by the door.

The scene that greeted them was eclectic, the social set from Sydney mingling with the local farmers and wives, but all attired for the event. Women twirled about resplendent in ball gowns while elegantly suited men, some in tailcoats and bow ties, guided them around the intricacies of the crowded dance floor, hopefully keeping collision to a minimum.

'Shall we?'

Jenna didn't even bother to answer as James took her in his arms, whirling her out onto the floor and into the melee. They both loved to dance.

Phil was confronted, as always. Oh God how he hated all this.

'Why don't you get us a drink, darling,' Adele tactfully suggested, knowing exactly how he felt and loving him for suffering in silence as he did. 'I'll find us a table over there on the side.'

He nodded gratefully. He'd down a few in quick succession and get up the nerve to confront the dance floor. He was a terrible dancer. But Adele wasn't, and it was only fair she enjoy herself.

He needn't have worried. Upon looking back as he headed for the drinks counter, he saw a gentleman already approaching her, offering his arm. She turned to her husband as if seeking permission. He gave another grateful nod.

The night proved a triumph. As planned, Phil got a bit drunk, which wasn't difficult for he was not a heavy drinker, but occasions like this demanded some help. Towards the end of the evening he and Adele found themselves dancing nearly as much as James and Jenna, who'd rarely left the floor.

'Do you remember me teaching you how to dance?' Jenna had asked as they'd nimbly quick-stepped their way between the couples. 'It was after Adele's wedding, the grand party back at the Big House.'

'Of course I remember.'

'I was always in love with you,' she said, 'I think from the day we first met. But that's when I decided you'd be the man I would marry.'

'And I'm so glad you did.' He held her even closer, lost in the happiness of this very special night and the knowledge he was to become a father all over again.

The ball was coming to an end. And all too soon it seemed. James was suddenly aware that he'd been so distracted he hadn't taken advantage of the opportunities on offer; he hadn't mingled with as many of the important dignitaries as he'd intended to. It didn't really matter, he supposed, but such contacts could prove valuable. If not from a practical point of view then most certainly with regard to one's image. Being seen hobnobbing with the social elite from Sydney was an all-important element of the Tirranna Picnic Races.

As Jenna, Adele and Phil left to collect their wraps and hats from the cloakroom, he excused himself.

'Grab my hat for me will you, Phil,' he said. 'Be with you shortly, just need to say a brief hello.' And he made a beeline for Alfred Lord Beasley, who was holding court with several guests at the drinks counter; two men whom James didn't recognise, tail-coated and clearly from Sydney, and one middle-aged society matron whom he knew well, as did everyone in the district. Millicent Ashley-Barton was considered the doyen of Goulburn and he really should have greeted her earlier. But no matter, he decided, Beasley's presence was of the greater significance.

Alfred Lord Beasley, a regular visitor to the Tirranna Picnic Races was, in James' opinion, an awful English fop, but being aristocracy his attendance was always reported in the newspapers. Rumour had it he'd been a 'remittance man', sent to the colonies a good fifteen years previously by his father, Howard Lord Beasley who had considered the youngest of his sons a wastrel. Over the ensuing years Howard appeared to have forgotten Alfred's existence altogether, although the remittances had obviously continued. Alfred, who had no right to his father's title, had adopted the use of 'Lord', and so it appeared had everyone else. Given his lineage, he was feted by all, including James, who had invited him to Glenfinnan two years previously when they'd been celebrating Jenna's second Challenge Cup win.

'My dear Millicent, such a wonderful evening.'

James greeted Millicent Ashley-Barton, who responded with gracious dignity although in truth she was just a little miffed he had taken so long to seek her out.

'And Alfred.' He then turned his attention to Beasley, hand extended. 'Good to see you again.'

'Ah. James, yes, good to see you too, old man.' Alfred's response was effusive and the two shook hands warmly. 'Too bad your mare didn't come home, she looked like a winner there for a minute.'

'Yes, she did, didn't she?'

'Allow me to introduce . . .'

Alfred made the introductions to the two men, a double-barrelled name, Mr someone-Smythe and a colourless little Englishman in his sixties, Professor Henderson.

'And this is one of the most prominent breeders of the finest Merinos in Australia,' Alfred said in true grandiose style, 'the owner of Glenfinnan Sheep Station himself, Mr James McKinnon.'

James didn't bother correcting the man, so many people these days left out the 'Brereton', who cared anyway?

'How do you do, gentlemen.'

As hands were shaken he was pleased to observe a nearby journalist from the *Goulburn Post* scribbling away in a notebook. He recognised the fellow and even gave him a friendly nod. A paragraph was bound to appear in the social pages of the *Sydney Morning Herald,* all of which was excellent, not only for his personal profile but that of Glenfinnan.

Alfred, well lubricated as usual, was keen for a chat, but James, having had his presence noted, was equally keen to make his departure.

'Your glorious wife, dear chap,' Alfred was saying, 'where is she? Saw the two of you on the dance floor, what. Heavens above, you never left it, one would think you were twenty . . .' A guffaw followed. 'But by God what a horse breeder she is, your wife. I'd so like to chat to her about Ebony Lass, and the gelding, year before last, what's-his-name, who took out the Challenge Cup . . .'

James broke into the man's insufferable monologue. 'Actually, Jenna's waiting for me out the front, Alfred, together with my business partner and sister-in-law. I'm to drive them back home to Glenfinnan, and . . .' He slipped a hand inside his tailcoat and with a flamboyant gesture withdrew the fob watch from the pocket of his impeccably starched white vest. Being in formal dress, he had chosen to detach the piece from its chain. 'Good heavens above, is that the time,' he said, flashing the dial at Alfred and pretending horror, 'half past eleven, they'll have been waiting for a whole ten minutes now. I really must go.'

He was about to return the watch to his vest and move off, but one of the two men to whom he'd just been introduced, the colourless little Professor Henderson, stopped him.

'No, please, Mr McKinnon, one moment, I beg of you.'

The man's plea seemed quite urgent and James halted.

'Your watch, sir. Please, may I see it?'

'Yes, of course.' James was not in the least surprised. The watch often received comment from those with good taste. He very much enjoyed showing it off.

The professor took the watch from him, produced a pince-nez from the breast pocket of his tailcoat and clipping the spectacles to his nose examined the piece closely.

'My goodness,' he said in breathless amazement, 'I have seen only one of these before in my entire life.' He turned the piece over in his hands, appearing to caress it. 'And even then not "in the flesh" so to speak.'

Then came the pronouncement that chilled James to the very core.

The little man looked up at him with pallid, grey eyes. 'The only time I have seen a watch like this,' he said, 'was in the portrait of the Grenfell brothers that hangs on the walls of the ground-floor foyer in Sydney's Grenfell Emporium.'

'Really? How interesting.' James smiled and held out his hand for the watch.

The professor passed it to him, albeit with reluctance, he would clearly have liked to examine it far more closely and for far longer. He tucked the pince-nez back into his breast pocket.

'I'm sure there must be many fine pieces like this,' James said pleasantly as he returned the watch to his vest.

'Oh no, to the contrary, there are only eight in the entire world,' Professor Henderson replied, not attempting to hide his excitement. 'Do you not know of the watch's history, sir?' In the slight pause that followed, Hubert Henderson gathered that James McKinnon did *not* know. 'Its antiquity is of great significance, I can assure you, Mr McKinnon. Where did you get the piece, may I ask?'

What fucking business is that of yours? James' mind screamed. He wanted to kill this little man. But his reply was amiable, his voice and demeanour most agreeable. 'It was gifted to me by my father upon his death many years ago.'

'I see, I see.' Hubert Henderson was nodding eagerly, desperate to ascertain more information. 'And was your father a military man?'

'No,' James replied, 'my father was a shearer.'

'Amazing, quite amazing.' Hubert decided that perhaps he should explain just a little about himself. 'I am a military historian, you see, and I have a great interest in antiquities, particularly those of a military nature. The two, as you can imagine, tend to go hand in hand,' he added with a light, self-deprecating chortle as if in stating the obvious he'd made some sort of joke. Then, after clearing his throat, he was once again in deadly earnest. 'So how did your father, a shearer, happen to come by the watch, might I ask?'

If we were alone, James thought, *you would be dead by now.* 'My father also was gifted it,' he said, 'by a wealthy farmer whose life he saved.'

'I see, I see,' Hubert Henderson had a habit of repeating himself when excited, and he was very excited now. 'And had this farmer been a military man by any chance?'

'Not that I know of,' James replied.

It was at that moment a thoroughly fed-up Millicent Ashley-Barton chose to interrupt.

'If you'll excuse me, gentlemen, I really must circulate and say my farewells before the evening is altogether over.' She was both irritated and bored by this unnecessary talk of watches. So was Alfred Beasley, she could tell. He was nudging his friend and signalling for another drink.

'Goodbye, Alfred,' she said and she swanned off, not bothering to farewell the others who had so rudely ignored her.

'Ah yes, bye-bye Millicent,' Alfred replied before turning to his friend. 'Another for you too, Walter? Best say yes, they'll stop serving soon. The whole shindig's supposed to be over by midnight.'

While the two men turned their attention to final drinks, Hubert Henderson honed in on James.

'I would love to discuss the background of this watch with you, Mr McKinnon. My colleagues in the Royal Historical Society will be thrilled to hear of its existence. May I suggest—'

'Most certainly you may,' James agreed graciously, 'but not at this moment, I'm afraid, my wife and . . .'

'Yes, yes, of course, I realise this. But some time tomorrow? I'm staying at Mandelsons Hotel. Might we meet in the morning, or perhaps for lunch?'

'Any time during the day would be impossible I'm afraid.' James' smile was warm and friendly, but his mind was racing ahead trying to formulate a plan. Whatever this plan might prove to be it would no doubt require the cover of darkness. 'You must understand that the work of a sheep farmer takes place during the hours of daylight.'

Another smile, apologetic and charming. 'Daylight is the farmer's friend, Professor Henderson.'

'Yes, yes, of course, of course.' Hubert was nodding overtime now. He'd planned to return to Sydney tomorrow, but the investigation of the watch must take ultimate priority. He would stay in Goulburn an extra night. 'May I perhaps suggest dinner then? They serve an excellent meal at Mandelsons, so I've found.'

'They do indeed,' James agreed. *Yes,* he thought, *that might work. The hotel is rarely busy on a Monday night, and any racegoers booked in are bound to have caught the train back to Sydney during the day.*

'Excellent.' Hubert Henderson beamed happily. 'Shall we say seven o'clock?'

'Seven o'clock,' James agreed, offering his hand. 'I shall see you then, Professor. We'll meet in the bar.'

'Excellent, excellent.' Then a hasty reminder. 'You won't forget to bring the watch, will you, Mr McKinnon?'

'Oh no, I shan't forget the watch,' James assured him.

He then turned towards Alfred Lord Beasley who had distanced himself and was now several paces away, lolling against the drinks counter chatting with his good friend Walter Crighton-Smythe.

'Goodnight, Alfred,' James called, and he gave a wave to the double-barrelled Mr someone-Smythe.

'Ah yes, goodnight, old chap, regards to that clever little wife of yours,' Alfred called back while Mr someone-Smythe returned the wave.

The others were waiting outside, Phil with James' top hat, which he'd retrieved from the cloakroom.

'What took you so long?' Jenna asked as he donned his hat and they set off for the car.

'Got cornered by Alfred Beasley,' James said, 'who sends his regards to my "clever little wife".'

'How patronising.'

'Not at all. He thinks you're a marvellous horse breeder.'

'And he's quite right.' Jenna gave a toss of her head. 'Just not so marvellous in my choice of jockey, but things will be different next year.'

'Oh by the way,' James said, 'I'm to have dinner at Mandelsons with a friend of Beasley's tomorrow, a Professor Henderson. Don't know his first name, just met him tonight.'

'A *professor*,' Jenna pretended to be impressed, 'my, my.'

'Yes, he's a professor of history and evidently very keen to meet up for a chat with me.'

'Why? What about?'

'I have no idea, my love. No idea whatsoever. But he seems a nice enough chap. Might be interesting.'

James had decided that whatever action he was to take must be conducted as overtly as possible. There could be no sneaking about in the dark this time. No creeping off into the night as he'd intended had Delia's death proved necessary. This time whatever was to take place – and something obviously *had* to take place – must be perceived as accidental. Perhaps even witnessed. How on earth was he to go about it?

They piled into the car, all four, and during the drive home as they chatted on animatedly about the ball, James included, his mind continued to tick over.

'Do call me Hubert, please,' the little man eagerly insisted as they seated themselves at a table in the near-empty front bar, having decided upon a drink before adjourning to the restaurant. 'I've been impatiently awaiting our chat all day,' he went on, 'can't tell you how thrilled I am by the discovery of your watch.' Rubbing his hands together gleefully and even appearing to bounce up and down in his chair a little, the professor looked for all the world like an excited ten-year-old let loose in a lolly shop.

James smiled graciously. 'And you're to call me James,' he said. He found the fellow's childlike enthusiasm quite repellent. He had from the moment Henderson had arrived in the bar beaming excitedly and accepting the large glass of cognac awaiting him with a protestation almost girlish.

'Oh goodness, I rarely drink spirits,' the man had gushed, 'but perhaps just this once, yes? We have a great deal to celebrate after all, don't we? My, my, we do, the discovery of so rare an antiquity.'

'Quite,' James had replied, 'which is why I have purchased the very finest aged cognac. Only the best will do for such an occasion.'

Then the professor had suggested they sit at the table in the corner, which was positioned right under the lamp in its wall bracket, where the light would be best in order to examine the watch.

James himself had arrived a good twenty minutes earlier than arranged in order to study the conditions and the layout of the hotel. He'd been pleased to note they were much as he'd envisaged they would be. Or rather as he'd hoped they would be, given his earlier recollections of Mandelsons.

He'd entered via the main foyer instead of the doors that led into the front bar directly from the street. There was only one person in attendance at the reception desk, a young man, the night clerk or night manager, whatever his title might be, but no one else. *Good,* he'd thought, *that's good.* And towards the rear of the foyer was the staircase, which led up to the first-floor accommodation level. He'd crossed to the reception counter and discovered that he couldn't quite see the top of the staircase from here. *Good,* he'd thought, *yes, that's very good.*

'I'm to meet one of your hotel guests, Professor Henderson,' he'd told the clerk. 'We're dining here tonight and I believe I'm a little early. Will you tell him when he comes downstairs that Mr McKinnon is waiting in the bar?'

'Yes, of course, sir,' the young man replied, and he gestured towards the doors that led from the foyer into the front bar and from there into the restaurant. 'Do please go on through.'

As they sat, Hubert took a tentative sip of his cognac. 'My, my, it is rather strong, isn't it,' he said.

'Yes, but quite delicious I think you'll find,' James replied, encouraging him to take a second sip.

Hubert obligingly sipped. 'Yes, yes,' he said, only too eager to please, nodding away in what appeared to be his customary manner, 'very warming, isn't it, very rich, very mellow.'

The man obviously had just one thing on his mind, so James withdrew the watch from his vest pocket, unfastening the gold chain he was now wearing given his less formal attire, and placed both watch and chain on the table.

'Ah.' The professor put down his glass, gave an audible sigh of reverence and picked up the watch, briefly fingering the heavy, gold chain. 'Most attractive,' he said. 'The chain, of course, remained a personal choice of the recipient; the watches were made to be awarded as handpieces only.' He then lost all interest in the chain, withdrew his pince-nez from his breast pocket, clipped the spectacles to his nose and settled down to examine the watch itself. 'Marvellous,' he breathed, 'to think I am actually holding one of these pieces in my hand. Absolutely marvellous!'

James' irritation, already intense, was on the rise, but he didn't let it show, his manner conveying nothing but charm and an avid interest he didn't feel.

'Perhaps you'd enlighten me, Hubert. As you gathered last night I am at a loss with regard to the watch's history. You said there were only eight of these pieces in the entire world?'

'Yes, yes, of course, James, of course,' Hubert replied all aflutter. 'How remiss of me, I'm just overly excited, you see. Such a find!'

'I'll drink to that.'

James raised his glass encouragingly and Hubert followed suit. They clinked and drank, James barely sipping his cognac, Hubert taking a healthy swig of his, keen to get on with his story.

'The watches were made on the orders of Field Marshall Lord Raglan, Commander of the British troops during the Crimean War,' he explained, 'and they were to be awarded to eight officers in commemoration of the Battle of Balaclava on the 25th of October 1854.' He held the watch out to James, stabbing an eager finger at the centre of its face. 'See the letter "B", right here in the middle. And they were made by a famous Swiss watchmaker living in London, a fellow by the name of Francois Brenel who was a friend of Raglan's.' Once again an eager finger pointed out the feature at the top of the watch near the winder. 'See, here, the watchmaker's initials, "FB".'

'Yes,' James said, 'I had presumed that was a watchmaker's mark. So how did these pieces end up in general circulation?' he asked. He was genuinely interested now. *How the hell did Charles Grenfell happen to come by it?*

'That's the whole point, you see,' Hubert went on excitedly, loving every minute of this discussion, aware that he was on the verge of a great discovery, 'no one really knows. The watches were collected by a British Army officer, after which they disappeared from history. They were never distributed to the eight officers Raglan had them made for and the actual names of the officers were known to no one but Raglan himself. However, he died in Sevastopol in the Crimea on the 28th of June, barely eight months later, so the identities of these intended recipients remain a mystery. There is much conjecture, of course, but no proof to be found.'

'How very intriguing,' James said thoughtfully, sipping at his cognac, the little professor by now automatically following his example.

'Yes, yes, indeed,' Hubert agreed after taking a healthy swig. 'Over the years,' he continued, 'the watches have purportedly appeared and disappeared on any number of occasions, some reports genuine, others not, and they're now considered almost the stuff of legend.' His eyes were alight with sheer elation. 'So you can understand my excitement upon this discovery.'

'I can, my friend, I certainly can.' James once again raised his glass, and there was another salutation. The professor had nearly finished his cognac now, which had been a double. *So far so good,* James thought.

'One of the watches is in the St Petersburg Museum in Russia,' Hubert went on, 'another is reportedly in private Turkish hands in Istanbul, and three are believed to be somewhere in the British military system, whether in private hands or regimental property it is not known. Which leaves three that are totally untraceable. Until now, my dear James,' he declared exultantly, 'until now!' And this time it was Hubert who proposed the toast.

They drained their glasses and James stood, pocketing the watch and chain.

'Shall we continue this discussion over dinner?' he suggested.

'Yes, yes,' Hubert agreed, feeling just a little unsteady as he rose to his feet. He needed food. Cognac on an empty stomach was not a good idea, he decided.

They adjourned to the dining room where James was pleased to note there were only two couples dining. As he'd anticipated, Monday was not a busy night.

They sat, Hubert thrusting a hand into his coat pocket to produce a small notebook, which he'd purchased at the newsagent that very morning.

'I do hope you won't mind,' he said, 'if I make the occasional note now and then. There's so much I'd like to enquire of you. I've already jotted down some bits and pieces, but I haven't as yet written to my colleagues at the Royal Historical Society in London, I've been waiting until we'd had our chat.'

Thank God for that, James thought. 'I don't mind in the least, Hubert. Feel free to jot away.'

As the professor ferreted about for his fountain pen, James beckoned the waiter over.

They took a brief look at the menu, Hubert ordering the roast lamb and James beef steak, medium-rare.

'By way of a change,' he said lightly. 'As you can imagine, we eat a great deal of lamb at Glenfinnan.'

'Yes, yes, of course you would.' The professor nodded and gave an ingratiating chortle to show he really did get the joke. 'You would, yes, yes, of course you would.'

You really are the most irritating man, James thought as he ordered a bottle of the hotel's finest shiraz.

'We'll have the wine right away, thank you,' he instructed the waiter, then he watched as Hubert opened the notepad.

From his position on the opposite side of the table James could read quite clearly, although upside down, the name 'James McKinnon', and beside it 'Glenfinnan Sheep Station'. There was a date below and several other scrawls, but he didn't bother studying any further. Hubert was by now poised, Waterman's fountain pen – 'the brand-new "safety" version, guaranteed not to leak' – in hand, all ready to embark upon his interview. It appeared he intended far more than 'an occasional note now and then'.

Hubert did. Without hesitation, he launched himself into the plethora of questions he'd planned.

'You said you'd been gifted the watch upon your father's death,' he started out, 'and that your father was a shearer . . .'

'Yes, that's correct.' These were obviously the scrawled notes under the heading, James thought.

'But the McKinnon family has been established at Glenfinnan for several generations.' Hubert appeared somewhat confused. 'So your father . . .'

'I'm not a McKinnon by birth, Hubert.'

'Oh.' This declaration stopped the little man in his tracks.

'I married Alastair McKinnon's youngest daughter. The family name I have adopted for my wife and children is actually Brereton-McKinnon.'

'Ah.' Still an element of confusion. 'But Lord Beasley introduced you as—'

'Yes, I know he did. Alfred is always confusing my name.' Hubert's referral to Alfred as 'Lord Beasley' pleased James, it intimated the two were not the close friends he had presumed them to be. 'Alfred Beasley is such an admirer of my wife and her family, he chooses to think of us all as McKinnons. Which I don't really mind,' he added with a shrug, 'many people do the same. But I was born a Brereton.'

'I see, I see.' The scratch of the fountain pen as Hubert jotted down the name. 'And so your father was?' he queried without even looking up.

'George Brereton,' James replied, nodding to the waiter who'd arrived with the wine. 'He was an Englishman, a widower who migrated to Australia with his very small son, and became a shearer in Central Western Queensland, which is where I grew up.'

As Hubert's fountain pen continued to frantically scratch, James sipped from the taster the waiter had poured and gestured he fill both glasses, which he did before disappearing and leaving the bottle on the table.

'I see, I see. That would mean, I take it'—Hubert finally looked up from his notebook—'that the wealthy farmer who gifted the watch to your father was from Queensland?'

'That's correct.'

'And his name? What was this farmer's name?' A fanatical light burned in Hubert's eyes and his voice all but shook, knowing he was on the verge of a major breakthrough.

'I have no idea, I'm afraid. Now, Hubert, please do try this wine, it's an excellent shiraz, one of my personal favourites.'

Realising he was back to square one, the professor's disappointment was so palpable he appeared to physically deflate before James' very eyes. But he did as he was told, and sampled the shiraz, which was indeed delicious, he very much enjoyed a good red wine. Then something occurred to him. Perhaps it was the wine hitting the cognac that brought a whole new thought crashing into his brain.

'Amazing isn't it,' he mused, 'quite amazing, that two of the eight watches have been discovered in Australia of all places. The one I saw in the Grenfell portrait barely a month or so ago, and now this one left to you by your father.'

'Not that amazing, really,' James calmly replied, although he was surprised Hubert appeared to have only just registered the coincidence. 'Many military officers were gifted land in the colonies by a grateful British government. Glenfinnan itself is the perfect example. The property was originally a soldier settlement granted to the McKinnon ancestor who fought in the Battle of Waterloo.'

'Ah, yes, of course, there is that.' Hubert adopted his nodding routine, accepting instantly the plausibility of such reasoning. 'Yes, there is certainly that. The members of the historical society have agreed that the three watches unaccounted for may well have found their way into military hands.' He sipped his wine thoughtfully, mulling over the matter.

'Did you discover any military background to the watch you saw in the Grenfell portrait?' James enquired. Now here was an area that was of definite interest. Just what action had the professor taken upon identifying the watch?

'No, not a wretched thing,' Hubert replied crossly, 'and it certainly wasn't for want of trying, I can tell you. Oh my goodness, the trouble I went to. Came up against a brick wall every single time. The Grenfell family proved most unhelpful.'

'Oh really?' James was fascinated. 'In what way?'

Ten minutes later, when the meals arrived, Hubert had well and truly launched into both his story and the wine. Hungry as he was, or rather as he'd thought he'd been, the professor was by now so carried away he barely touched his food. James signalled the waiter for another bottle.

It turned out the oldest of the three brothers in the portrait, Thaddeus Grenfell, had died ten years previously, he told James, his wife's death following two years later, and the family had decided the portrait which had hung in their home was to be displayed in the grand foyer of the Grenfell Emporium.

'The youngest brother,' Hubert explained, 'the one displaying the watch, and I might add *displaying* is the operative word – you should just see the way he's showing it off to the artist as if it's some sort of trophy . . .'

I have seen it, and you're quite right, he certainly was, James thought, recalling the posture and the arrogance only too well.

'. . . which of course, was very convenient for purposes of identification,' Hubert went on, 'but which also led me to believe he knew of its history that he should exhibit the piece in such a triumphant manner. Anyway, this youngest brother, Charles, died quite some time ago. A heart attack evidently, and it's his daughter who is managing the emporium. The middle brother, Geoffrey, is unwell I was told, hence Miss Grenfell has taken over the management.'

Miss Grenfell, James thought, wondering which of Charles' daughters it might be, Evelyn or Dora. He remembered them both with great clarity, pretty young women.

That was fourteen years ago, he thought, *they'd both be well into their thirties now. So one of them has devoted herself to the family business instead of marrying, it would appear. Interesting.*

'I naturally asked to see Miss Grenfell, whom I discovered to be a rather sour-tempered woman, not remotely interested in my enquiries. Said she knew nothing about the watch, except for the fact that it was no longer in the family, which as you can imagine was hugely disappointing news. And then she said she was far too busy to chat on any longer. She did, however, suggest I speak to her mother who was at least sympathetic to my cause.'

Clementine, James thought, remembering feeling sorry for the sad-faced woman who'd had the misfortune of being married to such a hideous man as Charles.

Hubert downed the remains of his wine and James poured him another as he continued, unabated.

'I visited Mrs Grenfell at her house in Elizabeth Bay and found her to be most pleasant. Certainly to begin with. We even took tea together. She was very interested in the watch and its history.'

Hubert couldn't help but recall how very promising their interview had been at the outset.

'Dear me,' Mrs Grenfell had said, 'it would seem Charles knew of the watch's history, which would certainly account for his excitement upon being presented with the piece. He truly was thrilled to own it. Which is why he posed for the portrait the way he did, showing it off, so to speak. It was a gift from his brothers as a birthday present, you see, shortly before they sat for the portrait.' She'd appeared thoughtful. 'I'm surprised he didn't tell me of its historic value,' she'd said. 'Although perhaps he feared he might get into trouble, given the fact that experts like you, Professor, are seeking the whereabouts of these valuable watches which were intended for military recipients.

Perhaps all three brothers knew of the watch's history and feared there might be some troublesome complications.'

'Where did the brothers purchase the piece?' he'd asked.

'From an antique shop I believe, at least that's what they told me.'

'Would you know which particular antique shop?'

'Not a clue, I'm so sorry.' A regretful shake of her head, Clementine really would have liked to have been of help.

'Perhaps I may visit the other Mr Grenfell?' he'd asked tentatively, not wishing to sound tasteless, but meaning 'the one who's still alive'.

'Out of the question, I'm afraid.' Another shake of the head, sad this time. 'Geoffrey is quite brain-addled. He had a stroke several years ago and is in a sanatorium. He can't even speak, the poor dear.'

Hubert had then decided it was time to get to the nitty-gritty. He'd been told the watch was no longer in the family's possession, but surely they must have some idea of its whereabouts.

'Mrs Grenfell,' he'd said purposefully, but again he trusted with good taste, 'I hope you won't mind my asking, but after your husband's heart attack, what happened to the watch? Did the family sell it? And if so, to whom?'

Hubert drained his glass of red wine and gazed directly at James, his eyes by now bleary, his roast lamb virtually untouched, gravy congealing on the plate.

'That's when she closed off altogether,' he said.

James, who had finished his steak, which he'd found quite delicious, refilled the professor's glass. They were nearly halfway through the second bottle by now. Or rather, Hubert was.

'Why would she do that, I wonder?' He didn't wonder at all, he knew exactly why.

'Can't even hazard a guess. But she called a halt to our morning tea, which I found just a little rude from a lady of obvious breeding like Mrs Grenfell. Simply said she had no idea what had happened to the watch. That none of them had. It was presumably stolen when her poor husband was taken to the hospital. Then she said she really must get on with her day. And that was that. Most odd.'

'Most odd indeed.' *Poor Clementine,* James thought, *still living the lie to this day that her debauched husband died of a heart attack instead of admitting he was murdered and robbed in a Woolloomooloo brothel.* 'Would you like some dessert, Hubert?'

Hubert looked down at his roast lamb, which appeared singularly unappetising.

'I'm not sure about dessert,' he said. 'I'm actually not all that hungry.'

'I don't fancy dessert either,' James agreed and he signalled the waiter for the bill. 'I have a much better idea. What say we adjourn to your room and polish off this excellent shiraz? I'm so much enjoying our chat and have so many further questions I long to ask. For instance, you really do believe that the Grenfell brothers knew about the watch and its history?'

'Yes, yes.' The professor nodded furiously, in response to both the question and the idea. He would willingly talk about the watch all night, particularly with a glass of red in hand. 'This I truly do believe.'

The waiter arrived with the bill, which James settled, despite the professor's protestations.

'No, no, James,' Hubert said, 'the dinner is to go on my hotel account. *I* invited *you* to dinner if you recall. The invitation was most definitely mine.'

He's slurring his words, James thought, pleased that the waiter was witness to the fact, *good, very good.*

'Wouldn't hear of it old man,' he insisted, 'we're in my home town and as such you are my guest.' He smiled graciously at the waiter who returned a bow and disappeared. 'Come along now, Hubert.'

Hubert rose a little unsteadily. 'In fact,' he went on as if there'd been no interruption whatsoever to their conversation, 'I believe the brothers, all three, would be able to tell me what happened to the watch. But with two dead and the third *non compos mentis* I suppose I shall never know.'

'Don't forget your notebook,' James reminded him.

'Ah, yes.'

Hubert returned the notebook to his coat pocket, James picked up the bottle of wine, and they walked out of the restaurant and through the front bar, James pleased to observe that the professor was quite noticeably unstable on his feet.

'And what's more,' Hubert continued as they went, 'the family members, too, have some inkling. Or at least Mrs Grenfell does. I mean *stolen when her husband was taken to hospital!* I ask you! Am I really to believe that? There's some secret afoot, James, I'll swear to it.'

He was still talking, still slurring his words, still unsteady on his feet, in fact quite visibly inebriated, as they entered the hotel foyer.

'Here, old man, let me give you a hand,' James said loudly for the benefit of the young night clerk behind the reception desk.

'I'm fine,' Hubert insisted as he started wobbling his way up the stairs, 'I'm absolutely fine.'

James nevertheless put his right arm, wine bottle dangling from his hand, supportively around the little man's shoulders as they set off together up the staircase to the first floor.

When they were at the top and out of sight it took only seconds.

The supportive arm that had been around Hubert's shoulders was suddenly around his face.

Standing behind him, James locked the man's head into the crook of his elbow, placed the palm of his left hand on Hubert's temple, then pushed and wrenched sharply to the right. He gave a loud cough in order to cover the sound of the crack, which he knew would be audible. Probably not to the clerk at the reception desk, but best to play safe. As Hubert's lifeless body slumped in his arms he dived a hand into the man's coat pocket and retrieved the notebook. Then he threw the body forcefully down the stairs, letting out a cry of alarm as he did so.

He quickly followed down the stairs himself, to arrive beside the body, which was lying prone, neck grotesquely twisted to a 180-degree angle, open eyes staring up at the ceiling. He got there at precisely the same moment as the night clerk, who'd raced from behind the counter.

'Oh dear God!' James exclaimed, distraught.

'He's broken his neck,' the desk clerk announced unnecessarily.

They called the police.

CHAPTER SEVENTEEN

'He insisted we take the bottle of red wine up to his room, he refused to stop drinking,' James told the police after the body had been collected for delivery to the city morgue. 'I agreed simply in order to assist him up the stairs, I knew he was drunk. It was my intention to see him safely to his room and leave. And then . . .' A despairing shake of the head. 'When we reached the first floor landing, his foot didn't even make the top step, he just slid out of my grasp.' James' face was a picture of anguish. 'If I hadn't been holding that wretched bottle of wine . . . I don't know . . . I might have been able to cling on to him . . . I might have . . .'

'Not your fault, sir,' the middle-aged sergeant assured him kindly, aware the poor man was tortured with guilt, 'not your fault at all, Mr McKinnon. You put it right out of your mind now. It was an accident, a tragic accident, that's what it was.'

James noted the lack of 'Brereton', which seemed to happen as a matter of course these days. He noted too, as he always did, the added degree of respect that accompanied the use of the name. *Very handy being a McKinnon,* he thought.

'Thank you, Sergeant,' he said. 'You're quite right of course. It was a terrible thing to have happened, but a tragic accident, no more. Not healthy to dwell too much upon it.'

'That is so, sir. Now you go along home. And you take care, mind.'

During the drive back to Glenfinnan, James' mind went over the evening, step by step. Not the dispatching of the professor, which had simply been necessary, but the story of the watch.

Had the Grenfell brothers been aware of the watch's history? he wondered. Had Charles? Was that why he'd been showing off the piece so ostentatiously in the portrait, as Hubert had surmised to be the case? Or had he just been showing off his new birthday present?

James tended to believe the latter himself, although either way the matter was not really of great importance. Something else was, though. Something else was of vast importance.

I've been lucky so far, he thought, *damn lucky. But the watch must never again see the light of day. Dear God, how many other 'military historians' or 'antique experts' might be out there hunting these lost relics of the past?*

What to do? He could throw it in the river. He could bury it in the outback. He could destroy it altogether, smash it to pieces. But he decided no, to all three options. On the one hand there would always be the possibility of its discovery. And on the other, the loss of the watch in any way would be to invite comment; he'd made such a show of the piece over the years. No, no, he would keep it.

But in truth there was another factor altogether governing James' decision. He was simply loath to part with the piece. He had become inordinately fond of the fob watch and chain gifted him by his father. It was all he had left of George Brereton, who in his mind was always George Wakefield. But he must never again wear the thing in public, he vowed. It must remain locked away in the deposit box that he kept in his wardrobe. Locked away just

as it had been all those years ago following the night he'd
killed Charles Grenfell.

Jenna was horrified to hear of the tragic accident, which
the following day made headlines in the *Goulburn
Post,* and which also warranted mention in the *Sydney
Morning Herald.*

'What a shocking thing to happen,' she said, 'and you
were witness to it, you poor darling, how absolutely awful.'

'I was far more than witness, my love,' he replied, 'I was
right there beside him, did my best to stop him falling, but
he just slipped right out of my grasp.'

James' story to Jenna that night had been exactly the
same as his story to the kindly police sergeant.

'Hubert was already drunk, and yet he insisted I drink
on with him in his room. I agreed simply in order to assist
him up the stairs. He was a fragile chap in his sixties and
I worried for his safety.' James shook his head, once again
in a distraught state. 'He broke his neck in the fall, it was
a terrible thing to see, such a terrible thing. And I could do
nothing to prevent it.'

'Oh my poor darling.' She put her arms around him
comfortingly. 'You mustn't blame yourself, it was a tragic
accident, not your fault in the least.'

Jenna's reaction had been exactly the same as the kindly
police sergeant's.

A day or so later, however, when her husband appeared
to have made a remarkably speedy recovery from the incident that had so traumatised him, Jenna felt safe in once
again raising the subject.

'What did he want to discuss over dinner?' she asked as
the two of them prepared for bed on the Wednesday night.
She was seated upon the little pink, padded stool before
her dressing table, looking thoughtfully into the mirror
as she brushed her hair. Jenna was proud of her fine head

of coppery hair, which she always brushed a hundred times before bed. 'What on earth did he talk about?'

'Who?' James was standing naked at the washstand, paying little attention, having just brushed his teeth and rinsed into the small bowl that sat beside the water jug and basin. He dabbed at his mouth with the hand towel. 'What did who talk about?' he asked, reaching for his nightshirt that hung over the back of the nearby chair.

'Professor Henderson. You said he was keen to meet up for a chat. What did he want to talk about?'

'That's a very interesting question, my love.' James slipped the nightshirt on over his head. 'Do you know, I really have no idea.' He sat on the edge of the bed, watching her admiringly in the mirror. *She truly does have the most beautiful hair,* he thought.

Jenna laughed, enjoying the admiration she could see in his eyes. 'Oh come along now, James,' she said and she twirled about on the stool to face him, 'you spent the whole evening having dinner with the man, you must know what he talked about.'

'Oh yes, I know what he talked about,' he replied, 'of course I know what he talked about.'

'What then?'

'Himself.'

'Himself?'

'Yes, he told me all about his connections with the Royal Historical Society in London, and his background as a military historian. Hubert was very much out to impress. In fact the entire evening was something of a history lesson, and a highly academic one at that. I learned a whole lot about Lord Raglan and the Crimean War.'

'How very tedious.'

'Yes it was rather.'

Jenna had stopped counting her brush strokes, but she was sure it had to be more than a hundred by now. She put down the hairbrush and looked at him with an expression of puzzlement bordering on comical.

'Why on earth should Professor Henderson wish to meet up with you for an academic discussion? You're a farmer, for goodness sake.'

'Yes, I was somewhat mystified by that myself,' James admitted, 'to start with anyway. But as I said, Hubert was out to impress.'

His reply had only increased Jenna's puzzlement. 'Why? For what reason? What purpose?'

'I didn't really understand until . . .' James hesitated, appearing to hedge as if reluctant to reveal the truth. 'Until he insisted I accompany him up to his room . . .' He left the rest unsaid.

Jenna's jaw gaped in amazement. 'You don't mean . . .?'

'I'm afraid I do, my love. At least this was my suspicion. I mean, what other reason could there have been?'

He patted the bed and she crossed to sit beside him, her expression now a mix of repugnance and disbelief.

'You think he was a . . .' She could barely bring herself to say it. 'A deviant? A homosexual?'

'Yes, I do believe so.'

'But you said he was a frail man in his sixties.'

'I've heard that the most unlikely men can have tendencies in that direction, some of them even quite elderly, as would appear so in Hubert's case.'

It had certainly been so with any number of men he'd accosted and robbed in Hyde Park, James remembered. The ordinary, the middle-aged, the elderly, so many of them indiscernible from the average man in the street. Impossible to tell, he'd found.

'How repulsive,' Jenna said.

'Yes, perhaps,' he agreed, 'although I couldn't help feeling a little sorry for Hubert, he seemed so lonely. So lonely and, as I said, so frail. Which is why I helped him up the stairs, poor fellow, I didn't want him to fall.' He shrugged regretfully. 'Fat lot of help I was as it turned out.'

'How could you possibly feel sorry for a degenerate creature like that?' Jenna was outraged. 'The man wished to defile you, he was depraved.'

Like your brother? James wondered. *Like your brother who was the best of men, and whom I loved dearly?* He felt irritated with Jenna now, time to end the conversation.

'Let's not talk of it any further, my love, the subject is painful to me.'

'Oh I'm so sorry, James, I'm so very, very sorry. How tactless I've been.' She kissed him and caressed him tenderly. 'Please do forgive me, please, please, my darling.'

He made love to her, grateful the matter had been so easily buried.

James had locked the fob watch away in his deposit box as planned and, with no official occasion that might have called upon his wearing it, the absence of the piece went unnoticed for a month or so. But he was aware he must replace it for he could not be seen without a watch and chain, which was his distinctive pattern of dress. So he set about purchasing another.

He ordered a Waltham pocket watch and chain from a catalogue that specialised in supplying only the top-quality brands of imported goods. Ironically it was a Grenfell Emporium catalogue, and the fob watch, which had been supplied directly by the American Waltham Watch Company, arrived barely six weeks later via Sydney. The Grenfell Emporium was renowned for its efficiency.

James immediately showed the piece off to the family, prepared to field the queries that would follow, his reason for its purchase at the ready.

'Very impressive,' Jenna said as they gathered about the kitchen table to admire the new acquisition, 'but why do you feel the need for another watch, James? You're so proud of the one your father left you.'

'That's precisely why, my love. Pa's watch is extremely precious to me, but it's old now, and fragile. It must be treated with care.'

'I like this one better,' Emily piped up. Emily, who would be eleven later in the year, was always quick to voice her opinion, 'it's more sparkly.'

Ted, now twelve, didn't really care either way, watches weren't of great interest to him. Although he could understand how his father would value Grandpa's watch, given the way it had been earned in such heroic fashion. Heck, Grandpa George had been gifted it for saving a bloke's life!

'Yeah, I reckon it's a good idea to look after Grandpa's watch, Dad,' he said, 'and this new one's a beauty, I like it.' Ted was a nice boy.

But two months later when fourteen-year-old Josh came home for his mid-year holidays, James was confronted with a different opinion altogether.

'Why aren't you wearing Grandpa's watch?' Josh demanded.

They were off to a family wedding in Goulburn, the youngest of Adriana's daughters was getting married at St Peter and Paul's Cathedral, and the whole tribe would be there. A very dressy affair.

James had completely forgotten that, of course, Josh hadn't seen the new watch and that it would now be necessary to embark upon the story all over again. But he did not receive the same reaction, or even lack thereof, from Josh, who held very strong views.

'If Grandpa George's watch is so old and fragile then it should be repaired, Dad,' he insisted, 'repaired and strengthened. It's a family heirloom. It should be worn with pride.'

'I agree with you, son. It is most certainly a family heirloom, which is why it is of such personal value to me. I treasure the watch deeply and refuse to risk its damage or theft. It will remain safely locked away in my deposit box for this very reason.'

Josh had no option but to accept the decision, although he still looked unconvinced.

'Besides,' James added with a smile, taking the Waltham from his vest pocket and flashing the dial at his son, 'you have to admit this one's much fancier.'

James returned his father's smile with his customary winning charm. 'Yep, Waltham's a top brand all right, Dad, one of the very best. Excellent choice, I agree, you couldn't have done better.'

Josh didn't actually agree at all, he vastly preferred his grandfather's watch. Quite a number of his schoolmates' fathers wore Waltham watches imported from America. A top brand certainly, flashy, expensive, but Grandpa's watch was far more stylish. And far, *far* more distinctive! No one had a watch like Grandpa George's. Josh thought his dad was mad for not wearing it. If it was his he'd be showing it off to all and sundry, his mates at school would be green with envy.

Josh continued to do exceedingly well at Sydney Grammar. His reports had been even more glowing this year than last. So glowing that it appeared the school wasn't quite sure what to do with the boy. He was outstripping his contemporaries to such a degree it was even suggested he be moved up a form the following year.

The maturity and focus of Joshua is far beyond that of the average fourteen-year-old, his mid-year report from the principal read. *His commitment to his studies, particularly in maths and all areas relating to business, is so total that his teachers feel he may be better placed with students a year above him. They further agree that Joshua would be perfectly capable of grasping the added complexities he would encounter should you choose to embrace this course of action, Mr Brereton-McKinnon . . .*

The principal went on further, obviously encouraging his suggested 'course of action', and after reading the entire report out to Jenna, James gave a laugh of triumph.

'You see, my love? Leonard Crompton was quite right. Our son has a touch of the genius.'

'Sounds to me,' Jenna drily replied, 'they just don't know how to handle a boy as precocious as Josh. He's always been mature for his age.'

'Possibly, possibly,' James agreed, 'but many a genius is, I'm sure.'

'We'll let Josh decide,' Jenna said. 'He might not want to leave his classmates behind and move up a year.'

'Very well, my love.' James was quite sure of his son's response.

He called the boy into his office and after reading out the report in its entirety he put the proposition to him.

'So what do you think, Josh? Do you want to move up a year? Your mother is of the opinion you might prefer to remain with your classmates.'

'No I'm perfectly happy to study with the older boys,' Josh replied. *Why on earth would I want to stay with my classmates? They're children.*

'Good for you, son.' James couldn't have been more delighted, this was just the response he'd expected.

Josh was pleased. Things were going exactly the way he'd planned. He would leave school when he was sixteen.

Jenna's pregnancy had been progressing satisfactorily and when Josh returned to Sydney for his third term she was barely a month from her due date of delivery. She wore her condition with pride, which many found most improper.

Refusing to obey the rules of etiquette and observe a period of confinement, she preferred instead to march down the streets of Goulburn, her huge belly leading the way.

Her ageing aunts were appalled, Adriana and Alexandra both chastising her in the strongest of terms.

'You don't even *need* to go into town,' Adriana expostulated, 'why do you *do* such a thing?'

'Because I can and because I want to.'

'But it's so unseemly to be seen in your state,' Alexandra said, 'it's simply not done.'

'Why not? My state is a perfectly normal state. I'm having a baby. What's wrong with that?'

The rest of the family didn't really care, choosing to give a collective shrug instead. Jenna was just being Jenna. She had never conformed and never would. And her husband didn't appear to mind, so where was the harm?

Far from minding, James was proud of his wife for flaunting the rules. He'd always admired Jenna's boldness.

Then came that night. That interminable night when the baby decided to make its arrival earlier than planned.

It actually started during the day, a late afternoon in mid-July, when Jenna began to experience painful cramps.

She was in the vegetable garden on her knees, cutting herbs with a pair of scissors, specifically rosemary and mint, for the dinner Maude would be cooking that night. It would be lamb again, a shoulder this time, the family surprisingly enough never got sick of lamb. But the way Maude cooked it, with plenty of rosemary embedded in the meat, and with mint sauce on the side, it was always tasty. Jenna herself made the mint sauce, just the way her mother had taught her when she was eight years old.

She stood, easing her aching back, and that's when the cramp first hit, steel fingers clenching into a fist, squeezing at her insides. She doubled over with the pain, dropping the scissors and the herbs, clutching at her stomach.

But she didn't fall. She must get back into the house, she told herself. She must not collapse out here.

The cramp eased enough for her to start on the trek towards the back verandah, but it wasn't long before the steel fingers once again closed into a fist. The cramps came in spasms and the trek to the verandah, then up the steps, then past the cookhouse and into the kitchen took forever. She staggered, then stopped, then staggered on, the waves of pain overtaking her until, when she finally reached the kitchen door she had barely strength enough to open it before collapsing on the floor.

Maude and Millie were both there in an instant, kneeling beside her.

'The baby,' Jenna muttered through clenched teeth, 'it's coming.'

Between them they helped her struggle to her feet, Maude taking the major weight as she issued orders to Millie.

'Get the men,' she said, 'we have to carry her upstairs.'

Millie raced off to fetch Boris from the stables, and also Wallace, who was bound to be working in the garage. There was no point in trying to find James, not at this stage anyway, he was working somewhere out on the property.

Maude had managed to get Jenna to the stairs, where she stood groaning in pain clinging to the railing when the men arrived.

One either side, they picked her up in their arms as gently as they could and carried her upstairs to her bedroom, Maude and Millie following close behind.

As they laid her down on the bed, Maude once again issued orders.

'The baby's coming,' she said in her customary, efficient way, although she was a little worried. The birth was premature, the baby wasn't due for a good three weeks, possibly four. 'You drive into town and fetch Doctor

Fulton,' she told her husband, and then to Boris, 'Where's the boss?'

'He's off fencing the western paddock with the boys.'

'Ride out and get him. Tell him the baby's coming.'

Maude's orders would have continued, but Millie was well ahead of her by now.

'I'll get towels and hot water,' she said, already making for the door, 'and I'll get scissors too in case it comes quickly.'

But the baby wasn't going to come quickly. The baby was dead.

It took the whole night for it to happen.

Maude and Millie remained by Jenna's side. Then the doctor was there, urging her to push, feeding a hand up inside her, trying to drag out the foetus that refused to budge.

James was there too, pacing up and down outside the closed bedroom door, waiting to hear the cry of a newborn, but hearing nothing but the screams of his wife as she writhed in agony.

Dawn was streaking the sky, offering a particularly spectacular sunrise when Jenna finally gave birth to a stillborn son. In a state of utter exhaustion she cuddled the infant to her, gazing down at the little face so breathlessly still.

Henry Fulton, a good doctor and a sensitive man, considered it kinder to allow her this moment of contact rather than hiding the carcass from her as most medical practitioners would. He even agreed when she insisted her husband be allowed to see the dead child, but only after the women in attendance had cleaned up the mess as best they could and placed a fresh counterpane over the bed. There'd been a lot of blood.

'We'll leave you alone for a moment or so,' he said tastefully as James entered the room. 'I'll come back in ten minutes,' he added, *to collect the body* remaining unsaid, 'after which you must rest, Mrs McKinnon.' And he left the room, together with Maude and Millie to whom he was most grateful. The two had been excellent attendants. But then most outback women were, he'd found.

'A boy,' Jenna whispered as James sat gingerly on the edge of the bed. 'Look.' She pulled aside the cloth Maude had wrapped around the baby, exposing the whole of the perfectly formed little body. 'Everything about him is flawless. He could be asleep, couldn't he? Look at him, James, look at his little toes and his little fingers. He's perfect in every way.' Tears were starting to well. 'Except he's not breathing. He's dead, our little boy, James. He's dead.'

'I know. I know.' James pushed the matted hair back from her face, the tears now rolling in rivulets, unchecked. 'He was not meant for this world, Jenna.'

'But why? What did I do to deserve this? I've always been strong and healthy, I've given birth to three strong, healthy children. Why did this one die? What did I do wrong?'

'There are no answers my love, these things just happen, that's all.'

'Oh no, these things don't just happen. This is retribution. We have done something terrible, James. We have done something terrible and this is our punishment.'

She was becoming distraught, which would surely not be doing her any good, James thought.

'There, there now, Jenna, calm yourself,' he said, taking the little body from her arms. He wouldn't wait for the doctor's return, this was not healthy. He stood.

'No, no,' she cried, 'give him back to me, give him back to me.'

'You must rest now, you heard what the doctor said . . .' He crossed to the door.

'Retribution,' she cried, hysteria sapping the very last of her strength. 'Our son's death is retribution, James.'

Retribution for what? he wondered. The notion was fanciful. Anything he may have done had been purely for the preservation of the McKinnon family name. Where was the guilt in that?

'Rest, my love.'

She was on the verge of passing out as he closed the door behind him.

'She's very upset,' he said to the doctor as Maude took the child's body from him.

'Understandably so,' Henry Fulton replied. 'I'll give her something to help her sleep.' He returned to the bedroom, but reappeared only moments later, carrying his medical bag. 'She's already asleep,' he said. 'I'll leave these with you should she awake distressed.' He handed James a bottle of pills. 'One every four hours if needed.'

'Thank you.'

James looked at the bundle in Maude's arms. The bundle that was the body of his son. Maude had wound the cloth entirely around the child, like a shroud. Nothing was visible. *Difficult to believe it's a body at all*, he thought, feeling strangely detached. He'd so wanted this child, he'd been so happy about the impending birth, and yet it had all come to this. To nothing. *How odd.*

Henry Fulton felt sorry for the man as he watched him gaze at the shrouded body of his son, which the family would no doubt bury somewhere on the property. He'd experienced moments like this before and such times were always poignant. But he had further sad news for James McKinnon.

'Your wife has survived a life-threatening experience, Mr McKinnon,' he said. 'She is strong and will regain her health, but I'm afraid I must inform you there will be no more children. Another pregnancy, another attempt to give birth, could prove very risky.'

James nodded. He'd been noting once again the lack of 'Brereton'. The doctor, too, referred to him simply as

'McKinnon'. But that was all right. He had no problem
with that.

Henry Fulton's manner then took on a certain degree
of heartiness, his intention being to raise the man's
spirits. 'You must be happy with the brood that you have,
Mr McKinnon. And they're a fine bunch, to be sure.
They're a very, very fine bunch, your children.'

They most certainly are, James thought, *and they
will go on to achieve very fine things. Particularly Josh.
Josh will be leading the brigade. The new generation of
McKinnons.*

'Thank you, Doctor. Would you like some breakfast
before Wallace drives you back to town?'

PART FOUR

CHAPTER EIGHTEEN

LONDON, 29 JUNE 1914

'Just what the world needs. Another Balkans War.'

'Dear God, when is there *not* a Balkans War? The Serbians and the Bosnians rarely do anything else, for them war's a bloody pastime.'

'And let's not forget the Herzegovinians. They love nothing more than a spot of bloodshed, second nature to them.'

At the plush Kelsey Club on The Strand, cigars were being vigorously puffed and brandy balloons waved about expansively as a bunch of elderly members lolled in the lounge's huge leather armchairs discussing the news, which had appeared in the morning's edition of *The Times*. Front page headlines had screamed that just the previous day, the Austrian Archduke Franz Ferdinand had been assassinated in Sarajevo.

'Shot right out in the open, he was. In broad daylight. His wife, Sophie, too.'

'The assassin was a Serb by the name of Princip, they say . . .'

'Dreadful man.' A voice from several tables away cut through the chat, a commanding bass baritone that brought the others to a halt.

'Who?' someone queried, turning to the voice. It was a voice he knew well, as did the other regular members of the Kelsey Club, for it was the voice of Colonel Edward Cranmer. 'Princip?'

'No, no,' came the dismissive response, 'Franz Ferdinand. Dreadful man.' An enormous cloud of smoke billowed from Cranmer's table while they waited for him to continue. Which, peering around the side of his armchair to face them, he did. 'Obsessed with trophy hunting. Killed every single animal on his estate, then shot his gamekeeper. Claimed it was a mistake, which is highly debatable, but one will never know of course. Travelled the world between '92 and '93 shooting whatever he could find; tigers and leopards in India, lions and elephants in Africa, even kangaroos and emus in Australia.'

Cranmer gave a bark of laughter and briefly turned to share a smile with the young man seated at his table, the comment having been made specifically for his benefit, before continuing. 'When he got to New York they took his weapons off him, and he was so frustrated with nothing to shoot they found him bashing squirrels to death in Central Park. Or so I heard. Dreadful fellow, simply dreadful.'

A further bark of laughter, a final swig from his balloon and Cranmer signalled the waiter for another brandy. He was aware he'd kept everyone entertained, as he always did, although his performance this time was really intended for his young companion. He settled back in his armchair leaving the others to amuse themselves.

'How about you, Josh? Ready to go again?'

Josh looked down at his brandy balloon, where it rested on the glossy surface of the large, ornately carved coffee table that sat between them. The glass was still half full. 'No thank you, Edward, I'm fine for the moment. Did Franz Ferdinand *really* shoot kangaroos and emus in Australia?'

'By Jove yes, and probably dozens more things besides. I'm not sure what other wild animals you have down there, but whatever they may be, you can rest assured he would have shot them.'

Despite their age difference, Josh McKinnon and Colonel Edward Cranmer had forged an excellent relationship. Cranmer found the young Australian remarkably mature. *Impossible to believe the boy's only just turned nineteen,* Edward thought, *I could swear I'm talking to a thirty-year-old.*

Cranmer himself was an impressive man in his early forties. Tall, imposing, very obviously of military bearing, neatly moustachioed but otherwise clean-shaven, he was not only witty, but knowledgeable. Josh had learned a great deal from Edward Cranmer since his arrival in London six months previously. And he intended to learn a great deal more. Cranmer was without doubt the most valuable of the contacts with which he'd been supplied, and there had been any number of influential connections provided him. The McKinnon name carried weight in many circles of London society.

Josh's life had progressed exactly as planned. He'd left school at sixteen, surprising his parents with the announcement he did not intend to go on to university.

'Why bother?' he'd said to his father. 'I can be of far greater assistance to you here at Glenfinnan.'

James had expostulated to start with, and vehemently. This was, after all, his 'genius' son of whom Leonard Crompton had predicted great things, even hinting at prime ministerial capabilities. Surely Josh wasn't content to come home and work as a farmhand.

'Of course not, Dad,' his son had replied, 'I'm going to take over the running of the property. I intend to operate our entire business portfolio. This is exactly what I've been training myself to do. It's what I was born to do.'

James would have argued further, but Jenna had put her foot very firmly down.

'He's right,' she'd announced. 'Glenfinnan is his destiny, James. He's a McKinnon and he's the next in line. Let Josh take his place earlier rather than later.'

The comment had piqued James. He'd felt very much on the outer. *Am I* not *a McKinnon,* he'd thought, *is that what you're intimating? And after all I've done for this family!* But he'd been given no right of reply as she'd blithely continued.

'Besides, you're a hopeless businessman, and poor Phil will be only too glad to rid himself of the burden he's been carrying all these years.'

James had wished she'd made the remark with humour, but she hadn't. Since the loss of her baby, Jenna had become hard, he decided.

As predicted, Phil had been more than happy to relinquish the business reins of Glenfinnan, and Josh had proved vastly superior at the task anyway. So superior that he fired the accountant who handled the books and hired an assistant instead. Twenty-four-year-old Terence Dimbleby was a fully licensed accountant whom Josh personally trained in the management of Glenfinnan. By the age of seventeen young Josh McKinnon was running the whole show.

There is indeed a streak of genius in my son, James thought. Far from feeling on the outer, these days James could not have been more proud.

Several months after his eighteenth birthday, with the full permission of his glowing parents, Josh had set sail for London where the family name was well known in wool circles, thus offering him entry into the upper echelons of society. His intention was to remain there for one year, feting the many already established business connections and working to create new ones. Terence Dimbleby could hold the fort back home, Josh trusted him implicitly.

Arriving on Christmas Day, 1913, he'd taken up rooms in a highly respectable boarding house in Belgravia, which catered exclusively to those of the upper classes, or at least those with the money to claim they were, after which he'd quickly gained entrance to several clubs through family connections. One such connection was Colonel Edward Cranmer of the British Army Transport and Supply Corp. Cranmer, Officer in Charge of Acquisitions, was well aware of the McKinnon name as a wool supplier to the British Army over the years. He'd been more than happy to welcome young Josh to London, and the two had become firm friends.

'They're quite right you know, those old fogies,' Edward said as the waiter arrived with his fresh brandy, placing it before him on the heavy, mahogany coffee table, 'there will be a war.'

'Yes, I would think so,' Josh agreed, 'but it'll be strictly regional, wouldn't you say? Much along the lines of "another Balkans dispute" as they said.' Josh made a habit of reading *The Times* religiously every morning, and had his own views. 'From what I've gathered the Austrians will welcome a legitimate excuse to declare war on Serbia, and after they've dispatched the Serbs, it'll be over. Honour satisfied. Shouldn't last long.'

'I wouldn't be too sure about that,' Edward replied ominously. 'It's all in the lap of the cousins really, isn't it?'

A pause followed. The remark had been deliberately enigmatic and as Cranmer puffed at his cigar he was aware he'd garnered the lad's total attention, which, as always, he very much enjoyed. The young Australian was a sponge, soaking up any drop of information that came his way. It was very flattering, Edward found, to have such a fiercely intelligent young fellow so focused upon one's every word. He launched into his firmly held belief, which was far more than simple theory and which would conclude with some sound advice to Josh McKinnon.

'The German, Austro-Hungarian and Russian governments are answerable to a Kaiser, an Emperor and a Tsar,' he pronounced, 'all three of whom see war as the only way to preserve the *status quo* and maintain their royal houses. Our own good King George is either blind to the fact or simply fails to understand his cousins' infantile attitude to military confrontation. Dangerous to be so *blasé*, in my opinion.'

Edward rested his half-finished cigar in the Waterford cut-crystal ashtray where it sat smouldering as he took a sip of his brandy. 'Wilhelm ll of Germany was an *enfant terrible* and is now an *homme terrible,* utterly obsessed with war, while his dilatory cousin, the Romanov, Nicholas ll is a weak individual only too delighted to play at rattling sabres. They're like children with a box of matches and between them they'll start a war, mark my words. This assassination of Franz Ferdinand is just the spark they need. Before long the whole of Europe will have dissolved into war.'

The brandy balloon was replaced on the coffee table, and the cigar resumed as Edward lounged back in his chair. 'Britain will be dragged into the fracas, and God knows who else along with her. Her dominions? The whole world?' A plume of smoke spiralled into the air like an exclamation mark. 'Mind you, her dominions really *are* the whole world aren't they, more or less, the parts that matter anyway. Oh no, I don't think this will be along the lines of "another Balkans dispute", my friend. Not at all. This will be war on a global scale!'

A last puff, leisurely this time, producing a final cloud of smoke. The cigar was finished now, or if not, Edward wanted no more of it. He leaned forward and ground it into the ashtray, the force of his action matching the force of his words, for here followed his advice. 'And when this war comes, as it inevitably will, my dear McKinnon,' he said, his eyes boring into those of his young friend, 'primary producers, especially those of wool and cotton and leather, will find themselves in a very enviable position financially. Or they will if they have the right contacts and know how to take advantage of the situation. Do you get my drift?'

'Oh yes.' Josh nodded. His brandy balloon remained untouched upon the coffee table. He'd been transfixed throughout Edward Cranmer's entire tirade. 'Oh yes, I get your drift.'

'Good.' Edward smiled. 'I thought you might. We must talk more on the matter.'

And they did. They talked a great deal more on the matter. Josh was very keen to be of use to the military should war break out. As an Australian and a proud member of the British Empire it was his bounden duty to do so.

Exactly one week later, on 5 July, Josh McKinnon left the UK from Plymouth aboard the Blue Star Line vessel SS *Lady Meredith,* bound for Australia. He would miss London. Along with the progress he'd made in business circles – the meetings with Glenfinnan's established buyers, the creation of potential new clients, the feting of influential men in positions of power, all of which had been most successful – he'd found considerable entertainment in London.

Not all the clubs he'd frequented had been as respectable as the Kelsey Club. There were many gentlemen's establishments catering for those of the upper classes that, along with fine brandy, excellent dining and comradely chat among like-minded men, offered further delights. There were those clubs with additional lounge rooms out the back where fine-looking women draped their desirable bodies invitingly in armchairs and chaises longues, and where there were rooms upstairs that could be discreetly visited.

While indulging his hedonistic side, Josh had discovered a number of useful business contacts in such clubs. Influential English gentlemen came in all varieties, he'd found, which made life most interesting.

But there was the seedier side of London that he'd also enjoyed, the one that offered no business opportunities at all. Josh liked to prowl the streets late at night, just as he had in Sydney when he'd been no more than a boy. He didn't sleep with the whores who sold their wares in Soho for fear of catching the pox, but he liked to watch them. He liked to loiter in the shadows, avoiding the street lamps, watching not just the whores, but people in general, people in the lighted windows of houses and bars and brothels, or those walking in the street, going about their business, whatever that might be. He liked watching people who didn't know they were being watched. It gave him a feeling of power.

Yes, he thought as he boarded the SS *Lady Meredith*, he would miss London. He had certainly looked forward to a further six months in the city. But the assassination of Archduke Franz Ferdinand had put a halt to his plans. He had new plans now, and they must be acted upon with haste if Edward Cranmer's theory on war was to prove correct.

Josh arrived in Sydney on the 15th of August, the very day the Australian Army opened recruitment offices in army barracks around the country, seeking soldiers for overseas service with the newly formed Australian Imperial Force. Britain had declared war on Germany on the 4th of August, and just as Edward Cranmer had predicted, she had called upon her dominions.

*

'I'm gonna join the army,' Zac declared eagerly, he was just raring to go.

'Why?' Josh demanded. 'Why the hell would you want to do that?'

The twins, together with Josh and young Ted, were once again huddled behind the Catons' tractor shed on a cold Saturday morning in mid-August. They hadn't even bothered to kick the footy around – they'd been too eager to hear Josh's stories, which he'd shared only too willingly.

'*Why?* Because I'd get to travel overseas, of course,' Zac replied as if the question had come from a simpleton, 'I'd get to see the world like you have, mate. And I'd get to fight in a war and I'd get *paid* for it. *That's why!*'

'Nup.' Josh gave his customary good-natured grin. 'Wouldn't work that way, Zac. At least I don't reckon it would. You'd get paid an absolute pittance to train for months, after which you wouldn't get sent overseas because the war would be over by then and you'd have missed out. Not worth the effort, mate.'

'Sounds like good advice to me,' Sam replied. 'Let the professional army blokes go in first, then we'll wait and see what happens, eh, Zac?'

Zac nodded reluctantly. And seventeen-year-old Ted, who was too young to have signed up for anything, went along with the gang, as usual. They always ended up doing what Josh suggested anyway.

For all his sophisticated travels and his adventures in London, Josh appeared not to have changed in the least. The four were as close as they'd been throughout their childhood. In fact they might have been exactly the same boys. But then Josh was something of a chameleon. Josh could be whatever he perceived people wished him to be. A rare talent.

Despite his advice to Zac, Josh very much hoped that the war would not be short-lived. He vividly recalled

Edward Cranmer's words. *'This will be war on a global scale,'* Cranmer had said. And surely war on a global scale was not likely to be short-lived. In any event, Josh had decided to move quickly, having already arranged things with his father. Or rather, having already informed his father of his intentions; a little convincing had been required before the practical arrangements had been set in place.

'Melbourne! Why Melbourne?' James had been astounded, and also mystified by his son's announcement. 'You've only just returned home, Josh, why on earth would you need to go to Melbourne?'

'Because that's where the military operational head-quarters are, Dad. That's where my contacts with the army officers are, particularly those in the Transport and Supply Corp. I have a personal letter of introduction to the officer in charge of acquisitions himself. And from Colonel Edward Cranmer no less.'

'Cranmer, yes,' the name instantly registered with James, 'British Army Acquisitions, we supplied wool for their military some time back.'

'Exactly. And we shall again. Cranmer proved my most valuable contact in London and he's put me in touch with his equivalent in Melbourne, a Major Keith Manning. He's already written to Manning, who's expecting my arrival. We must set up a McKinnon sales office in Melbourne, Dad, so we can deal directly with Military Acquisitions—'

In his excitement, Josh would have continued, but James interrupted.

'A business proposition?' His expression was decidedly dubious, this could pose a threat to the family name. 'We wouldn't want to be seen to profit from the war, son.'

'Of course not!' Josh's expression mirrored his father's horror at the mere suggestion. 'Good God no! To the contrary, we'd be serving our country.'

'Oh yes?' James needed convincing.

'Absolutely.' His son was happy to spell things out. 'According to Edward Cranmer, the Australian military will need clever, proficient businessmen to work hand in hand with their Transport and Supply Corp. To leave the whole process in the hands of inexperienced army officers, he says, would be to court disaster.'

These had been Edward's exact words, but now in his eagerness Josh was off and running on his own.

'The AIF has only just been set up, Dad, and like many new enterprises, they'll lack those with experience in areas they're not accustomed to dealing with. And by that I mean the supply of goods for their men who are fighting overseas. They haven't been called upon to do this before. They'll need help.'

Josh had by now convinced himself of the nobility of his cause and he closed his argument with fervour. 'We wouldn't just be selling goods to the army, we'd be ensuring the quality and the quantity and the smooth delivery of product essential to our soldiers at war in foreign lands. We'd be doing our patriotic duty, Dad!' he concluded triumphantly. 'That's something to be proud of.'

It was a *fait accompli*. Unable to refute his son's reasoning, James agreed, and they spent the following hour discussing the logistics of the exercise; the necessary transfer of funds required, the period of time Josh would need to set up the Melbourne office and other pertinent details.

'We'll have to sort things out here with Terence too,' James said finally, which he realised was a somewhat ineffectual remark given the fact that Terence Dimbleby had looked after all aspects of Glenfinnan's business for the past six months.

'Oh yes, I'll sort things out with Terence, Dad, don't you worry about that.'

Josh had already 'sorted things out' with Terence. He'd spoken to his assistant before he'd approached his father.

It had been necessary. Terence was essential to the overall plan. And of course Terence had been most keen to be involved; he and Josh spoke the same language when it came to business.

Josh had chosen his assistant with care. Terence Dimbleby was not only a clever accountant, he was cunning and not averse to bending the rules just a little when needed. Josh had recognised his type in an instant. Inoffensive to look at, even a trifle plain some might say, but shrewd, and beneath the colourless exterior rested a greedy streak of ambition. All Terence needed was a leader, and that leader was Josh.

As for Terence Dimbleby, he had no issue at all with the fact he must take orders from a very young man a whole seven years his junior. He'd sensed the power in Josh McKinnon and had been in awe of him from their very first meeting. Although he would never admit it, for he had never expressed himself sexually in any way whatsoever, Terence was a little in love with Josh McKinnon.

Josh had recognised that too, which was another reason he'd hired the man.

Major Keith Manning of the Australian Army Transport and Supply Corp proved not dissimilar to Colonel Edward Cranmer. Not as imposing perhaps, nor as witty, but of military bearing, tall, in his early forties and, most importantly, sharing very similar views. He was delighted to meet Josh, and offered the warmest welcome when they met at Melbourne's army headquarters in St Kilda Road.

'You certainly come highly recommended, Mr McKinnon,' he said as they shook hands, 'Colonel Cranmer informs me you're just what we need. Come on through to my office.'

He led the way to the Acquisitions Department and they settled down to talk. Keith Manning was keen to voice the problems he was facing and as Josh listened he could hear Edward Cranmer's voice loud and clear.

'I can tell you categorically, Mr McKinnon, the Army's Quartermaster-General and the Director of Equipment are seriously handicapped by the lack of training and business experience among officers on their staff,' the major said. 'This state of war in which we now find ourselves has revealed the entire section to be a dumping ground of misfits, men simply unqualified in the practice of trade and procurement.'

Just as Edward predicted they would be, Josh thought.

'A respected business name like yours will be a great advantage to the military, Mr McKinnon,' Manning went on. 'With your expertise, and that of your partners, we will hopefully be able to coordinate our dealings and sort out this mess.'

Partners . . . Josh was aware he was being confronted by a whole new enterprise about which he knew little, but business was business, wasn't it? . . . *Yes, I know who my partners will be,* he thought. *At least I hope I do.*

Although Manning had been his first port of call upon arriving in Melbourne, Josh had been supplied with several other names courtesy of Edward Cranmer, one being Henry Hitchcock, owner of a sheep and cattle property in south-western Victoria.

'Hitchcock's the fellow you need,' Edward had said. 'He's supplied leather goods to the British military in the past, he knows his business.'

Another had been a man by the name of Darcy Willard.

'I've actually met this chap here in London,' Edward had said, 'didn't altogether take to him I must say. Came to the club, bit flashy for my liking, but he's from a very wealthy family and has links everywhere. We've done business with him from time to time. Could be handy for you.'

Let's hope he is, Josh now thought.

'I shall be only too happy to oblige, Major,' he replied, 'as will my partners, I'm sure. Leave things with me and I'll get back to you shortly. In the meantime if your staff could list for me all the major supplies and quantities you're currently seeking . . .'

'Yes, of course.'

Henry Hitchcock was equally welcoming when Josh visited his farm, a property called Braedalbin 25 miles south-west of Melbourne.

'Mr McKinnon, I've been looking forward to meeting you,' he said, huge paw extended. 'Colonel Cranmer says you're a *very* young man with a *very* big future.' He gave a hearty guffaw, which Josh found fractionally jarring as they shook. Although he wasn't sure whether it was the man's oafish heartiness or his property that most jarred. Braedalbin was not exactly the wealthy spread he'd been expecting. It wasn't a large farm at all, or it hadn't appeared to be on his journey from the railway station in the trap Hitchcock had sent to collect him; the driver, a young farmhand, pointing out the property's boundaries as they went. Most surprising that Hitchcock had managed to successfully supply leather goods to the British military, Josh had thought.

But as they sat on the back verandah drinking mugs of tea supplied by Hitchcock's worn and weathered wife, all was eventually revealed. Although the process was frustratingly slow to start with.

'Thank you, Mrs Hitchcock,' Josh said, acknowledging the mug she plonked on the table beside him, and receiving a terse nod in reply.

'Yes, thank you, my dearest heart, thank you.' A jovial acknowledgement from her husband received the same response and she disappeared.

Josh found the Hitchcock pair, both in their late forties, farcical to the point where they might have stepped out of a cartoon gracing the pages of *Punch*. Everything about Henry was large, signalling the good life; his overall build, his belly, his voice, his ill-kempt, but healthy growth of beard. And everything about his wife was gnarled, emaciated, signalling a life of deprivation. All Josh could see in the two of them was a joke, the reversal of Jack Sprat and his wife. Unable to take them seriously, he was beginning to think his trip out into the countryside had been a complete waste of time.

'Looking forward to doing business with you, young Josh,' Henry said expansively, lolling back in his rattan chair.

Are you really? Josh thought with derision while managing to return a weak smile. Henry had not only insisted upon a first-name basis right from the start, this was now the third time he'd added the 'young', which Josh found overly familiar and downright patronising.

'Nice healthy countryside around here, as you can see,' Henry went on, waving a hefty arm about at the view, 'good grazing land.'

'Yes, it certainly is,' Josh politely replied, wondering how soon he'd be able to make his departure. The man was a buffoon.

'Of course you're wondering "how does he do it?" aren't you?'

'Um . . . Sorry, how does who do what?' Josh was taken aback. The benignly good-humoured eyes that met his had suddenly turned shrewd. Henry Hitchcock was 'reading' him.

'You're wondering how I manage to produce ample leather for the supply of goods to the British Army given Braedalbin's relatively small acreage.' Henry had been reading young McKinnon, and reading him correctly, from the moment of his arrival.

Realising he'd been caught out, Josh answered truthfully. 'Yes, as a matter of fact, that's exactly what I've been wondering,' he said.

'Ah, well, young Josh . . .' The humour was back now, but not in a cartoonish way, rather in a knowing way – crafty and calculating. Henry was anything but a buffoon. 'I have partners in crime, as they say.' He tapped a forefinger to the side of his nose in the classic conspiratorial gesture and smiled. 'If you deal with me you'll be taking on more than just one partner, mate. You'll be gaining a team.'

Henry could see in an instant he'd garnered young McKinnon's full attention. 'I sense you'd like to hear more, am I right?'

'I would, Henry, yes I most certainly would.'

'Sun's over the yardarm, time for a beer.' Henry stood, tossed the dregs from his teacup over the verandah railing and strode to the back flywire door that led directly into the breakfast room. 'Hey, Violet,' he yelled, 'bring us some beer, will you heart? We've got business to discuss, me and young Josh.'

He resumed the rattan chair, his manner now brisk and efficient. 'You'll be dealing with two other blokes,' he said. 'Mick Lawrence, who owns the next door property a mile or so up the road, and Darcy Willard, who lives in the city.'

Josh nodded. 'I know of Darcy Willard. I haven't yet met him, but I was told to look him up. Colonel Cranmer gave me his name.'

'Yes, Cranmer would,' Henry agreed, 'they know each other, more or less.' Then he added with a smile that was sly. 'Mick Lawrence is the one Cranmer *doesn't* know about, the "silent partner" so to speak.'

At that moment Mrs Hitchcock, who had now become Violet, appeared with a bottle of beer and two glasses, which she placed on the table, sharing a meaningful look with her husband as she did so. 'Do you want me to ride over and get Mick?'

'If you would be so kind, heart, yes. That would be an excellent idea.'

Violet – who to Josh looked like anything *but* a 'Violet', surely 'Agnes' or 'Edith' would have been more apt – was as shrewd as her husband and equally knowledgeable in all business matters conducted at Braedalbin. Josh was slowly coming to realise these two were not in the least the simple, cartoonish pair he'd initially found them to be.

He spent the next several hours at Braedalbin, Mick Lawrence eventually joining them. In physical appearance, Mick very much reminded him of Phil Caton, a gangly, sun-weathered farmer, but Josh sensed a vast difference between the two. Phil Caton was an open book, an honest man, whereas in Mick there was cunning. Mick was out to seek advantage over others, and in the shiftiness of his eyes, it showed.

Violet also joined them, that is after she'd set out a platter of bread and cheese and fetched a fresh supply of beer. She contributed her two penneth what's more, which impressed Josh, although he did wonder why the woman appeared incapable of producing a smile, particularly as both men were so convivial.

They're a gang of thieves, the three of them, he thought, *which may well serve my purpose.*

Mick Lawrence's place in the scheme of things was simple. Mick scoured rural Victoria, locating small farms whose owners were in debt. He bought up poor stock in sheep and cattle and had them transported to his neighbouring property, which in acreage was far bigger than Braedalbin.

'But we keep the Braedalbin name on our supplies,' he said with a grin. 'Braedalbin's known to run healthy stock. You know, makes a better impression and all that.'

The McKinnon name would make a far greater impression, Josh thought, but he said nothing, sipping his beer, listening to them go on.

'Course the British Army's got no idea the leather goods they buy are of inferior quality,' Mick added proudly, 'they wouldn't know if their bums were on fire.'

They presumably wouldn't know cloth made from low-grade wool rather than high-quality Glenfinnan fibre either, Josh thought. Things were beginning to fall neatly into place as fresh ideas occurred. He recalled the major's words. *'A respected business name like yours will be a great advantage to the military, Mr McKinnon.'* Well, *there's no name more respected in the wool industry than Glenfinnan, is there?*

'You haven't met Darcy Willard yet, have you?' It was Violet, once again cutting through his thoughts and through the conversation in general.

The question was rhetorical, Violet knew full well he hadn't met Darcy. She'd been standing by the flywire door listening to every word of her husband's earlier conversation with Josh McKinnon.

'Darcy's the most valuable link in the chain,' she said. 'He's got contacts with all the manufacturers. Leather goods, clothing, you name it. Transport companies too.' Violet eyed Josh up and down, assessing him in the most unashamed fashion. 'You'll get on real well with Darcy, you will. You're birds of a feather, you two. Upper-class types, flashy families dripping with money.'

Josh raised an eyebrow. Did she mean to be insulting or was she perhaps joking?

She was neither. Violet never joked and she intended no insult, she was merely stating things the way she saw them. She waved the scrawny claw of her hand at Henry and Mick.

'Darcy sees these two as a couple of oafs, thinks they're beneath him.' *Just the way you do,* was inherent in her tone. Violet had decided she didn't like Josh McKinnon. He was too young, too smooth, too handsome, too everything . . . But by God he'd be good for business. And she could tell he was as sharp as a tack.

'We look forward to working with you, Josh,' she said.

Violet, whom Josh had rightly gathered was very much the team leader, proved wrong about one thing. He did not 'get on real well' with Darcy Willard, although he pretended he did. And he certainly did not consider Darcy and he were 'birds of a feather'. In fact, he was insulted anyone could possibly make such a presumption.

There was no denying twenty-six-year-old Darcy Willard was good-looking and stylish, but he was a wastrel. Licentious and dissolute, the only asset Darcy brought to the business table was his highly respected 'old family' name and the wealth that accompanied it. The Willard name unlocked many a door, and the contacts that would be made available to the enterprise upon which Josh was about to embark appeared endless.

Major Keith Manning himself was most impressed. 'My, my,' he said, when Josh once again visited him at army headquarters, 'the McKinnons and the Willards, two fine, pioneering family names with which to be associated. We're proud to have formed such a connection, Mr McKinnon.' Keith Manning was speaking personally. This would not only impress his superiors, he greatly enjoyed mingling with the elite.

'And both families will be proud to lend all the support they can to the war effort, Major. We shall make a fine team,' said Josh.

Despite Josh's dislike of Darcy Willard, none would have guessed them to be anything but the best of friends. Least of all Darcy himself. In the eyes of others, including Darcy, they were very much as Violet had described them, although to most they would be depicted in a more flattering way as dashing young men-about-town from highly respected wealthy families. They were, furthermore, members of the Melbourne Club, which everyone knew embraced only the elite.

It was the public image Josh wished to present and the influential contacts to be made at the Melbourne Club were invaluable, but there were other clubs of less repute that he frequented, just as he had in London. And here, too, he was accompanied by Darcy. He would much have preferred to visit the brothels and gambling dens on his own, but forming an unbreakable bond of friendship with Darcy Willard in order to cement their business partnership was of far greater importance. So he suffered the man's company, womanising and gambling with him and listening to his drunken, dissipated ramblings. Darcy appeared also to consider them 'birds of a feather'.

'The good life's all that matters isn't it, Josh,' he said, words slurring, 'you and I both know that.' Wine sloshed from his glass as he waved it about, the girl wriggling invitingly on his lap in the hope of urging him upstairs so she could get him over and done with and move on to the next. 'Wine, women and song, everything people go on about, they're all purchasable commodities. What you need for the good life is *money*.' Another wave of the glass, another slosh of wine. 'Lots and lots of *money*! You and I both know that.'

They were in the dimly lit bar and lounge of one of their favoured bordellos in Little Lonsdale Street, Melbourne's seamy district known fondly as 'Little Lon', and Darcy was behaving in typical fashion. Josh, who very much enjoyed the hedonistic pleasures of life, returned his normal comradely smile, but he didn't in the least agree with Darcy. Certainly 'the good life' was to his taste, but this was not why one set out to make money. One didn't accumulate wealth in order to fritter it away; one accumulated wealth in order to attain power; 'the good life' was simply an added bonus.

Power was all-important to Josh. The power to rule, the power to be a leader of men, respected and, yes, perhaps even feared by others. But Darcy Willard was too stupid and too self-indulgent to recognise the true value of power.

He watched with distaste as Darcy continued to slosh wine about and share his vulgar philosophy on 'the good life' as the pinnacle of attainment. Josh couldn't abide a man who couldn't hold his liquor, which to him was a sure sign of weakness. Much as he appreciated fine wines and good brandy, he never overindulged himself, taking care always not to exceed the limits of his tolerance. *God how I hate drunks,* he thought, *and Darcy's the worst kind.* Even the whore wriggling on his lap appeared irritated as she copped another dose of wine in her face. *And who can blame her,* he thought, *the man's a complete drunkard. A hopeless gambler to boot. In fact, Darcy's a useless human being all round, except for his family.*

Josh got on very well with Darcy's family; both parents, his two hard-working older brothers and his younger sister. But most particularly Darcy's father, who was delighted, and secretly relieved, to see his youngest son enter a business relationship with an impressive young man of good family like Josh McKinnon. Sixty-three-year-old Iain Willard, respected pillar of the community, was well aware of his son's predilection for the seedier side of life. Young McKinnon, obviously a very clever and ambitious fellow, would keep Darcy on the straight and narrow, he decided. Besides which, it was high time his son set his sights upon some form of sustainable career instead of dillydallying about relying upon the odd opportunity that came his way purely because he was a Willard. The boy had been offered various positions within the family firm, but had proved mediocre at every single one, professing boredom. Well it now appeared something had aroused his interest. Iain was grateful to Josh McKinnon.

'Good luck to you, boys,' he'd said, shaking Josh's hand vigorously, while gracing his son with a congratulatory smile. 'Your enterprise appears an excellent proposition, most soundly thought out. I promise no interference, but I assure you both that you shall have my full support.'

Which had meant not only the support of the Willard name and contacts, but whatever financial assistance might be required in the initial stages of setting up the business. Little wonder Josh was prepared to suffer whatever Darcy dished out.

'I think your young lady here's keen to get going, Darce,' he said, smiling at the whore who smiled back, wishing she was bedding him instead of the drunkard. He smiled at his own girl who was sitting sedately by his side, sipping a glass of pretend champagne and enjoying being treated with courtesy. 'Let's go upstairs, shall we?'

There was a lot to be done over the next month or so in Melbourne, not least being the acquisition of a suitable property to house the new offices of McKinnon & Willard Enterprises.

Like Iain Willard, James McKinnon had not been averse to the business link between their two families, although he had at first voiced his reluctance to enter into an actual partnership.

'The McKinnon name has always stood on its own, Josh,' he'd said when his son had informed him of his plans via telephonic communication.

James had been one of the first in the Goulburn district to have a telephone connection installed on his property. Following the delivery of Jenna's stillborn baby and the knowledge that she might well have died under such circumstances, he had made the installation a priority.

'One never knows when an emergency may present itself,' he'd announced.

Josh was now deeply thankful for his father's prescience, not so much for the sake of emergencies, but telephonic communication was essential for business purposes.

'The McKinnon name will still stand on its own, Dad,' he'd assured his father during their conversation. 'We'll be joining forces with the Willards purely in order to supply the army with essential provisions and support the war effort, as agreed with the military.' Josh had decided that sounded good enough, at least he hoped it did; his father was, after all, no businessman. But he added a further comment to help seal the deal. 'And I have to tell you, the Army Acquisitions Department is delighted to be connected with two such respected families. Those were Major Manning's exact words to me, Dad.'

There was little James could say in response to that. Particularly when he learned Iain Willard was happy to share equally in the cost of establishing a Melbourne office for the new business partnership formed between their sons.

The property Josh and Darcy chose for their headquarters was a three-storey Victorian building in Collins Street. The ground floor already housed a thriving printery, but they leased the upper two floors in the name of McKinnon & Willard Enterprises, the second floor becoming their official office, the third a private apartment for Josh, who shifted out of his suite at the Grand Hotel to take up residence.

'Your own private apartment in the very heart of the city,' Darcy remarked with a supercilious smirk. 'You *are* moving up in the world, aren't you?'

'Not at all,' Josh said, returning an easy smile, 'the Grand Hotel's far more elegant and far more fashionable; if I was out to impress I'd continue to stay there. But it's good to have one of us on site the whole time, Darce.

Of course you're quite welcome to move in with me if you like.' *Perish the thought!* 'There are two bedrooms, old chap, and you're more than welcome.'

'Good God no, too crowded.' Darcy's handsome face twisted into a look of abhorrence. 'I need my space! Particularly if I'm to *entertain,*' he added with another smirk, lascivious this time. 'You know what I mean . . .'

Courtesy of his father, Darcy owned a very pleasant house in South Yarra, not far from his parents' lavish Toorak residence, and the parties he held were known, among the younger set anyway, for their debauchery. As far as Darcy was concerned, this was essential for his image as one who had attained 'the good life'.

'Of course,' Josh replied with a laugh, 'wouldn't want to cramp your style.' He breathed a sigh of relief.

Over the ensuing several months, the two set about with diligence, establishing their contacts and arranging business deals, even Darcy, in his inimitable way.

'Oliver's come to a number of my parties,' he said. Oliver Blackwell was the representative from the Commonwealth Government Harness Factory with whom Darcy had conducted leather sales in the past. 'And he likes sex, preferably rough sex, dominatrix style, so I think we should fete that side of him. Take him to brothels free of charge, wine him and dine him, set him up so he's in our debt.'

'Good idea.' Josh was gratified to discover Darcy's dissolute side could be used to advantage.

And Darcy proved quite right. Oliver was eager to provide the army with ready-made leather goods for a decently negotiated price and a bonus of 'the good life' thrown in.

The Willard name also offered introduction to a clothing manufacturer in Geelong who was contracted to produce uniforms, blankets, socks and other army supplies made from fine Merino wool, which would be delivered to their textile factory for processing early in the new year. It didn't matter to either Josh or Darcy that Braedalbin had no Merinos; that indeed Braedalbin had no fine fibre at all, but could produce third-grade wool only. Josh had the ready answer.

'It's time we brought Glenfinnan into the game, Darce,' he said. 'According to Major Manning, the army wants the McKinnon name. And when it comes to wool, the McKinnon name means Glenfinnan.'

A week or so later, towards the end of November, Josh caught the train to Goulburn. But he'd be back before Christmas, he promised Darcy.

'I'll have everything arranged by then, Darce,' he said. 'Come the new year we'll be up and running.' He laughed. 'More than that, old chap, come the new year there'll be no stopping us.'

James picked up Josh from Goulburn Railway Station, Ted and Emily with him as always, and there was a warm homecoming when they arrived at Glenfinnan. Jenna had even arranged a garden party for the following day, inviting the entire extended family and staff and any number of neighbours. November was such a wonderful month for garden parties and what better way to welcome home the pride and joy of the McKinnon family.

Josh very much enjoyed the reunion, particularly with Ted, Zac and Sam, regaling his brother and cousins yet again with stories. But he'd returned to Glenfinnan for a reason other than family, and there was really only one person he needed to see.

'I'll call upon you at the office tomorrow,' he said to Terence Dimbleby at the garden party. 'Around ten o'clock. We have a great deal to talk about.'

Terence had coffee and biscuits ready when Josh arrived the following morning, the rich buttery shortbread biscuits he knew Josh loved, and they talked for a good two hours. Or rather Josh did. Terence listened, attentively, as Terence always did, understanding every word, every requirement, and eager, as he always was, to be of assistance.

'So we'll need new McKinnon/Glenfinnan stencils for the Braedalbin wool bales,' Josh said in conclusion, having explained all the arrangements he'd set up in Melbourne. 'You must have those ready in a couple of weeks so I can take them back with me, I'll be leaving before Christmas.'

Terence added this to the notes he'd been busily scribbling down in his pad. He was deeply disappointed to hear Josh would be leaving so soon, having presumed he'd be staying for the festive season.

'And you'll need to provide regular reports on the samples that have supposedly been taken from the Braedalbin wool,' Josh continued. 'You can just base these on previous Glenfinnan reports. It'll all be fake, but the army won't know. They're a disorganised bunch, nothing gets checked. They're leaving everything to us. Which makes it all so bloody easy,' he added with a conspiratorial smile.

Terence returned a special smile of his own, he so loved the way they spoke the same language. 'I'll get onto it straight away,' he said.

'You're a wonder, Terence.' Josh rose to his feet. 'Don't know what I'd do without you,' he said, giving the man a fond pat on the shoulder. 'Where do you get that marvellous shortbread, by the way?'

'The bakery in Bourke Street,' Terence replied. He'd made a special trip into Goulburn the moment he'd heard Josh was returning to Glenfinnan.

The family, too, was disappointed to discover Josh was not staying for Christmas.

'And for New Year's Eve,' Jenna protested, 'we always have a big party on New Year's Eve, you know that.'

'Yes, Mum, of course I know that,' he replied, 'and I'm truly sorry I have to miss it, but there's still such a lot to get done in Melbourne, and we want to be ready to go as soon as possible in the new year.'

'At least stay for Christmas, son,' James suggested, 'that's only a couple of weeks away.'

'Wish I could, Dad, but the army needs us. They're relying on us in a very big way. We can't afford to be slack.'

Two weeks later, Josh returned to Melbourne, satisfied everything was set for a prosperous future.

CHAPTER NINETEEN

The first soldiers of the Australian Infantry Force had departed for overseas in early November. The entire convoy had included twenty-six Australian and ten New Zealand troopships, together with escorting battleships and the cruiser HMAS *Sydney*. Stretching three miles in length and carrying thirty thousand troops, the fleet had finally arrived at Alexandria, the men disembarking on the 3rd of December. The troops had then been transported to Mena on the outskirts of Cairo where they'd set up camp beside the grand Pyramid of Cheops.

To the general soldiers of the AIF, their destination came as a complete surprise; their officers hadn't told them they were going to Egypt.

'What the hell are we doing here?' men asked one another.

'Haven't got the foggiest, mate, I thought we were going to France.'

'Yeah, me too. Or England.'

'Well, somewhere in Europe anyway. We're fighting the bloody Huns, aren't we?'

The average soldier hadn't known that the entente powers of Britain, France and Russia sought to weaken the Ottoman Empire. They didn't even know the Ottoman Empire had entered the war, that Turkey had allied itself to their enemy, Germany. And over the ensuing tedious months as they trained relentlessly in the Egyptian desert, wishing they could join the battle that raged in Europe, they had no inkling of the strategy their British commanders had in mind. The average soldier was kept completely in the dark about the military campaign to which he had been assigned.

The British Army's objective was to force a passage through the Dardanelles exposing the Ottoman capital of Constantinople to bombardment by Allied battleships. With the capture of Constantinople, Turkey would thus be defeated and the Allied forces would gain possession of the Suez Canal, opening a supply route through the Black Sea to the ports of Russia. However, when in February and March the following year attempts by the Allied fleet proved unsuccessful, a new plan was devised. There would be an amphibious landing. It would take place in April 1915. The 11th and 12th Battalions AIF would be the first troops ashore, and the site of their landing would be the Gallipoli Peninsula. Neither the troops themselves, nor the citizens of Australia were yet aware of this.

Josh encountered his first major problem in March. He recognised immediately it was something he should have anticipated, but things had been progressing so smoothly he'd given no thought to the matter. With hindsight he realised this had been downright stupid of him. Completely out of character, furthermore.

'There's something a bit dodgy going on here isn't there, Josh?'

Kevin Cavanagh of Cavanagh Clothing Manufacturers had paid a personal visit to Josh at his Collins Street offices, which was most unusual. Cavanagh's was a large, thriving business housed in Geelong and as a rule Kevin sent his minions.

'Dodgy, Kev? How do you mean?'

There was a tap at the door, and both men paused as Josh's secretary, Dorothy, a pleasant, but plain woman in her thirties, entered with a tea tray, which she placed on the large coffee table that sat between their armchairs. Josh had deliberately chosen a plain secretary; any attractive woman would have been instant prey to Darcy.

'Thank you, Dottie.' He smiled as she picked up the teapot about to pour. 'I'll play mother.'

'Of course.' She returned the smile. 'I've brought you some almond shortbread biscuits too.' She knew these were his favourites.

'So I see.' Another smile and a grateful nod.

Dottie quietly left the office. Oh God, every time he smiled at her that way she wanted to swoon.

Kevin Cavanagh waited until the secretary had closed the door before turning back to Josh. 'Come on now, mate, you know exactly what I mean.'

Aware he was cornered, Josh decided to play the innocent, just for a while anyway. Which path was Kev likely to take? He was accusative, certainly, but he didn't appear angry.

'Why don't you enlighten me, Kev,' he said pleasantly as he poured the tea. 'I'm a little in the dark here.'

Kevin laughed. He had to admire the bloke's audacity. Young Josh McKinnon was a canny bastard all right. He knew how to play the game, you had to give him that.

Kevin Cavanagh was no slouch himself. A rather handsome, granite-faced Englishman in his mid-fifties, he'd played many a game in his lifetime, working his way up from the factory floor of a textile mill in Manchester to become a self-made businessman with his very own manufacturing company. Of course marrying the boss's daughter had helped – the oldest of four, the spinsterish one the boss had been happy to part with – as had opening a branch of the boss's business in Australia where wool reigned supreme. And with the boss long dead, the factory was not only his, but now bore his name. Kev knew exactly how to play the game. Just as he knew a fellow game-player when he met one.

'I recently read the reports of the Glenfinnan wool samples that your assistant sent down to the factory,' he said, accepting the cup of tea James passed him, and adding a teaspoon of sugar from the sugar bowl.

'Oh yes?' Josh concentrated upon pouring his own cup, stirring in his own sugar. He was surprised Kevin Cavanagh should display such a personal interest in the basics; this was surely a job to be assigned to others. 'They would have read rather well, I should think,' he said. 'Would you care for some shortbread?' He offered the plate.

'Thank you, yes.' Kevin accepted a biscuit, placed it on his saucer, and sat comfortably back in his leather armchair, crossing his legs as he took a sip of his tea. He wore clothes elegantly, as befitted the owner of a clothing manufacture company, even an owner who had sprung from the factory floors of Manchester.

'Oh yes, the reports were most impressive,' he said, pausing to take a nibble of his shortbread. 'These are excellent.' He examined the biscuit. 'They'd have to come from Scotland, wouldn't they? All the best shortbread comes from Scotland.'

'Yes, they're imported,' Josh replied. 'So if you're happy with the reports, what appears to be the problem?'

'They're not reports on the wool we're working with, are they?'

'They're reports on Glenfinnan wool,' Josh replied, still prepared to brazen it out if possible.

'Yes, that I believe, and I've followed my enquiries back to the textile factory who tell me the bales arrive bearing the Glenfinnan stamp.'

'So?'

'So we both know, don't we, Josh, that the wool does *not* come from Glenfinnan.' Kevin uncrossed his legs, leaned forward and placed his cup and saucer on the coffee table. He was now prepared to talk business. 'We both know don't we Josh, that the woollen fabric my company is working with is not of the finest quality it boasts to be.'

As their eyes locked, Josh knew he'd met his match.

'Did you really think, matey,' Kev said, the Mancunian accent, barely discernible as a rule, now coming to the fore, 'that I wouldn't recognise that fact?'

He's not angry, Josh thought, *we might be able to come up with a deal here.*

'What do you intend to do about it?' he asked boldly.

'What would you *like* me to do about it?' Kevin's response was equally bold.

'Join forces with us?' Though posed as a question they both knew it was an out-and-out offer.

'I was hoping you might say that.' Kevin's grin was attractively triumphant. He did so enjoy the company of fellow game-players. 'You're a smart young man, Josh. Your ties with the military are exceptional. I admire the way you've secured your army contracts so effortlessly, very clever indeed.'

'Thank you.'

Josh accepted the compliment as his due, although he was aware he'd done little to earn it. The ease with which Major Keith Manning had been manipulated bordered on the laughable. Right from the start, the man had been swayed by the prospect of an association with the likes of the McKinnon and Willard families, which had been most convenient. Then as time had progressed it had become evident the major loved nothing more than mingling with the elite. The Melbourne Club, which had long been attractive to the upper echelons of the military, had become a regular base for the business meetings they conducted, and Keith Manning wore his connections to all select branches of society with consummate pride. Focusing upon this aspect of his nature, Josh had worked hard to cultivate a personal friendship with Manning, earning his trust as a like-minded man of integrity. In doing so he had carefully avoided any inclusion of Darcy Willard when they socialised.

'Keep clear of Manning, Darce,' he'd instructed, 'he's not your type.'

'Ah. A wowser you mean.' Darcy had taken no offence.

'Exactly.'

Josh's tactics had worked. He and the major had become good friends, despite their age difference. Just as he had become good friends with Colonel Cranmer in London. They respected each other. Most importantly, Keith Manning was a soldier held in the highest regard by his men. And the many officers in acquisitions and the general area of supply and demand obeyed the major's every order without question.

The major was honest, Josh knew this; there was no doubting the fact. But in his own way Keith Manning had been bought, albeit unwittingly, by the social connections offered him.

And now it appeared Kevin Cavanagh must be bought. Josh wondered exactly what additional services, apart from his silence, Kev might bring to the partnership.

'So what are your views on the direction we should follow?' The question could be interpreted ambiguously. He might have been asking, *How much do you want for your silence?* Or perhaps, *What input are you offering?*

Kevin chose to answer the latter option. To begin with anyway. And his input was offered with sublime confidence.

'We're well into production already,' he said, 'I see no reason not to continue along the same lines. As you say, the army doesn't seem to recognise quality, it's durability they're after, which is only natural. We'll keep on with the uniforms and the socks. And one hardly needs fine wool to make army blankets,' he added with a laugh.

Kevin took another sip of his tea before continuing. Knowing he was being tested along the lines of what assets he might bring to the partnership, he was not prepared to be found wanting. 'I'm not sure if you're aware, but the Australian Army has a contract for the production of blankets with John Vicars & Co out of Sydney . . .'

Kevin could tell by young McKinnon's expression, subtle though it was, that he hadn't known this. *Good,* he thought.

'Which won't affect us in the least,' he continued. 'My enquiries lead me to believe the army's need for blankets will be infinite. They'll accept supplies from knitting mills all over Victoria and our factory will churn them out with the best. Two for every soldier, Josh, that's a lot of wool.'

'It is indeed.'

'We'll need good fibre for the slouch hats though,' Kevin went on, 'can't skimp there. The slouch hat is destined to become iconic, open to close inspection, needs to be made of the best wool felt.'

'All of which can be arranged.' Josh was pleased, Kev's input was obviously going to prove valuable.

Knowing he'd passed the test, Kevin was equally pleased. 'I have other ideas that can be addressed over time,' he said, 'all of which I'm sure will appeal.' *Now let's get down to business,* was inherent in his tone as he continued. 'So perhaps we might agree on a three-way split? McKinnon & Willard Enterprises to remain as is, but with a silent partner brought into the mix. What would you say to that?'

Josh's pause was minimal, for effect more than anything.

'I would say yes,' he replied.

'And what would Darcy Willard say?'

'Nothing. Darcy will do whatever I tell him. So long as he's kept in an ample supply of liquor, women and the good life in general he'll have no complaint.'

Kev rightly gathered from such a comment that young McKinnon had little time for Darcy Willard.

'I'll arrange a meeting between the three of us to formalise the arrangement,' Josh said, 'but in the meantime, shall we toast to our new partnership, you and I?'

'Excellent idea.'

He stood. 'Brandy or Scotch?'

'Scotch for me, thanks.'

'Scotch it is.' Josh smiled as he crossed to the drinks cabinet.

The amphibious landings at the Gallipoli Peninsula had proved disastrous. On the first day alone over six hundred troops of the 11th and 12th Battalions AIF had been killed, and the carnage continued relentlessly in the days and weeks that ensued. But it was to prove some time before the news reached home and Australians became aware of the devastating statistics. The British Army refused to make public any details of casualty numbers or to admit to the military ineptitude of command that had led to such a catastrophic outcome.

The Australian government, too, was reluctant to release the true story. Given their agreement to provide a quota of troops for the British, they were wary about scaring off volunteers, and with the loss of such numbers, recruitment drives were in full force. Further troops were needed.

But gradually, as the telegrams arrived informing families their men had been killed or wounded or lost in action, the news seeped from household to household. Australians were slowly learning the awful truth of the Gallipoli Campaign.

Still the recruitment drives continued, as relentlessly as the campaign itself, or so it seemed. The more troops lost, the more troops needed. The war appeared set upon devouring a whole generation of young men. Those who served with the Australian and New Zealand Army Corps, those now known as Anzacs.

But the worst was yet to come. Between the 6th and the 10th of August 1915, over two thousand Anzacs died at the Battle of Lone Pine. And during that same four-day period in an attack at The Nek, which was intended by British command to be purely a diversionary tactic, nearly four hundred Australians were killed and wounded.

'Two hundred and thirty-four killed and one hundred and thirty-eight wounded to be precise,' Keith Manning told Josh in hushed tones as they sat sharing a beer at the Melbourne Club. 'In approximately one hour, I believe.'

Keith was fully aware he should not be sharing these details with a civilian, and he would certainly not be doing so with any civilian other than Josh McKinnon. But Josh was different. Josh had become a true friend, one who could be trusted, and it was good to talk to a friend who existed outside the military.

'In one hour,' Josh gasped, 'good God almighty.'

'They only had to charge twenty-five yards,' Keith went on, 'and not one of them made it. They were all mowed down as they ran. At least that's what I was told.'

'Jesus.'

'Yep.' He downed the remains of his beer. 'Terrible business,' he muttered, 'bloody terrible.'

Barely one week later, Jenna telephoned her son.

'You have to come home, Josh,' she said. 'You have to come home and stop Ted signing up. Zac and Sam too. They're determined to go off to war, all three of them. Adele and I are worried sick.'

'I can't come home, Mum,' he replied. 'We've never been busier. We've never been more needed.' *We've never made more money,* he thought. 'I can't just drop everything and come back to Glenfinnan.'

'You have to,' she insisted. 'You're the only one who can stop them. You're the only one the boys will listen to, you know that. Your father and Phil aren't making any inroads whatsoever, and we're getting desperate.'

Josh felt a surge of irritation. What was he expected to do, for God's sake? But he didn't allow his annoyance to show.

'I'll come home when I can, Mum,' he assured her calmly, although he knew he wouldn't be going home for quite some time, not while the war was producing such a profit. Kevin Cavanagh's latest idea was proving immensely successful. McKinnon & Willard Enterprises no longer relied purely on army contracts, although the demand for the production and exportation of military supplies was ever-burgeoning. They'd recently branched into the import business as well. There had been a wartime change in the government's rulings, and they now ran a clandestine operation bringing in goods that had been banned from importation; household items for the most part, which had been manufactured in Germany or enemy allied countries. As Josh and Kevin had agreed, there was such a lot of money to be made from a war.

'Tell the boys to stay put until I get back to Glenfinnan,' he said. *That'll have to do for the moment,* he thought. 'Tell them not to sign up until we've talked things over . . .'

His mother was about to interrupt, he could tell, so he continued, the voice of reason, but also authority, calming her fears. *Fobbing her off.*

'Don't you worry, Mum. Through my contacts in the military I have inside knowledge and I'll be able to properly advise the boys. I'll come home and sort things out. I promise I will. All in good time.'

And Jenna had had to be satisfied with that.

A month later, however, when Josh had still not returned to Glenfinnan, the McKinnon women took matters into their own hands. A meeting was called, and a decision made.

Late one bright, September morning, right out of the blue, Josh's sister arrived in Melbourne. She simply fronted up to the offices of McKinnon & Willard Enterprises, suitcase in hand.

'Em!' Josh rose from the chair behind his desk, utterly flabbergasted.

His secretary, Dottie, had ushered her in from the reception area and there she was, larger than life and breathtakingly beautiful. Emily McKinnon, just turned seventeen, bold as brass, bonnet-less, coppery red hair a brazen beacon. Em had always stood out in a crowd.

'What the heck are you doing here?'

'I caught the overnight train,' she said. Which didn't answer the question.

'Why?'

'To see you of course.' She plonked down her suitcase and looked approvingly about at his office. 'Very fancy,' she remarked, 'and you have an apartment upstairs, don't you. I may be staying a few days. Are you going to put me up?' In typical fashion, she was being deliberately confronting.

'Why on earth didn't you telephone me?'

'Because Mum and Aunty Adele both knew you'd try to fob me off. I've been elected to bring you home. Or rather I elected myself, but with their permission. Does that very nice secretary of yours supply a cup of tea by any chance?'

Exasperated, Josh was forced to give in. 'Take a seat,' he said, circling the desk and gesturing to one of the arm-chairs in the office's lounge area. He popped his head out into reception. 'Dottie, would you round us up a pot of tea, please?'

He made the request quietly and closed the door behind him, hoping Darcy hadn't heard. They had adjoining offices that opened onto the reception area and Darcy was currently next door, having made one of his random appearances at the workplace. Whether or not he was actually working was another matter altogether, but he liked to pretend an air of importance from time to time.

'So are you going to put me up in your apartment?' Emily repeated her request.

And rather imperiously, Josh thought. He did wish she'd keep her voice down. 'No,' he replied, sitting in the armchair beside her.

'Why ever not?' she demanded. 'You have a spare bedroom, don't you?'

'Because my business partner, Darcy, quite often stays overnight, Em,' he said, lowering his voice, signalling she should do the same. Darcy rarely stayed overnight, except on the odd occasion when he'd end up so drunk he could barely walk, but the last thing Josh wanted was Darcy Willard drooling over his sister, either drunk or sober. The more he kept Em away from the Collins Street offices altogether, the better.

There was a tap on the other side of the adjoining door and, right on cue, Darcy popped his head through.

'Did I hear you order some tea from Dottie,' he queried, 'and without including me? Oh my goodness . . .' He suddenly noticed the beautiful girl who'd turned to look at him. 'Hello, who do we have here?' A redhead, he simply adored redheads. *And so young,* he thought, *so deliciously young!*

'This is my *sister*, Darcy.' Josh's voice held the sternest of warnings. He rose to his feet. Just as he'd expected, Darcy was drooling. 'Emily, this is Darcy Willard.'

'How do you do, Miss McKinnon.' Darcy read the warning correctly and was on his best behaviour as he crossed to Emily and took the gloved hand she offered. He didn't shake it, however, raising it to his lips instead, a flirtatious twinkle in his eye.

'How do you do, Mr Willard.' Emily smiled politely. She, too, had read the warning in her brother's voice, which had been none too subtle, but she considered it unnecessary. Darcy was handsome, there was no denying the fact, but she recognised his type. Darcy Willard was a rogue; straight from the pages of a Jane Austen novel. The wicked glint in his eyes signalled a desire to seduce, and she was personally affronted that his name should be Darcy. *Pride and Prejudice*'s 'Mr Darcy' was surely every girl's favourite. Her look to her brother assured him there was no need to worry on her account.

'Shall I stay for tea?' Darcy enquired. It was not a request, but an automatic assumption for, to Josh's extreme annoyance, he'd already seated himself in the armchair opposite Emily.

'Be my guest,' he replied.

Darcy launched immediately into the requisite small talk, dripping charm as he always did with pretty young women. How fortunate she'd encountered such pleasant weather upon her arrival, he said. Melbourne could be so unpredictable, even in the spring.

Emily nodded, maintaining a polite façade, but aware that his roaming gaze was checking out every inch of her.

The tea arrived, together with Dottie's specially selected almond shortbread, and Darcy's small talk continued. How long was she staying in Melbourne? Possibly a few days, she replied. And she'd come to pay a visit to her brother, how nice. No, she'd come to fulfil her duty and persuade her brother to return to Glenfinnan, she said bluntly.

'Oh. Really?' Here suddenly was news of interest. Darcy had been quite happy simply feasting his eyes on this glorious young thing, but he was now alerted to a possible problem. Josh was heading back to Glenfinnan? Now? With business as it was? Army requirements were at a peak, and of even greater importance, their recent foray into illicit importation needed to be strictly governed.

The timing seemed most odd to Darcy and he felt a flash of concern. Josh and Kevin handled everything, and Kevin didn't like him, he knew that. What on earth would he do without Josh? He cast a querying glance at his partner.

'Emily and I have a few matters to chat about, Darce,' Josh said with a comradely smile while cursing his mother, his aunt and his sister. *Damn the McKinnon women*, he thought. 'Just family stuff, you know how it is.'

'Ah.' Darcy relaxed. 'Yes, yes, of course.'

To Emily, the exchange between the two appeared patronising, as did her brother's tone, and she started to bristle. She didn't like being talked down to by men. She was a fierce advocate of women's rights and would not be belittled. But she said nothing for the moment and the matter was glossed over until ten minutes later Josh stood, calling a halt to morning tea. Which seemed a little premature, they'd only had one cup and there was a whole half a pot left.

'Time we made a move, Em,' he announced.

A move? she wondered. *To where?*

But before she could enquire, he continued.

'I'm booking Emily into the Grand Hotel,' he said to Darcy. Then back to her he said, 'You'll love the Grand, Em. We'll get you the best suite they have and it's only just around the corner.'

She forgave him in an instant, feeling a wave of affection. *He's doing this to protect me from Darcy Willard,* she thought. *But you really don't need to, Josh. I can look after myself.*

'How thrilling,' she said, rising to her feet, genuinely excited, she knew of the Grand. 'I've heard it's the most marvellous hotel.'

'About the most marvellous in the whole country.' He flashed her the fondest of smiles. He dearly loved his little sister, just as he dearly loved his whole family, but he had plans and would not be deterred. Nothing and no one, not even those he loved, would distract Josh McKinnon from his chosen path.

He wondered how long it would take for his family to realise this. How long would it be before Emily realised she must go home to Glenfinnan without him? Or if she proved stubborn and refused to give in, would he be forced to return for a short visit? No. He dare not leave Darcy in charge, even for the briefest period. Or Kevin for that matter. Darcy was incompetent and Kevin untrustworthy. Kev was a slippery customer. They played the role of mates, but Kev would rob him or undermine him at the first opportunity.

'Come on, Em,' he said, picking up her suitcase, 'let's go.'

They made their farewells to Darcy who rose to his feet, bewildered by the speed of their departure and wondering what had happened to morning tea.

No, Josh decided as they stepped out into Collins Street, the family would just have to cope without him. And why must he be the arbiter anyway? If Ted and the twins were determined to sign up and go to war then let them. Zac and Sam were twenty years old and Ted was eighteen. They were of age, they could make their own decisions. *The McKinnon women have always been domineering,* he told himself. *It's high time they released the hold they have over their sons.*

Josh determined to convince Emily of this fact over the following days. She must be made aware that her brother and cousins should be left to make their own decisions.

But as things turned out, there proved no need for any form of persuasion. He was surprised to discover, and barely an hour and a half later, that his sister was in entire agreement.

'Yes, you're quite right,' Emily said as they discussed the situation over lunch at the Grand Hotel. Having booked her into a suite, they'd adjourned to the dining room. 'Mum and Auntie Adele are being over-protective. I hate this war, but if the boys want to join up, it's their choice. I think Dad and Uncle Phil agree, actually, but McKinnon mothers have always been bossy, haven't they?'

Josh was bewildered. If she'd been sent to Melbourne to bring him back, she was hardly going about things the right way, was she? He watched as she tucked into her fish fillet with a healthy appetite while maintaining impeccable table manners. She seemed so at home in the elegant Grand Hotel. They'd been well brought up, certainly, their mother had always been strict about social etiquette, and he was aware too that Emily had been to Sydney on any number of occasions, but at heart she was still a country girl, wasn't she? Why, only fifteen minutes ago she'd displayed such childlike glee upon viewing her suite overlooking Spring Street.

'Oh it's glorious, Josh,' she'd declared ecstatically, twirling about then hanging out the window to gawk at the view. 'Look. That's Parliament House! I've seen it in the newspapers. Oh and look, look! There's a protest being held right there on the front steps.'

Yet here in the dining room, she was a confident young woman, stylish, forthright and with strongly formed views. The child-adult mix was attractive, but confusing.

'Adriana and Alexandra would be just as bossy,' Emily blithely went on, referring to her grand aunts, 'except their sons are too old to join up, and their grandsons are too young. If any offspring of those two threatened to go to war believe me they'd be joining forces with the McKinnon mothers' brigade.' She took another mouthful of her fish.

'This is absolutely delicious. Snapper, isn't it? I can't remember what it said on the menu.' She halted briefly. 'What's the matter? You haven't even touched your steak.'

Josh continued to stare at her, puzzled. 'You told me you'd been sent here to bring me back home,' he said with an element of accusation.

'Yes, that's right,' she agreed. 'That's what Mum and Auntie Adele think I'm doing here. But I lied.'

'Why? Why *are* you here then, Em?'

'I wanted to see Melbourne, of course.' She looked at him as if he was foolish for not having realised this. 'Mum would never have let me come on my own without a valid reason. She thinks you were expecting me. She thinks you were there to pick me up at the train station this morning. I told her you would be. I told her we talked on the telephone and you promised you'd look after me. But I told her she wouldn't be able to talk to you herself because I'm the only one you trust, and if she interfered in any way you might change your mind.'

'You clever girl,' he said admiringly, 'you clever, clever girl.'

'Thank you.' She smiled, the compliment pleasing her, particularly coming from Josh whom, like her brother Ted, she'd idolised throughout her childhood. 'Now, please, do eat your steak before it gets cold.' She'd finished her fish and was now attacking her salad. 'May we have dessert?' she asked.

'Of course.'

They made their plans over dessert. Emily would stay in Melbourne for several days, exploring the city's beautiful buildings and theatres as she so longed to do, after which she would telephone her mother and aunt, admit defeat, and return to Glenfinnan.

'I convinced them I'd be able to talk you into coming home, Josh,' she said, 'but I don't think you should. I don't agree with this war,' she added rebelliously, 'despite Empire and all that, I don't think we should be a part of it. But your work here is of such importance to our boys overseas, and you're doing so well. Dad is of the same mind, you know. He's awfully proud of you.'

The remark pleased Josh immensely.

Emily thrived in Melbourne. So much so that within just one week their carefully laid plan had completely backfired.

'This is the most exciting city in the country,' she enthused to her brother. 'Far more so than Sydney. There's a sense of purpose here in Melbourne, which is quite inspiring. People really *care* about things. *Important* things. Things that *matter*!' She paused. 'Perhaps it's because this is the home of our federal parliament,' she said thoughtfully, 'but I find Melburnians far more politically activated than their Sydney counterparts.'

Josh found both her fervour and her newly inspired 'sense of purpose' amusing. Just how well did she know Melbourne's 'Sydney counterparts'? he wondered. But he was not altogether surprised. Em had always been forthright in voicing her opinions, which now appeared to have taken on a political slant.

It was true. The activist in Emily had been fully awakened. She had met Adela Pankhurst and the well-known Melbourne suffragette, Vida Goldstein, during a rally on the steps of Parliament House, and she now had no intention of returning to Glenfinnan.

'Adela is one of Emmeline Pankhurst's daughters,' she proudly explained to Josh. '*Pankhurst*,' she added with a touch of impatience when he appeared disinterested. 'The famous suffragette currently fighting to gain English women the vote?'

He nodded. Yes, of course he knew who Emmeline Pankhurst was, but he was nonetheless uninterested.

'Apparently Adela had a falling out with her mother two years ago, and Emmeline gave her a ticket to Australia together with twenty pounds and told her to emigrate. They haven't been in touch with each other since. And they probably never will be again.'

'I see. She told you all this herself, did she?'

'No not directly, I heard it from members of the organisation she and Vida have formed.' Bridling at his apparent disdain, Emily was immediately on the defensive. 'But I *have* met her, Josh, and I *have* talked to her. She was very nice and we got on very well, and what's more I've joined up.'

'Joined up with what?'

'The Women's Peace Army, of course. We are against the war. Adela herself is currently touring the country arguing the importance of feminist opposition to militarism. I shall remain here and fight the cause.'

Josh could have laughed out loud. *So much for bringing me home to Glenfinnan,* he thought.

He found it even harder to quell his amusement as he explained the situation to his mother.

'I was all prepared to come home, Mum,' he assured Jenna when she telephoned yet again seeking news – he'd fobbed her off on the previous two occasions saying 'any time now' – 'but Em won't budge, I'm afraid. She's totally committed to the Women's Peace Army cause here in Melbourne and refuses to leave. But don't worry, I'll look after her, I promise.'

His dilemma had been solved most satisfactorily. He'd now had to assure his family that he would *not* come home, that he would remain in Melbourne and take care of his little sister. At least until she regained her senses. This activism of hers, they all agreed, was no more than a passing fad.

Well, well, how the tables have turned, Josh thought.

He blessed Adela Pankhurst and her fellow suffragettes.

As the Gallipoli Campaign continued upon its deadly course, wreaking countless casualties on both sides while achieving no Allied advantage whatsoever, more and more troops were needed. Australia's recruitment targets were not being met, and particularly it seemed in New South Wales. To remedy these embarrassing shortfalls, residents of country towns launched a series of recruiting marches intended to encourage men to enlist by following the example set by the marchers themselves. The initial march in October 1915 was led by local plumber William T. Hitchen, captain of the Gilgandra Rifle Club. It became known as 'The Cooee March', and eight other regional centres organised similar marches, which ensued over the next four months. Along each route, local communities fed and housed the men, as the closer they came to Sydney the greater their numbers grew. And the closer they came and the greater their numbers, the more publicity the marches engendered. Hurrahs resounded across the state. The commitment from rural New South Wales was total, the country boys were coming to town.

One such march set off from Wagga Wagga on the 1st of December 1915 to arrive in Sydney on the 7th of January 1916. Starting out with eighty-eight potential soldiers and growing exponentially with each town along the way, the distance overall would be 350 miles. Word was passed around. This was to be known as 'The Kangaroo March', and one of the towns through which it would pass was Goulburn.

'That's us,' Zac said when the news reached them. 'The Kangaroo March. That's us! It's a sign.'

'Yep,' his brother Sam agreed.

Sam had been delaying his decision, he wasn't quite sure why. Perhaps because their mother had kept telling them to wait until Josh came home, because Josh had so much inside information about the military and the war, and Josh would be able to offer them the correct advice. But Josh hadn't come home, and there came a time when a bloke had to follow his gut feelings, Sam resolved. Besides which, he was sick of Zac's nagging. Zac had been straining at the leash for altogether too long.

Yep, Sam thought, *this is definitely a sign*.

Once they'd made their decision, their younger cousin Ted was right along with them, he too raring to go. Ted, who at eighteen was now a strong, robust young man, needed his father's permission, but James readily gave it, and fight as she might, Jenna was allowed little say in the end.

'Let the boy go, my love,' James insisted. 'If I was his age I'd want to sign up. And he'll be with the twins,' he added reassuringly.

The three of them rode into Goulburn the very next day where they enlisted at the AIF Recruitment Office that had been set up in the centre of town.

'When those blokes come marching through here,' Zac declared as they sat in the pub sharing a celebratory beer, 'we'll be waiting for them, ready, willing and able.'

And they were. With the well wishes of family, friends and neighbours who turned up to cheer them on, albeit some with a heavy sense of trepidation, the gangly twins Zac and Sam and their nuggetty young cousin, Ted, proudly joined the Kangaroo marchers bound for Sydney.

They enjoyed every step of the way. Young, fit and healthy, 8.8 miles a day was no more than a pleasant, brisk walk for the boys, and the welcome they received in every town along the route proved nothing short of a party. They were not only comfortably housed by the locals, they were feted and fed like royalty, or so they declared.

'Wined and dined like there's no tomorrow,' Zac said. 'We'll be fat by the time we get to Sydney.'

The march finished at Campbelltown on the outskirts of the city. The Kangaroo recruits were then transported by train into Sydney, where they were to be housed at Randwick Racecourse. It was here their training would begin, after which they would be posted overseas, first to the AIF base camp in Egypt for further training, then on to the battlefields of France.

Zac, Sam and young Ted were about to embark upon the adventure of a lifetime. It was 1916 and they were going to war.

CHAPTER TWENTY

The Gallipoli Campaign had proved an ignominious defeat for the British. It had, furthermore, resulted in a disastrous loss of life for Australia with over eight thousand troops dead and more than nineteen thousand wounded. The only element of the entire operation to prove successful had been the well-planned and efficiently conducted evacuation towards the end of 1915. Over five nights, from the 15th to the 20th of December, thirty-six thousand troops were withdrawn from the peninsula, smuggled out under the cover of darkness to waiting transport ships. These war-torn men would live to fight again on the battlefields of France.

But first, after being returned to the base camp at Mena where they would spend Christmas thankful to be alive, they must help train the new troops that were to arrive in the early months of the following year. Fresh-faced young troops who to the battle-weary Gallipoli veterans appeared no more than boys.

Among these boys were brothers Zac and Sam Caton and their cousin, Ted McKinnon, all of whom upon arrival, found themselves attached to the newly formed 54th Battalion, 14th Brigade, 5th Division.

The AIF had been restructured into five divisions following Gallipoli, and the 5th, which was chiefly composed of raw volunteers, was the last Australian division to leave Egypt, bound for the port city of Marseilles in France.

Their departure didn't come about until June, at which stage the boys' letters home were full of excitement.

'We're finally on our way!' Zac wrote. *'And I tell you what, about bloody time! These months of training have been boring as hell. Can't wait to be in the thick of things . . .'*

'Look out France, here we come,' Sam wrote. *'Gosh I hope we get to see the Eiffel Tower . . .'*

The twins wrote sparse letters and always a combined effort, a paragraph from Zac, then a paragraph from Sam. Theirs were 'duty' letters intended to be passed around among the family.

Ted's letters home were altogether different. They were far more detailed as Ted really enjoyed writing. He'd loved telling his mum and dad all about Cairo and the Sphynx and the Pyramids and even the desert itself. His brother and his sister too. He'd written to Josh in Melbourne, and also to Emily who was now living in Sydney.

'The bazaar in Cairo has to be seen to be believed,' he'd written. *'It's called Khan el-Khalili and it's something right out of "The Arabian Nights". And as for the grand Pyramid of Cheops, well that just beggars description. How did they do it? You have to ask yourself that, truly you do. Unbelievable! And the magnitude of the desert! When you can get away on your own, as I do now and then, particularly of an early evening when things have quietened down, the desert is overwhelming. You get the funniest feeling. Well I do anyway, don't know about the other blokes. But this really is a different world, an ancient world . . .'*

On and on he would go. Ted loved to wax rhapsodic. Now, with France beckoning, he was thrilled by the prospect of what lay ahead. He'd have a lot to write about when he got to France.

And he did! From the moment they arrived in Marseilles, Ted was carried away by the sights and the sounds and the people of yet another world altogether.

'Marseilles is the biggest city imaginable,' he wrote. 'And the busiest, you should just see the port! And it's the oldest too. Somebody actually told me it's the oldest city in the whole of France. It certainly looks it. Being here you feel like you've stepped back in time . . .'

Then of the troops' journey across France by train in open carriages to Armentieres in the north near the Belgian border . . .

'We've been passing by the prettiest villages. Some only around the size of a small country town you'd see back home – you know the sort, blink and you miss it – but of course they're totally different over here. Cobblestone streets, little stone terrace houses with wooden shutters, really old, always with a church in the middle. And the people! Crikey, the people here are amazing. They come out of the village to line up beside the tracks as we pass by. They line up for miles. Women and children and old men – course the young blokes are all off fighting – and they wave and salute and throw kisses. They're so happy to see us . . .'

Ted wrote three letters a week for three weeks in a row. One to his mum and dad, one to Josh and one to Emily. The words just poured out, he couldn't stop.

Zac and Sam teased him endlessly about the way he was always scribbling.

'Give it a rest, mate,' they'd jeer good-naturedly, 'you're not writing a bloody novel for God's sake.'

But maybe he was. Or maybe he would one day. There was so much to see, so much to take in, he just had to write it down. Besides, what else was a bloke to do after endless marches and drills? They'd been transported from Armentieres to the camp and trenches near a town called

Fromelles, and the training hadn't let up from the moment they'd arrived.

Ted didn't write about the camp and the training though. They could hear the sound of artillery and gunfire from the not-too-distant front by now and he had a feeling they were soon going to be 'in the thick of things' as Zac was wont to say. The army wouldn't let him write about that sort of stuff anyway. And what was the point? He only wanted to write about the good parts. The travel parts.

'Maybe I'll be a travel writer one day,' he wrote to his sister. He and Emily were both keen readers and had always discussed books. *'Mark Twain started out as a travel writer, didn't he? What a way to earn a living, eh, Em? Fancy getting paid to travel the world and write about it!'*

The Battle of Fromelles commenced on the 19th of July and lasted just twenty-four hours, a period which was later described as 'the worst twenty-four hours in Australia's history' and a 'tactical abortion that should never have happened'. Intended by the British as a feint to prevent German reserves moving south to the Somme, where a large Allied attack had begun, the Battle of Fromelles proved an unmitigated failure. During one day and night more than two thousand Australian troops were slaughtered and even greater numbers were to die from their wounds. In excess of five and a half thousand casualties was to become the final count.

The fresh young troops of the Australian 5th Division had been introduced to the Western Front in a baptism of fire. The initial assault had been ordered to take place over open ground and in broad daylight. Under clear observation, the troops had charged directly into heavy fire from the German lines. Hardly surprising such tactics had resulted in a blood bath.

Ted McKinnon was one of the lucky ones. He did not lie groaning in agony among the mortally wounded who would take so long to die. He was among those who'd been struck in the first minutes of battle. Young Ted McKinnon would have felt no pain. He'd been dead before his body had hit the ground.

His cousins, Zac and Sam Caton, had miraculously survived. They didn't know how. Zac and Sam had simply charged along with the others, screaming their lungs out mindlessly, expecting the bullets to hit at any moment. But like those other survivors, and there *had* been survivors, they'd somehow made it through. They hadn't copped it and now lived to fight another day. But they'd never be the same. They'd been blooded, and in the most horrific way.

The Battle of Fromelles had taken place barely one month after the 5th Division had arrived in France and mail from the front was slow finding its way to Australia. Ted was dead by the time his letters reached home.

His family had been informed of his death well before the mail arrived. Then the letters started to turn up. And in numbers. Ted's letters from France. Three letters a week, written over three weeks. They arrived in a deluge. To his parents, James and Jenna, delivered from the Goulburn post office to the property of Glenfinnan. To his older brother, Josh, delivered to the offices of McKinnon & Willard in Melbourne. To his younger sister, Emily, delivered to the boarding house for young ladies in Sydney, accommodation which had been carefully selected for her by the Women's Peace Army.

Ted's letters had a profound effect upon the whole family, all of whom were already mourning his death. In late August they congregated at Glenfinnan to share their loss, Josh arriving from Melbourne, Emily from Sydney, and they read their letters out loud to one another, weeping, exchanging stories of yesteryear, even laughing at childhood memories. The whole extended family turned up, from ageing aunts to grandchildren and countless cousins. It was a healthy experience, akin to a wake, and Ted's voice was there with them. Young, fresh and vital.

There was, however, one hostile element to the proceedings – at least there was to start with.

Across the crowded room of immediate family, and aunts and uncles and cousins and small grandchildren, Jenna's eyes found those of her son. And her eyes bore accusation – the same accusation she'd hurled at him during the telephone conversation they'd had upon the news of Ted's death.

'Why didn't you come home,' she'd demanded, and it hadn't been a question, but a condemnation. 'You promised! You could have stopped them from going. You told me that through your contacts with the military you had inside knowledge and you'd be able to properly advise the boys. That's what you said, Josh! *"I'll come home and sort things out."* That's what you *said*!'

It had been grief speaking, of course. She'd known deep down they were powerless, all of them – that the boys would eventually go off to war, that in her demands of Josh she'd been buying time. But she'd blamed him anyway, and she'd felt she had every right. She still did. And now, in this crowded room of family, she glared at him balefully.

But as Ted continued to talk to them through his letters, Jenna felt her anger and bitterness slowly fade.

'*Crikey Em, I wouldn't have missed this for quids . . .*'

They were reading the letters sequentially and this was Emily's turn, the last letter to her, dated just the day before the Battle of Fromelles.

'*Whatever happens, I've seen so much! The places, the people, the cultures . . . The things I've learned. Gosh, this world is a wonderful place. So much bigger than you and I ever envisaged, even when we talked about the books we'd read. You'll have to travel, Em, honest, you really will have to travel . . .'*

Jenna gave up at that stage. What was the point in accusation? Ted was gone. Ted had been destined to go, and there was little Josh could have done to prevent it.

The effect Ted's letters had upon the family was indeed profound.

The 'duty' letters from Zac and Sam would continue to arrive, sparsely written as always, but there would be a different flavour to them from now on. Hardened. Zac and Sam were no longer young.

Josh was glad he'd returned to Glenfinnan. He was deeply saddened by the loss of the little brother to whom he had been such a hero. He would miss Ted. It was good to see the family again too. He loved his family. Family was important. A successful man should have strong family ties, in Josh's opinion. Why, just look at his father. Such a fine patriarch, presenting such a noble figure, respected by all.

Josh watched his father admiringly as James gave a speech to the family gathering honouring Ted. *That will be me one day,* he thought. One day he would marry and one day he would have children, and one day that would be him standing there addressing his clan. *I'll be the most successful and the most powerful patriarch the family has ever known,* he told himself, the notion filling him with pride.

He stayed at Glenfinnan for a whole two weeks, as did his sister, Emily, she too basking in the warmth of family while mourning her brother. Despite the separate paths they'd chosen, it seemed to Em they'd never been closer. That Ted was bringing them all together.

But inevitably the very paths they'd chosen demanded they make their departure. Two weeks was as long as Josh dared leave Darcy on the loose in Melbourne, and Emily, now a prominent leader of the Women's Peace Army branch that had been established in Sydney, was driven to return.

'We've already designed the pamphlets,' she said, 'we're only waiting for Hughes to announce the date of the damned thing – sometime in October, or so we've heard . . .'

It was several days before she and Josh were to leave, and Emily was informing the assembled dinner table of the Women's Peace Army's plans to influence the forthcoming plebiscite. The gathering included not only her parents but the Catons – her aunt and uncle, Adele and Phil, and her cousins, eighteen-year-old Mathilda, known as Hildy, and young Tom who was fifteen. The two families had always been close, but now more than ever, Adele supporting Jenna in her grief while both prayed for the safe return of the twins.

'Hughes is absolutely set upon a referendum,' Emily went on. 'He maintains conscription will be essential if Australia is to sustain its contribution to the war effort.'

Prime Minister William Morris (Billy) Hughes, a strong supporter of Australia's participation in the war, was an equally strong believer in the need for conscription. Particularly now, given the latest massive numbers of casualties – twenty-eight thousand men killed, wounded and missing in action during July and August alone.

Emily thumped an assertive fist on the table, rattling the nearby dishes and cutlery. 'Well damn Billy Hughes, I say, and damn this war!' She was now in full soapbox mode, and might have been preaching the cause at Speakers' Corner in Sydney's Domain the way she did on a Sunday. 'We don't need more boys going to their deaths. There's been more than enough death already. And we certainly don't need mandatory conscription!'

'Hear! Hear!' Jenna, Adele and Hildy loudly voiced agreement, all three sisters to the Cause, while young Tom looked startled, and James and Phil exchanged glances that were a mix of amusement and admiration. Em was pretty impressive. But then she always had been, even as a child.

'We'll be handing out thousands of pamphlets,' she continued, 'and there'll be campaigns and rallies and protests all over Sydney. All over the entire *country*,' she said emphatically, 'including right here in Goulburn. I'll send you a box of pamphlets, Mum. You and Auntie Adele and Hildy can round up the locals and make sure they vote no.'

'We shall, Em,' Jenna assured her daughter, Adele and Hildy nodding vigorously, 'we most certainly shall.'

Josh smiled, appearing to enjoy the exchange and even approve the sentiment expressed, but remaining silent nonetheless. He was ambivalent to the situation himself. He could hardly profess to anti-war sentiments, could he? Not when business was at its peak and he was making so much money from the conflict. But it was important his work be viewed from the right perspective, along the altruistic lines of his invaluable assistance to the military, and to the war effort in general.

When the conversation about Billy Hughes and the forthcoming plebiscite had finally died down, his father gave him the perfect opening.

'I'm delighted with Glenfinnan's input to the "Diggers Vest" campaign son,' he said. 'I've been a bit out of touch with our military connections, leaving everything to you as I have, and I'm grateful to you for including us in it. Indeed proud to be part of such a worthy cause.'

Josh smiled. 'I'm glad to hear that, Dad, I hoped you would be. It's the least we can do of course,' he added modestly, 'but you're right, it's a fine campaign, and I'm glad we're part of it too. More than a part, I might add.

We helped initiate the campaign and we remain one of the leading providers of sheepskins for the Diggers Vests.'

'Excellent.' James beamed at his son. 'Excellent news!'

Good for you, Terence, Josh thought. *Your plan certainly paid off. Good for you, mate!*

Josh recalled he'd initially been sceptical of Terence Dimbleby's idea.

'A not-for-profit campaign,' he'd queried, 'how will that benefit us? We're not a charity, Terence.'

But Terence had been uncharacteristically adamant. 'We should not only become a part of this campaign, Josh,' he'd replied, 'we should be seen to lead the way.'

The campaign was a noble one. Hearing of the hardship suffered by the troops overseas, many of whom were freezing to death or dying of pneumonia in the muddy trenches of war, the Australian public had responded with a practical form of assistance. An appeal had been launched with the help of the press to provide the men of the Australian Expeditionary Forces with tanned sheepskin waistcoats for warmth. Notices had been posted on shop windows and advertisements had appeared in the pages of newspapers all over the country.

SEND HIM A SHEEPSKIN VEST:
Have you a soldier in camp or leaving for foreign battlefields?
Send him a Sheepskin Vest.
IT MAY SAVE HIS LIFE.

The ads had gone on to explain that the vests would be 'efficiently tailored from specially chosen oak-bark-tanned skins of natural wool; bound with leather; secured with straps, and reversible'.

'MADE TO ORDER. SEND ONLY THE CHEST MEASURE.'

The waistcoats would become known as 'Diggers Vests' and the ads didn't lie; they *did* save lives.

'Glenfinnan must be among the first woolgrowers to donate sheepskins,' Terence had insisted. 'No, let's make sure we're the *first,*' he'd said, 'and let's make sure we donate the *most!*'

Terence Dimbleby, the canny, but meek and mild accountant, was rarely so assertive. Josh had been forced to listen.

'If Glenfinnan leads the way in this venture,' Terence had explained, 'it would be difficult to suspect McKinnon & Willard of unethical procedures. Don't you see? The Diggers Vests would help form a perfect smokescreen.'

Josh had agreed at the time, albeit reluctantly, but Terence had proved right. By 1916, over seven and a half thousand waistcoats had been sent to soldiers at the front, and with every ensuing month the numbers had grown. Innumerable lives had been saved, and all those involved; the woolgrowers, the wool brokers who arranged the tanning, the Red Cross volunteers who helped with the manufacture of the vests, and more, were lauded as heroes.

Well done, Terence, Josh thought as he basked in his father's admiration, *you crafty bugger, well done.*

Josh had had many a productive meeting with Terence Dimbleby over the past fortnight. His trip home to Glenfinnan had proved not only a pleasurable reminder of the importance of family, but a lesson in clever accountancy and impeccable book-keeping. Terence's records of all business conducted by McKinnon & Willard Enterprises was masterfully camouflaged.

'You're a true genius, mate,' he'd said, 'well done.'

And Terence had basked in his friend's admiration. How he wished Josh could remain here at Glenfinnan. He'd missed him so.

Upon his return to Melbourne, on a mid-Wednesday morning, having caught the overnight train from Goulburn, Josh was greeted with potential disaster. His worries about leaving Darcy Willard on his own had not been unwarranted. He'd known Darcy needed to be held on the tightest of leashes or else kept away altogether from any form of business connection, but he'd hoped two weeks wouldn't be asking too much. He'd been wrong.

'Had a visit from your good friend Major Manning on Monday,' Kevin Cavanagh said tightly, his whole manner displaying a rage that was barely controllable. 'I'm here to tell you that your little mate, Darcy, might have cost us our contract with the military.'

Kev had been waiting in Josh's office the very day and the very hour of his return, Dottie having informed him of her employer's expected time of arrival. And Kev was fuming.

'What the hell's he done?' Josh was already cursing himself.

'Behaved like the useless fool he is at the Melbourne Club on Saturday, or so I'm told. Manning said he was drunk as a lord.'

Damn, Josh thought, *he shouldn't have gone to the Melbourne Club without me, Darce knows that.* 'So?' he queried brightly. 'It's no crime to be drunk, Kev, even in the Melbourne Club.'

'It's a bloody crime when the bastard opens his big, fat gob to the officer responsible for our army contracts.' Kev was snarling now. 'And in front of one of that officer's own superiors!'

Oh dear God no! Josh thought. *Darcy's been told he's never to approach Keith Manning on his own.* 'All right,' he said, offering no pretence now, but resigned to hearing the worst. 'What happened? Tell me. What did he do?'

'How the hell should I know, I wasn't there!' Kev's temper was not abating in the least, if anything it was on the rise as he relived his humiliation. 'The prick probably big-mouthed about how valuable he is, about him and his family name, and how lucky the army is to have the Willards onside, I've no fucking idea what he said, but Manning turned up at my office in Geelong! He couldn't find you, so he came to me! And he wanted answers! Well, I ask you, what the hell was I supposed to *do*?'

'Calm down now, Kev, calm down,' Josh placated the man, who appeared on the verge of exploding. 'Take a seat and let me get you a drink.'

Once Kevin was seated and they both had a Scotch in hand, he continued.

'So what *did* you do, mate?'

'I pleaded ignorance of course. And I ate humble pie,' Kev replied, taking a hefty swig of his Scotch. 'Which is something I do not enjoy doing,' he added scathingly, 'I can promise you that. But what choice did I have?'

Kev had hated his meeting with Keith Manning. It had taken him right back to his early days in England when he'd kowtowed to the factory boss on a daily basis before discovering that courting the man's plain daughter was the way to get on. Kev didn't like kowtowing. He didn't like kowtowing one bit. But he was good at it.

'I'm only a manufacturer, Major Manning,' he'd said, sounding pathetic, painting himself as an insignificant cog in the whole enterprise. 'I'm afraid I know nothing about the operational side of McKinnon & Willard. And I must admit to having little personal connection with either gentleman concerned. I merely supply the orders that are handed me, no more than that.'

The major had accepted the paltry role he played in the scheme of things, but Kev had found the response he'd received equally demeaning in its dismissiveness.

'Very well. I shall pay a visit to your employer,' Manning had replied, as if Kev were a mere lackey. 'We'll see what

Willard has to say about the disgraceful behaviour of his son. The army will not be treated with such disrespect.' And Keith Manning had stormed out of the office.

'You'll have to do something about your friend,' Kev said, still simmering at the memory. 'That bastard could bring us all crashing down if the military decide to dig a bit deeper into who they're dealing with. I'm a partner in this enterprise, Josh, don't you forget that. You two might be the names, but I'm the *true* partner behind McKinnon & Willard, and I will not have my business brought to ruin by your snotty-nosed little rich-prick mate . . .'

But Josh wasn't listening. 'So Manning came to your office on Monday,' he said. 'The day before yesterday. And when he left he told you he was going to pay a visit to Willard.' *Jesus Christ, Darcy might have already brought us unstuck,* he thought as he downed the remains of his Scotch. A chain of events had been set in motion and anything could have happened by now.

He grabbed his overcoat and made for the door. 'See you later, Kev,' he barked, 'I'll be in touch as soon as I've sorted out this mess.'

'Good luck,' Kev called, and as he downed his own Scotch he wondered in which direction Josh was headed and who he was headed for. Willard or Manning? It was a toss-up either way, he decided.

The Willards' Toorak mansion was in Kooyong Road, and like most Toorak mansions was most impressive, this particular one having been designed and built in the 1850s during the gold-rush era. Josh had been a guest at the family residence on a number of occasions and was certain he would find Darcy's father there, Iain Willard choosing to work from his home these days. Although now in his sixties and semi-retired, Willard senior still played an active part in the highly successful organisation founded by his father. His two hard-working older sons ostensibly ran the business, but it was a well-known fact that Iain, the patriarch, remained the true power behind the Willard throne.

Iain Willard's father, Edward, had arrived in Melbourne in 1860 with his upper-class English wife, Olivia, his two young sons and one small daughter. Himself upper class and a highly regarded London architect, he'd been sought out by the Victorian colonial government to design and supervise the construction of several large government buildings in central Melbourne.

The extraordinarily fast expansion of Victoria that had followed the gold rush had proved fortuitous for Edward, who had entered into private partnership with a number of business-minded men to design and build municipal buildings in Ballarat, Bendigo and Geelong. He had also undertaken the design and building of post offices for the Victorian government, making Willard a highly respected name, not only in architectural design, but in governmental achievement.

Edward's young daughter, Cynthia, had married well, entering Melbourne high society, and his two sons, Iain and Anthony, had graduated from the University of Melbourne, Iain following his father into architecture, Anthony graduating in law. Both brothers had entered the senior ranks of the now powerful Willard organisation, but Iain, the elder and a natural-born leader, would be the one to take up the reins of the Willard conglomerate upon the death of his father.

Emulating his sister's example, Iain too had married well, his wife, Virginia being of impeccable lineage. Four children had followed, three sons and a daughter born to bear the proud name of Willard, and upon achieving adulthood they had gone on to do so with dignity. But one son was letting down the team. One son had been letting down the team for a long time now.

Iain Willard was at his wit's end as to what he must do with his reprobate son. Darcy was a threat to the Willard name. He was also a threat to his father's marriage for Iain had come to lay the blame squarely upon Virginia. She'd indulged the boy! That was the problem! As her youngest son, Darcy had always been her favourite. Virginia had pampered and spoilt him throughout his entire childhood. And now this! This latest unforgiveable escapade!

Iain had been driven to despair by the visit from Major Keith Manning. To think the boy had humiliated the family by drunkenly boasting of his connections, of his value to the army, of his elevated status . . . And at the Melbourne Club of all places. In the company of military and business associates of standing.

Iain Willard's apology was heartfelt, and even a little moving, given the fact he was a proud man, and arrogant at times, aware of his standing in the community. Iain was not accustomed to offering apologies.

'I am most sorry to hear this has occurred, Major Manning,' he'd said in all sincerity. 'I beg your forgiveness, I truly do. My son is a disgrace to our family. If you can see your way clear to once again put your trust in the Willard name, I assure you, such a thing will never happen again.'

Darcy's drunken indiscretion had been so blatantly public that the major had threatened the army contracts with McKinnon & Willard Enterprises might well be jeopardised.

'There must be respect in our business dealings at all times, Mr Willard,' he'd said, 'the military cannot afford to be so openly insulted.'

'There must certainly be respect,' Iain had agreed, 'and there shall be. You will no longer be dealing with my son, Major Manning, but with me. And, of course,' he'd added, 'with Josh McKinnon, who is the principal businessman behind the partnership. It would be most unfair if my son's unforgivable behaviour were to threaten Josh's career and advancement. He's a fine young man, and he comes from an excellent family. A family whom I hold in the highest esteem.'

'As do I,' Keith Manning said. 'The army is proud to be associated with the McKinnon name. And I agree with you, Josh is indeed a fine young man.'

'I must admit,' Iain said with a tone of deep regret, 'I had hoped this partnership between my son and Josh McKinnon might have led Darcy to mend his ways. But apparently he remains the lost cause he's always been.' The regretful tone took on a sudden edge of bitterness. 'Darcy's was an indulged childhood,' he continued, 'he was spoilt terribly by his mother. I very much blame my wife.'

The major appeared nonplussed by the sharing of such intimate information, which Iain realised may have been a little indiscreet on his part, so he quickly changed the subject.

'I trust there will be no disruption to the army contracts with McKinnon & Willard Enterprises, Major Manning,' he said, 'and I presume you will continue dealing directly with young Josh as you say you have been up to date. In the meantime, you may rest assured that the Willard behind the scenes will be none other than my good self. You need suffer no further contact with my son.'

Iain's promise had proved enough. The men had shaken hands and Keith Manning had departed.

Two days later, when Josh arrived, Iain Willard was fully prepared. He'd anticipated a visit from young Josh McKinnon.

'Will you stay for lunch?' he enquired, ushering him into the front drawing room. 'Just the two of us. My wife is having a very nice chicken salad prepared even as we speak. We can dine out on the terrace. A little chill, but such a pleasant day for September.'

Josh hadn't known what to expect. As he'd left the offices in Collins Street and hailed a taxi he hadn't even been sure which way he was heading. Who should he see first? Keith Manning or Iain Willard?

'Toorak,' he heard himself say to the taxi driver.

Willard, he decided. He wondered whether Darcy's father would hold him in any way responsible for his son's shameful behaviour. Hopefully not. But Willard senior would at least be able to give him the lay of the land. Were they in or were they out of favour with the military? Iain Willard would surely know. And if they were 'out', then he would just have to front up to Keith Manning and grovel for all he was worth. God how he hated Darcy.

He was heartened by the reception that greeted him at the Toorak mansion. Iain, whom he found at times rather pompous, and even condescending, was extremely welcoming.

'Thank you, sir,' he replied, 'lunch would be lovely.'

They dined on the tessellated tiled terrace overlooking the lavish gardens of topiary and flowerbeds, all of which Josh found far too ornate. He much preferred the outlook from the wooden verandahs of Glenfinnan, where the gardens were informal and where beyond lay the paddocks and the rich grazing lands of the Goulburn plains. *Each to his own,* he thought. There were kings of commerce in all areas, some with city properties like this, others with country estates like Glenfinnan. *And Glenfinnan will one day be mine,* he told himself. The prospect was profoundly pleasing.

As Iain recounted every word of his meeting with Keith Manning, and as Josh listened, he felt a surge of relief. *So we're safe,* he thought, *they're not going to cancel our contracts.*

He was grateful to Iain Willard. The man had obviously behaved with great dignity, admitting to his disgrace of a son, even taking the blame for Darcy. Or rather laying the blame on his wife's shoulders.

'As I told the major,' Iain said, topping up his glass of riesling for the fourth time – he was drinking rather heavily for the middle of the day, Josh thought – 'the boy's been spoilt the whole of his life. My wife dotes on him. She excuses everything he does, always has. I put his behaviour down to just that. A mother's indulgence.'

Josh was amused. Willard was talking to him as an equal and referring to Darcy as 'the boy', yet Darcy was seven years older than he was. *How interesting,* he thought. Interesting, too, the friction between Iain Willard and his wife, which was probably why the man seemed tense. The rift in their marriage was plainly evident, and all due to Darcy, or so it would appear.

Virginia, a stylish woman of around sixty, had person-ally greeted him when the staff had been informed he would be staying for lunch.

'Hello, Josh,' she'd said, popping her head into the drawing room, 'how nice to see you.'

'Hello, Mrs Willard.'

But when she'd stepped out onto the terrace to join them for lunch, the maid having set the table for three, she'd been very rudely halted in her tracks.

'No, Virginia,' her husband had ordered, 'we'll be dining on our own, just the two of us. For *obvious* reasons,' he'd added disdainfully. 'As you must be aware, we have much to discuss.'

'Of course, dear.' She'd given Josh a brittle smile and retired, the maid clearing her place at the table. A humiliat-ing experience for the lady of the house.

And now here was Iain Willard, laying the entire blame for Darcy upon his wife. There had obviously been a huge row between the two of them over this most recent episode. *Poor woman,* Josh thought, *it can't possibly be all her fault. I only hope Darcy copped a good dressing down.*

Darcy had. Darcy had copped the full wrath of his father, Iain venting his rage about the betrayal of family. 'You have besmirched our name!' he'd screamed. On and on he'd gone until Darcy had burst into tears and his mother had intervened, as she always did.

'Don't yell at him like that,' she'd yelled herself, raising her voice to be heard above his. 'He's not like the others. He's not strong, he can't take it.'

That had been the final straw for Iain. That had been the moment when, for the first time in the whole of their married life, he'd wanted to hit his wife. He'd stormed from the room instead.

'I don't know if Darcy would have turned out like this,' he now said to Josh, ignoring his half-eaten meal, which was of no interest, and concentrating on the riesling instead, 'had it not been for Virginia's excessive pampering. She's treated him since infanthood as if he were a consumptive or an invalid suffering a debilitating weakness when he's never had a day's illness in his life. And of course he has played on this fact, he's manipulated his mother with consummate ease. Darcy's a wastrel, but she can't seem to see that.'

Iain drained the glass and poured himself another, the last in the bottle. 'How can one boy be so different from his brothers? *Why* is he so different, I ask you! How can such a thing happen?'

Iain Willard didn't really appear to be asking Josh at all, but agonising to himself more than anything. Josh, however, decided to answer the question regardless of its rhetorical nature, simply because he found the subject of great interest.

'I believe it's impossible to tell,' he said, pushing his plate aside. Having thoroughly enjoyed his meal, he was now happy to focus upon conversation. 'I suppose it's just one of nature's many mysteries, but I believe no brothers are ever truly alike. I was always distinctly different from my younger brother, Ted. He and I came from quite different worlds.' *It's true, isn't it?* he thought, recalling the simplicity of Ted's nature, the warmth, the lack of guile. *What a lovely boy he'd been.*

Iain, jolted from what he now saw as his own bout of self-indulgence, felt a surge of guilt. He knew young Ted McKinnon had died in battle barely two months previously. Why, he'd written to the boy's father, James, offering his condolences. Although he'd not met the man, their sons were in business together, it was only right he should do so. He'd also offered Josh his sympathy at the time, but today, the very day of the lad's return from Glenfinnan, he'd said not a word on the matter. He'd been too distracted. How unforgiveable.

'I'm so sorry, Josh,' he said, 'please do accept my apology. Your family reunion must have been most moving, and you will surely be—'

'It's quite all right, sir, thank you.' Josh's smile instantly signalled no apology was necessary. 'Ted died bravely serving his country and we're proud of him. We've said our goodbyes, we've shared our grief, and we thank you for your sympathy.'

The subject had been changed, and to Josh's advantage, or so he felt. He had Willard's full attention and it was time now to pursue the vital issue of his independence with regard to the dealings of McKinnon & Willard Enterprises. Iain's promise to Keith Manning that he would substitute for his son could pose a definite threat. The last thing they needed was Iain Willard breathing down their necks.

'You mustn't worry about Darcy, Mr Willard. I can keep him in check, I promise you. His untoward behaviour only occurred because he was left on his own, but this will never happen again. If by any chance I'm called away, I have trustworthy staff who can deputise for me.'

Kevin Cavanagh was the 'staff' to whom Josh was referring, but as Kev came to mind an idea occurred. *Yes*, he thought, *yes, damn it, why not?*

'As a matter of fact, sir, if I may confide in you . . .' Intent upon impressing, Josh lowered his voice and leaned forward conspiratorially despite the fact there was not a soul within earshot. 'I have a secret partner. One who, now being aware of Darcy's tendency to indiscretion, will prove of great assistance.'

'A secret partner?' Iain automatically followed suit, lowering his voice, aware he was being treated to confidential information, but mystified nonetheless.

'Well, not a *partner* as such,' Josh corrected himself, 'the business has always been exclusively McKinnon & Willard, as you know. But from the outset I've been aware of Darcy's . . .' He hesitated, searching for the least offensive term. 'Shortcomings, shall we say?' He smiled as if they were talking about a wayward child. 'And as a safeguard I have placed my trust in a businessman with whom we conduct the majority of our dealings. You may know of him. Kevin Cavanagh of Cavanagh Clothing Manufacturers?'

'Yes.' Iain nodded. 'I haven't met the man personally, but I know of Cavanagh's. They're a large company, based in Geelong.'

'Yes, that's the one. Kevin is an extremely clever man, hard-working and trustworthy as his highly successful business attests. Given this recent episode, he is now aware of the problems that can arise from Darcy's undisciplined behaviour, which of course has not reflected well on him either, considering his association with McKinnon & Willard. Kevin has promised me that, in my absence, he will keep a strict eye on Darcy and ensure there is no further trouble.'

Josh sat back in his chair, raised his glass of riesling, which as yet he'd barely touched, and smiled reassuringly. 'Kevin and I will look after your son, Mr Willard,' he said, 'you need concern yourself no longer. You have enough on your hands as it is.'

'I'll drink to that,' Iain replied, not bothering to disguise a heartfelt sigh of relief that the whole mess now appeared successfully resolved.

They clinked wine glasses and sipped, Iain wishing his youngest son could be half the man Josh McKinnon was. He picked up the small hand bell and rang for the maid to come clear the table.

'I'm grateful to you, Josh,' he said. 'Your father is a lucky man to have such a son.'

'Thank you, sir.'

But before the maid could arrive, someone else appeared on the terrace, summoned by the bell. She'd been waiting.

'Hello, Josh.'

'Hello, Gwendolyn.'

Josh rose from the table as she swanned over to them, her pretty pastel gown and her cream-coloured woollen wrap billowing about her like a cloud.

'May I join you, Daddy?' she enquired, although she was already in the act of sitting, Josh having pulled out a chair for her as she'd clearly expected him to.

'Of course, dear,' Iain said with an indulgent smile. He was as spoiling of his only daughter as his wife was of their youngest son. But that was a father's prerogative, surely.

'Mummy told me you'd arrived and that you were staying for lunch.' Gwendolyn's attention was focused solely upon Josh. 'But she said you were having a business meeting and that I wasn't to interrupt. So I've been waiting for the bell.' She laughed flirtatiously.

The maid arrived as if on cue and began to clear the dishes.

'Are we having coffee?' Gwendolyn enquired.

'Of course,' her father replied with a nod to the maid.

'So the business meeting is over?' Gwendolyn smiled brightly from her father to Josh and back again.

'It is,' Iain said.

'Satisfactorily?'

'Yes.'

'Oh I'm so glad.'

Gwendolyn could well imagine what the meeting had been about. The row over Darcy had caused irreparable damage to her parents' relationship, which was shaky at the best of times. She wasn't sure exactly what had happened, but it appeared Darcy had got drunk and disgraced the family. Hardly an unusual occurrence, but on this particular occasion he'd obviously gone too far altogether.

My goodness, the fracas, she recalled, *the worst screaming match they've ever had.* Then, changing the subject, she put on her very serious, caring face.

'I've been thinking of you, Josh,' she said, 'and your trip home to the family, and how sad it must have been. I offer you my *deepest* sympathy.' She *had* been thinking of Josh, although not really of his family and his dead brother. Just Josh. He was so immensely attractive.

'Thank you, Gwendolyn, how kind.' Josh's smile conveyed the sincerest gratitude, but he didn't believe a word she said. He knew she fancied him and that she didn't care one whit about the death of his brother.

Josh found twenty-year-old Gwendolyn eminently readable, and he liked her for it. Beneath her prettiness, and she was certainly pretty with her bouncing fair hair and her coquettish smile, he sensed a hardness. Here was a spoilt little rich girl accustomed to getting what she wanted, but if it didn't come her way, she might just be ruthless enough to go out and get it for herself. An attractive quality, in Josh's opinion.

The coffee arrived, and as conversation turned to the general events of the day, Gwendolyn openly flirted with Josh. He flirted back in his own fashion, but surreptitiously, tastefully, careful not to arouse her father's suspicion that he may have an ulterior motive. He was, after all, a rung or two down the social ladder from the Willards.

But even as he shared with her a 'special' smile, the possibility crossed his mind, and surprisingly enough for the very first time.

I could certainly do worse, he thought, *in fact I really couldn't do any better, could I? I wonder how she'd take to a life in the country?*

'Which way do you think the referendum will go, Josh?' she asked. 'Do you think the population will vote "yes" or "no"? What is your opinion?'

She was out to prove herself now, bringing up matters of substance in order to show off her intelligence, and there was no denying she was intelligent, but again she didn't care one whit about the referendum, or the war for that matter. This was just another way of flirting.

'I think the public will vote "no",' he said. 'But the issue is contentious, I think the margin will be narrow.'

Josh was aware of Iain Willard's benign presence at the table. He was enjoying their exchange, the pompous arrogance of the past now replaced by gratitude. A wealth of gratitude. Was it possible Iain might even welcome him as a son-in-law? *McKinnon and Willard,* Josh thought, *why not?*

An hour later, having arrived at the Toorak mansion with a feeling of dread, Josh left with a distinct sense of victory. Darcy's ruinous behaviour may have taken a fortuitous turn. A near disaster might one day prove a triumph. Who could tell? *Something to think about anyway.*

CHAPTER TWENTY-ONE

Prime Minister Billy Hughes' national plebiscite for conscription had failed. But by the narrowest of margins. In the referendum that had divided the nation, 1,087,557 citizens had voted 'yes' and 1,160,033 'no'. The battle had remained bitter to the end, politically, socially and religiously, but the people of Australia had spoken. The aim of the *Military Service Referendum Act 1916* had been defeated.

Meanwhile, as the year drew to a close, the battle that had been raging overseas slowly ground to a halt, troops digging in to wait out the worst of the northern hemisphere winter. But everyone knew the respite was minimal, that it would be only a matter of time before this bloodiest of wars would once again wreak havoc on the world.

'A triumphant win by the women of Australia!' Emily declared, conversation having turned to the referendum. 'The mothers, the wives, the sisters and daughters have saved this country's young men from barbarous slaughter!' Emily, at her soapbox best, was claiming personal victory for the Women's Peace Army.

Josh laughed out loud. 'I think the trade unionists, the Roman Catholics and the socialists might have had a bit to do with it, Em.'

'Besides which,' Adele added drily, 'the *barbarous slaughter* as you call it is hardly over.'

'I know, Auntie Adele.' Realising she'd gone too far, Em felt instantly mortified. She'd just been showing off, no more, but how tasteless of her. Zac and Sam were still in France and would soon be back 'in the thick of things', as Zac himself was wont to say. 'I'm sorry, truly I am. I didn't mean . . .'

'Of course you didn't, darling . . .' Adele's smile, although wan, was forgiving. 'You're only being you.'

It was shortly before Christmas and the family had once again gathered at Glenfinnan. They were currently seated on the verandah having drinks before dinner, the early evening air balmy and inviting, the heat of the midsummer sun having waned.

'Fancy a walk, Josh?' James rose to his feet. 'I'd like to have a bit of chat if that's all right with you.'

Josh stood, realising this was neither a question nor an invitation, but a command. 'Sure, Dad.'

'Bring your beer.' James nodded to the assembled family. 'Excuse us for a moment, won't be long.'

Jenna looked a query at her husband. She and James had picked up Josh from the railway station barely an hour ago. Why hadn't he had his 'chat' on the way home?

James would have done exactly that had Jenna not insisted upon coming along for the drive. This was a chat he did not wish to have in Jenna's company.

He gave her a reassuring smile, then father and son walked down the verandah steps and into the garden, beer glasses in hand, a companionable pair.

Josh was happy to see his family again. He was comfortable, too, in the knowledge that Darcy would not run amok this time. Darcy was too terrified of Kevin Cavanagh.

'You fuck me around one more time, mate,' Kev had said, 'and I'll kill you, I swear I will. Or I'll have somebody do the job for me. I've worked hard to make my business what it is today, and I won't be mucked around by a snotty-nosed little bastard like you!'

They'd met in the offices of McKinnon & Willard where Kev had read Darcy the riot act in no uncertain terms. Even Josh had been taken aback by just how tough the normally stylish Kev could be, for Kev had reverted to the man that always lay beneath. The hard-hitting, working-class man who'd emanated from the backstreets of Manchester.

'If you need to let off steam,' he'd ordered, 'you go to your sleazy dives and your brothels, understand? You don't go near the Melbourne Club, and you stay well clear of anyone we do business with, you got that? All me and Josh want from you is your family bloody name and your family bloody contacts. Do you understand me? You got all that?'

Darcy hadn't said a word, just nodded furiously.

Josh had been pleased, although he'd felt it wise he should remain on friendly terms with Darcy.

'Better do as he says, Darce,' he'd advised after Kev had gone. 'But don't you worry, when I get back we'll have some fun. We'll go to Little Lon and get drunk, line up some girls, have a really good night out. Just stay low while I'm away, all right? It's only for two weeks.'

'Yes, yes, of course, Josh, of course.' More furious nodding.

Father and son strolled leisurely through the gardens, James leading the way to his favourite bench with a prime view of the surrounding countryside.

'I heard some slightly unsettling news a while back,' he said as they walked, 'about your partner, Darcy.'

'Really?' *Good grief,* Josh thought, *fancy that.* He wasn't altogether surprised, strangely enough. He'd wondered if word might get back to James McKinnon. Gossip ran rife among families of prominence, and such news tended to travel, even interstate, particularly between Melbourne and Sydney. He hadn't really expected it to reach Glenfinnan though. Someone must have telephoned his father.

They'd arrived at the bench.

'Yes,' James said as they both sat. 'Rumour has it Darcy disgraced the Willard name.'

'That's right. He did. Got drunk as a lord at the Melbourne Club.' Josh gave a light laugh, underplaying the seriousness of the incident and took a swig of his beer. 'Made an absolute fool of himself. His father was furious.'

James turned to look at his son, his expression grave. This was no matter to be treated lightly. 'You are in a business partnership with this young man, Josh,' he said, the ice-blue eyes issuing a warning loud and clear. 'Your association with Darcy must pose no risk to us. The McKinnon name, and also that of Glenfinnan, must be protected at all cost.'

'Oh I know that, Dad, and it *is* protected, I promise you,' Josh hastily replied, aware he may have played the moment incorrectly. 'I've cleared everything with the Willards and also the military. There's no possibility Darcy's behaviour can in any way reflect badly upon us.'

'Glad to hear it, son, glad to hear it.' Relieved, James took a swig of his beer. 'The most important thing to consider at all times is our family's good name.'

Josh didn't entirely agree with that concept. *Do you know how much money I'm making for this family?* he wanted to say. *We're getting richer by the minute, and all because of me!* But he had a feeling his father might not approve, given the fact their profits, both legal and illegal, came directly from the war.

'The McKinnon name is quite safe with me, Dad,' he said.

Father and son shared a smile, drained their glasses and returned to the house. Dinner would soon be served.

Following the meal, the family retired to the main lounge where coffee was served, and port or brandy for those who wished. James and Josh availed themselves of the brandy, James in particular did enjoy a fine cognac, which always, even after all these years, reminded him of Ben. Phil reneged on the offer, he rarely drank anything but beer, while Jenna and Adele refused not only the liquor, but the coffee too, vastly preferring a cup of tea. Young Hildy, however, eagerly accepted a coffee; the Catons drank nothing but tea at their house. Uncle James was so *modern* in Hildy's opinion.

'Read the boys' letter out, Mum,' she urged once they were all comfortably settled, the ceiling fan whirring away pleasantly, relieving the sultry heat of the evening.

Adele cast a querying glance at her sister. Reading the letter from her sons was so reminiscent of the way they'd read out Ted's letters to the family when they'd gathered for his wake, and in this very room. But Jenna nodded eagerly.

'Please, Adele, do,' she said, 'I long to hear their voices.'

Adele took the letter from the breast pocket of her blouse where it sat, two small pages neatly folded. She'd been fully prepared to share it with the others.

Given the approach of Christmas, the twins had put a little more effort into their letter than the usual brief 'duty' missive, although they still shared in the writing, just several short paragraphs apiece.

'Hope this reaches you in time for Christmas,' Zac wrote. *'Knowing the army it'll probably get to you around April, but it's still November as I write this and the Red Cross Christmas parcels are already starting to arrive, so who can tell? Maybe they're putting in a bit of extra effort to keep us blokes happy.*

'I must say things aren't really too bad at the moment. Pretty quiet in fact. We actually heard a birdcall the

other day. Don't know what sort of bird would want to hang around a place like this, but it was a change from the sound of constant artillery and gunfire. Geez that bloody racket drives a bloke mad. Makes you deaf, honest it does. You get this ringing in your ears that just won't go away, even when you're not in the thick of things.

'Anyway, enough of all that. I'll be thinking of you at Christmas and sending my love. Over to Sam and cheers for now, Zac.'

Sam's contribution was equally sparse, although perhaps thought out with a little more care.

'Zac's right about the bird call. Strangest thing to hear. Don't know what sort of bird it was, we couldn't see it, but the call was there all right. Not as pretty as a magpie, but not as mournful as a crow either. Quite tuneful, actually. A very nice sound indeed.

'We got your letter saying there was a Christmas parcel on its way, but it hasn't arrived yet in case you're wondering why we're not mentioning it here. Don't worry. It'll get to us eventually.

'Like Zac said, we're not doing too bad now that things have quietened down a bit. By golly it's cold though. We always reckon our winter nights at Glenfinnan are cold, and they are, but this is a different sort of cold. This is the wet sort that gets into your bones, you know what I mean? We'd be lost here without our Diggers Vests, I can tell you that much. I boast like mad to all the blokes that our family supplies the sheepskins. And for nothing what's more. So does Zac. We both show off. Makes us feel like real heroes.

'Well that's it from me. Have a beaut Christmas and lots of love, Sam.'

At the mention of the Diggers Vests, James shared a look with his son. He was so proud of Josh.

There was a pause as Adele carefully re-folded the pages and tucked the letter back into the breast pocket of her blouse.

Then from Hildy: 'I wonder what sort of bird it was.'

And from her father, Phil: 'I hope they've got our parcel by now, in time for Christmas.'

After which the conversation took off in varied directions. The twins were safe, and that was all that mattered.

The two weeks of his stay went by so quickly that Josh was loath to return to Melbourne; it seemed only yesterday he'd arrived at Glenfinnan. He loved the place and wished he could remain. But the brand-new year of 1917 was upon them and business called.

He and Emily commiserated with one another. She too wanted to stay, but must return to Sydney.

'What on earth for?' he asked. 'You and your women have single-handedly won the referendum,' he added jokingly, 'what more do you want?'

'We're protesting against unemployment and high prices of course,' she replied as if there were surely no need for enquiry. 'Something must be done to save the women and children of the unemployed. Many are struggling in the most appalling conditions, some virtually without food! There's been a closure of retail outlets, Josh,' she went on forcefully, 'causing shortages, forcing higher prices, feeding the black market, which is thriving . . . The government must be brought to task. All these things need to be addressed.'

'Good for you, Em, good for you,' he remarked humorously, but with just a touch of condescension. *Of course the black market is thriving,* he thought. *Everyone's profiting from the war. Everyone with brains, anyway.*

Upon his return, Josh was quick to fulfil his promise to Darcy, and the Saturday after his arrival saw the two of them at Nell Gwynn's Tavern in Little Lon, the red-light district of Melbourne.

Nell Gwynn's wasn't a tavern at all, although it certainly bore the resemblance of one. At least the façade and the interior of the downstairs dining area did. The front was white-washed with wooden beams running vertically up the walls in mock-Tudor style, the multi-paned windows were framed with wood, and the large wooden sign that swung on hinges above the main doors bore a picture of Nell Gwynn, with the words 'Tavern and Bar' beneath. Inside the main doors, the Tudor theme was maintained throughout the dining area and bar, which was as noisy and colourful and bawdy as it might well have been during the time of Nell herself, favoured mistress of England's seventeenth century King Charles II.

There was even a flamboyantly buxom hostess. A Londoner in her mid-forties, perennially jolly, appropriately called Nell, and dressed in period costume welcomed the diners as they arrived, adding to the overall atmosphere. There was no denying Nell Gwynn's Tavern and Bar was picturesque.

Upstairs, however, told a different tale, as did the two conjoined houses that sat either side of the tavern, all of which were owned by the same management and all of which had interconnecting doors. Here there was no attempt to create 'atmosphere' for there was no need. No one came to Nell Gwynn's Tavern to dine, or if they did they were disappointed, the standard of cuisine being the management's least concern. Food was served, naturally, together with copious supplies of liquor, but the clients were there for the women. Women of all description and available for every sexual purpose imaginable. Nell's, known among the trade as 'Naughty Nell's', was a brothel famous not only for its variety, but also its versatility. You could be anyone you wanted to be, and you could do anything you wanted to do at Naughty Nell's.

Little wonder it was a favourite haunt of Darcy Willard's. Little wonder, too, that Josh considered it one of the safest places he and Darcy could frequent. Here anonymity reigned. No one cared who was who or who did what to whom. People just took no notice of what went on in a place like Nell's. Not even Darcy could cause trouble at Nell Gwynn's Tavern.

Having returned through the side entrance from the brothel next door, Josh sat at the bar in the noisy lounge area that adjoined the restaurant and ordered a whisky – fine Scotch and cognac not featuring among the abundant supply of liquor to hand. He hadn't taken long with his girl, booking her for a 'short time' only and choosing to be fellated, aware of a possible lack of hygiene at an establishment like Nell's. But one could never really tell, could one? He was very selective as a rule. The whores he availed himself of were those who worked discreetly at the most expensive gentlemen's clubs and who were therefore presumed to be particularly fastidious. After all, one got what one paid for, didn't one?

What a specious argument, he now thought, *there's always a risk.* He smiled to himself, the memory returning as it so often did. That first time. When he'd been, what, all of thirteen, was it? Sam's voice, warning him about the pox: *'I heard somewhere that the pox can take a little while to show.'* And how for the whole of the school holidays he'd worried himself sick. Strange how childhood memories stayed with one. Well, he'd never caught the pox, or any form of sexual disease for that matter, and he didn't intend to. One must practise caution. As best one could, anyway.

His whisky arrived and he sipped at it as he sat back to wait for Darcy, who would be some time yet. Darcy had opted for the brothel on the other side of Nell's where they specialised in sexual fetishes – sadism, masochism, bondage and the like. He'd booked his favourite domina-trix for a full hour.

Josh studied those around him, the girls coming onto the men so wantonly they were all but fornicating right here in the lounge. And the men. You could tell by the lust in their eyes what it was they were after. That one wanted to be beaten the way Darcy liked it, he'd probably squeal like a pig. That one over there, the one twisting the girl's nipples through her scanty blouse, he wanted to do the beating. The whore would have to get extra money, wouldn't she? At least you'd hope she would.

Watching them all, Josh couldn't really pretend that he visited sleazy establishments like Nell's just to keep Darcy satisfied. The truth was he enjoyed this darker side of life. He always had, hadn't he? He liked watching others. Analys-ing them, getting inside their heads without their knowing. Made him feel so above them. Fed his sense of power.

Darcy finally appeared forty minutes later, fronting up to the bar where Josh remained patiently waiting with the same glass of whisky, as yet unfinished. It was filthy stuff when one was accustomed to the best.

Josh continued to wait just as patiently while Darcy downed several large whiskies one after the other. And he continued to listen as Darcy raved on about 'the good life' and how much he'd missed Josh while he'd been at Glenfinnan.

'I always enjoy myself when I'm out on the town with you, Josh,' he gushed, 'we're made for each other, you and I. But I behaved myself while you were away, didn't I?' he added, clearly seeking praise. 'I was a good boy, wasn't I? I did as I was told.'

'Yes, you were a very good boy, Darce,' Josh replied with a benign smile, 'I'm proud of you.'

Darcy gurgled with childish delight and called for another double whisky. He really did behave like a naughty ten-year-old, Josh thought with a mix of interest and disgust, the interest being vague and the disgust profound. Darcy had been drunk before he'd gone off with his dominatrix and he was now determined not to leave this place until he was barely able to walk. What pushed a man to that extreme? A mother's indulgence, as Iain Willard believed? Surely not. There was an inherent weakness in Darcy.

'Time to go, Darce,' he said at long last, although Darcy appeared not to hear. He was now in avid conversation with the barman, a huge, amiable man called Rolf who doubled as a bouncer, of which there were quite a number at Nell's, any fights being quickly bundled outside.

'Come on mate, we're off,' Josh insisted. His tone remained good-natured enough, but nonetheless commanding. He was not prepared to carry Darcy Willard out into the street.

As they weaved their way towards the front doors, they were joined by none other than the hostess herself. Nell made a habit of not only greeting new arrivals, but farewelling her regular 'guests' as she liked to refer to the clients.

'See you anon, gents,' she said, her plump face beaming with bonhomie. 'Nice to have you back, I must say. Don't leave it so long next time.'

'We won't, we won't,' Darcy assured her, his voice by now slurred.

'Yes, we'll be back.' Josh gave the woman a smile and a polite nod. Nell always looked after them personally, with a special welcome and a drink on the house. He suspected she was not just the colourful hostess she presented herself to be, but the brothel's madam, appointed by the management, whoever 'the management' might be. If so, she did a good job, ran a good house.

'Night, Nell,' he said. 'See you next time.'

'You shall, good sirs, you certainly shall.'

Nell had been pleased to welcome these two back. They were obviously upper class, given their dress and their manner of speech, and she liked to personally welcome any upper-class gents who chose to slum it at her place. She didn't own Nell Gwynn's of course, although dear God how she'd like to, but she always thought of it as 'her place'. When classy gents put in an appearance she always upped the price without their knowing it, and without noting it down in the books for management. All of which was easy, 'management' being a wealthy consortium of landlords whose interest was principally in property value and rentals. They left the running of the brothel to her.

Yep, you two can afford it, she thought as she watched one of them support the other while they walked down the street in search of a taxi. She'd slugged them good and proper, and the money would go directly to her girls. *And my girls need all the dosh they can get in these hard times,* she thought. Nell was a real mother to her girls.

The height of the northern hemisphere winter was over and the battlefields of France once again ignited with a vengeance, both German and Allied Forces focusing upon the use of heavy artillery in their desperate bid for victory.

General Douglas Haig, Commander in Chief of the Allied Forces, had been warned about the disastrous choice of terrain upon which the British planned to launch their attack. The ground that was intended as a battlefield had been reclaimed from the sea, he had been told by French authorities. The intricate drainage system of dykes and culverts had been preserved over the centuries, farmers who worked the land were under penalty to keep the construction maintained at all times. Should any form of bombardment take place, why, he was told, the land would revert to the marshland it had once been. This was certainly not the land upon which to launch a battle! Haig and his generals had refused to listen.

The dire warnings that had gone unheeded proved accurate, and drastically so. Within only weeks of shelling the land had become a quagmire. Trenches were impossible to maintain under the constant bombardment. In the first battle alone half the newly designed British tanks were swallowed up by the mud, and the ones that weren't proved of little use. It was found essential that tracks be laid down in order for troops to advance, and should a man stray from these tracks he might find himself buried alive in the mud. As the enemy barrage relentlessly continued this was to become the fate of many.

Back in London, Haig was advised of the appalling conditions and warned of the prospect of failure, but still he refused to listen. Such opinions were not welcome. The battle must continue as planned.

And so it did. Over the ensuing months, battle after battle laid waste to land and lives, swallowing all in the mire of a war that was horrific.

Darcy Willard was bored. He'd enjoyed swanning around as a successful businessman, one half of a partnership that bore his name, McKinnon & Willard Enterprises, no less. Most impressive. His father had been proud of him what's more, he'd said as much right to his face. 'Proud to see you doing so well my boy,' Iain Willard had said, patting him on the back. But those days were long gone. His father despised him now, Darcy knew it. His father had never understood him. No one did. No one ever had. Except Mummy. Mummy had always known he was delicate.

Darcy was more than bored, he was unhappy. Being a partner in McKinnon & Willard Enterprises had not only been fun, it had given him a purpose in life. But now he was forbidden to take any active part whatsoever in the business. He wasn't even allowed to go to the Melbourne Club! That hideous Kevin Cavanagh might kill him if he did. Even Josh had put his foot down, and Josh was his best friend.

'You have to keep a low profile at all times, Darce,' Josh had said, and although he'd said it nicely, it had been an order not a request. 'If there's one more mess-up your father will insist upon taking over the Willard half of the partnership and God only knows what would happen then. We're done for if your dad discovers even a quarter of what we're up to.'

'So I'm useless then, am I?' Darcy had whined.

'Of course you're not, mate,' Josh had assured him. 'You're one half of the partnership, but you're the *silent* half, all right?' He'd given a winning smile and a cheeky wink the way only Josh could as he'd added, 'Besides, we have a lot of fun when we're out together, don't we?'

'Yes.' There was that, Darcy supposed. 'Yes, we do. We're a good team, you and me.' Playtime was more important than ever to Darcy these days. Playtime was all he had left.

Josh was totally fed up. By now it was August and Darcy Willard had become a millstone around his neck, threatening to bring them all down with his drunkenness and disgusting self-indulgence, all of which was worse than ever. He didn't dare admit to Kev what a risk he considered Darcy and his big mouth to be, because who could tell? Kev might well follow through with his threat and kill the bloke. All Josh could do was keep Darcy entertained as best he could. And as safely as he could. Which meant Nell Gwynn's Tavern.

The visits to Nell's had become regular now, mostly on a Saturday night. If Darcy wanted to party throughout the week he did so at his home in South Yarra, where he'd provide whores and liquor for the debauched circle of friends who'd been bludging off him for years. Josh saw no risk in this and was thankful to leave Darcy to his own devices. But Nell's was becoming tedious. Half the time he didn't even avail himself of a whore, although he'd come to know the women, several of whom he liked. Instead, he'd sit at the bar with a drink, observing those around him and having an occasional chat with Rolf the barman while Darcy was being looked after in the next-door brothel.

For a barman and bouncer in a whorehouse, Rolf had turned out to be something of a surprise. Big and burly as was to be expected, he was also a happily married family man with two small children he adored. Which Josh found rather odd. He'd met many a barman and bouncer over the years, but never one quite like Rolf. Refreshing in a way, he supposed, although the man could at times be a terrible bore. *Ah well,* he thought, *at least there's now a decent drink to be had.*

With Nell's permission, and a very large tip included each visit, Josh's own supply of liquor had been made available. Rolf himself ensured a bottle of fine cognac sat in a cupboard beneath the bar at all times, and he kept it in reserve just for Josh. Josh rarely had more than two drinks a night, perhaps three at the most, and savouring a fine cognac certainly helped pass the time.

'Turning ten's a big thing in a boy's life,' Rolf said with a sage-like nod as he leaned on the counter drying freshly washed glasses with a tea towel that didn't look too clean. 'So's a boy getting his first bike, and the two go hand in hand, at least they do in my opinion.' He plonked down the glass and picked up another. 'I got me first bike the day I turned ten, proudest moment of me life, it was.' A sorrowful shake of his head now. 'Bloody shame I can't do the same for my Ronnie.'

It was a half past eleven and there was the sort of lull that occasionally occurred, even on a Saturday night, when clients had eaten and got drunk and were now off with the whores of their choice. A log fire crackled comfortingly in the large open hearth, several men lolled around in the lounge area drinking, several girls chatted together waiting for their services to be called upon, but the bar itself was not busy. Which left Rolf free to bemoan the fact that having tried every avenue available, he'd discovered a bicycle was impossible to come by.

'It's the war you see,' he went on, still working away with his tea towel, glass after glass. 'There's shortages everywhere, particularly of imported stuff, you know, things made in Germany and all that. You can't get that sort of stuff for love or money. And I've got the money all right. Saved up for it I did, saved up specially, got enough to buy him the best there is. But you reckon I can find one? Not a bike to be had, I tell you, not a bike to be had . . .'

Josh drained the last of his cognac, and this was his second glass. 'I'll have another thanks, Rolf,' he said. A third was his limit, but Rolf was being particularly boring tonight. Josh did wish the bar would pick up a bit so the man would be put to work, it wasn't this slow as a rule surely, not on a Saturday.

'Right you are, Boss, coming right up.' Rolf called everyone Boss, which the clients appeared to like, but then the clients liked Rolf. He was a nice man.

Diving a hand into the cupboard beneath the bar, he reappeared with the bottle and started pouring a healthy measure into Josh's glass.

'Yeah, so poor little Ronnie . . .' He took up from exactly where he'd left off. 'Doesn't seem fair . . .'

'Keep your eye on that for me,' Josh said as he stood. 'Be back in a minute. Nature calls.'

He checked the clock on the wall as he left for the men's room out the back. Darcy's hour was up, he'd return to the bar any minute, let him cope with Rolf. Darce just loved a chat, and so long as his glass kept being refilled he'd sit and listen for hours. In fact with the whisky flowing he'd probably find Rolf riveting company.

Josh took his time in the men's room and upon re-emerging was pleased to see, across the other side of the lounge, that Darcy was seated at the bar and that he and Rolf were engaged in conversation. *Good.* He'd be able to relax with his cognac while Darcy took the brunt of Rolf's interminable tenth birthday woes.

But something wasn't quite right, he realised. Nell had gravitated to the bar and was listening to the two of them, and by the look on her face she didn't appear at all happy with what she was hearing. Darcy, furthermore, wasn't listening. Darcy was the one doing the talking, and at the top of his voice.

Josh strode across the lounge and before he was even halfway to the bar he could hear Darcy quite clearly.

'Course we can, mate,' he was boasting, a drunken hand waving about airily, 'me and my mates can get you any-thing you want, anything at all. We've got deals happening everywhere. A bike's no trouble.'

Rolf's big beefy face was a mask of happiness, and he beamed at Josh as he arrived at the bar.

'Did you hear that, Boss? Your mate here reckons he can find me a bike.' Rolf wasn't even questioning why Josh himself hadn't mentioned the fact, all Rolf was thinking of was Ronnie's tenth birthday.

'And the best bike there is, what's more,' Darcy said, raising his glass of whisky in a salute, he just loved showing off, 'the very best one there is.' He downed his drink in one hit.

Josh was all too aware of Nell standing nearby, scowling her disapproval. He wondered if anyone else in the lounge had heard. Darcy had been loud, as Darcy always was. He didn't look around to check, though, it wouldn't do to appear anxious. He smiled instead, the smile of an indulgent parent.

'I think you've had a bit too much to drink, old man,' he said, 'we can't achieve the impossible, simply can't be done.' Then he turned the full charm of his smile on Nell. 'No rabbits out of hats I'm afraid,' he added with a light laugh.

But Nell didn't appear amused. Her eyes studied them both craftily. She knew exactly what she'd heard. These two rich bastards were dealing with the black market, probably doing a roaring trade. Blood money it was, in her opinion. Didn't they know how tough things were? Particularly for the women, with their men off to war and children to be fed. Jesus Christ, crowds of women were demonstrating outside Parliament House practically every day. She'd seen them there herself, same was happening in Sydney, she'd read about it in the papers. Thousands of women protesting against unemployment and shortages and high prices. *And you two are raking in the dough? Shame on you!*

She made no comment, but turned away, bustling off to busy herself in the dining room.

Having read the accusation in the woman's eyes, Josh cursed Darcy. But he kept up the façade.

'Come along, old man, time to get you home, you're rambling.' He heaved Darcy to his feet.

'Hang on, hang on,' Darcy protested, 'I need another drink.'

'No you don't.'

'What about your own drink, Boss?' Rolf gestured to the untouched glass. 'You haven't had your brandy.'

Josh picked up the glass and swilled back the cognac. 'I have now,' he said with a cheery grin. Then he all but dragged Darcy away.

From the hastiness of their departure, Darcy gathered that Josh was displeased, but he couldn't for the life of him understand why. 'Nothing to worry about, Josh,' he muttered, 'Rolf's a good mate, he wouldn't tell on us, and he only wants a bike for his boy, what's wrong with that?'

'Everything,' Josh hissed through clenched teeth. *God, the man's an idiot,* he thought.

'And nobody would have found out anyway,' Darcy rambled on. 'We're at Nell's, no one knows who we are and no one cares.'

There is at least that, Josh thought thankfully. But who knew when and where Darcy would again open his big, fat mouth. He was too much of a risk, something had to be done. *I'll have a talk with Kev,* he decided, *Kev will work things out. It's the only way.*

They passed through the dining room, collecting their heavy overcoats from the reception area. Outside the night was freezing.

He turned back to wave to Nell. 'Night, Nell,' he called as usual. 'See you next time.'

'Yeah, see you next time.' She waved in return, but didn't accompany them to the door. *Bastards,* she thought as she watched them walk out of the tavern. *What right did they have! Who the hell did those two think they were!*

But back in the lounge there were several who knew exactly who those two were. They didn't know the pair personally, but they'd seen them at the Melbourne Club, and here at Nell's too on a number of occasions. The three middle-aged chums seated together in the lounge often slummed it at Nell's, as did any number of successful businessmen who liked a bit of rough trade, but they never advertised the fact, always arriving in dun-coloured great-coats and nondescript outfits. They never strutted about in their finery like young Josh McKinnon and Darcy Willard, who really were an arrogant pair.

Lounging in armchairs with glasses of cheap whisky they'd watched the whole scene and heard every word. Now they huddled together quietly chatting.

So our two naughty young chaps are into the black market . . . Well, well, who'd have thought it . . . From such impeccable families . . .

The chums were fascinated. They wouldn't rat on Josh and Darcy of course, it just wasn't done. And what the hell anyway, there were others among the upper classes who dabbled in the black market, they were hardly alone. *But McKinnon and Willard?* This was certainly fodder for gossip!

Less than one week later, Darcy Willard disappeared under the most mysterious of circumstances. He always called in to see his mother on a Monday or Tuesday when they would lunch together, but he hadn't turned up. And he wasn't at his flat. He was simply nowhere to be found. Another week went by and still there was no sign of him. His family was frantic, particularly his mother, who was by now hysterical.

Josh McKinnon had naturally been the first person Iain Willard had sought out for information regarding his son's possible whereabouts. He'd called in to the offices of McKinnon & Willard on the Friday seeking news, but Josh had had no idea.

'I'm sorry, sir, but I haven't had any contact with Darcy for close on a week now,' Josh had said. 'He doesn't come into the office much these days, and the last time I saw him was on Saturday night. We went to a rather seedy bar called Nell Gwynn's in Little Lonsdale Street,' he'd

admitted shamefacedly, 'and I haven't seen him since then.'
All of which was absolutely true.

Three weeks later there was still no sign of Darcy.

Well done, Kev, Josh thought. He didn't ask Kev precisely what had been done, or how or by whom, and he didn't intend to. But it appeared the problem of Darcy Willard had been solved.

CHAPTER TWENTY-TWO

S am lay on his back in the mud looking up at the dull-grey sky. *Where was the colour?* he wondered. There was no colour. No colour anywhere. Just grey. And you couldn't really call grey a colour, could you? His mind was wandering now. There were different sorts of grey though. There was the heavy lead-grey of the mud he was lying in, and there was the dull misty-grey of the sky, and there was the shiny metallic-grey of the water in the craters of no-man's-land.

He turned his head and gazed to the right, gratified to discover he could still move his head at all, nothing else seemed to be working, and he could see the stark outline of a tree forking its way up into that dull-grey sky. *Amazing the tree is still standing*, he thought. Even though it was dead, only a stunted skeleton, it looked defiant somehow. And the silhouette of its trunk and few remaining branches were black. A relief from all the grey, he supposed, but it still wasn't colour. Because black wasn't a colour, was it? Black was the absence of colour, he'd learned that at school.

He turned his head to the left and gazed at his brother. Zac was grey too. Covered in mud, like they all were, and like they'd all been for God knows how long. But Zac's face, even right up close as it was, his cheek only inches away, was a pallid grey, no flesh tone to be seen at all.

He looked peaceful though, so very peaceful, and Sam was glad about that. His groans had been bloody awful.

They'd copped it together, charging out of the shell hole where they'd taken cover for a few minutes, charging and screaming like a couple of lunatics. And down they'd gone. Simultaneously. He hadn't really felt much himself, just an almighty thump to the chest, and then he must have blacked out. But when he'd come to, after who knew how long, minutes, hours, impossible to tell, there was Zac to his left, barely a yard away, and Zac was in agony. A gut shot. Sam had slithered on his belly through the mud to join him.

'It's all right, Zac, it's all right,' he'd said, stupidly, because it wasn't all right, but he was desperate to offer some sort of comfort. 'I'm here, I'm here.'

He'd manoeuvred himself onto his side and with his right arm he'd held his brother close. His other arm didn't seem to work, it was just trailing uselessly in the mud.

'Hang on,' he'd said over and over, 'hang on, Zac, the stretcher bearers'll be here any minute. They'll get you back to the line and you'll be looked after. Just hang on, mate.' It would be a long time yet until night, and the stretcher bearers only ever arrived under the cover of darkness, but he hadn't known what else to say.

It hadn't done any good anyway, Zac's groans hadn't abated as the pain had devoured him. They'd been awful, those groans. They hadn't really been groans at all. They'd been non-human noises that didn't sound like his brother. Unrecognisable. Coming from another place. But Sam had kept cuddling him, kept murmuring words that were not being heard and could therefore be of no comfort. What else was he to do?

On and on he went. The gunfire had ceased by then and it seemed to him they were all alone, just the two of them there in the mud, him talking, Zac groaning in that horrible way.

Until at long last . . . A pause. The groans stopped and then there was silence. And finally a whisper.

'Sam?' Only a whisper. But it was Zac's voice.

'Yes,' he'd breathed. 'Yes, it's me, Zac. I'm here.'

Another pause. Brief this time. An exhalation that might have been a sigh of relief. And it was over. The agony and the life, both were over. But Zac had known in his final moment that his brother was with him. Could death really be this kind? Sam had wondered.

Now he lay on his back in the mud looking up at the dull-grey sky, thankful that beside him Zac appeared so peacefully asleep. He wondered whether he'd still be alive himself when the stretcher bearers arrived. He wasn't in pain. He just felt numb. Numb all over. Was he dying? And why was there no colour? His mind kept wandering. Why was a battlefield always grey? Why had the whole world turned grey? Where had the colour gone? So many questions to be asked, so many answers eluding him.

The telegram informing the family of Zac's death arrived in mid-October. Private Zachary Caton had been killed in action during the First Battle of Passchendaele on the 12th of October.

At this stage there was no word about Sam, who would surely have been fighting alongside his brother. Adele and Phil Caton were left to mourn one son while they prayed for the other.

James telephoned Josh to tell him the news, following up with a request that was obviously a command.

'The family is gathering in order to honour Zac,' he said, 'much the way we did Ted. I want you to come home, Josh. Next week,' he added abruptly.

'Yes of course, Dad,' Josh replied, presuming the edge in his father's voice was evidence of grief. 'Any news of Sam?'

'Not as yet. I'm making enquiries through some connections I have.' Again the tone was brusque. 'I'll see you next week, son. Hopefully we'll have some news by then.'

Josh made the necessary arrangements with staff and informed Kev of his forthcoming trip interstate.

'I'll be gone for around two weeks or so,' he said.

'Fine,' Kev replied with a shrug, 'at least there's one element we won't need to worry about.'

'Yes, I suppose so.' Josh couldn't believe the man's nonchalance and, uncomfortable with the blatant reference to Darcy, wondered how he was expected to reply. He knew better than to question Kev, just as he knew Kev had no intention of sharing the secret he was harbouring. The secret that had been unspoken between them from the very beginning.

'We need to do something about Darcy, Kev,' he'd said following the episode at Nell Gwynn's, and then he'd told Kev what had happened.

'Leave it with me,' Kev had replied, and only days later Darcy had mysteriously vanished.

That was nearly six weeks ago, and the disappearance of the youngest son of the prominent Willard family had by now become headline news. Journalists were raising questions, providing answers, posing hypothetical scenarios. Had Darcy Willard been kidnapped by blackmailers? Was he being held for ransom? But his father had received no demand for payment. To the contrary, Iain Willard had offered a healthy reward for anyone who knew anything that might lead to his son's whereabouts. Had Darcy himself, known as something of a playboy, staged his own disappearance? And if so, why? Nothing had been forthcoming and conjecture was growing rife.

'*FOUL PLAY SUSPECTED*' the most recent newspaper headline had announced above a very handsome portrait shot of Darcy. But still no information was to hand, no body discovered.

When Josh had dumped the latest newspaper on Kevin's desk, Kev had given it no more than a perfunctory glance.

'Good riddance,' he'd said, and left it at that.

Josh admired the man's nonchalance, even while he found it a little unnerving.

'At least there's one element we won't need to worry about,' Kev had just said. *What the hell am I supposed to reply to that?* Josh wondered. *Nothing, I suppose. It's something we don't talk about.*

As was to be expected, the gathering at Glenfinnan was sombre. A second death, the family once again plunged into mourning.

'This wretched war,' James said to the assembled company. It was late afternoon and they were seated in the McKinnons' main lounge room at the Big House, a room that seemed now to have become associated with mourning. 'This wretched, wretched war.'

'Is there any war that *isn't* wretched?' Emily declared with her customary boldness. 'There's nothing noble about a war . . .'

She was about to go on, but catching sight of her aunt's eyes, swollen from weeping, she halted. The beautiful Adele, seated on the sofa beside her husband, was pale and gaunt, weighed down with grief and stricken with worry.

'Sorry,' Em said. Now was hardly the time for soapbox haranguing, was it? Her mother's glare told her as much. But glancing apologetically around the room, she caught the small nod of agreement from her cousin. Young Hildy very much admired the stance Em took on all issues of importance.

Emily and Josh had arrived earlier that same afternoon, James picking them up from the station. Josh had caught the overnight train to Sydney and they'd journeyed to Goulburn together, which had been most companionable.

Through his enquiries, James now had some good news to share with both of them.

'I found out only yesterday,' he said, 'so you two haven't heard as yet, but Sam is alive. He's been wounded and is currently hospitalised in England. I've been told he'll recover, but they don't know in what condition he'll be. Or if they do, they're not sharing it with us at this stage.'

Phil Caton put a comforting arm around his wife.

'I can gather no more than that, I'm afraid,' James went on, 'but it appears he won't be sent back into battle, which is something positive.'

'It certainly is,' Phil agreed firmly. 'Just a matter of time before Sam'll be coming home.' He gave his wife an extra squeeze, very gently, and Adele mustered a smile intended to be positive.

There was still an hour or so before dinner would be served – upon Jenna's insistence, they were to eat in the formal dining room tonight, as opposed to the breakfast room.

'It's only right,' she'd said, 'as a tribute to Zac. We'll have official toasts to him the way one does at a proper wake.'

The late-afternoon cups of tea hadn't seemed at all appropriate for toasts, so James now rose and crossed to the drinks cabinet.

'Time for something stronger than tea,' he suggested.

When glasses of Scotch and sherry had been poured, and when the maid had brought in a cold beer for Phil, they proposed their first toast of many to Zac. And also to Sam's full and hopefully speedy recovery. Then James turned to his son.

'Would you mind coming up to my office, Josh? Something I'd like to chat about. Bring your Scotch with you. Excuse us everyone, we won't be long.'

The invitation was casual, but Josh could tell the intent was serious. *A repetition of the Christmas lecture?* He wondered what criticism his father might have in mind this time. Probably something to do with Darcy. The press was bound to be as rife in Sydney as it had been in Melbourne, and his father always bought the Sydney newspapers.

He was right. The first thing he saw as he entered his father's office was the *Sydney Morning Herald* splayed out on the coffee table. Intentionally. The same handsome portrait shot of Darcy, and a very similar headline. *'POLICE SUSPECT FOUL PLAY'*.

'Yes, exactly,' James said, noting his son's glance at the newspaper. Choosing not to sit behind his desk, he gestured to the armchairs in the lounge area where the coffee table sat between them, the front page glaring up accusingly. 'I would have expected you to telephone me about this, Josh,' he said once they were seated, glasses in hand. 'Why didn't you?'

Despite the ice-blue eyes trained upon him, Josh felt no qualms, confident he had all the requisite answers.

'I'm sorry, Dad, I suppose I should have, but I really didn't think it necessary. Ever since last year's debacle, Darcy's played no part in the business dealings of McKinnon & Willard. I've refused to work with him, in fact. His own father accepts this and understands the reasons. Darcy simply can't be trusted.'

'I see,' James replied thoughtfully. 'So what do you make of this then?' He tapped a forefinger at the headline. 'Why would police suspect foul play? How could such a thing come to pass?'

Josh shook his head. 'No one knows,' he replied. 'I have as little idea as anyone else. I have no knowledge at all of where Darcy is, or where he might have gone.' *Which is true,* he thought. 'I haven't seen or heard from him for a whole six weeks. He's just disappeared from the face of the earth.'

'There are rumours, or so I've heard,' James said, slowly and with meaningful deliberation. 'Word has got around . . .'

What rumours? Josh thought. *What word?* Why was his father looking at him like that? Was there the vestige of suspicion in his eyes? For the first time, Josh felt a vague sense of unease.

'Word that Darcy Willard may have been tied up with the black market.'

'Really?' Josh feigned surprise even while his mind raced. *It has to be that night at Nell's. But who could have been there? Who talked? Nell herself? Surely not!* 'It's the first I've heard of it. Although I wouldn't put it past Darcy, I must say. He's a pretty unsavoury character.'

'Yes, so I believe.' James nodded thoughtfully. 'If this rumour is true, it could perhaps explain his disappearance and the suspicion of foul play. He may have crossed some racketeer, which would be dangerous. There are many ruthless characters dealing in the black market.'

'You're probably right,' Josh agreed. 'Yes, when you think about it that's probably just what happened. Poor old Darce, eh? I didn't like him much, I have to admit, but it's horrible to think he might have been murdered.'

'It's also a great pity, Josh, that your name is linked with his.' This was the factor of greatest concern to James, who didn't in the least care about Darcy Willard's fate. 'War profiteering is a shameful activity. It would bring disgrace to the McKinnon name if we were in any way connected—'

'Oh God no, Dad!' Josh interrupted, the mere thought appearing abhorrent to him. 'We profit from our dealings with the military,' he said, 'of course we do. We have contracts to fulfil and a business to run. But *war profiteering*!

Good God, that's a different matter altogether. I would never . . .'

'I know you wouldn't, son, I know you wouldn't.' James was gratified to put that ugly rumour to rest, he hadn't believed it anyway, not for one minute. Pure gossip-mongering. How dare such an inference be made of his son whose motivation was always impeccable! Good heavens, Josh had been the driving force behind the Diggers Vests, hadn't he? James vowed he would give these gossip-mongers a piece of his mind if he ever heard the subject raised again.

There was a great deal more he wished to discuss with his son, however, areas he felt were open to misinterpretation and could prove of some concern. But tonight was not the night, he decided. Tonight was about Zac.

He drained his glass of Scotch and smiled as he rose to his feet. 'How about we go for a ride in the morning? Just the two of us, what do you say?'

'I say that's a marvellous idea.' Josh returned the smile, drained his glass and stood.

Then they went downstairs to join the rest of the family.

The following morning was crystal clear. Cloudless and still, with barely a breath of breeze. But it was cold for a spring day in late October. Cold and invigorating.

'Perfect weather for a ride,' James remarked as they saddled up.

They were already mounted and about to set off, their horses feisty and eager to go, when an idea occurred to him.

'I'll race you to the old stone quarry,' he said. 'From here to the grove of trees at the bottom of the ridge.'

Why not? he decided. *It's the ideal place for a father-and-son chat.* They'd sit together on the large flat rock at the top of the ridge and they'd talk, the way he and Ben used to talk in the old days. The quarry was a place where honesty reigned, where secrets were shared and bonds were forged.

The race turned out to be close. Much of the time their mounts ran neck to neck, both horses and riders vying for the lead. It was a battle to the finish. But Josh proved the winner.

As they dismounted at the grove of trees beyond which the ground was rocky, James laughed. A little breathlessly. Perhaps from exertion, perhaps from exhilaration or perhaps from a mixture of both. It was such a joy to be in the company of his son.

'I'm happy to see that the good life in Melbourne hasn't blunted your equestrian skills,' he said approvingly. Josh had always been a fine horseman, even as a young boy.

'You're not too bad yourself, Dad.' Josh returned the compliment, his father was equally skilled.

They loosened the girths and left their horses grazing as they walked up to the top of the ridge where the view was spectacular across the breadth of the valley and down the steep slope to the stone quarry below.

'Magnificent, isn't it,' James said as they seated themselves on the large flat rock. 'I haven't been here for quite some time now. Don't know why.'

It was colder up here on the ridge and the air was no longer still. They pulled their coats tightly about them, raising their collars against the bite of the breeze.

As James gazed out at the view, Ben came to mind and he found himself reminiscing.

'This was Ben's favourite place. He and I used to sit here together and watch the sunset. It's a pity you never met Ben, you'd have liked him, Josh, he was quite a character.'

'Yes, so Mum's always told me.' Josh knew only too well who they were talking about; his mother's older brother who'd died before he was born. He'd seen pictures of Ben McKinnon, a handsome young man.

'There's a lot of history to this place,' James went on. 'That old well down there is convict-built,' he said, pointing to the circle of roughly hewn rocks topped with a rusty sheet of corrugated iron. 'Ben always used to say it'd be the perfect place to hide a body.'

He laughed at the memory. Then grew silent. And when he spoke again his tone was sombre, his expression grave as he continued to gaze out across the valley. 'If Ben hadn't died he would have inherited all this,' he said finally. 'Glenfinnan would have been Ben's, he was the rightful heir. It was Ben who bore the McKinnon name. Not me.'

Where was this leading? Josh wondered. Was there something his father was trying to tell him?

There was. And James decided it was time to get to the point. He turned to his son.

'We need to talk, Josh,' he said.

Josh nodded. 'Yes, I gathered you had something on your mind.'

'About the McKinnon name,' James went on barely pausing for breath. 'The McKinnon name and all it stands for.'

Josh felt a surge of impatience. Another lecture! They'd been through this last Christmas, he could recall his father's very words: 'the McKinnon name, and also that of Glenfinnan, must be protected at all cost.' And then there was last night's warning too, God, the man was becoming pedantic! *All right, all right, get on with it,* he thought, but he didn't allow his impatience to show.

'I must admit to having felt a little disturbed by the rumours that reached me,' James said, choosing his words with care. 'Not in regard to you, of course,' he added, 'I knew you would never involve yourself with black-market activities. But the thought that Darcy Willard might have done so without your knowledge was concerning. I wondered whether perhaps, because you two are in a business partnership, he may have channelled some of the profits through Glenfinnan in order to avoid detection.'

This was beginning to sound ominous, Josh thought, but he remained silent, waiting for his father to continue.

'Bearing such a possibility in mind,' James went on, 'I called in an expert accountant to examine the Glenfinnan books. And I have to admit to doing so without Terence Dimbleby's knowledge, in order to prevent any word getting back to Darcy Willard.'

You what! Josh was outraged. *You did what!* his mind screamed. He stared back at his father in shocked disbelief.

James continued with great haste, aware he'd offended his son. 'I have the utmost faith in Terence, I assure you, and I know how closely you and he work. As I said, I harboured no suspicion about your actions. Nor those of Terence, I can assure you. Indeed the books were discovered to have been meticulously kept, the transactions impeccably recorded, just as I'd expected they would be . . .'

It doesn't alter the fact you've been prying into our affairs though, does it? Josh was more than outraged now, he was incensed. *But . . .* he thought. *Go on! You're about to say 'but' . . .*

'But I discovered an anomaly that raised my concern.'

'And what would that be?' Josh kept his voice deadly calm.

'Glenfinnan has part ownership of a property in Victoria, a sheep and cattle property called Braedalbin.'

'That is correct.'

'Why was I not informed of this, Josh?'

'Because you left me in charge of all army contracts, Dad. Because I formed – and with your full approval, I might add – my own business partnership in order to do exactly that. And because the property is a sound investment. Where lies your problem?'

James was aware of his son's antagonism, which he'd expected, but he continued nonetheless. This was a problem that needed to be confronted.

'I had Braedalbin investigated, Josh,' he said. 'Upon my orders, inspection was carried out on the stock it was running, the yield of its materials, the quality of the leather and wool it was producing for manufacture . . .'

You've been spying on me, you bastard!

'And it would appear that Braedalbin's policy is quantity rather than quality. Would you not agree?'

'Of course I agree,' Josh replied coldly. 'The army needs quantity. We have delivery deadlines, bulk orders to fulfil.'

James continued, still calm, but now firm. He'd anticipated such a reaction, aware that his son would feel his authority had been undermined. 'The military also expects quality, Josh,' he said. 'Even army blankets are presumed by all to be made of Australian Merino wool. Yet,' he added, 'there is no such wool to be had from Braedalbin. There are no Merino sheep farmed at Braedalbin. Isn't that true?'

Josh glared back at his father. *How dare you criticise me,* he thought. *You're a bloody shearer who married into money. You know nothing about the world of commerce.*

James could see the anger seething there, but he wasn't about to back down. Josh had to be told.

'I don't doubt your motivation, son, your commitment to meeting bulk orders from the military, your need to deliver product efficiently. But you must avoid the selling out of our family name, which is linked with your business. Cutting corners as you've been doing could be perceived by others in a most unflattering light, perhaps even mistaken for war profiteering.' His smile issued a warning. 'And we both know how we feel about that, don't we?'

Then he got back to the matter at hand, which was of ultimate importance. He stood, intent upon lending impact to his statement. He had made his decision, it was now time to end this discussion.

'We must get rid of Braedalbin, Josh. We must get rid of that property altogether.'

We, Josh thought. *We! Where the hell do you come into all this?*

He also stood, facing his father defiantly. 'Have you noticed in your investigation of our books,' he said steely voiced, 'the amount of profit recorded? Have you seen just how much money Glenfinnan is making? We've never been richer! We've never been more powerful!' *Don't you realise that?* his mind demanded. *Can't you see what I've done for this family?* 'Money is power, Dad.'

Their eyes met. It was becoming a duel of wills.

'Money and power are nothing, Josh,' James said, 'nothing at all if you've lost your good name.'

'*What* name?' A white-hot anger suddenly engulfed Josh and he erupted, words spewing from him with a venom he'd never known he possessed. 'You *denied* your name, Dad! You accuse *me* of selling out! What about *you*?! You sold your name in order to become a McKinnon! You don't even wear Grandpa George's watch! The Brereton name means nothing to you!'

The eruption had shocked Josh as much as his father, and even as his anger subsided he wondered where it had come from. Had he burst out like that merely as a method of self-defence, he wondered, or had it come from somewhere deep within?

The two stood together in silence, father and son, both momentarily lost in reflections of the past.

James was thinking of his father, George Wakefield, and how there'd never been a Brereton family name. But he could hardly tell his son that, could he? And Grandpa George's watch? There was no such thing. The watch Josh so valued had been stolen from a dead man in a Woolloomooloo brothel. *A man called Charles Grenfell,* James thought, *a man I murdered.* He could hardly tell his son that either. He recalled how he'd murdered another man too, the poor little professor, Hubert whatever-his-name-was. Hubert would have exposed the watch as one of just eight in the world made on the orders of Lord Raglan commemorating the Battle of Balaclava. Hardly Grandpa George's watch! And it could be traced to Charles Grenfell.

There was so much he couldn't tell his son, James thought. Apart from the one thing of any real value. The McKinnon name and the need to protect it. Dear God, he'd been prepared to kill his own sister in order to do so.

He turned and looked away at the view over the valley. 'It is true I have devoted myself to the McKinnon name, Josh,' he said evenly, 'just as you must. It is your duty to do so.'

But Josh barely heard him. Josh was thinking of Grandpa George and all the wonderful tales he'd been told over the years. Grandpa George, the famous gun shearer . . . Grandpa George who'd saved the rich farmer from drowning, and how the rich farmer had gifted him the beautiful pocket watch . . . Grandpa George who'd tested his son with the true meaning of 'Baa Baa Black Sheep' . . .

Have you forgotten that, Dad? he wondered. *You tested me exactly the same way. You tested Ted too.*

His wild outburst of anger now over, he studied his father dispassionately, as if from a distance, far, far away.

'I thought you idolised Grandpa George,' he said, and there was a touch of contempt in the way he said it. 'Ted thought so too.'

James could hear the disdain in his son's voice, but he chose to ignore it. The fantasy was over. The past could not be repaired, there had been too many lies. They must look to the future.

And this is the future, he thought as he walked the several steps to the edge of the ridge, still staring out at the boundless plains. *Glenfinnan is the future.*

'You will stop as of now, Josh, do you hear me? You will do as I say. You will sell Braedalbin and you will cease all activity that might appear in any way suspect. You will devote yourself to Glenfinnan and the McKinnon name. That is an order.'

Josh continued to study his father. *You're a weak man after all,* he thought. The notion surprised him. He'd always seen his father as a bold man, a leader of men. *But you're not, are you? You're just one of the sheep, conforming to type like all the others. You're a fraud, Dad. A fraud who doesn't deserve the position of leader.*

He joined his father, looking out over the view of the valley, and then down at the stone quarry below.

'Better not get too close to the edge, Dad,' he warned, 'you wouldn't want to slip. It's a pretty treacherous fall down there.'

Instinctively, James glanced down. Then before he knew it he was falling. No, not falling. Hurtling. He was hurtling down the steep, rocky slope at such a pace there was no holding on, try as he might, and the rocks were hurtling along with him. It seemed to go on forever. Until suddenly everything went black.

He didn't know how long it was before he regained consciousness, but when he did, he was befuddled, his brain jangled from the experience, unable to comprehend what had happened. Had he slipped? Josh had warned him. But he didn't remember slipping. And he'd travelled at such speed.

He lay on his back, blinking unseeingly, everything a blur, and at first he was unaware of his son's presence.

Josh had scarpered down from the ridge to the grove of trees where a narrow track led to the base of the quarry.

He was now kneeling beside his father, gazing at the broken body and the eyelids that were flickering.

James tried to move, but found he couldn't. The slightest attempt and his whole being screamed with pain. His bones were broken. But he was alive.

The blur receded. His vision returned. He looked up to see his son, and realised in that instant what had happened. He hadn't slipped at all.

He opened his mouth to speak, but no sound came out. *You pushed me,* he thought. He could feel the hands in the small of his back. *You pushed me!*

Then even as his eyes made the accusation, he saw the rock that his son had picked up. He saw the rock raised high above his son's head.

The last image James had was of the rock plunging towards him. Then nothing.

Josh remained kneeling there for a moment or so.

Sorry, Dad. Did he think it or did he say it out loud? he wondered, he really wasn't sure. But he had no regrets as he stared down at the body of his father. This was simply something that had had to be done. There'd been no other way.

His mind remained a blank as he hefted the body over his shoulders and started on the laborious trip back up the track.

Upon finally reaching the convict-built well at the bottom of the ridge, he recalled his father's words: *Ben used to say it'd be the perfect place to hide a body.* The remark now seemed blackly humorous.

And that was when he *did* start to think. What tale was he to tell of his father's death? A fall from his horse was the most plausible, even the best of riders had been known to fall from their horse, and the result could be fatal. The fatal injury, however, would most commonly be a broken neck. His father's injuries were not consistent with a fall from a horse. Such a terrible smash to the head.

No, he decided as he heaved the body over the saddle, it had to be the truth. His father had slipped and fallen down the deadly, cliff-like slopes of the old stone quarry. A tragic accident. Everyone would believe that.

Everyone did. There was no other possible explanation.

The death of James McKinnon was mourned by all. Hundreds turned up for his funeral, which was held in St Peter and Paul's Cathedral. Family, neighbours, friends, half of Goulburn it seemed. He was a McKinnon, after all.

A month later, in sorting through his father's possessions, the first thing Josh did was lay claim to the watch. Grandpa George's gold watch and chain. He would wear it at all times and display it with pride whenever possible. He was twenty-two years old and the new patriarch of Glenfinnan. But he was much, much more than a McKinnon. He was the grandson of George Brereton.

EPILOGUE

1920

Josh sat in his armchair on the extravagantly tiled front verandah of his brand-new house overlooking the courtyard that was flanked by formal gardens. Far in the distance he could see the original Glenfinnan House, where his mother Jenna still lived, and where his sister Emily stayed when she visited from Sydney. But this house, two storeys of solid brick, complete with marble entrance hall and central tower was much bigger and grander, and more to his taste. This was the Big House these days.

Neither his mother nor his sister particularly liked the new house.

'A bit too flashy for me,' Jenna would say.

'Downright vulgar,' was Em's opinion, 'doesn't fit the landscape.'

But Josh didn't care. He'd outlived the days of wooden verandahs with wicker chairs and overgrown flowerbeds. Besides, it was only right a man of his standing should boast such a house. It was very much to his wife's taste too, Gwendolyn adored it.

'So deliciously modern,' she would say, 'and with just a touch of decadence. One must move with the times.'

He quite agreed, the twenties was destined to be a decade of growth and excitement. Josh had great plans for the twenties.

He looked down at the cradle that sat beside him. It was a fine cradle, mahogany, he'd ordered it through the Grenfell Emporium catalogue and had it freighted from Sydney. He'd been rocking it with his foot, but stopped now. Little Louis appeared to be waking up.

'Hey, Gwennie,' he called through to the front hallway where he knew his wife was arranging the central flower display in order to impress the visitors who would shortly be teeming through the house. The Tirranna Picnic Races were to commence tomorrow and hordes were already arriving from Sydney. 'Hey, Gwennie, I think you might need to call for a bottle, he's waking up.'

Gwendolyn appeared through the open front doors, a bunch of long-stemmed roses in her hand. A picture in pastel pink, she was glowing. She loved the way he called her Gwennie. Diminutives had never been allowed in the Willard household, they were considered altogether too common. 'Gwennie' would simply not do.

She sat beside her husband, both gazing down at their six-month-old son. Little Louis was definitely awake now, gurgling adorably.

'Sing to him, Josh,' she said. 'You know how he loves it when you sing to him.'

So Josh sang. Very slowly and tunefully. He had a pleasing voice.

'Baa baa Black Sheep,
Have you any wool?
Yes, sir, yes, sir,
Three bags full;
One for the master,
One for the dame,

And one for the little boy
Who lives down the lane.'
He would teach his son the truth behind those lyrics one day.

ACKNOWLEDGEMENTS

Love and thanks as always to That Man Bruce Venables, my husband, for his help, encouragement and at times downright inspiration.

Thanks, too, to those dear friends who offer support and expertise of the most practical kind: James Laurie, Sue Greaves, Colin Julin, and also to Susan Mackie-Hookway for her constant encouragement.

I must offer a special vote of thanks this time around to the inimitable Warren Brown AM, matchless not only in his all-round talent and versatility, but also his generosity of spirit. (Just ask anyone – they'll agree.) Thanks for the tours of Goulburn and its surrounds, Warren, and thanks for the warm introduction to so many helpful local identities, and thanks for the wonderful stay at your home in Middle Arm with Tanya and Ollie, and thanks for . . . well, for just being you!

Speaking of Goulburn locals, I must thank the welcoming bunch Warren gathered together for a lovely morning tea at the Goulburn Soldiers Club: Terry and Cecily Hayes, Noel and Jan Lawton, Archie and Aileen Coggan, and Trevor and Shirley Mills. It was great to meet you all and share in your stories (and what about those gorgeous scones!).

My thanks to Monique Hayes and Fran O'Flynn of Goulburn Mulwaree Library, and an extra special thanks to you, Fran, for the additional links and material you forwarded – most helpful.

During my visits to Goulburn I very much enjoyed staying at the Abbey Motel, where I received the warmest attention from Amanda Connor and Paula St Vincent. A special thanks to you, Amanda, for the amount of trouble you went to in making up the enlarged city map for me.

My thanks to Michelle Mackey of the Goulburn Visitor Information Centre.

My thanks also to Kerry Collins, whom I met at the Coolo Pub. (If you read this book, Kerry, you'll note how a particular house in Australia Street features in one chapter!) And hello to Tina, hostess supremo behind the bar. I enjoyed my visits to the Coolavin and our chats about its history as the Southern Railway Hotel.

Many thanks as always to my publisher, Beverley Cousins; my editors, Brandon VanOver and Lauren Finger; my publicist, Jessica Malpass; and the many other members of the hard-working team at Penguin Random House Australia.

Among my research sources I would particularly like to recognise:

Springfield: The Story of a Sheep Station, Peter Taylor, Allen & Unwin Australia, 1987. This publication was invaluable to me.

I would also like to recognise:

1914: The Year the World Ended, Paul Ham, Random House Australia, 2013,

The Great War, Les Carlyon, Pan Macmillan Australia, 2006,

Clothes in Australia: A Pictorial History 1788–1980s, Cedric Flower, Kangaroo Press, 1984.